Morning Sun

THE
STORY
OF
MADAM
BUTTERFLY'S
BOY

LAIRD KOENIG

PROSPECTA PRESS

Print edition ISBN 978–1-935212–90–4
Ebook edition ISBN 978–1-935212–89–8

Book and cover design by Barbara Aronica-Buck

Published by
Prospecta Press
P.O. Box 3131
Westport, CT 06880
(203) 454–4454
www.prospectapress.com

Morning Sun

CHAPTER ONE

It was the month of March and, of course, it was raining in Bremerton, Washington, across Puget Sound from Seattle. Every electric light in the navy base and the grade school had been burning since morning. The 3:10 bell ended the school day with baseball called off.

Samuel Adams Pinkerton, seventh-grader, surprised the kids in third, bursting into their classroom to pick up his kid brother. Here was the school's star first-baseman who'd come himself to take skinny, bespectacled Benjy home. He knelt, buckling on his brother's canvas raincoat and pulling his cap down over his blond curls. Sam straightened Benjy's glasses as the eight-year-old stood straight, basking in his classmates' respect.

Released, the kids raced out into the rain, a shrieking flock of gulls. One mother waited in her brand-new 1913 Ford Model-T Runabout. Five others held umbrellas. Sam and Benjy's mother hadn't come to school for months, not even for Sam's biggest game.

"Ready?" Sam looked down at Benjy and challenged. "Beat you home!"

Benjy met the challenge with a vigorous nod. "It's a go!"

Diving into the downpour meant a quarter-mile dash through the icy rain.

Benjy fought to keep up, but his asthma had him sniffling and blinking behind wet glasses. Sam was the first to see their house. He reached for Benjy's hand. Douglas firs and bare maples rose above the clapboard bungalow the navy had assigned their lieutenant commander father, now on duty up in Alaska. Their house was a dark blur in the rain; no window glowing with light. Their mother rarely left the house. They paused, wondered if what they'd both been dreading for weeks had happened.

Benjy, shaking uncontrollably, gasped his fear. "We can't. Not alone. The navy—they'll get someone to go in first—"

Sam didn't answer.

"Sam?" Benjy whispered.

Not since last summer, when he had been caught in an undertow while swimming, had Sam felt such overwhelming dread. Icy water had swept over his head hurling him far out from shore, away from life. He'd fought drowning. Somehow he'd found the strength to touch bottom. Somehow he'd gotten back to land. Today, staring at his own home, dark as a tomb, he felt powerless to fight that same overwhelming dread.

Benjy, in tears, tightened his hold on his brother's hand to stop him with desperate cries. "No! We can't go in." Frantic, Benjy was tugging Sam's hand, to hold him back. He felt Sam pulling him across the front yard. Their boots echoed hollowly on the wooden porch steps. At the door Sam reached for the knob.

"No!" Benjy shrank back.

"I have to," Sam whispered. "You stay out here if you want to."

Benjy gripped his brother's hand following him into the dark, bitter cold, their breath turning to white mist. Neither of Kate Pinkerton's sons needed to glance into the kitchen to know that their mother had set out no after-school graham crackers and milk.

Sam pried off Benjy's hand in order to shed his raincoat and sodden hat. Benjy, shaking violently, pulled off his wet glasses to watch his brother, but dropped them. Now he was at the foot of the stairs' blue carpeting leading up into the dark.

"No! Don't!" Benjy wailed.

"Just shut up." Sam, desperate to hold onto whatever courage he could muster, was forcing himself to take his first step. On the fifth stair he stood motionless. Benjy hadn't moved. Sam knew he was sharing their terrible memory—that Christmas more than a year ago when their father, home from duty, had raced down these stairs, slammed the front door and never returned.

Sam reached the second floor three steps from his mother's closed bedroom door. His heart beat as loud as the rain on the roof as he tapped on the door. "Mom, we're home," his voice was small. "Okay if I come in?"

After silence he pulled off his boots, carefully pushed open the door and switched on the inside light. Drawn curtains held the bedroom deep in shadow. Across the room on tangled white linen lay his mother, in her favorite blue silk robe, the one she'd so often told her boys was "Alice blue." She never seemed to tire of telling them the color was named after the daughter of President Theodore Roosevelt, whom she'd met once before she married their father back East, in Baltimore.

Now she lay on her back, the blue silk she loved fallen open exposing bare white naked legs. Suddenly nothing was more important than that no one see her white nakedness.

Without looking at her, he tiptoed to the bed and drew the blue silk across her. Her bare right arm dangled from the bed. Out of reach on the carpet glinted the silver hypodermic needle. Her secret, the secret no one else must ever see. He'd overheard Dr. Sorenson leave her this needle for her worst times when she fully realized that the man she loved had left and that he was never coming home to her and her boys.

He hid the thing, thrusting it in her bed-table drawer. He struggled for breath against his pounding heart. His mother, without her Lady Esther face powder, was a terrible ash gray. Her glasses, like those President Wilson wore in the portrait at school, glittered, lying crooked across her face. Her almost white eyes, once blue as Benjy's, stared up at him.

Hugging himself he backed away from her eyes and out of the room, picking up his wet boots and creeping down the stairs.

Without a word Sam put his hand on Benjy's shoulder and guided him into the kitchen. Benjy, gasping but silent, watched Sam pick up the telephone to ask the operator for the navy base. "Sir, this is Lieutenant Commander Benjamin Franklin Pinkerton's son, Samuel. I'm at home here with my brother and we're all alone in our house. Our father's on duty up in Alaska—" His voice stuck in his throat. "Sir, my mother—something's happened." His voice broke. "She's in her bedroom upstairs and—and my brother and I need help—" He choked with tears but struggled on. "Please, sir, if you can get here as soon as you can." He gave the chaplain their address, hung the speaker back on its hook, and without another word, pulled Benjy close.

CHAPTER TWO

A heavy black overcoat filled the front door. Carrying a small black bag and with only a nod for the boys, the doctor and his smell of cigar smoke hoisted himself up the stairs. Another man, also in black, was in the door. He was a thin, pale young man who seemed hesitant about entering, a young navy officer who'd dashed through the rain without an overcoat. On his black uniform sleeves gleamed a stripe-and-a-half of gold under a cross the boys knew was the sign of a chaplain. He wiped his feet and stepped in, coughing and wiping his nose. The officer introduced himself as Lieutenant J. G. Stanley Lobaugh, urging the boys to call him "Stanley."

To Sam, the man of God looked more like a gawky Minnesota farm kid sniffling with a winter cold. Taking off his hat he appeared even younger, his head shaved nearly to the top tuft of haystack blond hair. The boys heard him talking about being here to bring the comfort of Jesus. He said he knew Sam would be a tower of strength for his brother; did they understand that he'd already been praying for them? He waited for them to nod before he patted their shoulders, turned and mounted the stairs.

With neither adult telling them what to do, they stood stricken at the bottom of the stairs.

"Young men?" The sympathetic voice calling belonged to the chaplain. "Samuel and Benjamin? We'll all be leaving the house in a few minutes. The doctor and I want you to find a couple of cardboard cartons and fill them with a change of clothes—winter clothes—along with anything you want to take with you. Can you do that?"

Sam nodded before he realized the officer at the top of the stairs was waiting for his answer. He cleared his throat. "Yes, sir."

He found some cartons and herded Benjy into their bedroom at the back of the house where the bunk beds were still unmade from morning. Benjy, holding his empty carton, stared helplessly at an open chest of drawers.

"The chaplain says to just put what you need in one box."

Benjy didn't stir. Sam drew clothes from his own drawer. Blinking back tears, he'd filled his box, his new baseball mitt on top. He tucked in his most precious possession, baseball cards bound with a rubber band, the newest of which was the precious Ty Cobb he'd traded only last week with his shortstop, Eddie Walters, a Siwash Indian with a blue tooth who was his best friend.

Benjy hadn't moved. "How about it? You need help?"

Benjy shook too hard to answer. Sam took his carton and filled it for him till a very small voice asked. "Can I take my *Wizard of Oz?*"

Sam tossed the heavy book on top of Benjy's clothes. They carried their boxes back to the foot of the stairs. At last Dr. Sorenson's heavy tread was followed by the chaplain's lighter step. "We know you two boys are going to show us what strong young men you are."

We're not young men, Goddamnit, we're kids and our mother's dead! Sam wanted to shout at the two men in black.

"We can count on you to make your father proud of you."

"He's in Alaska," Sam announced.

"Yes," the chaplain said, "the navy knows and right now we're telegraphing and bound to reach him in no time." He underscored his and the Lord's assurance by patting the older boy's shoulders. By now the doctor had gone into the kitchen to telephone. "Samuel?" the chaplain was looking squarely at Sam. "We're counting on you, Samuel."

Sam nodded. The chaplain crouched down to look into his younger brother's face.

"And this is Benjamin."

"Yes. We—I mean, I call him Benjy," Sam announced. "He's seven. I'm eleven."

The chaplain still held his Bible. "Upstairs, I prayed for your mother. Would you two young men like to join me in prayer?"

"I guess," Benjy said.

"Okay," Sam corrected his brother. "I mean, yes, sir."

Lieutenant Lobaugh opened his Bible at exactly the place Sam knew he'd go. He began intoning the 23rd Psalm. "The Lord is my shepherd." Sam knew that one, but was overwhelmed, knowing that at this moment what he'd remember forever was not the promise of comfort, but that his mother was dead upstairs

"Samuel," the doctor appeared at the kitchen door. "Can you run and find us another carton and show Chaplain Lobaugh and myself where your mother kept her important papers?"

In the living room Sam slid out the bottom drawer of the Duncan Phyfe desk his mother had shipped all the way from Baltimore, an emblem of her eastern home here in the raw Pacific Northwest. The two men in black stood over Sam as he lifted out papers, file folders, and letters tied with ribbon she dropped into the carton.

After the bottom drawer was emptied, Sam and Benjy continued to do exactly as they were told. This meant helping Benjy pull on a dry winter coat. And a scarf. Sam found a coat for himself and then both of them followed the two men in black out the front door.

In the back seat of the Reo, Benjy burrowed in his brother's arms, crying. Though fighting his own tears Sam was listening hard to hear how the grownup world in the front seat was determining their fate. From what he could make out the doctor and the chaplain both confessed themselves somewhat at a loss as to their next move. The neighboring navy houses were vacant. The Lieutenant Commander's wife seemed to have no family here on the west coast. At this point both men in the front seat turned to her sons.

"We all know your mother seldom left the house. But do you know if she had any close friends?" the doctor asked.

"Anyone we can contact?" the chaplain added.

Sam shook his head. "She was from back East."

The men gazed ahead through the windshield wipers. For tonight, at least, the adult world decided Kate Pinkerton's sons belonged at the Bachelor Officers' Quarters at the naval base while telegraphers went to work to reach their father in Alaskan waters.

The doctor, lighting a cigar, filled the car with smoke all the way to the navy base with Sam still straining to hear the two men. The chaplain was the more hopeful of the two. With the help of the Lord the navy would reach their father in Alaska, while at the same time his office telephone would reach long-distance, across the country, to Kate Pinkerton's family in Baltimore, Maryland.

When the boys got out, Doctor Sorenson leaned across the back seat offering his firm handshake. Leaving them in the rain, but in the hands of the Lord, he added his promise to look in on them after dinner.

While Lieutenant Commander Pinkerton's boys waited on a hard, shellacked bench in the chaplain's office, the BOQ readied their room. The chaplain studied his notes, picked up his telephone and urged them to pray with him to be able to reach their mother's family in Baltimore.

Sam felt such a miracle unlikely, but the excited chaplain was nodding, sharing his wonder with the boys. "I've got the Showalters, your mother's mother and father. "Yes—" Speaking on the phone he stifled his excitement to drop his voice to a grownup seriousness imparting the heart-breaking news. "Your grandparents," he covered the mouthpiece and whispered to the boys.

"Benjy, listen. Right now Chaplain Lobaugh's actually talking to Mom's mother—our grandma and granddad—all the way across the entire country—three thousand miles away."

The chaplain's hand still covered the speaker as he cast an encouraging look to the boys. After several moments' exchange, it was time for the three of them to pray and thank the Lord with all their hearts. The Showalters would be on their way to cross the country to take them and their daughter home. Sam wiped back tears of relief watching the young chaplain nodding at the phone.

The chaplain hung up the phone and in enormous relief, blew his nose. Thank God, the boys weren't alone. God had answered their prayers with family—their mother's people, who loved them so much they were coming three thousand miles to take them home to Baltimore.

For three days, while the Showalters crossed the country, the navy kept trying to reach their father. Lieutenant Lobaugh, God's pale young man who had wrought the miracle of the telephone, refused to admit defeat and encouraged them to keep praying. After nearly four days of cabling, the navy was still unable to reach him.

On the fifth day the boys were in the day room, building a fort of Lincoln Logs, when the chaplain rushed in, breathless with wonderful news. No. Not Alaska but Dr. and Mrs. Showalter from Baltimore had just this very morning arrived on the Empire Builder at the King Street Station in Seattle and called from the New Washington Hotel. Talk about love. Yes, they were here in Seattle and waiting for their Kate's boys.

The navy had outfitted the boys with new suits of gray Melton, knickers with stout new elastic to hold black stockings up to their knees.

Full of good wishes from the young officers at the BOQ, Sam and Benjy left with brand-new valises and Benjy's humidifier in a shopping bag. The chaplain, still sniffling with his winter cold, double-checked the papers in his black leather briefcase, important papers from their mother's desk.

At the ferry slip, boarding the Illawah as foot passengers under a pale but encouraging March sun, a brisk breeze carried the tang of salt and acrid creosote along with smoke from the lumber mill, sending flags snapping. On board they chugged out from Bremerton onto the wind-whipped whitecaps of Puget Sound.

The chaplain and Benjy retreated to the hot, stuffy saloon, but Sam braved the cold wind to stand at the rail. He clung to a box of Crackerjack praying that the navy would still get word to his father before he and Benjy left Seattle with their mother's family. One by one, he tossed Crackerjack to the seagulls, swooping and screaming in flashes of white and gray.

No one saw him alone at the rail, wiping his tears as he said goodbye to Bremerton and his baseball team.

Would he ever be back?

He stared down at the swirling icy water of the Sound, already distancing him from his past. Wherever life took him, he knew that he'd never stop climbing the stairs of that dark house to his mother's bedroom, and covering her white skin with the Alice-blue silk robe she loved.

CHAPTER THREE

On the streetcar ride up Seattle's Second Avenue, Chaplain Lobaugh's beneficence, besides Crackerjack, included hoarhound drops. Sam accepted one though he was certain it would never melt in his mouth, dry with worry about meeting his grandparents.

"Samuel," the chaplain said, looking ahead up the street. "We're almost there. Is Benjy ready?"

Sam straightened the glasses on his brother's worried face. The chaplain lowered his voice and Sam knew he was about to repeat the assurance he'd already offered so many times. "Samuel, tell your brother again that there's not a reason in the world for either of you to be concerned. Just imagine. Your mother's parents love and want you so much they've just traveled three thousand miles, across the entire United States, for you."

"What about my father?"

"The navy won't stop till we reach him. Even after you leave Seattle we'll always know where to reach you." He offered another hoarhound drop. "And you know what I think? It wouldn't surprise me if after he does get back to Bremerton the navy might post him east—perhaps right there in Annapolis where you'll all be together again. So there's nothing for you two to worry about. Okay?"

Sam felt trapped into nodding his agreement. "Okay."

"Here we go!" With the streetcar's bell clanging to a stop, the navy hurried them. Sam reached for Benjy's valise and humidifier.

They reached the revolving door of the hotel and saw a resplendent, rosy-faced Santa Claus without a beard, a grand figure glittering with more gold braid than an admiral, who commandeered their valises and shopping bag.

Inside the revolving door, they entered a world of gleaming marble, mahogany, and a grove of potted palms. Sam pulled off his cap and then Benjy's. The chaplain spied a sleek young man at the hotel desk, in a closely tailored black cutaway coat, emphasizing his Arrow-Collar-Man blond handsomeness. With a smile he left his post and seemed to glide across the marble, while alerting uniformed men, studded with shining buttons, to whisk away the valises.

"Good morning, Chaplain Lobaugh." The hotelier's smile bestowed itself on Benjy. "Of course. This young man has to be Benjamin Franklin Pinkerton. Am I right? Benjamin?"

Benjy gulped, sniffled, but managed a nod.

Adept at intuiting every need of his guests, their host turned them by the shoulders in the direction of a door beyond the palms. "First, if I know boys, perhaps you'll want to visit our gentlemen's room."

Sam led Benjy into a gleaming white tile and porcelain chamber, magnified in a wall of mirrors. A smiling black man appeared and led Benjy, in alarm, to a shoeshine stand. Enthroned and rigid in panic, Benjy stared down at the old man with curly silver hair, who smiled and hummed at his work, making Benjy's high-top boots gleam.

In the wall of mirrors Sam caught sight of an eleven-year-old boy who'd be twelve in June, some kid betraying uncertainty and twisting his cap. He realized this was himself, no longer Sam but Samuel, dressed like some sissified dude from the East he'd seen in the movies. Now it was him saying goodbye to the Pacific Northwest and that kid who played baseball in the rain, who liked to imagine himself another Huck Finn in his favorite book by Mister Mark Twain. Huck smoked a pipe and swore a blue streak. Huck wasn't this kid the navy had dressed carefully in this tight, gray suit. Huck had shaggy hair, not this straight hair. Sam wondered if this sturdy first baseman in his choking celluloid collar looked eastern enough for his Baltimore grandparents. This was the beginning of a new life—how his grandparents would see him for the first time. Would they like him? "Oh, Jesus," he struggled for breath, "they just have to like me."

He yanked up his long black stockings, making sure he covered his skinned knees.

The black man chuckled and released Benjy. Sam was next. The washroom man laughed his deep laugh as if there was nothing in the world he'd rather be doing than shining this white boy's boots that had already been spit-polished back at the BOQ.

Duly shined, both boys now faced the whiskbroom. On trips here to Seattle Sam had been with his father who, of course, was an officer and a gentleman. Lieutenant Commander Pinkerton knew how to treat these men, who served forever smiling in washrooms. He voice squawked. "If my father was here he'd give you a tip."

"This time it's my pleasure, young sir."

Sam nudged Benjy to mumble his thanks and both fled the washroom.

The Navy and the elegant hotel man lined up the Showalter grandsons for a final inspection. Hair was smoothed. On order Sam showed a smile of even white teeth. Black ties were drawn tight against adam's apples. Mourning bands were straightened.

As the four glided up in the elevator. "Supposing," their host began in a reverential hush, "if I were to tell you two young men that President Theodore Roosevelt himself was a recent guest in this very same hotel. That's why you'll see a bronze plaque outside the presidential suite. Now, suppose I were to ask either of you who it is the New Washington is proud to have staying with us in that same suite?" The elevator continued to rise. "If you answered it's your very own grandfather and grandmother you'd be right."

The chaplain smiled down at his boys. Their host continued in his respect, "Top, top people. Doctor Howard Showalter just happens to be Johns Hopkins' most renowned surgeon. That's in Baltimore—Baltimore, Maryland. Southerners of course." He murmured a shared social reality to the chaplain. "Mrs. Showalter brought her colored maid with them. Imagine, all the way across the country. Fortunately we've put her in quite a nice boarding house for negroes over on Yesler Way."

They stepped out onto thick carpeting for a long trudge to the brass plaque—*The Presidential Suite*. At the lustrously polished mahogany door their host assured himself with the chaplain of one point. "When the doctor called did he make it clear to you, as he did to us, their Benjamin is to come in first?"

The door opened. Here was the Negro maid in a white cap and apron, a tall, thin woman, her light skin closer to brown than black. Her Caucasian features possessed such great dignity that Sam decided they were proof she came from his mother's East. At her first sight of Benjy her hands flew to her breast and clasped. Her eyes, white, wide and shining, matched her smile of joy in a face of radiant happiness. "Oh, yes, yes, yes! Doctor and the Missus surely are expecting this young man! Come in! Come in! Our Benjamin! With Miss Kate gone what a blessing you are for this family." She tugged his hands but he wasn't budging, refusing to take a step. The hotel man and the chaplain both prodded him to follow the kind woman. Still Benjy refused to move. Close to terror, he looked up at Sam. He grabbed his brother's hand and the two pushed rudely past the maid.

CHAPTER FOUR

The sitting room at the end of the corridor glowed in the light of lamps under huge shades illuminating heavy, upholstered furniture worthy of a president of The United States. Benjy tightened his hand on Sam's. Thick carpeting hushed their boots.

Amidst the heavy furniture and lamps no one was waiting for them. For a long moment neither said a word. Across the room a door opened.

Across a window's pale light a commanding silhouette moved, a woman, heavyset and even taller than their mother. Her raven black dress trailing the floor sparkled with jet beads. Light caught her face. Sam's heart stopped. Yes. Unmistakably, here was their mother's mother, older, of course, and heavier, but similar, down to her daughter's glittering pince-nez glasses. A sudden cry of joy rose as she rushed straight at Benjy, but she stopped herself. Instead of swooping him into her arms she was prolonging this first moment of joy. "My Kate's Benjamin," she cried, raising her arms.

"Howard!" Her excited voice filled the room. "Howard! Hurry! Our Benjamin's here!"

Benjy, stunned with fear, gasped when Sam pried his hand off, urging him to allow himself to be swept up in those black wings. Her head, with its handsome gray hair rolled like a cushion, drew back for a long, deep look of love at the boy.

"Our Kate's boy," she cried again, her warmth and love enveloping her startled grandson. She pulled back long enough to take off her glasses, dabbing her eyes.

Yes, Sam knew the chaplain had been right. The brothers had nothing to worry about. The older brother had only to wait, ready to be overwhelmed with love.

"Howard!" Calling again, she was moving Benjy to the window for a closer look, when across the room a door flung open. A man so huge and heavy he all but filled the doorway burst in, pulling a cloth belt tight on his brown flannel robe. His heaviness carried the scent of pine soap as he rushed past Sam. At the window his wife stepped back presenting their grandson to the excited man. Dr. Howard Showalter of Johns Hopkins stopped himself, one hand sweeping a few strands of hair back across his unusually large head. His pince-nez glasses, like his late daughter's, glinted in his large red face.

"Yes! Yes! Yes!" he exclaimed, gathering Benjy into a bear hug while raising the lad to eye level. "Our Katie's boy! My first grandson!"

Benjy, all but suffocated with love, shot Sam a look of alarm, warning his brother that his turn was next.

"Just you look at him, Mother!"

To Sam, their grandfather's accent sounded even more Southern than his wife's.

"Look. Written all over him. Our Katie. Our Katie's blue, blue eyes. And look at his chin, Mother. See? Even that little cleft of hers. And glasses—just like our own Katie at his age."

Sam realized how embarrassed he must look twisting his cap. Fortunately, no one but Benjy was looking at him, the couple too thrilled that they had yet to give his older brother a single glance. How long was he supposed to stand here waiting all by himself? He heard his own stifled voice. "I'm Samuel Adams Pinkerton! You're my grandfather. I'm your grandson, too."

Neither grownup so much as glanced at him. Only Benjy, held back by the large woman, was looking at him. The important people from Baltimore made it clear that, as far as they were concerned, he wasn't in this room. Slowly Sam fought the awful sense he was being deliberately overlooked. No, he told himself, that couldn't be. It was only his little brother they loved and wanted. Their every move made it clear. As for Sam, no longer could he feel simply left out. They were deliberately telling him he was not one of them.

Nothing could stave off the creeping sense of dread. He was alone. But why? He shocked himself hearing his cry. "I'm Samuel Adams Pinkerton!" His voice was far bolder, far more insistent than he'd intended. And yet, even after his outburst, neither grandparent turned from their Benjy.

He heard his next cry, this time a polite, feeble cry for help. "I'm Sam—Samuel Adams Pinkerton . . ."

Mrs. Showalter's dark silhouette, with its hard beads glittering in the window's silver light, drew bewildered Benjy closer, the lad casting imploring looks to Sam to rescue him. The woman was giving her husband a significant nod, another grown-up signal that she was taking Benjy firmly by the hand. With tear-filled eyes never leaving Sam, Benjy was at a loss to understand why he was being taken from his brother and led stumbling through an open door.

"Sam!" The door closed on Benjy's screams.

Too late Sam sprang for the door only to slam into the enormous brown robe. Breathing in deep anger the man held Sam, while sliding one hand over his bald head.

Sam fought to push past him. "Sir, Benjy needs me. He has asthma something awful. It's bad for him to get excited—"

For the first time the doctor spoke. "Suppose you let his grandmother and I do the worrying about our boy."

The door shut away Benjy's wails. "I made it perfectly clear to the navy you were not to be here. Only Benjamin. You are to go with your father—"

Sam swiped his eyes, spilling scalding tears. "He's way off up in Alaska!"

"Don't argue with me. Get the chaplain in here this minute."

Sam, shaking from head to foot, couldn't move. The heavy face above him, now red and frowning, glared down, cold eyes behind glass. "You will do as you're told." With that command he turned from the boy who didn't belong here and faced the window. Sensing the boy hadn't moved, his voice sharpened like breaking ice. "Damn you! Do as you're told. Get the chaplain in here right this minute."

Now shaking even more violently, Sam was frozen to the carpet. When the doctor sensed he was refusing to obey he turned from the window. Two steps brought the doctor looming over him. "Before you go," he edged his deep anger with sarcasm, a weapon against which no child can defend himself, "don't stand there and try to pretend you didn't know. Not with us."

Sam managed to utter, "Know what?"

"For nine years you must have known the wife and I sent our Benjamin birthday and Christmas presents. Never one single thing to you, and you never asked why?"

"I always got your presents," Sam cried. "Mom always made me write a thank you."

The doctor sighed a deep sigh. "Even if she never told you the truth, no way could you possibly believe our Kate was your mother. Now go, get the chaplain."

He was in the undertow sweeping him out into icy water, desperate but unable to touch bottom or cry out for help. Confusion added to his terror. And shame. Already shaking, he lost his fight to hold back tears. Why was this hateful old man, his own mother's father, saying these terrible things?

He heard himself crying out. "You're lying. Everything you're saying is a lie! So shut up! Just shut up!" Scalding tears ran down his face. "She was my mother and she loved me so just shut up!" Suddenly he was a fierce young animal. "Mom loved me and I loved her so damn you for saying that . . ."

"Listen to me, young Pinkerton. Because of you the wife and I have had no choice all these years but to live our lives up to this minute telling no one our Kate's secret—"

Sam shook his head violently. "Stop lying!"

"Then it's clear. She never told you her secret?"

Sam's eyes spilling tears, rose, searching the man's face.

"Her secret that no one besides your father—and her mother and I have had to share—"

"Then it's true. Our Kate, so soft-hearted all these years, couldn't bring herself to tell you the truth."

"My Mom never, ever lied to me," Sam wailed. "Not once—not ever!"

"Samuel Adams Pinkerton. Yes? You were born in Japan. If my daughter couldn't bear to tell you the truth—was there nothing in your blood telling you? If you never guessed, then now you must know, you are the living lie born of a Japanese woman and your father."

"Shut up! Shut up!"

"My Kate loved him. Her tragedy was she loved that bastard so much she swore she'd tell the world his son by that Jap woman was hers."

"You're the liar. Not Mom—"

"Yes, my Kitty brought you back to America believing her love would stand by her and make the world accept her lie." The doctor's large hands clenched into fists ready to strike the man who broke his daughter's heart. "That bastard!"

"And you hate my father so much—" Sam fought through broken sobs, "that's why you're taking it out on me—"

"Don't you dare raise your voice to me, young man."

"Benjy's my brother and he's our father, goddammit!"

"Benjamin is my Kate's son. My grandson will be a Showalter."

"Pinkerton! That's our name!"

"You'll stay a Pinkerton. Your Christian name. Have you never asked yourself why your name isn't Benjamin like your father's? No. Never asked yourself that? Your father saved his name to give to my Kate's American son."

"You're lying—"

"Ask your own father—"

"He's not here!" Sam cried back. "He's in Alaska."

"Then you're his. Benjamin is ours. Not you."

The doctor's heavy bulk turned back to the window to watch silver rain trickling down the glass. He heaved a profound sigh of loss. "She's gone, but thank God, at least we have our Benjamin."

"You're lying about me—wherever Benjy goes, I go. He's my brother."

Benjy's grandfather watched the rain. "Even at your age you must have seen how that man you call your father broke my Kitty's heart—the way that bastard deserted her as if she were a Japanese woman—All these years . . . After he left her in Bremerton and broke her heart, we begged her to come home—come home without you. Leave you to your father."

"He's in Alaska," Sam cried. "He loves me and Benjy."

"Tears won't help any of us. Until your father comes back for you— if he ever does come back—you stay in Bremerton. The chaplain will arrange something for you. Now leave us and get the chaplain in here."

Dr. Showalter, a man the world obeyed, had dismissed the boy. But Sam was still there when the door to the next room opened. Benjy was scuffling against his grandmother and shrieking for Sam.

"Benjy," Sam cried. "Tell them! Tell them you're my brother!"

"Sam!" Benjy answered, wailing and struggling fiercely against Mrs. Showalter. The woman's voice fiercely rasped. "Howard, why is that creature still here?"

"Sam!" Benjy shrieked, "Sam!"

The doctor, as determined as his wife to keep the struggling boys apart, held Sam as he called to his frantic little brother being swept into the next room.

"Benjy!"

"Howard!" Mrs. Showalter's shrill cry cut through Benjy's screams. The woman closed the door but not before Sam heard her furious hiss. "Howard, make it clear to that damned chaplain—tell him I'd sooner have a nigger in my family than a Jap!"

Sam tore himself from the doctor, and blind with tears, ran down the hall to the outside mahogany door.

CHAPTER FIVE

Out in the corridor the chaplain sprang up from a little gold bench, closing his Bible. The sight of Sam, wild and in tears, so startled him that raw shock edged his voice. "For heaven's sake, Samuel. What in the world's going on?" Words jammed Sam's racking, silent sobs rushing to the navy, hugging the astonished officer.

"Samuel, tell me." The startled officer, uneasy at such sudden intimacy, allowed the wildly distraught boy to cling to him. "Samuel, whatever's happened in there, you wait right here. I'll talk to them."

He slid his Bible into his black briefcase and obediently followed the doctor into the suite. The gleaming mahogany door closed behind him.

"Don't move," the chaplain had insisted. Don't move. Without Benjy, where could he go? Benjy was still behind that door with those angry, hateful old people. They wanted Benjy, not Sam. They hated Sam.

Shuddering against the cold marble wall, he saw that his only hope against those terrible lies the Showalters had spat at him was the chaplain. For a moment he was standing beside his mother in the navy chapel. He was holding the hymnal for both of them. She was singing the hymn she'd sung so often since their father left. "What a friend we have in Jesus. Take it to the Lord in prayer."

He had no need to turn, he sensed that mahogany door opening. He heard the chaplain cough and held his breath. The chaplain stood there, carrying his officer's hat and briefcase and looking straight at him without smiling. "Samuel, this is partly—perhaps mostly—my fault. This morning when we talked by telephone the doctor said he and Mrs. Showalter didn't want to see you, but that was all he said. He didn't explain why they only wanted Benjy to come to them. To tell you the truth I couldn't imagine a reason in the world they wouldn't want you and love you every bit as much as Benjy . . ."

His hand tightened on the trembling boy's shoulder. "Samuel, no matter how difficult this is for both of us, you must tell me and the navy the truth. About your mother. You never knew? About your father. About Japan. Right now I have to ask, Samuel, is what the Showalters are telling me, is that—the Lord's truth?"

"You already believe them," words muffled against the wall. "So just shut up."

"Please don't talk to me like that, Samuel. I'm here to help." The chaplain's hand went to his shoulder, but Sam twisted from under his hand.

"I want you to look at these papers they brought from Baltimore."

Sam shook his head against being shown proof that he deserved to be hated.

"Look at me, Samuel." Lieutenant Lobaugh held Sam while positioning himself to look at him as if for the first time. Only his mother with her pince-nez glasses had ever studied his face so closely. The chaplain sighed. "Almost blond hair," he murmured. "Gray eyes. Not slanted. And anyone can see you're going to be tall. It's almost impossible to believe."

"Shut the hell up—"

"You're not helping either of us, Samuel. First we both have to face the truth. The Showalters tell me that back in Baltimore they have letters and a photograph from your mother they've kept secret from the world for nine years. The truth seems to be, your real mother was Japanese—"

Sam jerked around violently, his face a fierce challenge, straight into the chaplain's eyes. "Lies! Because they hate my father so much for what he did to my mother. They're taking it out on me—lying about me! Look at me! A Jap? Me? How could anyone ever accuse me of being a Jap!"

The chaplain drew another breath. Still looking into Sam's eyes he began again. "Sam—it's all in the letter their daughter mailed from Japan—"

"They're lying! Mom was never in Japan! Okay, maybe my dad could have been over there in the navy, but if Mom ever was, she would have told me!"

"Their daughter married your father—Lieutenant Junior Grade Benjamin Franklin Pinkerton—at the Naval Academy at Annapolis. After the wedding they only had time for a short honeymoon at a place called the Greenbrier in Virginia, before he was ordered to Norfolk for sea duty. Mrs. Pinkerton went back to living at home till she got word from the Philippines to meet Lieutenant Pinkerton in Nagasaki." He paused for a moment repeating what he'd been told. "Nagasaki, that's in Japan, where he'd take leave from the navy so they could meet over there and have a real honeymoon sailing back to the States on a passenger liner—"

Sam shook his head vehemently. "Mom was never, ever in Japan."

The chaplain snapped open his briefcase to find a letter. "Samuel, this came from the bottom drawer of your mother's desk. If you'd look, please look, you'll see it's on stationery with the letterhead of the United States Consul in Nagasaki."

"So what! Mom was never there—"

"Dated July 20, 1904. Here's the man's signature. If you'll look you'd see the name is Arthur Sharpless. Just a simple note wishing Lieutenant and Mrs. Benjamin Franklin Pinkerton a happy and safe voyage home to the States on the SS Samuel Adams with their boy—"

"It doesn't prove a goddamned thing—"

"This second paper, which looks like some kind of important document, is in Japanese, which none of us can read—" He glanced at the paper and sighed. "You and I will need to get it translated. Samuel, will you please help both of us and look at me?" He looked at the flimsy paper. "Who knows, but this could explain everything."

"Because I'm no Jap." Sam thrust his face close to the chaplain demanding, "Do I look Japanese?"

"Samuel, I'm trying to help you. None of us knows what this says, but the Showalters have a letter from their daughter they've saved all these years. Mrs. Pinkerton wrote that in Japan she'd discovered your father had a wife there—in Nagasaki. Not a real wife, of course, but the mother of his two-year old son." The chaplain continued, as much for himself as for Sam, trying to fathom a twelve-year-old secret. "Mrs. Pinkerton wrote her parents that she loved your father so much that even if his son was from another race, the boy looked enough like him that she insisted on taking him home with them to call him her own son." The chaplain's arm crept back on Sam's shoulder but he jerked away.

"Sam, are you hearing what I'm saying?"

"Not when you're lying!"

The chaplain began again, his voice low, scarcely a whisper. "They have another letter your mother wrote in 1904 they've never shown a soul. It came from the Moana Hotel in Waikiki where Kate Pinkerton wrote that she and your father had you baptized in the Plymouth Congregational Church in Honolulu, Hawaii. They named you Samuel Adams Pinkerton after their ship, the Samuel Adams, that brought them home.

They say her letter even included a snapshot of a two-year-old little boy in a sailor suit standing on the beach—"

"So where the hell is it?"

"Mrs. Showalter said she tore it into a million pieces—"

"See? All lies because they hate my father so much." Defiant, but choked with sobs, his cry was weak.

The chaplain had been thorough. "I checked his record, his fitness jacket. After Lieutenant Pinkerton and his wife got back to the States, he served a tour of duty on Coronado Island in San Diego. That's where Benjamin was born. Do you remember San Diego?"

Sam refused a nod. To remember sunshine, palm trees, and a fox terrier in a back yard with a croquet court would be adding evidence to the Showalters' lies about letters and documents they were using against him.

"Your brother, Benjamin Franklin Pinkerton, was born in San Diego on October 14, 1906—"

"You think I don't remember?" he snapped. "He's my brother—"

"Of course, and no one's saying you both don't have the same father. You would have been about five when your father was assigned to Bremerton and you came to live there—" All the rest about Bremerton was unassailable, the recent truth. The chaplain allowed more sympathy to warm his voice. "Samuel, I can only imagine how difficult this must be for you." After a silence, he said, "Samuel, I want you to pray with me."

Sam shook his head. "To hell with praying—"

"After all the Navy and I've tried to do for you, I know you don't mean that."

"Look at me!" Instead of looking at Sam the chaplain stared down at the flimsy paper neither could read. "Look at me!" Sam cried. "Look at my eyes! They don't slant. Mom always called them slate gray. And not black. And my hair." He yanked down the evidence of his forelock. "You call this black? As for me, I've barely ever seen a Jap."

"Let's not start things off with a word like that from you, Samuel. People from Japan are called *Japanese*."

"The only Japs I've ever seen were in *The Mikado* but they were only white guys with paint on their faces. At home—Mom and I—we never talked about Japan. Not once! Not ever!"

"After I see the Showalters about Benjy, the first thing you and I do, Samuel, is take this paper with its Japanese writing to Japantown and find someone to translate it."

"Why?" Sam demanded, "when it's all lies!"

The chaplain closed his briefcase and picked up his hat. "You hang onto it while I go back and finalize the arrangements about Benjy. I'll say it again. I'll do what I can to change their minds about you but I have to ask you to be prepared for—for whatever we find."

"They can't take Benjy without my father knowing what they're doing."

"It's unfortunate that your father's still out of reach so what I'm saying now is very important, Samuel. You understand? While I'm gone I want you to think about what Dr. Sorensen and I asked you and Benjamin in the car. Remember? If Mrs. Pinkerton and your father had any close friends we could get in touch with. Someone who might want to take you in."

"How could she have any friends when she almost never left the house?"

"Then please, try to think if your father had any relatives. Even good friends. I'm sure you must know some of his friends. What about Christmas cards?"

"None, ever, from Michigan where he was born. What's wrong with the goddamn navy that they can't find him?"

"Words like that don't help, Samuel. You know the navy's doing everything we can—"

Sam slumped back on the bench. After a long silence his voice was small and defeated. "You told Benjy and me you were getting married."

"The last week in May."

"I mean if—if Mom's mother and father really don't want me—I mean till my dad comes back, maybe I could come and work for you and Mrs. Lobaugh." When the chaplain said nothing he rushed on. "I'm a good worker. I could earn my board and keep . . ."

"I know you would, Samuel. The thing is, Millie and I have a life of our own to start. People would know you weren't our son, and, knowing you, you wouldn't want us to lie about who you are."

Sam tightened with rage. "You know damned well I'm not Japanese!"

"What I'm going to say now, Samuel, I'd give anything not to say.

The truth is, there are people in this world, like the Showalters, who are—who feel uncomfortable around anyone different from themselves—like foreign people and people with mixed blood. I'll do what I can. I'll try my best to convince them not to separate you two, but—as I said, I can't hold out much hope." He rose, dug out a handkerchief and mopped his nose.

"They can't take Benjy—not without me!"

"Now you sit right here and hang on to this paper. We'll get it translated. When we know more—even if it proves what the Showalters are saying—you and I will get back to my office and make some telephone calls. Believe it or not, Samuel, there are people—good Christian people in this world—willing to reach out and give a young man like yourself a good home." He added, "And besides good people there are places—"

Sam's gasp was a cry of betrayal, "You mean like an orphanage?"

"No one is saying that—"

"Yes, you are! Like Oliver Twist. Where they send kids nobody wants—Or worse, reform school."

"Samuel, don't. This is 1913. You and I will keep trying to reach your father. You're not the first eleven-year-old boy who—for a time—has had to face the world—"

"Where people lie and call me a Jap?"

"Samuel, please. Whatever Our Lord made you, you are still His precious child. Hang onto that paper and promise me you won't budge an inch."

"You're on their side, goddamn you," he cursed silently as the door closed. With his heart pounding he knew what he must do. This paper, this flimsy paper his mother had kept all these years, must be important. Once he had it translated it would prove that the whole goddamn world of grownups was lying about him and Japan.

Without a minute to lose before the Showalters left the hotel with Benjy, he'd race back here with the paper translated and prove he wasn't half Japanese. That meant he'd have to dash out of here, find somebody Japanese to translate the document, and hightail it back here to the New Washington Hotel. Then he'd prove those goddamned grownups were lying. Sliding the paper into his breast pocket, he raced wildly down the long corridor.

CHAPTER SIX

He spun himself through the revolving door and out onto Second Avenue into the rain. Noon and Seattle were indifferent to rain. Laughing young women in hobble skirts and big hats, secretaries and shop girls arm in arm, were hurrying to mid-day lunches. Young men in box-back suits from offices were smoking cigarettes and cigars with elaborate grownup gestures. Mothers pushing prams and herding toddlers shared the sidewalks with older people carrying shopping bags bulging with fresh vegetables, salmon and Dungeness crab from the Pike Place Market. Seattle. He'd only been here with his mother. He raced down First Avenue toward the market where he knew he'd find the largest number of people who didn't look like himself. He dodged around an old woman squatting on the sidewalk selling hand-woven baskets, her crumpled cedar-colored face all but hidden within a cocoon of blankets. He'd heard someone say she was a local American Indian. Here were a few black men and others who might be Filipinos, some kind of Orientals—Asians—or whatever they were called. Noontime Seattle was filled with people the Showalters would hate. Asians, he recognized with their black hair, black or if old, gray. Mostly it was their dark eyes kids in school called "slant-eyed Chinks," and shaped nothing like his. Since white people like the Showalters hated the Japanese so much he guessed they probably kept to themselves in the poorer part of town the Pinkertons never visited.

He rushed to a cadaverous news vendor, a white man with thin eyelids and a stubbled face and strong breath from a bottle of whiskey poking out of his pocket. "Please, Sir, where's Japantown?" He asked his question twice, but the man refused to answer. He turned to a tall policeman holding a chunk of ice against his red cheek nursing a toothache.

"Japs?" The policeman grimaced and rubbed his cheek. "The Chinks are over on Jackson Street, Japs up in Japantown around Yesler. You know where the King Street Railroad Station, is? But a kid like you doesn't want to go poking around there."

"Is it dangerous?" Sam's voice was small.

"The Japs eat with chopsticks. Raw fish. Even dog. No place for a god-fearing American boy."

By now his black socks flapped around his bare legs as he raced past shops, banks, vaudeville theatres and nickelodeons. Climbing a hill he looked down on the towers of Seattle's two railroad stations. If he'd arrived at Seattle's Japantown, it was this street, a dismal huddle of shabby little one-story buildings. Yes. The storefront signs were the same kind of strokes that matched the black ink on his precious document.

He recoiled. No street in Bremerton reeked with the smell he caught coming from a fish market. He cringed at the sight of an octopus dangling on hooks. He couldn't believe that anyone—not even Japanese—ate such slimy things.

He saw more of those strange brush markings on newspapers for sale outside grocery stores, proof he must be among Japanese people under umbrellas, hurrying past him in the rain. Was there someone here he could stop to decode his secret?

The officer with the toothache had warned him to be careful here in this shabby part of town. After all, these were people the Hearst newspapers called "The Yellow Peril." He sneaked looks under their umbrellas. "Almond eyes." That was how people more polite than the Hearst newspapers described any Asian.

Yamamoto Antiques. The sign in English slowed him to a stop. The small shop's window offered a look into a world of painted screens, bronze statues, and silk robes. Here was Japan in America. He took a deep breath, squared his shoulders and pulled open the door.

A bell tinkled.

In the shop's dim light he sniffed something unfamiliar. He guessed it must be incense curling up from a little brass, dragon-shaped burner. Deep within the shop, among shadows, screens gleamed in gold leaf.

As he drew out his paper he startled. From among the statues, in the shadows, a tiny woman in a dark blue kimono emerged from a back room. He'd never seen a woman so tiny, not even as tall as the younger girls in Benjy's class in their Bremerton school. Her gray hair was drawn back above black eyes that appeared somewhat slanted to him.

One step into Japan and he was already in a stranger world than he could imagine. Her hands weren't barring him from her shop but pointing to her golden floor mats of tightly woven rice straw under his big wet boots. He froze, as still as one of her statues, then stepped back. Looking down, he nodded. He understood how precious the gleaming straw was to her. She returned his nod. Now that her mats were saved she looked up at him and the paper he held out to her. She seemed to sense its importance. Without moving an inch onto the mats he reached out to hand the paper to her. To his horror she had scuttled down and was scrambling on her knees at his feet. Mortified, he held his breath. She was taking off his boots.

Scarlet with embarrassment he blurted out the urgent business bringing him here. This letter. It was in Japanese. Would she please translate it for him?

Having taken off his boots she stood, coming barely above his waist. "First," she spoke in a small voice. "First, tea."

"No. I'm sorry. No time," Sam's voice was loud, probably another sacrilege in this strange land. "Please, will you read this for me?"

Nodding gravely, she smoothed back her gray hair. Her voice was as tiny as the rest of her. "If I can find my glasses."

She melted back into the shadows, leaving him feeling more the foreigner in his own land. Sam, the first baseman, Huck Finn, and totally alone in a world among shiny gods and screens. The brass gods gleamed, and all of them seemed to be staring straight at him. To his right stood a folding panel on which black crows rose above windblown grass in their flight across a full moon. In another panel the bright round eyes of white herons were so real he could swear they were alive.

Daring a closer look, he tiptoed on his stocking feet onto the woman's golden mats. One step and he forgot all about those eyes watching and drew in his breath. The moment overwhelmed him. There was no dread of an undertow but a gentle current floating him away from life in Seattle on a rainy day. Within this little shop scented with incense he was in a dream world far away from this terrible, dark day.

To feel the dream even more deeply he knelt down on the mats and smoothed his hands over the silky straw. If he pulled off his socks his bare feet could feel even more of what—a memory?

"Tatami," the woman's voice entered his dream. She smiled and nodded at the floor.

"Tatami mats. Like Japan."

When the boy didn't move she looked at him as if she might be calling him back from some distant shore. She was reminding him politely why he was here; she was reaching for his letter. With infinite care she carried it to a countertop and carefully smoothed it.

Now Sam, back from his dream, was alive and fighting to calm his excitement. He managed to whisper. "Japanese writing?"

She took a long moment to hang her round glasses on her little face before she nodded. Yes, the nod said, this was, indeed, Japanese writing. Reading aloud her voice was still scarcely a whisper. "Nagasaki City," she announced. "Nagasaki Prefecture." He bent closer, desperate to catch every word.

"Month of June. Day 21. Year, 1902." She stopped to consider. "Does not say reign of emperor. Maybe date is Western-style calendar." Intent, puzzled, she read on in silence, but stopped. She drew off her glasses, folded them, and shook her gray head.

"Where did you get this?" she asked.

"What is it?"

"Please, I asked you. Where did you get this?"

"Some grownups told me it came from Nagasaki." Breathless with urgency, he cried, "Is it about someone named Pinkerton?"

"Sorry. I cannot say more." She folded the paper, turned away, smoothed her hair and slowly shook her head from side to side. "Sorry."

"Please—please. Tell me. What does it say?"

"This is about religion—Christian religion."

"Please. Whatever it says, please tell me."

"I am sorry." She folded the paper. "I am not a Christian. It is better that you ask someone who understands these things—"

"But you can read it and tell me what it says, can't you?"

"For me not to tell is better. In Nagasaki are many Christians. I am from Okayama. I am Shinto. Also Buddhist. You understand?"

"No."

"No. Of course you do not understand." She returned the paper to him. She ducked her head in apology. "Sorry."

"Please, if you won't tell me what it says, please tell me someone who will."

She plucked a card from a black lacquer bowl and presented it to him, then added an indelible pencil. "Write what I say."

Before he took the pencil he returned to imploring. "Please—won't you please read it to me?"

"Write, please. Write 'Mission Church of Christ. Yesler Way.' You know Yesler Way?"

He nodded that if he had to, yes, he could find the address.

"Two streets." Her bird-like hand emerged from her long kimono sleeve indicating that after leaving her shop he must turn to the left. "The people there are *hakujin*. Not Japanese. Missionaries. They have a church in Nagasaki. It is best they tell you what you wish to know."

Confused, but not utterly defeated in his first encounter with the Japanese people, he was enough in command to step off the tatami mats and pull on his boots, this time without her help. "Thank you," he said to the bowing woman. He left her and her golden mats, gleaming brass gods, and the heron's round eyes.

Out in the drizzle of the street he followed her directions to an even more dismal street. Ahead stood a whitewashed former shop blazoned with two large crosses in sky blue paint. A large sign above the front door announced serious Christian intent here in Seattle's Japanese part of town.

MISSION CHURCH OF CHRIST
Seattle and Nagasaki
REVEREND WENDELL S. SNYDER

Below, he recognized a smaller sign's writing as Japanese. His chilled fingers trembling with excitement felt inside his breast pocket for the paper. He summoned the courage he'd need to push open the door. Now—right now—he'd find the preacher, show him the paper and know the truth he prayed would prove those damned grownups were lying.

Once armed with the truth he'd still have time to race back to the hotel and Benjy before they took him to the train and left for Baltimore. On that train he'd be with his mother. No way would his own mother lie to him all these years. Not even to protect him from the truth.

He reached out to push open the door. "Nagasaki," he told himself. "That's where the chaplain said Dad had been in the Navy." He touched the paper from Japan. He didn't move. Should he put whatever his Japanese secret might be in the hands of a stranger—another grownup as white as the Showalters and the chaplain? First he'd need time to get to know this Reverend Snyder before he could trust him. Until he felt he could trust this stranger completely, his secret and his life, were still his own.

CHAPTER SEVEN

He took a deep breath and tapped on the front door. No one answered. He knocked harder. Still no answer. He pushed the door, found it unlocked and stepped into the chill of the storefront church whitewashed as outside and smelling sharply of fresh calcimine. Glowing pastel-colored light filtered in from side windows covered with paper imitation stained-glass. Ferocious clanging came from a back room. Someone was banging on metal.

He passed an altar, a simple table mounted with a cross at the back of the room. To his left, beyond an open door, he saw a toilet bowl standing in a pool of water. A man sprawled in the water was hammering and muttering at a pipe.

He inched forward. "Please, Sir. Where can I find Reverend Snyder?"

The clangs drowned him out. He began again. "Please?" He shouted loud enough that the man answered him by thrusting up a big, square hand.

"Fetch me that wrench. The biggest one."

Sam splashed through the puddle to a metal toolbox and lifted out the heavy iron tool. "Please, Sir. I'm looking for Reverend Snyder."

Sam waited. The plumber heaved himself to his feet to change his angle of attack against the pipe. His sweaty power filled the room. He was not quite six feet tall, and stocky with bare, heavily muscled arms and wide shoulders holding up bib overalls. His square face under dangling strings of sandy hair was blunt as a boxer dog's. His large dark-brown eyes glared at the offending porcelain. "Sister Ellen!" His sudden command roared so loud, his young visitor jumped. "Fetch a mop in here on the double!"

"Sir," Sam dared speak. "Sir, may I talk with you?"

"Not while I've got Noah's Flood to dry up."

"I can help mop up, sir."

The man with the massive shoulders and arms of a heavyweight prizefighter continued to scowl down at the flood at their feet. Clearly, Sam could see this was no time to talk about Japan. The ease he felt telling his first lie surprised him. "Sir, the Lord told me to come here."

"The Lord didn't tell you that on a Wednesday morning you belong in school?" The preacher tossed the wrench with a clang into the metal box. He turned his dark eyes, far more penetrating than Chaplain Lobaugh's pale gaze, on Sam. No one had to tell him this rugged man had experienced a different side of life than the navy's chaplain. Sam had seen men like this in Bremerton. If he weren't a preacher, he'd make a hell of a mean drunk.

"Actually, sir, my father used to tell me all about Japan and the good work missionaries are doing over there."

The preacher scrubbed his hands on his bib overalls and reached down fitting the wrench to the pipe. "Your father's been in Japan?"

"He was over there. Twice. He was a Lieutenant in the navy in Nagasaki—like your sign out front says. Maybe you knew him over there?"

The preacher grunted with the effort of working the pipe. "U.S. Navy officers on leave in Nagasaki don't generally drop by asking to have their souls saved." The preacher turned his head and shot Sam a look that told the lad to be careful, that this man of the Lord knew when boys were lying. "You're not by any chance a Roman Catholic, are you?"

"No, sir," Sam declared vigorously. "I'm a protestant. Navy chapel and Bremerton Presbyterian Sunday School." He hoped that answer was enough, and scoured his memory for anything besides Alaska his father had told about his days at sea. "The thing is, my dad told me all about Admiral Perry opening up Japan and how Nagasaki was the closest city to China and full of foreigners."

The preacher had stemmed the flood. "Where's he now—your father?"

"He's up in Alaska, but the navy doesn't know where."

Without turning to glance at the boy, the preacher-plumber said, "And that armband? Your mother?"

"She died last week."

"I'm sorry to hear about your mother." Reverend Snyder gave the pipe an added tug and continued to consider the stanched flood in which he stood. "When you're not playing hooky where do you live?"

"Bremerton. Or did." He was telling the truth part of the time, saving lying till it was absolutely necessary. "Now, without my Mom, the navy says they're going to send me to an orphanage."

"No people here in the Northwest?"

"No, Sir."

"And you thought you might duck in here looking to get in out of the rain."

"I could work for you, Sir, for you and the church."

"And suppose you tell me how I'm supposed to know if it wasn't Satan himself who sent you here?"

Sam's heart jammed in his throat. "I pray, sir. I pray all the time."

"We'd know, all right, the wife and I, if you were a limb of Satan." The back of the preacher's heavy arm rubbed across his face.

"Please, Sir. I could work for you. Earn my keep."

"You have a name?"

"Samuel Adams Pinkerton."

"Tell you what, Samuel Adams Pinkerton, before we pack you back to Bremerton, besides knowing the work end of a mop, you think you can handle a magic lantern?"

"Yes, sir, I ran one at school," he declared, thrilled not to be lying.

A woman with a shiny face framed by straight blonde hair cut like a Dutch boy's and caught above the ears with barrettes appeared in the door with a mop. Sam guessed she was thirty, but she looked older without a hint of his mother's pale blonde elegance. Her face was mottled red and white, the skin of a farm wife never defiled by lipstick or Lady Esther face powder. Her thin, gray dress and frayed blue sweater were what the wife of a man in bib overalls would wear.

For a moment her gaze locked on him. Her husband turned and for the first time appraised the young volunteer, this soldier for Christ, this nearly twelve-year-old boy in a gray suit with a band of mourning and sagging black stockings. Both the preacher and wife held him with long, penetrating gazes. Sam stood straight. He held his breath.

He was still holding his breath when, with a thrust of her chin, the skinny woman thrust the mop on him—an order to get to work.

Without another word her chin motioned her husband into a kitchen in back of the altar, and the two Snyders disappeared. Had he passed the test? With the mop in his hand he felt relief along with pangs of hunger. His stomach, without a bite to eat since Bremerton, was growling but he ignored it while starting to mop Noah's flood.

By midday he'd dried the floor and scrubbed the toilet. On a folding chair by the table that served as an altar, he found a baloney sandwich and a glass of milk.

CHAPTER EIGHT

All the rest of the day he sweated in the brand-new suit he'd worn to look his best for his grandparents. Besides the toilet floor he'd scrubbed the worn kitchen linoleum and now, with evening coming, he was put to work setting up for a church supper. Without being told what to do he was carrying tables and unfolding wooden chairs in what the Snyders referred to as the meeting room. From the kitchen he brought in bowls and plates and bunches of tin knives and forks. He carried a slide projector to the middle of the room and positioned it to throw images past the altar onto a whitewashed wall.

The Snyders said little. They didn't bother with kind words, and he was determined, no matter what chore they set him to, never to complain.

At five o'clock he helped three Japanese women to carry pots and bowls covered with dishcloths into the kitchen. An hour later the tabernacle's Japanese congregation of two dozen—mostly small, old, quiet people bundled in dark, Western-style clothes with a few in kimonos, filled the folding chairs.

Mrs. Snyder, in a dark brown bombazine dress, suddenly became "Sister Ellen," banging an upright piano with fierce enthusiasm. Her hymn built into a rollicking fanfare, which brought Reverend Snyder into the room, looking far more like a minister in a black suit than the morning's plumber with a wrench. His strong basso joined Sister Ellen's and his wildly waving big hands raised his congregation's voices into song—"Bringing the Sheaves." Sam added his own small voice.

As twenty-seven chairs screeched up to the tables, Grace was invoked while the Japanese flock sat before ample servings of meat loaf, canned peas, mashed potatoes and gravy. Sam managed to snatch his own dinner between scraping plates and stacking them in the sink for later washing.

After drying his hands he was ordered to the magic lantern. But for himself and the Reverend and Sister Ellen at the piano—everyone around him was Japanese. Real Japanese. Stealing closer looks, he could see they didn't all look exactly alike, but without exception they did have black or gray hair and dark eyes. Many noisily picked their teeth. Others smothered coughs and sniffles. A few wore gauze facemasks, limiting their winter colds to themselves.

The lights dimmed. The preacher snapped his clicker, and the white wall sprang alive with the first hand-tinted slides. The congregation sat like children, staring at another little white storefront church in Eau Claire, Wisconsin. A second click and the wall filled with a photograph of the mission's founder, The Reverend Elwood R. Peterson, a stern-looking man. Sister Ellen's proud smile reminded the congregation that he was her reverend father. The third slide, a small tabernacle, was not white but brick and overtinted a deep, liver color.

"Our mission in Japan." The preacher's resonant basso filled every corner of the meeting room. "Urakami, actually. Those of you from Nagasaki know it's three miles up the hill from that Godless city. As most of you brothers and sisters know, The Lord is calling Sister Ellen and me to return to our mission there in April."

The next set of slides had nothing to do with Japan. Black-and-white Bible pictures from the engravings of Gustave Doré depicted Hell in lurid bursts of flame and smoke where the stark naked damned agonized in an awesome repertoire of horrible tortures. Doré's last set of pictures illustrated rewarding calm as a white-robed Jesus walked through the Holy Land, his hand bestowing blessings.

Seventy-two slides in all and Sam only got one upside down.

Light startled the room. Sister Ellen battered the upright and the reverend's thunder and waving arms encouraged a louder "Rock of Ages." This strong, muscular American seemed to levitate, rising heavenward, higher and higher, intoning his sermon from the Book of Hosea. Words climbed while Sam struggled to stay awake. He dropped his head, nodding off, till a spirited anthem banging from the piano shot him to his feet to assist the preacher, holding a wicker basket and collecting a few coins.

At the front door many bowed to the reverend. Most of the men seemed reluctant to allow his big, strong hand to grip and shake his goodness into them.

Sam had spotted an army cot in the storage room behind steamer trunks and offered a silent prayer that it be his for spend the night on. After the service he heard himself telling the truth to the Snyders. Because he'd been helping do the Lord's Work all day and evening, he'd missed his last ferry to Bremerton.

He set up the cot. Sister Ellen handed him two thin blankets and stood over him till he got down on his knees to give thanks for his blessings.

His first day as a runaway. So far, he told himself, he should be thankful—after a fiercely hard day's work—for a baloney sandwich and snatches of dinner and a roof over his head. That morning had been a lifetime ago, racing from the hotel, praying as soon as his document was translated, he'd race back to the Showalters and prove he wasn't Japanese. He'd prove he belonged with his brother. He wound his blanket tighter. During the day Benjy had left on the train to Baltimore. Now his prayers he said were for his mother. He pictured her in the baggage car in her coffin. Was she wearing her gold pince-nez glasses? No amount of tears or prayers would bring her back. He prayed for poor little Benjy. He prayed again for that ultimate miracle—his father back from Alaska, holding him tight and taking him away from the Snyders and the Japanese people he'd been with tonight.

Suddenly he threw back the thin blankets and reached into his jacket hanging over a chair to make sure he still had his document from Japan. Drifting to sleep, he was back in the antique shop standing among the gold-leaf screens, smelling burning incense and feeling his stockinged feet touching those smooth rice mats. "Tatami," the little sparrow of a woman had called them. In that moment, just before falling asleep, just below the surface of his mind, came a vague drifting sense of a woman's face coming close as fabric as soft as silk covered his eyes.

CHAPTER NINE

Shivering, he woke long before dawn. He wound his thin blanket closer. Now that he knew he wouldn't be joining Benjy in Baltimore he would have to get the Snyders to ask him to cross the ocean with them. Japan. Scary, what an adventure leaving all the world he'd ever known. Yes. Japan, but it meant giving up all hope his father was coming for him. It meant trusting those people in the next room with his document. But not yet. Drawing his blanket tighter he told himself not to be scared. What kid in Bremerton ever had such an adventure to look forward to? Why ask what Huck Finn would do. He'd light out for the unknown on a wonderful new adventure. Besides, not even Huck had known the call of smooth tatami under his feet or felt that faint memory of silk and a woman's face. For the next eight days no true believer ever made himself more useful, sweeping and dusting, scrubbing floors, folding and unfolding chairs, spackling and calcimining walls, scouring pots and pans, stacking hymnals and Bibles, and mopping the toilet that no wrench could totally quell.

Serving without complaint, chanting what seemed a million amens and shouting hallelujah on cue, he was conscientiously, faithfully serving the Lord and the Snyders. Any free moment they sent him out on the streets handing out tracts—"Where Will You Spend Eternity?"

On his third day with the Snyders he'd telephoned Bremerton. Twice he reached the chaplain's office, and once the chaplain himself. The navy had no word of his father. "Samuel," the chaplain was upset, astonished to hear from his charge who'd so completely disappeared. He smothered his surprise with the utmost gravity. "Samuel, you must tell me and the navy where you are—"

Without a word Sam dropped the telephone receiver back on its hook. From the first day he'd come to them out of the rain he'd heard the missionaries planning to return to their mission in Nagasaki.

On a March morning with the wind rattling the imitation stained-glass windows, the preacher and his skinny wife ordered him to the kitchen table. For this important meeting he smoothed his shaggy hair and looked as solemn as he could manage.

The preacher seemed prepared to deliver a sermon, to speak with solemnity to the runaway who'd come to them off the street. "Samuel Pinkerton Adams. That's what you call yourself."

"Yes, Sir."

"Do you believe in God?"

"Yes, Brother Wendell." Sam quickly added, "Oh, yes, Sister Ellen."

"Your mother's dead and you still have no word from this Pinkerton—your father?"

"No word, Sir—Ma'am."

The preacher was only just beginning. "You have telephoned the navy since you've been here with us?"

"Yes, sir."

"Today we have decided to call you Brother Samuel. Do you know what that means?"

"That you and Sister Ellen know I live to serve Jesus?"

Sister Ellen closed her eyes. Her thin lips were close to a smile.

"What would you say, Brother Samuel, if we were to tell you that Sister Ellen and I have talked this over with the Lord and find it is His will that you will serve with us in Japan?"

Sam smothered a wild burst of joy determined to only show the humble gravity of one who has received what the Snyders so often spoke of as "the Call." His answer must convince them it came purely from his love to serve The Lord. Oh, yes, he told them with wet eyes. He felt it too. He'd long known he had no choice but to serve them and the Lord.

This husband and wife studied him, examining him as closely as any passage in scripture. Could they guess, he wondered, how closely yet surreptitiously he'd been studying them? For weeks he'd asked himself if he could cross the Pacific Ocean with these people he had yet to trust with his secret. They'd be in Nagasaki, the very city where the American consul had written the letter taken from his mother's desk. Over there with the Snyders he'd continue to pose as a missionary, pretending to love Jesus. Of course they'd work him like the slave he was but he'd have a roof over his head and Sister Ellen's plain cooking. Once there he faced the very real possibility of the document proving what the Showalters claimed, that he was half-Japanese. On the remote chance that charge could be true—once he was there in her city he'd find his father's Japanese wife, his first mother. If he were Japanese, over there he would have a mother and a family.

Japan!

"Japan, Samuel?" The preacher and his wife waited for his answer.

Sam managed grave solemnity. "Praise The Lord."

The preacher lifted both huge, square hands signaling them down on their knees on the kitchen's worn linoleum.

CHAPTER TEN

The last night in Seattle before sailing they worked till five in the morning packing Bibles and hymnals in wooden crates. In the morning down on Seattle's Alaskan Way the Reverend and Mrs. Snyder boarded the Japanese passenger ship, the nineteen-thousand-ton *Tenyo Maru's* second class, while Sam entered the lower depths of one of Doré's pictures of hell. Sweating in the hot depths of steerage, he was the only non-Asian, crowded in with its eight hundred and seventeen third class passengers. He'd expected bunks or U.S. Navy-style hammocks. Instead he'd sleep on a ratty quilt on a vibrating metal floor. Under the low ceiling the air was thick with smoke and smelled of frying food and acrid blasts of hot oil from the giant engines throbbing under his shoes. There was no place he'd rather be. He hugged himself in excitement.

To reach his sleeping mat meant crawling over men sprawled like worms in a jar, scratching and farting loudly and with alarming frequency. Some slurped tea but more downed sake from pottery bottles. There wasn't a one who didn't smoke.

On his quilt he pulled out his Bible and stared at its thin pages with a heavy heart. Brother Wendell had divided the Book's 1,272 pages into the 17 days the *Tenyo Maru* was expected to be at sea. He had to read and, more importantly, let 75 pages of the Word of God a day, into his heart. The print was small and the light dim.

The Asians who clustered around him were not all Japanese. Many seemed to be from other countries, chattering in their own languages.

Often, when he looked up from the Holy Book, he'd watch two old men a few feet away in a thick cloud of cigarette smoke, playing a board game with white and black stones. The older of the two was forever rubbing his bald head and scratching inside his gray kimono to help him think. His shaggy-haired opponent, peering at the stones through thick glasses, was draped in an oversized and threadbare Western suit of faded gray. Nearby other neighbors, a noisy batch of six, were spewing pumpkin seed hulls. Down here most of his fellow passengers were ragged and poor, bent and worn. Some were agricultural workers finishing labor contracts in the States. Besides the Japanese they were Chinese, Koreans, and Filipinos.

"Until the Oriental accepts the Lord Jesus as his Savior," Brother Wendell had thundered in Seattle, "he will always and forever be a creature unlike ourselves—a heathen doomed to live in darkness and desperate in his need of salvation."

"Well, here we are," Sam told himself looking through the gloom at these other heathens who didn't appear to realize they were doomed to hellfire.

Fresh air was only available outside his dungeon at a tiny stretch of rail where the salty wind sharpened his appetite for the little wooden boxes of white boiled rice, pickles dyed vivid acid-green and pink, and what for the first few days he hoped wasn't octopus.

On the morning of his sixteenth day at sea he was frowning over the *Tenth Chapter of the Book of Acts* when a thrill roused the crowd from their quilts to elbow each other onto their narrow patch of deck. Up, in the bluest of skies, seagulls, the sure sign of land, were swooping and squawking. Off to the right a fat little buddha of a man let out a yelp of glee spotting their first *sampan* with tattered brown sails. Ahead, across the silvery sea, dark green mountains rose over a cluster of gray piers and low tile roofs. Hours before they docked he and his cardboard suitcase were first in line emerging from steerage. Reaching the gangplank and brimming with excitement he saw more Japanese than he'd ever seen, tying up the *Tenyo Maru* against a pier with a band striking up a brassy welcome.

He was in Japan, but from here and the gray wharves, it could have been Seattle, except for the white flags with blazoning red suns flapping overhead.

He was the first to race down the gangplank. Ahead, on the pier, amidst the music and excitement, first class passengers were calling and waving to family and friends. Through the crush of passengers and porters down on the dock he reached an unusually solemn Brother Wendell and Sister Ellen who were overseeing their luggage and crates. The preacher's large hand signaled Sam to stop grinning. "Compose yourself," he hissed to remind Sam that with these first steps he must never forget he was a white boy in Japan, a Christian in a heathen land.

"Your Bible," he said under his breath, "carry it so everyone can see it. Since you don't have a passport you'll have to convince the immigration police you're our son."

Wild with excitement, Sam couldn't wait to see Japan beyond the gray docks—*The National Geographic* views he'd seen in the Bremerton school library—Mount Fuji, pagodas, cherry trees, willows, and lovely ladies in silk.

Brother Wendell stoutly refused the services of barelegged men with short jackets hardly covering their asses who were pulling rickshaws and carts among the clanging streetcars. Determined businessmen, dressed identically in dark Western-style suits, and wearing white Panama hats, seemed propelled in a massive rush. Old women, dark little wrens bent with age within dark kimonos, skittered on clogs. Younger women flashed by in colorful kimonos. Others, in the latest European and American styles, hurried on perilously high heels.

In the train station he stifled a gasp of surprise, for nothing about the ascetic Snyders prepared him for the luxury of their second class compartment. For the Snyders, this was apparently an ethnic necessity. Third Class would have been beneath the standing of any Westerner. Inside the compartment the heavy mahogany woodwork and elegance of frothy lace curtains, white antimacassars, and bud vases with carnations were adornment to be sternly ignored by the pious.

Since Sister Ellen had seen Japan before and was therefore relieved of any curiosity, she went straight to work darning Brother Wendell's socks. With her thrust of chin she ordered Sam to sit next to the window for the light to read his Bible.

He kept his head down on the Book but slid surreptitious glances at the first sights of Japan passing by. Japan! So far this far-off exotic land seemed nothing but shabby, gray, industrial warehouses. Soon, the real Japan, the *National Geographic* Japan, emerged as they rattled across checkerboard farmland dotted with low, thatch-roof houses among squares of glinting water and bright green rice shoots.

"Look!" He was so thrilled by the landscape he forgot his attention to scripture and burst with excitement. "Look! Rice paddies!" A frown from the Snyders sent him back to the Book and the *Revelations,* a Lamb standing on Mount Sion, and "with him a hundred and forty *and* four thousand having his Father's name written in their foreheads."

He tested the thickness of the pages left. Only seven more chapters to go.

He kept his head down, reading in silence, sliding ever more of his secret glances at the landscape, filled with straight rows of green. Out the window he saw men and women in blue work clothes wading in mud, bent double under wide-bowl hats.

He betrayed himself by gasping his delight at the sight of a hillside foaming in blossoms as white as the compartment's lace. "Cherry blossoms!" he breathed happily to himself. Yes. Here it was. Picture postcard Japan. Sister Ellen glanced up from Brother Wendell's wool sock. Her finger with a split nail tapped his open book, an order to address himself to the Lord, as she cast a disdainful glance at the blossoms. "Late this year. Can't begin to compare with ours at home in Eau Claire."

The train hooted and curled around a hill into a sudden sun spangling the ocean. Another curve sped them through a bamboo grove's feathery branches and a world of deep green. In a sudden flash he glimpsed a giant wooden temple and a file of priests in white, certainly more than worth the gasp he smothered just in time. Japanese priests! A temple! Those priests out there—heathens for whose souls they'd just crossed the Pacific.

More and more masses of stone monuments went by within bamboo groves on hummocks at the edge of rice paddies. A few stones appeared to be new, but most were worn down to stubs and mossy with age.

"Not even cemeteries," Sister Ellen huffed with another disapproving glance. "Only stone markers. They cremate their dead. Ashes. No rising for them on the Day of Judgment."

Awed, Sam was amazed by the number of the dead these stones memorialized till he reminded himself that Japan, unlike America, was a very old country where people had been dying for centuries. Brother Wendell shattered his thoughts returning him to The Lord. "You've finished the last chapter of *Revelations?*"

"No, sir. But just about."

From the green, gold and blue of his first day in Japan Sam bent down concentrating on the small print. Chapter Nineteen, Verse Eleven.

In the train outside their compartment clanging bells were summoning businessmen in Western suits and women in colorful silk kimonos hurrying through the passageway. Sam guessed this was the first call to the dining car, which the pilgrims from Seattle and Eau Claire ignored. No need to risk Japanese food. In Kobe Sister Ellen had packed a basket with egg-salad and baloney sandwiches, root beer and sarsaparilla. With knives and forks and a mouthful of egg salad Sam squirmed with secret pleasure wondering what they'd say if he confessed that on board the *Tenyo Maru* he'd not only become expert with chopsticks, but had eaten raw octopus.

They clanged through a blazing red sunset into night.

Japan was passing by in the dark, fields, forests, and mountains in silhouette against a starry sky. Night here in Japan was different, much darker than in the States, with only gleams pinpointing the black. The cities and towns they traveled through shone with only a few lanterns and gaslights, nothing here in Japan as brightly lit by electricity as in the States.

Brother Wendell snored. All night Sister Ellen seemed unable to clear her nose.

In the morning—which meant those last five pages of the Holy Bible—he was given time out and handed peeled oranges and greasily delicious, very American, crullers. They'd rattled on for hours when Sam, the first to hear a bell with a different tone, sensed their train was nearing their destination.

Nagasaki!

CHAPTER ELEVEN

The train came to a shuddering stop. Outside their window, swarming porters were fighting each other to unload the foreigners' baggage and lug their crates from the baggage car. Such clamoring eagerness for work stiffened the preacher with righteous anger. Not only as a man of God, but as an American from Wisconsin, he was offended that these Japanese dared challenge his American self-reliance. The preacher was making it clear he was his own porter.

Sam wrestled crates full of salvation—Bibles and hymnals and religious tracts—imported by Christian America here deep into godless Japan. By the time he'd trundled the last lot out to the street, still wearing the suit from his audience with the Showalters, he was streaming sweat.

In the April sprinkle outside the station a crowd of rickshaw pullers surrounded the pale Americans, offering themselves as man-powered transport, which fired Reverend Snyder's even greater missionary wrath. "Rickshaws! An abomination." He glared at the rough, muscular men. "Our Lord did not create man in his image—even heathens—to serve as a beast of burden."

"I guess," Sam, juggling crates, said to himself, "that doesn't include me."

The preacher, on fire with righteousness, thrust the brawling Japanese aside and plunged into the street, peering to the right and left to catch sight of the faithful converts from Urakami delegated to meet them here at the station.

Sam heaped the last of their crates and baggage into a pile taller than him. A stubby and muscular carter, sturdy as a tree trunk, tossed aside the onion he'd been gnawing to come trotting over, lifting his head, showing huge brown teeth and emitting foul breath. Before the Americans could stop him, he was strapping their baggage onto his cart. Sister Ellen cried out her alarm, fluttering her bony hands, shrilling out dismissal, which the Japanese totally ignored.

Sudden thunder cracked in the black sky over Nagasaki. A downpour burst. The preacher, dashing back and taking cover from his search for the welcoming committee, was stymied, and hot enough to swear, "Where the hell's Ito?"

Sister Ellen proffered absolution for the missing Japanese delegates. "Perhaps Brother Hiroshi got the wrong date—"

By now the other train passengers had hired most of the rickshaws and were speeding off. "Hell's bells!" Brother Wendell snarled. In spite of this downpour he was standing on principle, waving off the carter and commanding Sam to unstrap their bags. The rickshaw man shrugged, produced another onion and trotted off. Brother Wendell had won the first round, which left the three of them standing in the rain, staring at the crates and luggage and three miles from the Urakami mission. Grumbling, the righteous preacher waved over an old, white-haired carter, who tottered forward, his scrawny body bare but for a short jacket and straw sandals. A straw hat hung over his narrow shoulders like a mushroom. Brother Wendell snorted.

"You have a horse?"

The old man bared stubs of brown teeth in a wide grin and thumped his narrow chest. These gaijins didn't need a horse—they had him. The preacher, with no cart and no horse in sight and a black sky threatening Noah's epic rain, cursed. With a grunt he gave special absolution for this image of God to serve as a beast of burden. Sam stood staring in awe at the cheeriness of the tough old troll, heaving crates and luggage and then hitching himself to the cart as his own horse. Brother Wendell sent the man ahead, trotting off to the mission in Urakami.

Sam was assigned two suitcases. The preacher marched his own two Christian soldiers onward up a long hill, making a detour to keep from passing under an enormous half-built church tower. Brother Wendell's heavy mouth set hard in smoldering resolve. Near this tower they were dangerously close to the enemy—the Roman Catholic Church.

The sun came out. The wet world shone. Sam looked down a muddy road crossing spring-green rice paddies and spotted their old man tottering along with his cart. Here it was—the one-story brick building he'd seen so often when showing the magic-lantern slide show. A sign in English and Japanese was so weathered the letters were close to invisible: Mission Church of Christ.

Ahead, in the April sunshine, stood eight old Japanese women and one man, all in dark kimonos. At last, the reception committee which hadn't been at the train station was waiting under paper umbrellas and bowing low. The Snyders returned their welcomers' formality with only the slightest of nods. Already Sam had seen enough bowing to sense the importance of the ritual.

The formality outside the church lasted only a moment before the faithful broke ranks and rushed forward on wooden clogs, bobbing and chattering their welcome. Sister Ellen surprised him. Shattering all protocol, she drew a wisp of a bent old woman into her arms.

Brother Wendell bestowed only half smiles and beatific nods. Sam overheard his murmur to his wife. "Only eleven. So where the hell's Ito?"

A wraith of an old man, trembling so that his umbrella shook, had something to say, but apparently was too choked with tears to risk speaking. Tentatively he drew a letter from his sleeve, which he presented to the preacher with a bow. As Brother Wendell read it his face turned to concrete. "It seems our fair-weather friend, Brother Ito, in whom we and The Lord have vouchsafed our trust, has taken himself a position at the Mitsubishi shipyards. He's allowed them to transfer him to Formosa."

Ito's father found a wispy, apologetic voice. Quivering with guilt, he was bowing lower. "We did not write. All of us were too ashamed."

The preacher's face could not hide his anger and bitter disappointment at this pitiful remnant of his congregation—the Urakami Mission he'd so often and so proudly spoken of in Seattle. Without a word he turned and strode quickly into his church.

Every Japanese stayed bowed.

Sister Ellen's smile faded, but she remained out in the sunlight pressing the hands of old friends. Sam stepped forward with his suitcases for his first look inside the rundown little church, all but knocking down a woman small as a child. Struggling to raise her head she peered straight up at him with clouded agate eyes. Her intensity held him. "Oh, God," he thought, "—the way she's looking at me—is she saying I'm Japanese?"

He bowed and fled into the empty tabernacle.

His heart sank. The place was empty, a near-ruin. Urakami's mission cried out for far more whitewash than Yesler Way's. It stank of mold and evidence of a nearby privy. Gray walls, once white, were splotched with stains from the rain and cracks from Japan's frequent earthquakes. The ceiling was still dripping from the morning's rain. Puddles glinted the floor. Broken window frames, patched with the same paper imitation stained glass as Seattle's, rattled in the spring breeze.

Sam saw he was not alone. The preacher, in shadow, was down on his knees before the bare table of an altar, his head buried in his hands, his shoulders shaking. Sam's heart tightened, sharing the man's desolation. Brother Wendell in tears? Knowing the man would never forgive him for seeing him like this, he stepped back out the door as quietly as he could.

CHAPTER TWELVE

The Snyders had taken a solemn vow—with The Lord's help—to re-open the church by the next Sunday. Their example of furiously working day and night demanded their indentured acolyte match their devotion in full measure their devotion. With his twelve-year-old energy he quickly got the hang of spackling earthquake cracks in the walls, mending broken floors, and climbing up and daubing the Western-style roof with tar. The unbeliever was paying the price for having lied about his devotion to the Lord.

He was eager to learn Japanese, but the Snyders never read or wrote in anything but English. Every night, after praying before falling asleep, he imagined a forbidden run to Nagasaki to find their version of a city hall. There they'd tell him where to find the American Consul. Whatever truth he finally learned, he promised himself he'd do the honorable thing by the Snyders. Whether he was Japanese or American, he was desperate to search for his mother and his family. He'd work at the mission as long as it took to pay off his passage across the Pacific.

In Urakami Sam whitewashed walls. He climbed up on the roof and staunch leaks. He patched window frames. He hammered the few rows of broken benches back together. He emptied ashes from the black-iron stove with a shovel. Hauling those ashes made him look black as a banjo player in a minstrel show he'd seen in Seattle. Brother Wendell barked and ordered him to follow him into an overgrown patch of weeds behind the church.

The preacher, working at his side with fierce efforts, attacked the hard earth, telling Sam that this was Mrs. Ishigura's resting place. Sam remembered the bent old lady with the agate eyes. The preacher was saying a hallelujah, for she'd died a proper Christian death. "No Japanese sin of cremation for her," he declared proudly, wiping sweat as they worked together heaving aside a boulder. "Burning we leave to the heathens. At the Last Judgment, our dead rise up and stand before the Lord God Jehovah."

In the hot May sun, Sam unbuttoned his shirt.

"Button up!" the senior gravedigger commanded. "Our flock is forever watching every move we make. Hard work is no sin, but we're the white race and that means we stay covered here for them to look up to."

In any religion the re-opening of the mission in one week, as promised, would have been a miracle. Under a Sunday morning's cloudless blue sky Sister Ellen, dressed in her best brown bombazine, greeted the sun on the Lord's day with a rapturous "Hallelujah!" and threw open the front door with a second joyous cry. The acolyte, solemn in his frayed gray Melton suit, posted himself in the aisle, bowing, welcoming the nineteen worshippers.

Last-night's rain pinged into a bucket accompanying the out-of-tune piano of Sister Ellen on "Brighten The Corner Where You Are." Brother Wendell's impressive appearance in his black suit made him look every inch the man to save lives. He mounted the two steps of the pulpit Sam had hammered together, smiling, bellowing the last notes of the hymn. In just one week he was bringing his Urakami mission back to life. His strongest sermon, delivered in Japanese, none of which Sam understood, was the old reliable "Where Will You Spend Eternity?" The faithful nineteen perched spellbound on benches until Sister Ellen's piano erupted in a rousing "Bringing in the Sheaves." Sam sprang to his feet and solemnly passed the plate collecting a pitiful amount of sen.

After the service Brother Wendell clamped Sam's shoulder so hard his acolyte pretended not to wince. "Nineteen today, but never you forget, Brother Samuel, Our Lord began with only twelve." Following the service, the triumphant pilgrims sat down to a real American Sunday dinner. The Shimura family, owners of the largest squares of rice paddies in the neighborhood, had brought an offering—lamb chops from New Zealand. Sister Ellen had been gifted with potatoes and leeks from other neighbors, the Imeis. The apple pie was hers alone.

"When we first took up our mission here," Brother Wendell explained to Sam, "you never saw meat. Certainly not lamb. Even now, the vast majority of Japanese don't know what it is, and don't want to know. They scarcely touch meat. What they eat is fish and they eat it raw. Some chicken. But no beef. No milk. No diary products. They hate cheese."

"Despise it," frowned Sister Ellen whose preacher father, Sam had been told many times, was also a dairy farmer in Wisconsin with two hundred Holsteins and fifty-one Ayrshires.

The preacher sucked a shred of pie sticking to his teeth and peeled a local *satsuma* orange. "In a few weeks, Sister Ellen's garden will be fruitful. Till then we'll fill in with what our flock provides with canned goods, till she can put up preserves."

"So you see," Sister Ellen said smiling. "Just because we're here in Japan doesn't mean we have to live like the Japanese."

The preacher worked a toothpick. "The truth is, the Oriental isn't like you or me. It all comes down to one simple fact—he puts no value whatsoever on human life. He doesn't have the same feeling for his fellow man that we do. With the exception, of course, of those good souls who were with us this morning. Thank Our Lord we've brought them to the truth. And with the Lord's help we'll bring more."

Sister Ellen shared the joy. "Thanks to us you've seen how they've let Jesus into their hearts. We love them, but that doesn't for one minute mean that even with our brothers and sisters here, there are not always going to be differences. They love us for bringing them Jesus, but to them we'll always be gaijin. Foreigners. Outsiders. Never Japanese."

Brother Wendell nodded gravely in agreement with his wife. "Don't you ever kid yourself on that score. You can live with these people all your life, reach out to them, but they'll never include you as one of them."

Sam was expected to answer that he understood this truth, but too large a chunk of apple pie jammed his windpipe.

The preacher had weighed the acolyte in his scales and so far, apparently, not found him grievously wanting. "What say you, Brother

Samuel? Sister Ellen and I are beginning to believe you feel the joy of giving your life to Our Lord. Are we right?"

Sam prayed the preacher couldn't read his mind, couldn't see that even at this solemn moment getting the apple pie down, he wasn't weighing the devotion of saving more Japanese, but counting the days till he could make his escape into Nagasaki. The preacher held him with one of his penetrating looks straight into his eyes. "Are we right, Brother Samuel?"

He dropped his head in the hope of looking pious. "Yes, Sir, Brother Wendell." They were waiting for a hallelujah and he obliged. Sister Ellen put aside her coffee cup. She turned her tight smile to her husband, whose big hand squeezed hers. "Yes, I have a pretty good notion that our Brother Samuel is learning the truth of what we're talking about. He knows no man can live in two worlds between darkness and light."

Her words followed Sam to bed. Most of the night he lay wide awake between two worlds staring at the white walls of his musty little cell, silvered by moonlight.

Tomorrow was Monday. Monday was always a good day to start anything. Tomorrow he'd race the three miles to Nagasaki. All night his heart pounded.

CHAPTER THIRTEEN

Like an early morning bird Sam was flying across the edges of rice paddies. Crickets shrilled. More roosters announced the new day. A bullfrog , startled to be wakened this early, jumped across his path with a complaining croak. A perfect omen. A dog yapped in the distance. He breathed in the smells of morning breakfast fires and the less pleasant whiff of farmers spreading night soil. He dashed under the Catholic cathedral's tower looming against the crimsoning sky and took the morning wind in his face as he raced down the streetcar tracks of the long hill.

Na-ga-sa-ki! Na-ga-saki! He ignored his dribbling socks flapping down around his ankles. He had no time to slow down long enough to hike them up. In his thumping heart he feared if he cut his pace for an instant the momentous consequences of what he was doing, would freeze him on the spot.

He stopped just long enough at the Nagasaki train station to gulp cold water and renew his pace, sprinting into a city of stone bridges spanning canals overhung with lacy, spring-green willows. The sparkling water was his shining way into the redbrick center of town.

Nagasaki!

He burst into the first wide city streets which he found empty but for a few rickshaws and delivery carts. A lone noodle man piped a whistle. Nagasaki on the freshest, clearest, most glorious day May had ever shone on the world of the rising sun.

The few Japanese on the streets gawked in amazement at the sprinting gaijin. Who was this bronze-haired foreign boy gasping for breath, his stockings flapping? What could explain why he was dashing as if the devils from his Christian brand of hell were after him?

He wanted to shout to everyone that at last he was in Nagasaki. He forced himself to slow enough to look around. City Hall? Where was City Hall? He seemed to be in the center of an enormous town with tall buildings, not very Japanese, not wood and paper, but big city buildings.

He told himself to slow down. He was in Nagasaki. He decided he might not be able to talk to or trust anyone in City Hall. He told himself to forget City Hall and go straight to the American Consul. That was where that letter had come from, written by a man who'd known his father. He'd help. Sharpless. He'd never forgotten that strange name. Of course that letter written to his father, that Chaplain Lobaugh still had in his briefcase, was dated nine years ago. If by some miracle—after nine years—the American Consul was still in Nagasaki, he'd have his father's friend, who knew everything about him, an American who wouldn't need any document to tell him, once and for all, who he was. Best of all, if his mother were Japanese, he might even know where she lived here in Nagasaki.

He poked his head inside a vegetable stall opening for the day. "A-mer-i-can Con-sul." He tried to pantomime his problem to a plump woman in a shabby gray kimono, her bright red face so startled by the foreigner she shrieked and dropped a tray of eggplants.

On the street, one by one, he snagged five others and each one recoiled with fright and bewilderment. A sixth, a dark little gnome with wild gray hair with a wooden bucket of writhing eels, howled a hyena laugh, jumped up and down, and, without answering, trotted off.

Directly in front of him was a big Western-style hotel. The Bellevue's sign was in English, as easy to read as its huge stone grandeur was intimidating. With spit-smoothed hair and straightened shoulders, he dared enter. This early in the day the lobby was hushed, almost empty. The desk clerk, a slender Japanese man with bright black eyes and shoe-polish black hair, was bobbing with servility before a tall German-speaking giant with brush-cropped hair who was tapping the counter with an impatient cane.

Sam, dripping sweat, waited his turn till the German left. The hotel man glanced at the boy—a gaijin, but a boy, and therefore worthy of no respect. Impatient, he scarcely listened to the question spoken in English and quickly penciled a map on hotel notepaper. The Bellevue was an X. The American Consulate was a circle. He connected a line threading through streets.

Back out on the streets carts rattled, shopkeepers opened shutters and crowds filled the sidewalks. Men in dark suits, office workers, women in kimonos and Western dress, draymen in short jackets, were bringing the city alive. From a side street a drum thumped. Flutes screeched. Monks in robes, with their heads hidden under mushroom-shaped straw hats, emerged locked in silence, as they carried begging bowls tranquilly among the pedestrians.

The building, the circle on his map, left him unconvinced. He needed to see an American flag. The stars and stripes were nowhere in view but he found a bronze plaque in English. *Consulate of the United States of America.* The front door was locked. The hour was probably still too early to open.

After an hour pacing the sidewalk, ignoring his growling stomach, a Japanese man no taller than a boy but wearing a uniform and carrying a flag emerged from the front door. He found a rope and unfurled the flag in the sunshine—red, white and blue—the first American flag Sam had seen since Seattle. Tears sprang into his eyes. He swallowed hard. Feelings so powerful so overwhelmed him that he turned to hide his tears from a tall American couple entering the building.

Inside, he found a reception area. Beyond the counter three chattering women clerks were dusting desks and busily arranging papers. A thin man in a tight black suit, masked by gauze over his mouth and nose, hurried past the counter carrying a stack of dossiers dangling with ribbons. His eyes above the mask made it clear he was looking past and not acknowledging the mere boy.

"Sir?"

The man was so startled he fumbled his dossiers.

"Sir, please?"

The man was flustered. His small hand signaled a young woman in a navy-blue silk dress to come to the counter and deflect the boy from the adult world. Her face was not pleasant—wide and flat—not the face of a picture-postcard Japanese maiden. Her lips barely covered long teeth and her eyes bulged. No, not a good face—Japanese or Western.

Sam shone his best smile on her and began his pantomime and simplified English. "Mister—Sharpless—here?" With his head he gestured at the offices. The woman, facing panic the first thing on Monday morning by this mere boy, bobbled her head. Sam tried again. He enunciated slowly, unfolding his flimsy paper on a counter top. Her retreat blocked, her bulging eyes blinked in horror that this gaijin was demanding she examine the document. With a gasp she turned and called for reinforcements. Two lady typists in kimonos, much prettier women than his frightened clerk, came running in their short steps to share the document. As they read no one looked directly at him, but continued chattering and casting solemn looks of disbelief among themselves until all three burst into giggles and tried to hurry off.

He stopped them. Again, he spoke very slowly. "Where? Mist-er Sharp-less."

All three froze, drew in hisses of air, apparently incredulous a foreign boy could be so demanding. Fighting to make himself understood, he heard himself saying *Nihongo wakarimassen,* the two first words he'd learned on board the *Tenyo Maru* and had found himself using constantly in his first weeks, confessing he knew no Japanese. The three darted terrified looks at one another, then raised and flapped their smooth little hands in front of their faces, signaling him to wait as they skittered from the reception area with his document. His heart stopped. They had his paper—the first time it had ever been out of his hands.

After five minutes that seemed like agonizing hours while he sweated in terror, a flawlessly groomed, plump man strode into the reception area with the document in hand. The black of his pomaded hair was repeated in a carefully-trimmed mustache he scratched with the nail of his little finger. With cool dignity he snapped open a black lacquer case and drew out a cigarette.

"Good morning, young man," his English was crisp, his manner suggested he'd been interrupted in some important, grownup business.

"Good morning, sir."

"Do I understand you are asking that someone here who speaks English can translate this item for you?"

"Yes, Sir."

"I am not the United States Consul."

"No, Sir?"

"Your American Consul graciously allows me to use an office here when I visit Nagasaki."

"Would that be Mister Sharpless, Sir?" Sam's spirits soared.

"No. The Consul is Mister McClure. Mister McClure is in Fukuoka this week." The Japanese gentleman pocketed the cigarette case and drew out from another, smaller black lacquer case a card. He presented it to Sam with a bow so minimal, Sam felt the ritual might be a slight mockery. Nevertheless, Sam returned the bow by bending double.

The card was embossed, Japanese on one side, English on the other.

Mr. Takeo Sato
Fine Japanese Porcelain
Nagasaki, London and New York

"Come." Still holding the paper Mr. Sato's cigarette signaled the boy into an office at the same moment a short, stocky woman in a gray kimono rushed in with a tea tray.

"Tea," Mr. Sato of Nagasaki, London, and New York announced in a somewhat gruff voice. "You will find everything in Japan begins with tea." He waved the gray kimono woman away, indicating that he himself would pour the tea into small, handle-less cups. From the tray he offered rubbery-looking cake on a vermilion lacquer saucer to Sam. Famished, Sam bit into a solid mass of white goo.

Mr. Sato placed Sam's paper on the desk. From the vest of his three-piece black suit, Mr. Sato drew a small yellow fan he flicked open to create his own personal breeze. Seating himself behind the desk, his dignity was impressive, close to imperial. His English, spoken with such precision, was a kind of English Sam had never heard before. "The Honorable Mr. Sharpless you asked about indeed was the American Consul here perhaps eight, maybe nine years ago."

"Is Mr. Sharpless still here in Nagasaki?"

"In a manner of speaking." Mr. Sato examined his tea cup as if he was considering a precious antique. "Mr. Sharpless is in Sakamoto International Cemetery buried beside the estimable Mrs. Sharpless. He died before I myself first came here."

Mr. Sato's cup touched his mustache as he drew in tea with a sucking sound. He picked up his fan and created another breeze. "You are visiting Japan?"

"Yes, sir, Mister Sato," Sam cringed at the momentousness of his first lie in Nagasaki, and prayed after things had already gone this far he'd find Mr. Sato was a man he could trust.

"A suggestion."

"Yes, sir."

"Gentlemen here prefer to address each other as *san* which expresses a degree of honorable respect."

Sam spoke on cue. "Sato-San?"

"Well done. First rate. Of course, you are visiting Japan with your mother and father."

"My grandparents." Another wince. Terrified to admit he was a runaway from the Snyders in Urakami, and sensing the need for corroborative detail, he added, "From Baltimore. Baltimore, Maryland in the United Sates of America. We're staying at the Bellevue Hotel."

"Of course, as I am myself. One may be permitted your name?"

"Samuel Adams Pinkerton." He prayed he could maintain weaving a logical web of lies with his story about traveling with his grandparents.

"Well, sir, Mr. Samuel Adams Pinkerton, this is why you have come here. This is what you wish to have translated?"

With his heart racing, Sam sensed his entire world was waiting here upon this paper.

"You did not ask the hotel to translate it?"

"Whatever this is, it looks so official that I thought the American Consul could explain it best."

Sato-San spread the paper on the desk, carefully unpeeled his wire-rimmed glasses from his round face, and polished them with a silk handkerchief. He looked down at the paper while Sam held his breath. Sato read the document in a glance. "Why is it that you have this?"

"I don't even know what it is."

"No?"

"No, Sir." Sam didn't dare breathe.

"Did you not see? This? Faint, like a watermark. See?" Sato held it up to the light bringing Sam close for a look. Within the brushstrokes of Japanese writing he'd never realized was a faint Christian cross.

"This appears to be from a Christian church—"

In his excitement Sam broke in. "Here in Nagasaki?"

"Something about a Christian baptism."

Sam kept his breathing shallow. No matter how his heart banged he mustn't show this man he was trusting him with his life. Sato raised his eyes and over his glasses gave him a long look. "This particular paper. How is it you come by this?"

"A friend," he felt the net of lies he was creating drawing closer. "Actually, someone who knew we'd be in Nagasaki," he fumbled scrabbling for an explanation—"This friend—who knew we'd be here—here in Nagasaki—asked us to find out about this paper—"

"And your grandparents? But you came alone?"

"Grandpa's sick. Grandma's looking after him."

"At the Bellevue Hotel?"

"Yes." Between his shoulder blades he felt a trickle of cold sweat. "No." The man might suggest they go there to meet these grandparents for himself. "I mean they've gone back to the boat where there's an American doctor. We sail tomorrow."

"What boat would that be?"

"Golly, Sir, I can't remember right now." He prayed for inspiration. "I mean with changing our plans and all—From the other boat."

Sato-San removed and held his glasses. Without them he stared at Sam. Did this man believe a word he was saying? He slid a glance in Sato-San's direction without meeting his gaze. He was putting out his cigarette before he smoothed the paper. "Go to this church. They will explain this. This is all you wish to know?"

"The church. Is it near here?"

"Not far." Again Sato-San's fan created his own breeze. "I have a son your age. In London. His English is very good, not at all like my truly miserable attempt." Had Sam understood this Japanese pretense at humility he would have known this London-living merchant was allowing himself an even higher achievement by downplaying his perfect English.

Sato-San smiled, a real smile. "Do I sense you wish me to help you find this church?"

CHAPTER FOURTEEN

Mr. Takeo Sato of Nagasaki, London, and New York—Sam's new and only friend in Japan—pulled on a Panama hat and moved so quickly for a plump man that Sam found himself trotting beside him. They hurried down a street under the colorful banners of a crowded bazaar and passed an open-air market with heaps of fresh fruit and vegetables, fish, and unidentifiable creatures. Chickens, looking no different from those in the States, hung by the legs still clucking and flapping.

Sato-San slowed for a minute to help Sam change his fifty-two cents American into Japanese coins, before he bustled them to a line of rickshaw men munching turnips and onions while awaiting fares. With a surprisingly agile hop the gentleman landed up on the springy seat of the first in a line of carriages. Ensconced, Sato-San flicked his yellow fan indicating the next rickshaw. "Hop in, Young Samuel Adams Pinkerton." Sam was so excited he sprang with a leap onto the carriage seat.

He'd actually climbed into a rickshaw the missionaries in Urakami so hated. He looked down at the man's bare muscular legs topped by a short jacket and mushroom-shaped straw hat, human locomotion waiting between two poles. The man took off with a jolt, tossing his inexperienced passenger back on his high perch. Ahead, Sato-San, totally relaxed, was fanning himself, relishing an English cigarette.

The two rickshaws, speeding on roller bearings, raced around wagons and carts and dodged screeching streetcars and honking automobiles. Sam clung to the armrests. His rickshaw man slapped his straw sandals on the cobblestones with a steady beat.

They whirled along the waterfront where *sampans* with tattered sails floated amid huge freighters and one enormous, proud white ocean liner from across the world. A left turn spun them onto a climbing steep hill that scarcely slowed either puller till they stopped outside a brick church.

Sam jumped down onto his own two feet as his new friend paid off both rickshaw men who bobbed their thanks and trotted off. His guide drew off his white Panama and fanned himself as he led Sam into the church.

Sato-San hurried them down the aisle past the chancel of what appeared to be a proper church, where real stained-glass windows glowed, unlike the Snyders' poor little paper-made imitations. From the apse Sato-San led the boy through a side door into an office.

"Good morning!" The happy chirp came from a rosy middle-aged woman in a spider web hairnet who popped up from her desk.

Sato-San bowed and remained bent. Sam folded himself double. When the porcelain dealer spoke, he introduced himself in a hush of near quivering respect.

"My new, young friend here—Young Mr. Samuel Adams Pinkerton of Baltimore, Maryland in the United Sates of America—carries a document that friends of his grandparents visiting Nagasaki have asked him to inquire about. It appears to have come from your church."

"Yes?" The cheery lady made it seem that anything was possible.

"Perhaps as long as ten years ago," Sam's friend continued.

"Of course. How can we help?"

"His friends and the two of us would be grateful beyond the telling, if, perhaps, you would do us the honor—the great favor—of looking at it."

The cheery woman nodded. Pink hands waved away her guest's formality, not only signaling them to come closer but lunging forward with a surprisingly sturdy handshake for both. In more happy chirps she declared herself Mrs. Lorna McKie, the minister's wife, who was delighted to help in any way. From Sato-San and with near reverential care, she accepted the flimsy paper.

One glance brightened her even rosier. "Aye to be sure. From here. One of ours." Her voice reminded Sam of Harry Lauder, a Scotsman on a Victrola record singing "Roamin' in the Gloamin'" back in Bremerton "Aye. Of course. You see? Dated 1902. Of course this was long before the Reverend McKie and I came on the scene here in Nagasaki. This records a baptism. And definitely from this very same church." She shared the document with Sato-San. "You see? Written in kanji and not hiragana or *katagana*. Kanji—that's our Reverend Yamaguchi for you. A fine man. Precise. Meticulous. Every single document in beautiful, traditional Japanese ink."

Pink hands flattened the thin paper on her desk and smoothed it with love. Her smile included both Sato-San and the Western lad. She asked Sato-San, "You've read this?"

"Only that it comes from your church. For the boy's sake I wanted to make certain."

"Yes, one of ours," she confirmed the document and the wisdom of their visit. While Sato-San nodded, pleased they had come to the right place, Mrs. McKie motioned Sam to her side. "You see? It's all quite simple. All down in black and white. A Japanese bride of an American Navy Lieutenant brought her son here for a Christian baptism." She closed her eyes and sighed. "To come here. How the girl must have loved him to defy the Japanese and all their gods to prove to her husband how deep was that love for him and his new son."

Sam was trembling so hard, barely able to pull in breaths as Mrs. McKie sniffed back tears explaining the extraordinariness of what the young Japanese wife must have faced coming here without the father. She turned to Sato-San and allowed herself only a moment to show something of a frown. "As you doubtlessly know, your Japanese—at least in our City Hall here in Nagasaki—quite dismissively refuse to issue any kind of records for our Christian activities." She studied the document borne so long next to Sam's heart. "But see for yourself. Here, the good Reverend Yamaguchi sets it out—clearly—the fact—as legally as only he could make it—this record of baptism of the young woman's child." Suddenly she left them, springing up and off across the room. "Hold on. With any luck I'm certain we can find out more about her. Will you please follow me?"

Sam was too excited to utter a word and had trouble breathing. Sato-San, in almost childlike glee, smiled at him making it clear how much he was enjoying playing detective, as they followed the minister's wife into a storeroom. At Sam's side he whispered, "Just like Mister Sherlock Holmes," sharing more glee, "close on the track of solving a case."

Mrs. McKie was glancing across shelves heaped with stacks of books and files and ribbon-tied dossiers. "Most of these," she explained, "go back donkey's years. Long before—as I said—the Reverend McKie and my time."

She lifted down a pile of files and ledgers, blew off dust, and searched out one dangling with tied indigo ribbon. "A bit dusty—but here—I think—we are." She was enjoying the search as much as Sato-Sam and already untying the ribbon. "Yes. 1902. Happily for us dear Reverend Yamaguchi, in this case, used the Western calendar. You know what the Chinese say don't you? 'Pale ink is better than the best memory.' Now what month did we say?"

"We didn't, Ma'am. Not yet." Sam startled himself he could actually produce a sound.

"And here we are precisely where the dear Reverend completed it. You see? June 21, 1902. A male child brought here by Nakamura, Eiko. Here." She thrust the book while turning it to Sato-San. "You two have a look while I scoot and put the kettle on."

Sato-San, in his eagerness, all but snatched the book from her to solve the mystery while drawing in a big breath. His little mustache quivered spreading above a smile, and, in triumph he spun the dossier around to display for Sam—a page more than a decade old. "Eleven years ago, you see? June 21, 1902. As Mrs. McKie said, Nakamura Eiko brought her infant son here." He was tapping the desktop happily with his folded yellow fan when their helpful Scotswoman returned. She leaned to him helping him to a closer look at the record.

"Yes, you see," she explained to the other grownup as if Sam were not here with them in Nagasaki, Japan. "Apparently the young mother came alone to have her son baptized. There's no record of the father—but here—you see? The estimable Reverend Yamaguchi explains. Lieutenant Benjamin Franklin Pinkerton was in port with the U.S. Navy. Before his father returned here to Nagasaki she wanted his son baptized in his faith."

Sato-San, seeing beyond his Sherlock Holmes excitement, frowned. "But wait. That's very unusual isn't it—a Christian church allowing a Japanese mother being Shinto and Buddhist—insisting on her child having a Christian baptism?"

"Perhaps." Their hostess smiled at both of them. "But our Reverend Yamaguchi was no stickler. Reverend Yamaguchi was what we'd call a true Christian."

Sato-San was keeping up with her. "We know the father was a gaijin. What do we know of the mother? Is there a mention here of a *koseki?*"

Sato-San and Mrs. McKie were off together hunting some detail beyond anything Sam could follow. Still, even in their shared excitement, they included the bewildered boy. Mrs. McKie was about to explain this clearly important detail they'd both found missing. Just then the tea kettle whistled and their hostess rushed out of the room, and Sato-San explained. "For the mother this document states no *koseki.*" Realizing this term meant nothing to the boy, he began again. "I must explain. *Koseki* is the family registration system we have in Japan. Everyone in Tenno's Empire of the Sun has a *koseki.* All this tells us is Nakamura Eiko was born in a village in a Kyushu prefecture in 1886." He drew out an English fountain pen to write the information on notepaper which Mrs. McKie handed him. He wrote carefully. "A village. Small. I do not know it."

"Nor I," admitted their hostess.

"Farming probably," Sato-San guessed. "Maybe pottery of some kind, but certainly nothing like Imari-ware or Satsuma—nothing elegant."

"Is she—?" Sam, too excited and having trouble breathing, was barely able to choke out his question. "Is she alive—are she and her family still there?"

"We have no idea," his Japanese friend explained. "What I'm doing is writing down the name of the village for you. Can you read kanji?"

"No," Sam admitted.

"I'll write down what I can in *romanji* that you can read." Translating

from the Chinese strokes indecipherable to Sam, he wrote in Roman letters and with considerable gravity, presented the important paper. "Do
not lose this."

Some happy thought struck the reverend's wife and she clapped her
hands. "Yes, I remember now. Nakamura Eiko." Mrs. McKie's cheery
Scot's voice sang out over her tray of teacups, which, unlike Sato-San's
Japanese, had handles. "Dear Takako, Reverend Yamaguchi's wife, told
me about a lovely little thing, only a lass—sixteen years old. Imagine, six-
teen and a mother. Well, I don't have to tell you it happens here. *Eiko.*
But it seems her friends back in her Murayama days called her *Cho-Cho
San.*" She translated for Sam. "It means Butterfly."

She hurried off again, leaving Sam and Sato-San, who didn't breathe
a word till she returned with a teapot and a plate of sponge cake. "Of
course, as I said, the Reverend McKie and I weren't here then. It's coming
back now—Takako's story. After the wedding, the couple had their reception up in a house on the top of the hill. Lovely party, except, apparently
for one spot of bother. More than a spot, actually. Butterfly's uncle, some
kind of priest—Shinto, I should think—burst in hurling curses at the
poor little thing for daring to marry her handsome American. The man
was barking mad. Frightened all the Japanese out of their wits, but the
bride, so Takako was told, was so besotted—so very much in love with
her American navy officer—that she had no intention of allowing her
uncle's curses to ruin the happiest day of her life."

"You know the house where they held the reception?" Sato-San
asked the question before Sam could get out the words.

"Somewhere at the top of the hill. The *koban* will tell you where."

Sam was so thrilled he could have hugged Sato-San and in a jitter
tried to excuse himself without another bite of cake, eager to dash from
the church and up the hill. Sato-San, in his role of detective, enjoyed the
boy's excitement, but was a Japanese gentleman and therefore infinitely
polite. "What do you say, Young Samuel, we finish Mrs. McKie's lovely
tea and *castera* and then you and I can trot up there to that *koban* and see
what we shall see?"

No tea and cake ever lasted longer before Sam was out in the sunshine racing ahead. At the top of the hill there it was, the little glass hut,
the *koban.* Sato-San, fighting wheezes, reached the top of hill, stopped to

catch his breath and pump his fan. He was enjoying himself hugely. "More than ever I feel in the middle of one of your Conan Doyle mysteries." He wiped his face with his silk handkerchief and, thrilled with their morning's detective work, pointed his fan at the little police box.

"Every neighborhood in Japan has one of these. Every single one of Tenno's subjects in each neighborhood is registered with the police. Very efficient. Something, perhaps, your own Baltimore—State of Maryland, USA—could use."

They burst into the little box surprising a bespectacled officer in a too-tight uniform and a mustache dripping with late morning noodles. Instantly Tenno's man put the bowl on a file case, wiped his mustache and pulled himself to stiff, military attention.

"Pink-er-ton," Sato-San enunciated the foreign name precisely to the officer who polished his spectacles and sucked in breath over steel teeth to help him think. He spoke Japanese, most of which Sam followed. He bobbed his head. Yes, up here many had heard about an American naval officer leasing one of these nearby houses. "Nine or ten years ago," he stated. "Maybe further back." Frowning, he seemed to twist his entire body in an effort to remember. He moved his noodle bowl and chopsticks from the file case, wiped his mustache, opened a drawer and dug into detailed records. "*Hai!*" He cried, straightening up with a triumphant grin full of metal teeth. "Pink-er-ton!" Even though his records were almost exactly a dozen years old, here it was—"Pink-er-ton."

Sato-San took the record. "Here it is, Young Samuel. Mrs. Benjamin Franklin Pinkerton. Last to live in the house. 1904." In his joy and excitement Sato-San shared his speechlessness at the *koban's* thoroughness with a triumphant look at Sam.

The police officer pointed out beyond the booth. "Third house on the very top of the hill. Over there—the one with that tall twisted pine tree in the garden."

Sam felt his heart ready to break through his chest. He'd never seen anything as wonderful as that pine tree. Under the tree, a traditional tile-roofed house was set back in a garden surrounded by a lattice fence. Too thrilled to hold back one second longer and with a total lack of Japanese manners, Sam rushed from the two men in another mad dash.

The officer studying the file peeled off his glasses. His smile faded.

Sam's new friend listened to what the officer was now able to recall hearing of the sadness darkening the house. Yes, the American Pinkerton had leased it for his wife. He shook his head that life can be so cruel. He'd heard young Madam Butterfly had taken her own life in that house. Yes. Seppuku. Everyone on this hill agreed hers had been an honorable, a Japanese death.

Both men stood in silence watching the boy, but no longer able to share his wonderful excitement. Sato-San closed his fan. Sam had reached the gate and was tugging frantically at the hanging bell. In a gruff voice the officer added more bad news. "Of course that would have been over eleven years ago—the American officer lived there with his Japanese wife."

At the gate Sam rang the old iron bell with increasing urgency. A neighbor dog barked. At the gate of his mother and father's wood and paper house he grew desperate. He kept ringing but, at the front panel door, not even a servant appeared.

CHAPTER FIFTEEN

Sato-San had thanked the policeman for the two of them, and without a word led the stunned boy from the gate. Slowly the two crossed the street into a garden of bright green spangles of new maple leaves amid dark pines. Their footsteps crunched a gravel path between giant ferns, coral-colored azaleas and bed of fluttering white and purple irises. Ahead was a traditional teahouse commanding a panoramic view of Nagasaki's harbor below.

Sato-San's fan indicated a low table covered with heavy felt in a vibrant, blood-red. He motioned for the boy, who hadn't said a word, to sit on a flat cushion facing him. For a long moment, and without a word, he studied the boy, who had yet to hear the worst.

Neither spoke.

Nagasaki's Harbors' breathtaking view did nothing to raise Sam's spirits. The morning sun was high in the cerulean sky full of fast-moving white clouds. Miles below the hill the harbor sparkled between verdant hills where ravines rose spattered with gray roof tiles of homes climbing up to the horizon. Sam shifted himself on his cushion to keep the tall pine tree in view. In a crushed voice he uttered, "She wasn't there, Sato-San. No one was there."

Sato-San considered his enameled cup and said nothing. He took out his black lacquer case, but without taking out a cigarette he closed it. He spoke very quietly. "You are eleven-years-old."

Sam didn't answer.

"Young Samuel?"

"Twelve. June twelfth—One week after I was baptized in 1904."

"Say nothing, young Samuel. For now simply allow me to talk." Sato-San gazed past the fluttering green maple leaves and down into the harbor. "This is the Japan I love. If I were a poet this should be all the inspiration I need." He whispered, *"Ah, Nagasaki, ah."* Sato-San smiled. "What I just said needs explaining." He put out his cigarette. "When Basho, Japan's greatest poet, traveled to Matsushima in the north to view the sight of the sea most Japanese believe to be the most beautiful in all our islands, the entire country waited for his Matsushima poem. You know what happened? Basho was so overcome by what he saw that all that great man was able to gasp was, *'Ah, Matsushima, ah.'* I share this feeling with our Basho when it comes to Nagasaki." His small, smooth hand rose and his fan swept the horizon, the hills, the bay. "You see—far over there? Smoke from the factories? The Mitsubishi shipyards. Not so beautiful but very important for Japan. On that hill to our left is the Glover Mansion and other Western-style houses where rich Europeans and Americans live. And that yellow tile roof? Ming yellow. Chinese. A temple to Confucius. And down there in the harbor is Dejima Island where the Dutch endured living like prisoners for two hundred years to be able to trade with us and take our porcelain back to Europe. Now Dejima is no longer an island but filled in and part of the world. Like Japan is now part of the world—"

Sam broke in. "Before you say anything about my mother, I have to tell you something—"

The small smooth hand rose. "In a minute you can tell me. I leave Nagasaki tomorrow, and as you and I sit here I am putting myself in that picture—a porcelain merchant pretending to be sitting like a poet in one of the old Chinese landscapes—a sage contemplating nature." He turned his face up to the sky. "May sunshine," he stopped.

"No, perhaps I speak too soon . . ."

A dark cloud passed over the sun. A sudden cold breeze whipped the maples and sent his white hat flying and rolling into a bed of iris. Sato-San looked to the youngster to hop up and retrieve it for him. When Sam didn't move he heaved himself to his feet and stepped to the flowerbed.

In silence the middle-aged Japanese studied the boy and told him what he saw. "Dark yellow hair and wide shoulders. Soon you will be tall. But now, Young Samuel, you are a boy and you have something you wish to tell me."

Sam had dropped his face into his hands.

"Young Samuel?" The fan rose, a signal holding both from speaking for still another moment. "Perhaps, it is best if I begin. I know your name is Pinkerton. At the *koban* when we were talking with the policeman, we learned where your mother lived. You ran so quickly to the house that neither of us could stop you."

Sam still looked at the pine tree against the dark clouds. "He told you she was dead."

"Yes." Sato-San said. "Now you know the truth."

Sam was determined to summon all his courage, but the words from his heart choked in his throat. "What else did he say?"

Because Sato-San didn't trust his voice he sounded gruff. "The record in the *koban* shows she died more than ten years ago." Light rain began to patter on the iris. He cast a look at the shelter of the teahouse but neither stirred. Sato-San said nothing, giving the boy time, however long it might take for him to find the strength to say what was in his heart.

For a long moment Sam said nothing. A bird in the bamboo grove beside them insisted on shrilling a one-note song. Down in the harbor the blast of a deep-throated-horn sounded close. At last, in a very small voice, Sam shared the rest of the truth. "My American mother's name was Kate Showalter. She married my father—Lieutenant Benjamin Franklin Pinkerton, United States Navy. She came over here to be with him." Now Sato-San turned to gaze at that pine tree and the house with its gray tile roof, wet and glistening in the rain. "Before he married my Japanese mother, he lived in that house."

"Yes. The *koban* record shows you were born there."

"Then he left that house—my mother and me." He fought tears admitting the rest of the heartbreaking truth. "The same way he left my American mother in our house in Bremerton."

It was raining now. Sato-San sat without moving.

"You said my Japanese mother died ten years ago?" Sam's voice was small.

"Yes, the officer said almost ten years ago," Sato-San explained.

"I would have been two." His voice was a whisper. "Two years old when they took me away from her."

Sato San's voice, as is often the case when grown men are deeply moved, was husky, sharing his young friend's heartbreak, intuiting his thoughts. "You said you are twelve."

Sam nodded. "Two when they took me away."

"Apparently the same day your mother died. You may want to go back to that policeman so he can assure you that your Japanese mother's death was with honor." He looked up at the dark sky. The rain was heavier now, the air thick and moist with the scent of the wet garden. "It's true. The police record shows seppuku. Can you understand suicide is no shame here in Japan? Sometimes it is the only way."

To get in out of the rain they took off their shoes and entered the teahouse. "You know where your father is?"

"Before we left America the damned navy kept saying they couldn't reach him. The awful thing is I don't even know for sure if he'd want me when he came back." He heard himself whining, and he knew people hated whiners. He couldn't stop himself. "My father. My mom's parents. No mother here in Japan—"

Sam looked at the cigarette Sato-San offered, took it and leaned into the flame from his friend's gold lighter. He drew in smoke and tried not to cough, eager to convince his friend that he'd had no choice but to lie to the Snyders—even that he had pretended deep belief in Jesus—"the Call"—in order to reach Japan. He coughed and Sato took the cigarette from him and stubbed it out. Sam rose and crossed the tatami to the window and swiped away the mist to study the pine tree and the tile roof of his mother's house, shining in the rain.

"I was born in that house." All the secrecy, all the confusion since the New Washington Hotel in Seattle was over. "I'm Japanese."

Sato-San continued to smoke. "So now we know."

Sam, grateful that his friend had used the word "we," continued to open his heart. "Sato-San? When I came to the consulate and you said you'd help me, did you know—I mean, did you suspect I was—Do I look Japanese? Tell me the honest-to-God truth."

"Did I suspect that you are half Japanese? No. Now—looking at you, Young Samuel, here in this dim light, I should say perhaps your gray eyes are not so round as we see in England, but no. I did not know. I would never guess you to be half-Japanese."

Sam squared his shoulders, determined to climb out of the depths of his chilled emptiness and find a future. "What I'm going to do is, I'm going to stay here in Japan. I'm going to find her family—my family."

"For that you'll want to keep that paper I gave you." Sato-San patted the cushion beside him encouraging his young friend to turn from the window and the pine tree. "Sit. Save her village for the future. You have faced far more than enough for one day. What is it your English Bible says? 'Sufficient unto the day is the evil thereof'? Today is no time to make more demands of yourself."

Again he confessed to his new friend how, ever since that dreadful morning with the Showalters and the chaplain, he'd lived months of loneliness, denying their charge—his true identity. These last weeks in Urakami he was feeling himself more and more Japanese, always in the hope that here in Japan he'd find his mother. In three hours in Nagasaki, in one morning with this kind man, at last he faced the truth of who he was. "Back in America you can't know how much people like the Showalters hate me for being Japanese."

"Go ahead. I'm listening," Sato-San said through his smoke.

"I know it was wrong to lie to the Snyders about Jesus, but if I hadn't lied they wouldn't have ever brought me here—and without a passport how can I ever get away from them?" Again he heard himself and told himself not to whine. "Out there in Urakami you should see the way they make me work and live like a slave—"

"I think we both believe what has been most serious is lying to them about your love for Jesus."

"It's true, but I swear to God, without telling them who I really am

I'll go on working for them. I'll pay off every red cent of my passage over here. I will, Sato-San, no matter how much I hate them!"

"You must honor them—"

"For more than my passage? For what?" he spat. "They're not my family. You don't know how rotten mean they are to me and won't let me have any life but theirs!" Fury propelled him into hot, reckless indulgence. "So don't give me any sermon about honor. I'm sorry, but you think the Snyders honor the Japanese? They call them heathens. They don't even want to try to understand them. All they're here for is to scare them about going to hell so they can make fake Christians out of them."

"Look at me, Young Samuel. Look at me and listen. You must tell them the truth. They are Christians. Forgiveness is the heart and soul of the Christian way."

"You don't know them. What I've done today—sneaking off and coming into town like this is bad enough—if they knew I've been lying about Jesus they'd send me straight to hell."

"That gate over there to that house under the pine tree is closed to you, young Samuel. You have no choice. Your people in Urakami are responsible for you. The truth is, I would not be honorable if I do not tell you what you face. You think I don't know? Yes, you were born in that house over there, but as your friend who knows the ways of my country and you do not, I must remind you—you are only half-Japanese."

"I'm Japanese! You just said so yourself. You wrote the name of my mother's village right here on this piece of paper!"

Sato was not the Londoner now, twisting his head several times and drawing in his breath, as Japanese men often do facing difficulty. He sucked in a long breath. "This is very difficult for me to say. Your father was American. One look at you says that. From now on you must insist you are an American."

"Lie?"

"Even if you looked totally Japanese, under Japanese law and to other Japanese, you can never be one of us."

Sam fought outrage fired by betrayal. "Now you're saying I wasn't born in that house right over there? You saw the proof. My mother was Japanese. I'll get one of those *koseki* things."

"Today you are a boy. Japanese and American. A foreigner with no place in either world. No place to go but back to those gaijin who have made you their son. You must tell them the truth!"

"They're not my goddamn family and never will be!"

Sato-San picked up his fan and with one hand opened and closed it twice before he slid it into his vest and reached for his hat. "You said Urakami? We must hurry. Believe me, young Samuel, we are friends, but I leave Nagasaki tomorrow. I said it before. I say it again. You are twelve years old, with no one else in the world but these gaijin." He pulled the limp Panama hat flopping over his head. "Come. We must hurry."

CHAPTER SIXTEEN

Sato-San, with Sam dragging his feet behind him, entered the mission kitchen. Sister Ellen, in her gray work dress, with her head wrapped in a kitchen towel, was chopping cabbage for sauerkraut. She covered her shock at the sight of the wet, but well-tailored Japanese merchant with the runaway Sam in the doorway. Drying her hands on her apron she called, "Brother Wendell!"

The preacher loomed, filling the door of his office. Thick, ink-stained fingers massaged his cheek fighting a toothache.

Sato-San plucked a tiny card case from his vest and, with a low bow of Japanese ceremony, presented himself to the gaijin missionary. His English took on a solemn voice Sam hadn't heard before. "The Honorable Reverend and Mrs. Snyder?"

Brother Wendell's hand massaged his cheek. "We speak Japanese. Sister Ellen and I are blessed to be able to bring the gospel to your people in your own language."

A plump Japanese hand rose. "Forgive me, Reverend Snyder, but may I suggest that since our young man is limited in his Japanese, we speak in English? It is important he understands both his position here with you and the fact of his being in Tenno's Japan."

Sam lowered his eyes, staring down at the broken concrete floor. Everything was honor and religion now. He was being remanded from the judgment of the Emperor's code of honor into the judgment of the Americans and their Western God.

"I met your young man today at the American Consulate in Nagasaki. We became friends. Before I leave your estimable place of worship, he will tell you why he came to the consulate and why I was with him when he made several truly remarkable discoveries about himself."

As Sato-San outlined his case, Sam stared at the floor unable to look up at the two solemn figures, statues in granite as unforgiving as Old Testament figures. As the facts mounted against him, damning him, what could he possibly say in his defense? His early dawn escape to Nagasaki was proof of guilt—ending months of terrible deceit—lies to the Snyders, lies about his devotion to their Lord.

He prayed, but only to keep his knees from buckling under him.

Sato-San signaled Samuel to present the document Mrs. McKie had translated for them.

Wendell Snyder snatched it and shoved on his wire-framed eyeglasses. As his wife drew close to his side, the two looked like they were sharing a hymnal. Here was absolute proof that a Japanese woman, a girl of seventeen, had brought her child to be baptized in a Christian church.

Silence filled the kitchen. The Snyders ignored the Japanese peacemaker and turned their solemn accusations on the trembling boy. The accused coughed, cleared his throat, and heard his feeble voice shaking, admitting that lies had brought him to Japan. At last his confession, his dreadful secret was out.

Sato-San raised his hand for silence, supplying the rest of Sam's confession. "This young man, son of a Japanese mother married to an American navy officer, discovered only hours ago that his mother was dead."

With a deep breath Brother Wendell examined the stranger's card and showed it to his wife. When Brother Wendell spoke it was with all the authority representing the laws of his Christian God while also acknowledging the man's Japanese code of honor. The preacher had never sounded so polite. "Thank you, Mister Sato."

Sato-San bowed. "Now, Honorable Reverend Snyder and Mrs. Snyder, with your permission, I must leave."

The preacher's huge hand shook the Japanese gentleman's hand and thanked him for performing his honorable duty. Mrs. Snyder added a grateful nod. The preacher cracked an order to Sam. "Boy, see Mr. Sato to the door. Then come straight back."

Sam knew the pointed omission of any name attached to an order was dreadful judgment. Withholding "Brother" threatened the first step in expulsion from the flock.

At the front door Sato-San bowed to the half-Japanese lad who bowed much lower and stayed bent. He waited. With his folded fan the man lifted Sam's chin in order to look straight into his gray eyes. "Young Samuel-San, this has been difficult for both of us. Today you may feel I betrayed you. No. The thing had to be done. To fail to tell these people the truth would betray you far more."

Sam fought stinging tears.

"You understand, do you not, that until you are old enough to be on your own you have no one else. No other place in the world. You must stay here—"

"I won't stay!" The cry made the words sound hollow against the adult world laying down the law by which he must live.

"To hell with honor. I'm not Japanese—only half."

Sato-San surprised him with a slight smile. "Yes, my friend, young Samuel, you will do the honorable thing. I sail for England tomorrow, but I will always remember you. With your permission, young Samuel Pinkerton, I will ask Lord Buddha to watch over you."

Sato-San applied his wilted hat to his head, turned and began his way across the muddy paddies in the direction of the streetcar line.

Brother Wendell and Sister Ellen stood precisely where he'd left them in the kitchen. In the preacher's strong hand was his precious paper that had been his only hold on life. Without a word Sister Ellen stepped into his bedroom cell off the kitchen and returned with a thin gray blanket.

"Strip!"

He quailed at the order. She jabbed him. "Did you or did you not hear me tell you to get out of those soaking wet clothes before you catch your death of pneumonia?"

With judgment hanging over his head, he dropped his sopping jacket, pulled off his black tie, and undid his celluloid collar. He slid down his suspenders and peeled the wet shirt from his shivering white torso. He bent and unbuttoned his boots and peeled down his black socks. Barefoot and shivering, he hesitated to unbuckle his belt holding up his knickers.

Sam skinned his knee pants down his shaking legs while the preacher's wife swooped up the armload of sodden clothes. Sister Ellen flung the gray blanket at him. "Down on your knees!"

Sam wound the blanket around him and his bare knees hit the cold cement. He bowed his head dutifully keeping his eyes down on the cold concrete.

The reverend's voice was low, solemn, and deeply grave. "Sister Ellen and I can only leave to God the sin your mother and father have handed down to you. How you face the world branded by mixed blood will forever be between you and Our Lord. As for your lies to us . . ." The preacher, massaging his aching jaw, sighed a profound sigh. "Only Jehovah himself knows their extent of your untruths. Only He can forgive. As for the three of us here in His house, we now stand waiting for you to begin by telling us what you think we should do about this."

Mrs. Snyder made it simple. "You understand? We are waiting for you to tell the Lord what we must do!"

Sam shook. He'd already admitted what he'd done, had proved he was half Japanese. What more did they want? They knew he had no other place in Japan, or on earth, to turn.

She pressed on. "Do we have to remind you to thank Him for the way we took you in off the streets—how we sacrificed to bring you across the sea because you swore to us you loved Him and promised to do His work?"

Sam's blanket slid from his shoulders as he tugged up the thin cover, his only defense.

"And don't you for one single minute think," Sister Ellen raised her voice, "this revelation of yours comes to us as the complete surprise you might suppose. Oh, no." She slid her hands back over her hairnet and glared righteousness. "From the minute you came to us on Yesler Way in Seattle, you think we haven't always known you were holding back—never giving yourself completely to us—forever refusing to be the open vessel Our Lord Jesus asks you to be."

With a long, deep breath, the preacher took over with a profound sigh, a man suffering. A man pushed beyond endurance. "Very well. Sister

Ellen and I with the help of Our Lord will make it simple enough for even you to understand. Suppose you tell us, Samuel Adams Pinkerton—or whatever your name is—why Sister Ellen and I are here."

He'd been hearing the answer to that question all the days of his servitude and managed a rasp. "To serve God."

"Lies and rushing off to the Doubting Cities—that is your idea of serving God?"

Until this moment he'd confessed the terrible truth. Now he knew that if he were ever to get up off his knees and start serving his sentence with the Snyders, he would have to swallow hard, and begin again with another lie. "Pray Jesus, let me serve."

CHAPTER SEVENTEEN

For five years Sam would serve the Snyders.

In November, 1918 he'd hear of the end to the world's four-year Great War. Although the fighting had taken place on the other side of the world from Urakami, the Empire of the Sun, a power that had already triumphed over Russia back in 1905, had joined the clash on the side of the Allies and marched into defeated Germany's territories in China. Japan was one of the Big Five at the League of Nations. Russia was now an ally, and, like other powers with warships in Asia, was dependent on Nagasaki's vital coaling stations and outfitters.

Urakami, far from cosmopolitan Nagasaki, escaped many of the tsunami changing the world. In the cities, Japan was lighting up, with more and more electric lights outshining the glow of paper lanterns. Riots in Tokyo had demanded the vote for all men over the age of twenty-five, although women were still outwardly silent, obedient as Sister Ellen firmly believed every Western woman ought to be.

Some news trickled into Urakami. Sam had learned enough Japanese to hear the congregation muttering about the new class of rich Japanese war profiteers in godless Nagasaki, building their elegant new villas and insisting on London tailoring, and beefsteak broiled rare. They were increasingly pushing aside the old aristocrats and continuing to demote what was left of the once proud samurais.

In five years the mission had added thirty-one crosses to the grave-yard. At Easter of 1918 the congregation reached its all-time high, but had stalled at a disappointing one hundred and seventeen. Sister Ellen gave birth to a baby girl of eight pounds and three ounces, a silent child God had given a harelip, Martha Elizabeth.

For five more years Benjy haunted Sam's thoughts, and never more than that day in June when Sam turned sixteen and had grown too tall even for Brother Wendell's Sears-Roebuck hand-me-downs. For the ninth time Sister Ellen had taken scissors to let out the old gray worsted suit the Navy had bought him. Finally she cut it into strips for a blanket, his last link with the States. Just as he'd outgrown his suit, he had to remind him-self that little Benjy would no longer be so little. Sam pictured Benjy living in a grand house with his grandparents, those top-top people who hated his father and his son by a Japanese woman.

Benjy. Many times in his head he'd composed letters to him. Half a dozen times he'd started to write him care of the post office in Baltimore beginning, of course, by asking him if the navy or Baltimore had ever received word from their father. Each time, determined not to sound like he was asking for sympathy, he wrote that he was happy that his little brother must be having a wonderful new life with the Showalters in Baltimore. As he wrote bitterness often crept in. Why the hell shouldn't he be having a wonderful new life over there? Of course he didn't write this. Even with his asthma, Benjy was the All-American boy, the beloved grandson of rich and powerful and deeply hateful people.

Write the truth? He'd sound like a whiner he vowed never to be. Still, who could he tell how frantic he was for the day he could break free of the Snyders and travel deep into the country to that remote village Sato-San had written on the card he kept hidden, to find his mother's family?

Write the post office in Baltimore? No. He didn't have Benjy's address, which was excuse enough to crumple any letter.

During weekdays, when the Japanese parishioners wouldn't see him, any castoff work garment he wore would serve. Sundays, however, it was unthinkable for him to appear in anything but Brother Wendell's discarded Sears Roebuck suit, shiny and frayed even after Sister Ellen let out the sleeves and cuffs. He was now taller than the reverend and still growing.

By sixteen his boy's face had sculpted itself into a youth's, with strong, regular Western features and even white teeth. His nose was not as long as *Tengu's*—that grotesque god with the beak the Japanese prefer to think typical of most Caucasians. His straight, bronze-colored hair, slate-gray eyes, and broad shoulders would make him stand out in any group of young men in America. In Japan he was a handsome gaijin giant.

The Snyders told no one of his ancestry. No longer was he Brother Samuel, but simply Samuel living with the secret shame it was their duty to remind him of—"his special cross to bear."

His only schooling had been his dictionary and the Bible. By now he'd read it five times from leatherette cover to cover. In it he'd found a soul mate—Jacob—and his seven long years of service to Laban to win his coveted Rachel. Poor Jacob had labored seven years only to be tricked into serving another seven to win his love, his Rachel, whom the Holy Text declared, "beautiful and well favored." The thought of Jacob possessing his woman who was beautiful and well-favored excited him, although what these exact attributes might be were still left to his imagination.

Only two things made his life at the mission bearable. Speaking the most basic Japanese, he was leading young men his age in a twice-weekly Bible class, and coaching a baseball team in the weeds in back of the grave-yard. He had to be careful to keep the richness of the language he was picking up from his baseball team out of the Snyders' hearing. An alarming amount of talk dealt more than frankly with sex, about which his young Japanese never stopped jabbering, delighting each other with colorful lewdness.

Among his baseball players the boy closest to being a friend was the shortstop, Kenji Uchida. At fifteen with his gap-toothed smile he was short but sturdy, grimy but full of spunk, a promising young athlete whose hours playing ball had to be stolen from coaxing his father's radishes and turnips up out of a Japan nourished with stinking night soil. After a ball-game, watching him wave and trudge off home, Sam saw his friend as trapped as he, a grimy farm boy doomed to stoop the rest of his life in muddy fields.

Not that sturdy, Kenji never felt sorry for himself. No. He crowed his delight to Sam at how he was finding release for his pent-up juices with two farm girls who did what farm girls have always done with farm boys. His detailed explanations of sensual bouts so shocked the missionary boy, he scarcely dared admit the cause of his own private thrashings.

He shrank in growing horror knowing all too well the dangers to which he was yielding. Sam well knew, looking for telltale hair growth on his offending right hand, that he was risking eternal damnation. Struggling with his soul, the sixteen-year-old faced his baseball players, armed with his Bible and Snyder-like solemnity. He declared incessant talk of sex on the baseball diamond, taboo. His boys, with no desire to be saved, yawped and shrieked with derisive glee. Not only eager to relate how they satisfied their fiery animal appetites they took to badgering the gaijin to join in on the fun. Shoji, the carpenter's skinny son, awed them by passing around postcard photos of naked Japanese ladies. None had been to Nagasaki's Maruyama pleasure district, which didn't stop them from whispering of its endless joys.

Alone and sixteen, a prisoner in his white calcimined cell, Sam suffered, a monk on fire. No young woman had ever dared set foot into his English class. The dumpy farm women of Urakami inspired no lust. That came from *The Sears Roebuck Catalog's* steel engravings of the most modest of Western ladies in brassieres and copious undergarments. Nothing aroused him more than the fantasy, inspired by the Old Testament, of Jacob, his fellow-indentured-servant and his "well-favored" Rachel. "Well-favored." The words haunted Sam. In his reverie Rachel appeared as an out-of-focus lantern-slide of Doré's cast on a whitewashed wall, inflaming his imagination, to guess how a woman's naked body might look under all those desert robes.

In a frantic fight against sin he plunged into the distraction of monkish scholarship, picking up his ink brush, gritting his teeth, and laboriously copying kanji. The Chinese brushstrokes of brain-tangling complexity that constitute Japanese writing can only be conquered by endless rote, infinite repetition. Grammar-school students must master eight hundred and eighty-one, a high school graduate, three thousand, a scholar, five thousand and beyond, into nearly endless thousands.

Not even his furious concentration on kanji kept Rachel from breaking in until, hot and bothered, he hurled aside his brush and ink. He feared at times, struggling against pounding hot blood, that a force greater than himself shook him with dread. Even worse than guilt, he feared Satan himself had entered his monk's cell. Who but the Devil could lash him on into hot sin so dreadful that his Bible declared that it was Jehovah Himself who'd slain Onan for doing exactly the same act?

How much longer, the sixteen-year-old asked himself, could he bear life under the Snyders? At least Jacob, for his labors, had the promise of a well-favored Rachel. Sam's servitude here in the muddy fields of Urakami, far from Jesus' "Godless Cities," was driving him, night after night, into unspeakable acts of sin here in the very house of God.

CHAPTER EIGHTEEN

Five years. Five long, long years and still in Urakami since Sato-San discovered his baptismal record and the name of his mother's village—Asahi-mura. He'd pored over maps. Her village, a dot here on the island of Kyushu, was deep in the mountains beyond a railroad tunneling through miles of solid Japanese rock. Kenji brought him a railway schedule, his only way to reach whomever might be left of his mother's family. without a sen how could he buy a ticket? Hop a freight? What surer way to get himself arrested in Japan? Oh, God, a young man without a passport and between two worlds couldn't dare risk that.

During one of his Bible classes, inspiration struck. Why not add English classes for the boys to the baseball? He'd charge only a pittance. What an inspired idea! He'd teach English, improve his own Japanese, and make money. Yes, it would have to be on the sly, for his fare to Asahi-Mura. Of course to initiate classes he needed Brother Wendell's permission. He rehearsed his proposal carefully. The reverend's face hardened till Sam quickly reverted to added deceit—presenting his enterprise as a commitment to the Lord to better serve the mission, for instance, earning enough to pay for his own Sears-Roebuck mail-order three-piece badly-needed black suit.

Lessons began with five young men, none of them members of the poor little church. One, a few years older, was a frequent visitor to the godless Nagasaki. Junnosuke not only had yen but produced a smuggled deck of what kids back in Bremerton called "the devil's pasteboards." All five of his students clamored for their gaijin sensei to forget about teaching them English so they could learn the game the English and Americans called *poka.*

Their games met out in back of the cemetery. Sam took great care keeping these tutoring lessons secret and found himself back in Bremerton dealing cards, wearing his inscrutable Huck Finn face.

Were his winning the wages of sin? The work of the devil? He was simply a sharper poker player, inspired by his dream of Asahi-Mura. With coins trickling in steadily and parsing out enough to the preacher to allow his English teaching, his secret poker game continued. Weeks became months. The pot grew. The trip looked feasible, then actually possible. With careful planning, along with his fare, he was setting aside enough to face certain banishment from the whitewashed sepulcher. On his return he'd still have enough yen to realize his dream—and what was more logical, than opening an English Language School in Nagasaki. In Japan, and especially Nagasaki, potential students were everywhere. In his new Sears Roebuck suit, he'd call on the vast Mitsubishi Industries, offering to teach their young trainees the commercial advantages of speaking English.

Counting the days till his escape he grew scrupulous, stoically trudging through the last of his servitude. Behind his pious mask, his ambition soared with the possibilities of finding his mother's people, then coming back and opening his English language school.

As for his sense of honor—at seventeen he had paid off the Snyders in full and many times over with six years of hard labor.

A month before his secret escape date to Asahi-Mura came a roar from the preacher's office. "Samuel!" Obediently, with his practiced smile, he waited in the doorway.

"Quite the young man now in our new Sears Roebuck suit, aren't we?" Whatever the preacher had to say he rose to his feet to accost Sam face to face. Though by now the *ainoko* was an inch taller, he knew better than to answer, acutely aware he was being scrutinized. "God has been watching you, Brother Samuel."

There it was—Brother. Apparently the preacher smelled nothing of his imminent escape. The term "Brother" was bringing him back into the fold.

"Yes, sir, Brother Wendell."

"You wish to leave Japan?"

The question was rhetorical. Of all people in Japan, the preacher knew best he had no place else to go. Sam, to prove admirably, convincingly serious, answered. "No sir, Brother Wendell."

"Are you saying you wish to stay on here in Japan?"

"With all my heart." Though lying was absolutely necessary, six years had only taught the young man to be forever on guard. "That is—I mean if you and Sister Ellen believe it is His will."

"The time has come when Sister Ellen and I and even our Martha Elizabeth cannot continue to pretend you are of our blood or race." The preacher's face was close, only inches away.

"Do you understand?"

"Yes, sir."

"I'd be less than honest if I didn't remind you, you are not a citizen of Japan. You never will be. Should you ever consider leaving us, you'd do well to remind yourself you have no passport, nothing that will allow you to stay on here. Of course, if you think you'd be welcome back in the States, you're always free to go to the docks and offer yourself to work your passage back. Difficult. No, without a passport I'd say impossible. You're what? Seventeen?" Brother Wendell asked, but Brother Wendell, as always, answered his own questions. "Surely you realize Sister Ellen and I cannot be expected to watch over you and know how you spend every minute of your day and night. You know as well as we, the Lord never takes his eyes off you. He knows when you are not giving Him your full measure of devotion. Until now, without a passport, we have allowed the Japanese government to believe you are some sort of distant kin. Without us, you know, the day will come as surely as God makes little green apples when the authorities will demand to know precisely who you are and what you are doing here."

The preacher had set the trap. It was closing with more questions, more of his own answers. His large hand clamped Sam's shoulder. "Seventeen is long past the time that you declare to us and to God what you intend to do with your life." Sam fought to keep looking straight into those eyes. "Of course, it may be that our work is not your true calling. I don't have to tell you that calling can only come from God. If there's any doubt whatsoever about your faith or our work here, now is the time to come clean. Confess. There is nothing to hold you here with us except your calling. Without that you know you are free to leave whenever you wish."

Sam said nothing.

"Nevertheless, you surely must know Sister Ellen and I never stop praying for you. You do know that?"

"Thank you, Brother Wendell."

"As for the sin of your mother and father, Sister Ellen and I have left that to God alone to judge. Since we are not here to add to your burden we have shared your secret with no one. Not even the church in Au Claire. Sister Ellen and I can only pray that through us and your own diligent prayer you find the strength to live with your burden. Search your soul, Brother Samuel." He lifted his heavy hand from Sam's shoulder, raising it high in witness. "Think on these things. You have no more time to waste. You must decide what to do with your life."

CHAPTER NINETEEN

All that connected Asahi-Mura with the rest of Japan and the twentieth century was the rackety little train and its station, a weather-beaten wooden shack scarcely worth a stop.

The day was dark with the December wind spitting rain on the single street that was little more than a rutted dirt road. The village was wet, wooden shabbiness—gray and brown but for one obscenely bright yellow sign—KODAK FILM. Beyond its one street, shabby farms huddled in stubby rice fields under circling crows.

At his first steps into the street he ignored the odor of an open sewer flanked by shops of flimsy wood and paper. One shop offered pungent smells from withered white radishes and wilted leeks along with a dash of orange color from a heap of persimmons. A dingy bakery displayed flies crawling on a few dispirited bean cakes. Suddenly the street's sole inhabitant staggered from a shop of primitive farm tools into a sake shed next door.

Sam stopped. Asahi-Mira. He made no move. He had no idea how to begin his search for his family.

The sake buyer burst from the shed hugging a glazed pottery jar and trotted off without a glance at the gaijin. A fierce yellow dog lunged out of an alleyway, straining on his leash, yapping his warning to those behind closed shutters that an unwelcome stranger—perhaps even *Tengu*—had come among them.

A wooden Buddhist temple at the end of the street looked older but more solid than the shops. Yes. It was Buddhist, because his shortstop friend, Kenji, had told him the arch above the entrance of a Buddhist temple follows the same curve as the brim of a samurai's helmet. Crossing the temple courtyard, he crunched gravel before he reached a heavy iron pot on a pedestal with smoldering incense rising from it. He breathed in its spicy scent, and, without realizing he was succumbing to a heathen practice, drew the smoke to him with both hands.

An altar at the top of the cypress-wood steps was open to the day. The shrine appeared deserted, but at a closer look, what he first thought was a small child became an old woman bent double, tossing coins into an open wooden chest. If she saw him she ignored him to clap her hands twice and ring a bell to let the Lord Buddha know she was here. Still without a glance at the tall young man, she turned and crept down the stairs, leaving him alone at the altar open to the December wind, blowing red and yellow leaves across the floor.

He held his breath. Could his mother be here at his side? After all, this was her village. On this same worn cypress floor she must have stood, calling on Lord Buddha before her family sent her to Nagasaki, before she married his father.

"Mother, are you here now?" He murmured a prayer for some sign, some sense of her presence. A crow shrieked, and he turned, startled to find the statue of the Lord Buddha who'd been sitting here forever, looking straight at him.

He was alone.

By now the rain had stopped. The sun gleamed on the steps he descended to find his way to the back of the building, where an old man was spreading leeks on a plank to catch a patch of sunlight and dry. His round head was shaved but bristling with gray hair. Sam bowed to the back of his patched gray robe and held himself respectfully silent till the priest turned. Sam offered an even more respectful good day, but the old man continued spreading the green and white vegetables without a glance at the tall young gaijin. The priest turned his head. Old eyes showed no surprise that this boy from a far-off land was bowing before him. With only the slightest nod, he acknowledged his young visitor.

With his limited Japanese Sam went straight to the heart of the matter bringing him here. He drew out the record of baptism and Sato-San's notepaper with the name of this village—Nakamura Eiko's village. The priest accepted the paper and held it while fumbling in his work coat sleeve drawing out wire spectacles.

He read the note, made something like a snort, but said nothing. Along with the note he held the Christian baptismal document. With his small hand the priest motioned his visitor up the back steps of the temple where he shucked off his clogs. Sam knew enough Japanese manners to unhook his boots to stockinged feet before he stepped through the sliding door into cluttered living quarters. It was a small room with threadbare mats warmed by a *kotatsu* brazier sunk in a pit in the floor. He waited for his host to sit at a low table close to the floor before he scrambled down on his knees awkwardly, displaying none of the old man's suppleness. Unable to tuck his legs under the table or fold them under his buttocks he perched on the worn tatami.

In complete silence he watched the priest slowly repeating a lifetime of ritual moves, opening a canister and pinching tea into a little iron pot, reaching for a thermos bottle from which he poured steaming water. Slowly and with infinite care he placed a small cup before his guest and himself. After examining the flimsy paper from the Christian church the priest finally spoke. "No *koseki?*" He shook his head in wonder. "Born here thirty-two years ago?" He shrugged, admitting such a possibility. He sipped tea. His voice sounded younger than he looked. "But, of course, in those days no one paid much attention to daughters or what became of them." Slowly he drew off his glasses, brought the notepaper close and considered the name. "Nakamura."

"Nakamura." At the sound of his mother's name, Sam held his

breath. The old man rubbed his spikey head. "Many Nakamura's here in Japan, but," he reached inside his robe and scratched himself. "I do not remember a single Nakamura at this temple. No." He scratched himself again and considered. "However . . ."

He crawled to reach behind him to a shelf and took down a ragged dossier dangling with black ribbons. Bringing it close to Sam, his hand was plump with remarkable silken skin, as his fingers slowly unloosed the temple's records. Sam held himself motionless, fighting all the while his eagerness to help.

"Funerals." The priest explained the loose documents in the folder. "Births. We Buddhists leave births to Shinto." He plucked through the papers with slow, painstaking care. "This Nakamura Eiko—she has a death name?"

"I don't know." A death-name? Always there was so much more he didn't know about his mother's family, Japan.

The priest slipped the papers back in the folder. "No. I did not think so. No Nakamuras."

In a loud voice Sam offered all the knowledge he had. "Perhaps they were Shinto."

"Of course," the priest said closing the dossier. "Shinto *and* Buddhist."

"Sir, are there other Buddhist temples here?"

"No. Many are gone. So many changes. One time the government drove three hundred thousand farmers off the land." Sam discovered the dim eyes leaving the past and considering his young guest. "United States? You are from the United States of America?"

"Yes, sir."

"Rincon Abraham." As if to explain his understanding of this young man's search here in far-off Japan, he was suggesting he knew something of the world, or at least the existence of the United States. "Here—in the last years of the old century—one hundred and ten thousand men left Japan. Many went to America to find work." He reached inside his robe for another scratch. "Many changes. Many villages gone . . ."

Sam's knees, tucked under him, suddenly were howling with pain. As he shifted himself he watched in the agonizingly long time it took the priest to re-tie the ribbons on the records and put them back on the shelf.

He raised his voice to speak of the wedding reception in that house under the pine tree. "In Nagasaki 1901." He repeated Mrs. McKie's report of the ruckus caused by the enraged Shinto priest.

Old shoulders jiggled with silent laughter. "So, a Shinto priest interrupted your mother's Christian wedding party."

"Yes. An uncle." Sam caught and held his breath, asking. "Could he still be here?"

"*Shin-to.*" Without teeth the sunken mouth worked to form the word. "What year did you say this Shinto priest showed such thoughtlessness?"

"1901."

"1901." Old shoulders shook as Sam prepared to hear a bout of coughing, but the wheezing priest was laughing, till suddenly he burst out the reason. "Wild Boar." He waggled both hands conjuring up some happy memory. "Yes. We called him Wild Boar. Truly, he was very ugly— like a wild boar—always crashing through the sacred forests he claimed to worship." He wheezed and wiped his eyes. "Wild Boar. Of course. He may have had a Nakamura connection. After his wife died he became even wilder. Yes. Yes," he chuckled. "Always making a ruckus. That could be Old Wild Boar."

Sam's heart banged. "Is he still here?"

The priest scrubbed his bristly head. "Gone. Gone for years."

"Would they know about him at the Shinto temple?"

"Are you finished with your tea?"

Sam bobbed his head vigorously.

"Come." The priest, though an old man, rose effortlessly, gracefully. At the door he slid his feet back into muddy clogs.

CHAPTER TWENTY

The priest pointed a folded fan to a small hill with a little wooden shrine hiding within a blaze of scarlet maples. They approached a *torii* gate, once bright vermilion, now faded and badly needing paint.

"Shinto." The old Buddhist bowed. Without another word he stunned Sam by turning and clopping off in his wooden getas, leaving him alone in the sparkle of sun and rain. In the direction of his disappearing robes, Sam bent low and hoped his unheard but heartfelt thanks expressed some of the gratitude and something like the sudden love he felt for this old man.

He climbed mossy rock steps, but froze. With a real pang of fear he was startled to find a wooden statue of a white fox grinning at him. The sly creature had something wicked about it, certainly its disturbing smile was unsettling enough to paralyze any foreigner. Was he a Shinto god? A fox? He hated to think this deity proved Brother Wendell's accusation that Japan's people, his people, were heathens worshipping foxes and maybe worse.

He edged past the grinning fox and two stone dogs, only one of which was snarling. The shrine itself was scarcely more than a cedar-wood hut weathered a gleaming silver under maples flaming red against dark cypresses soaring up as tall as any Douglas fir in Washington State. He bent to peer inside. It was dark. Empty. Mysterious. Rustling with autumn leaves that might well be the sound of breathing of gods.

He bumped into a heavy straw rope hanging from a brass bell. Looking around to make sure he was alone, he pulled the rope. On the bell's thunking sound he gasped. He shrank with embarrassment. At this moment, too stunned to consider eternity, a voice startled and held him, a voice soft as a breeze through the tall cypresses, an encounter with a god?

"Yes?" The voice spoke English.

A flash of the purest white and bright vermilion was coming toward him. Had pulling on the rope summoned her? A Shinto goddess? Likely a mortal, she looked at him like a silent doe. Scarcely more than a girl, she was a young woman completely unlike any fantasy woman, no Rachel clad in the Bible's dusty desert robes. Here was a slender girl lovely as a fresh lotus with gleaming dark eyes, smooth skin and shining black hair pulled back in a ponytail. Her snow-white blouse with long sleeves met her full skirt of bright vermilion. Softly, but with a solemnity suggesting concern for this stranger, her soft voice whispered. "May I help you?"

Sam eagerly jerked down his head and bowed, obeisance he hoped carried the proper degree of respect. "Is the Shinto priest here?"

"Yes."

"Here at the shrine?"

"In the village. Tonight we have a ceremony here at this shrine."

"Is his name Nakamura?"

"Ota. Gon-gúji Ota."

"Is there a priest here named Nakamura?"

"No."

"Do you know if there was ever a priest named Nakamura here?"

"I do not know. Gon-gúji Ota perhaps can tell you. If you like, you are welcome to stay for the ceremony."

"I am not Shinto."

At his confession she resisted a small smile. "I did not think you were."

"This evening?"

"Here. Once it is dark. Now I am sorry. If I cannot help you I must leave."

His heart melted as he watched this young woman, his first goddess, glide down the steps from the temple grounds past the rock and disappear, vermilion and white, across rice paddies bristling with stubble. A thought stopped his heart. Had his mother looked like this? Could this lovely creature, so flawless, so composed, everything a goddess should be, be one of his family? Why not? The village was small.

He returned to the muddy street, ate a persimmon and a handful of the same crackers Sato-San had offered at their first meeting.

Darkness fell.

A giant drum thudded drawing him back to the Shinto temple. A bonfire blazed before the shrine, drawing families with lanterns like fireflies moving across the fields and up the mossy steps to the fire. The drum, the largest he'd ever seen, filled the night like the beating heart of the world. Suddenly flutes shrieked. If there were a melody in the music Sam couldn't find it, but the drum beats matched the beats of his own heart—men and women, young mothers and fathers, children with lanterns happily waving their hands and moving their bodies through the firelight in time with the rhythm.

And the lovely priestess? He peered into the crowd hoping to catch a glimpse of her, but she was nowhere in the glow. A man in white robes with a full head of gray hair and wearing tiny spectacles dangling on his smooth, porcelain face spotted him and coming straight at him, carrying an earthenware jar and tiny saucers. With a nod he announced in Japanese, "You were looking for me? I am Gon-gúji Ota." Sam bowed, and the Shinto priest poured milky fluid from the jar into one of his shallow clay saucers. "First sake of the harvest." He held out the drink Sam knew to be alcohol. "Please to drink."

"Thank you, sir. No." Sam ducked his head in apology. "I mean, I don't drink alcohol."

"No?" The priest, offering the tiny cup, smiled. "It is holy. Sake." He added a nod to his smile. "If you change your mind this year there is plenty." After a slight bow he drank the sake he'd poured for Sam.

Sam offered, "The Buddhist priest sent me here."

"Ah, yes. Yamaguchi Sensei. He drinks sake. A lot of sake."

"I am looking for an old Shinto priest—Nakamura-San."

The priest drew in his breath. He understood the question. "Nakamura Sensei. I am told was here for many years."

"Where is he now?"

"Yufuin, the last I heard. In the mountains. A place for those who suffer lung disease. He was very old."

"Did you know him?"

"No. He was here, I believe, two priests ago. I heard only that he was ill."

"He's my great uncle."

"Yes?"

The porcelain face, expressionless, showed no surprise, but serious concern for the visitor. "This Nakamura Sensei. Do not hope too much. He was very old."

"Wild Boar," Sam offered. "That's what the Buddhist priest called him."

"Yes. They say he was remarkably hairy. I am also told he and the Buddhist priest long gone to our ancestors liked very much to drink sake together."

"I'm here to find what's left of my family. My Japanese family." In the flickering firelight the gaijin explained. "I'm half-Japanese."

The smooth face lit in the same glow he shared with Sam on this holy night, appeared to accept anything, no matter how remarkable. "And the other half?"

"American."

"You have lived in America?"

"For eleven years. But now I live here. Nagasaki. Actually, I have been with the Snyders in Urakami at the Mission for Christ."

"For you to be a Christian is natural. You are a Westerner."

"The Snyders are missionaries."

"I do not know your people, these Snyders, but I have read the Bible of Christianity. Much I like. Much I find very strange. Perhaps that is because Christianity asks questions Shinto does not."

Here in the firelight and music were surely the realest Japanese he'd ever seen. "I know my mother's family was here in 1887."

The priest held out another sake and when Sam again refused, shrugged and sipped it himself. "Perhaps a family in some nearby village."

"I was hoping—actually counting with all my heart on finding them here."

"You have an American family?"

"No." For a second he wondered if that meant that he'd given up on his father forever.

"No family, but you have your missionaries."

The priest signaled three women to be patient and told them he would bring sake to them in a moment. Sam wiped his eyes, counting on the smoke to explain his tears.

"No family?"

"Not yet. I'm hoping."

"If you are troubled, pray to your Christian God for help."

"I've tried that."

"Still you feel great sadness?"

He nodded.

"You feel your heart will break."

"Sometimes."

"Go on searching."

"I'll never stop."

The priest smiled. "Stop for tonight."

Shinto wisdom? The priest held out the earthenware jar tapping it with a saucer. "You are certain you do not drink sake?"

"No. Thank you."

"If you are half-Japanese, drink half."

"You said Shinto doesn't ask a lot of questions."

"Not what you'd call questions."

"What does it ask?"

The holy man's eyes, shining in the firelight, gestured to Sam to turn with him and look at the dancers, clapping and singing, turning the deep, dark night to joy. A nod encouraged him to step forward and join with the dancers lit by this fire in this forest—a world of man and nature sharing being alive. Sam didn't move. Both stood looking into the firelight and the dancing while the priest poured sake for his people. He hadn't forgotten Sam's question, and said, "What does Shinto ask? Tonight —this."

Through the holy man's eyes Sam was seeing what he'd never seen, feeling what he'd never felt. Here was a world outside the Snyders' walls— the edge of the deep forest, the night, the soft wind, the music, everything vibrantly alive. Yes, that thudding drum was his own heart beating. At no other moment of his young life had his senses felt sharper, more alert— an outsider looking on at an ancient tribe dancing and singing in the fire- light. Could it be that he was with his ancestors, his family going all the way back to the Sun Goddess?

Abruptly he stiffened with fright. Out of the surge of dancers, lung- ing straight at him, was some crazed primordial demon—silhouetted by flame—a woman dancing and wildly waving her arms, a heavy farm woman with the fire's glow flickering on a flat face under a wild tangle of flying black hair. The other dancers, seeing she was claiming him, stared, everyone roaring with laughter. Closer and closer she was bearing down on him, swaying her stumpy body to the drumbeat, and to Sam's terror and astonishment boldly claiming the young foreigner as her prize.

Wavering in the firelight, she slowed and swayed, her hands raised, claiming him, and with a wild burst of cackling her hands threw folds of her kimono up on naked, fleshy legs, undulating obscenely, closer and closer, tipping herself forward, thrusting black hair at the base of her belly at him.

"Stick your *Tengu* nose in here!" She shrieked as her entire body burst with more cackles. Dispelling any chance he might try pretending he didn't know what was being demanded of him, she clutched her clump of black pubic hair, grinning till she was slamming her naked flesh against his crotch. "Put it in there pretty boy and stay the night!"

In shock Sam staggered back. Shame scalded his face redder than the reflected firelight. "No, don't back away!" Shouts came from the other dancers happily joining in, egging on the hairy, wild woman.

How could they join in taking such glee in his mortification—all Asahi-Mura laughing, clapping, even pushing the young and terrified stranger with his white face toward the woman's naked belly. Gon-gúji Ota, the priest? Sam saw him grinning. What shocked Sam most of all was that no one but he was shocked. He staggered back, waving her off with both hands, finally shoving her back into the crowd. Someone cried. "No fucking? No dancing? No sake?"

Sam wasn't able to trust his voice or look at the woman he'd spurned, now spitting curses at him with everyone laughing and tugging her back into the crowd's wilder dancing. Now he was the only one not singing and clapping happily and never feeling so absurdly tall, enormous and stupid. Every instinct told him to turn and flee the fire and music and dancing at Asahi-Mura's Shinto shrine.

With a silent look that might have been sympathy, Gon-gúji Ota with his sake, was at his side, telling him to stay and risk belonging to the human race. "You have come from Nagasaki. Very far. I myself was once in Nagasaki. Very big. And now you are in Asahi-Mura, which is very small, and you are looking, but not drinking or dancing."

"My religion does not allow either."

The priest poured sake for a group of women crowding around them. A farm couple tugged at the stranger attempting to haul him out among the dancers.

"If you decide to dance," the priest dropped his voice so only Sam could hear, "no one in the village will tell your other Christians."

Sam found himself holding out his hand for one of the tiny saucers. The priest poured. Sam drank.

In the firelight smiling faces surrounded him. He drank his first sake and smiled back. He drank another. The bonfire burned brighter. Music filled the forest. Sake was like nothing he'd ever tasted in his entire life. Was it making him move to the music? Was he dancing? Whatever he was doing, he soon felt buoyant, never so buoyant, never so much a part of anything as this fire and music and the whole beating heart of the world.

CHAPTER TWENTY-ONE

The strong odor of onions cooking hit, and his stomach turned queasy. His hand went back to testing the floor. Where was he? To look around he'd have to dare look into the brutal glare of day. Eyes closed, his hand went groping. He seemed to be wrapped in a wadded kimono within a tangled quilt.

Chickens clucked. A dog barked. Daring to blink into his unknown world he shrank under the quilt. Now what was he hearing? Giggling? He pushed himself up on one elbow, wincing but keeping his eyes open. Blurred vision took him across wooden floor and mats to the sight of a stumpy man with bare legs and a small, shapeless woman. The giggles were coming from three children dancing with glee and covering their faces with their hands and shrieking with laughter.

A new wave of dizziness knocked him back down. Abruptly he fought a wave of sickness forcing him to stumble to his feet. From the raised wooden porch he plunged past a family into a farmyard to a stand of burdock into which he vomited till he was empty. Someone handed him a bamboo bucket of water to splash on his face and hands. Blinking, he made out the farmer's wife. Why the hell was she grinning? He looked down and saw he was wrapped in a gray padded kimono.

What was probably a father, a son, and two daughters stifled more giggles watching the woman lead this boy, enormous and looking like no one they'd ever seen, back to the open porch. He slumped back down, his face on the floor, watching a little girl bringing soup smelling strongly of onions bobbing in some horrible brew. The sight of white blobs and green seaweed had him clapping his hand over his mouth and stumbling off for another bout of vomiting.

Again, with the cheerful woman's help, he was led back to the porch, slumping onto his quilt with the whole family gathering and bending over him for a closer look.

At mid morning he forced himself onto his feet. The mother propped him up and got him to his feet with the entire family spellbound, watching her drop the kimono from this man. Too helpless to protest and unable to defend his nakedness he stood, this gaijin, this *tengu* they'd found in their forest. Without a stitch on his young body the family commented on the bronze hairs on his limbs and crotch. The oldest child, a girl of seven or eight, dared approach and run her hand over the fuzz on his forearm before she looked away in awe and disbelief.

The mother padded off and returned, brushing his black Sears Roebuck missionary suit free of last night's dirt and leaves. From his jacket she drew the pocket dictionary he was never without and the wonder of his return railroad ticket. The ticket was proof that this *tengu* creature had not fallen out of the sky into last night's Shinto celebration. The farmer reached for the ticket, squinted at it, pulled on clogs and jogged off from the house. With her brood looking on, the mother carefully restored their exotic creature to his Western best, their guest standing unsteadily while the second youngest girl pressed more smelly soup at him.

A quarter of an hour later the farmer came jogging back, breathing hard, waving a train schedule.

By noon the family squatted their guest down on threadbare tatami eating boiled sweet potato, leeks, and onions. By now, after each one of the family had dared to touch their *tengu,* curious smiles watched him eating boiled vegetables. In their exchange of words they seemed to agree that yes, he was some kind of human. When, out of simple good manners, he began to help stack the dishes, they rejected his offer. Instead, they propped their young giant with his back leaning against a wooden post safely out of the way of a paper wall into which he might stumble and crash.

December dusk came early and lamps were lit as the family filed into the house for what he sensed was some kind of ritual. They sat in a circle. At his feet they spread a wide square of green silk, clearly the most elegant thing they possessed. On this they placed a flat wooden box of boiled rice balls and green pickles along with a tightly sealed jar of sake and three bright-orange persimmons. Over these offerings the mother and the oldest daughter brought the four corners of the silk together. Finishing wrapping food for his journey back to wherever unlikely place he had come from, the entire family bowed and presented him the finest they had to offer. Then all five happily scrambled down on their knees and touched their foreheads on the mat. Sam, standing tall as an awkward stork, bobbed back to them, his thanks to his first Japanese family.

On the train Sam slumped his forehead against the cold glass windowpane while dark fields, bamboo groves, black tunnels and pine forests rumbled past in the night. True, he hadn't found his mother's family. Not yet, but every click of the train told him over and over, that he'd just had the happiest time of his life.

However, the piper must be paid.

Now that he'd touched base with his Japanese heritage, only a sense of honor was taking him back to the Snyders to make his farewell formal. He hated the idea, but he'd make Sato-San proud of him.

Crossing the dried-up rice paddies he squared his shoulders, determined to turn his farewell stride into the mission not only honorable, but one of personal triumph.

He left the green-silk *furoshiki* outside the front door. Sounds of hammering in the kitchen drew him through the empty church to the preacher standing on a sauerkraut crock, his face and bare shoulders smudged with the sooty task of fitting a pipe from the iron stove up through the roof.

Sister Ellen, with Martha Elizabeth on her hip, wiped the child's running nose and watched silently from the doorway. The preacher swiped a heavy arm across soot blackened raccoon eyes, refusing to look down at the banished soul. Sister Ellen mopped the child's nose. She was clenched in cold fury.

Too cheerfully he said, "I came to say goodbye."

The preacher struggled to join the two sooty pipes. "Get out."

Sam turned to go into his room to gather up his work clothes, his Bible, his few books. "Hold it right here," Brother Wendell commanded. Sister Ellen, her plain face shining with righteous fury, used the squalling child to block his way. He'd been ordered to leave—cast out forever. They were making it plain he was to take nothing with him, with no way to deny him his Sears Roebuck's shiny black suit.

"Goodbye," the preacher snapped without looking down from his sooty work, "except goodbye means God be with you." His voice took on the sharp crack of a tree limb breaking under winter ice. "You and I know God is not with you. You have no one. You are no one."

At the door Sam picked up the green *furoshiki* moving out into the cold but bright sunlight, choosing to take the words flung at him as his first step in his new life.

CHAPTER TWENTY-TWO

Now he ran. Racing down the hill into town, Sam's spirits soared high. At last! Free—gloriously, wonderfully free. From his years at the mission he'd taken nothing but his suit, his pocket dictionary, and his mother's document that tied him to some village not far from Asahi-Mura. The apple-green *furoshiki* was a gift from his people. As for money, his total savings after his railway fare was three yen and sixteen sen. No question about it, until he set up his teaching, he'd have to be careful. He'd have to make every sen last.

Striding boldly into Nagasaki, he turned each coin over three times before buying a toothbrush, a safety razor and shaving soap. In town he filled himself with the deep cold air of freedom, walking for miles carefully checking room rates, till he found the cheapest of all waterfront hotels.

A bony man at the desk with the hooded eyes of a predatory bird demanded two nights' payment in advance. The sky that began full of sunshine was turning dark. His grimy room was even darker, and snapping on an unshaded but dim light bulb sent a cockroach scuttling. The Western-style bed's dingy sheets were torn, with thin blankets splotched with stains.

It was, of course, the most beautiful room in the world. His room! Bursting with joy and hope, buoyed by the absolute conviction that money from teaching would soon be rolling in, he hopped on the bed and hugged his knees. He flung himself back on the bed folding his arms under his head. He'd escaped! At long, long last he was free. "Hold on!" Suddenly he was scolding himself and jumped up. "This was heaven, but no time for daydreaming!" He still had what was left of this dark winter afternoon to start his new life.

He raced down the stairs and out into the street and found a print shop he badgered into having business cards printed by first thing the next morning. A Chinese tailor stripped him and took his suit to snip off his frayed cuffs and sponge away Urakami and Asahi-Mura dirt while the owner huddled in a blanket, ready to dress and ascend to a new life.

He was careful and with every precious sen he spent he winced. A haircut and a new cheap white cotton dress shirt he justified as absolutely necessary—his investment in his English-teaching future.

The December dusk threatened rain, but he galloped like a colt through the city—his city. He'd been born here, and on his first day of freedom he was spreading his wings, a big, bronze-haired young man with a smile all over his face for everyone in the world.

It didn't cost a sen to wander, to exult in the sights and sounds of the city, all the while dodging streetcars and rickshaws and sprinting up hills to visit temples and the gods of fortune who were going to make his English Language Academy a huge success. Back down on the busy streets, he thrilled at the mellow glow of lanterns and the brightly lit department store windows. At music from the bars his pulse picked up the beat. "Come on and hear, come on and hear, Alexander's Ragtime Band" All of a sudden he was back in Bremerton in 1911, humming. He was still up at midnight, one of the few left on the street, never feeling more Japanese, still as happy as he'd been in the firelight with the drum pounding in Asahi-Mura.

He'd eaten the farmer's gift in the green silk, but nothing since. From a late-night stall he bought five rice balls and three persimmons.

Back in his dismal but glorious room, he munched three rice balls and two persimmons and put the rest aside for breakfast. He washed his hands in the basin before he tried on his brand-new shirt, the first new thing he'd owned since the navy had dressed him in Bremerton. A little snug across his shoulders but it gleamed pristine white. With a grimy towel he shined his boots. Tomorrow he'd be all spit and polish in his new shirt, his pressed suit, and gleaming leather. Elegant white business cards would convince clerks in offices, young Japanese executives, how blessed they'd be to have him for their teacher opening postwar opportunities for anyone wise enough to learn English. Tomorrow, Mitsubishi. Yes, he'd start at the very top with Mitsubishi.

Hours before light poked through the torn window shade, he bounded out of bed, gobbled his rice and persimmons, dressed in his all Western, black splendor and dashed to the street demanding the printing shop to open.

Oh, but the cards were thrilling. So crisp. So official. English on one side, Japanese on the other.

Mr. Samuel Adams Pinkerton
Assistant Professor of the English Language

He kissed his card. How he loved this entrée into the world, magnificent enough to impress anyone. As to teaching. It was no lie. Didn't he have real experience at the mission teaching English?

The December day was bitter cold, but it had him sweating on his long hike through industrial streets to reach the other side of the harbor and the Mitsubishi shipyards. At the gate he dusted off his shoes and yanked his tie close. The first gate was locked and didn't open. He found other doors guarded against his first foray into industrial Japanese life.

At the back door of the mighty Mitsubishi kingdom it took pluck and a quick quarterback dash to get him through the line of applicants. In a personnel office he was taller than the two slender young men in black serge Western-style suits he faced. Their shirts were white as his, their collars celluloid, their ties dark and modestly patterned. With extravagant solemnity he bowed and presented his card the proper way Sato-San had taught him, clamped with both thumbs.

The two young Mitsubishi employees studied his card and glanced at each other without even attempting to smother their smirks. The shorter man returned the card to Sam with overly elaborate politesse. "No." He insisted and fought on. "Please, keep it." Before they turned away he asked, "Do you speak English?" He was polite enough not to challenge either man. Covering his nervousness, he smiled, but realized he was showing too many teeth.

"I speak Engrish." The taller, a soft, tea-colored man fitted tightly into his three piece suit with cuffs that didn't need trimming, held the card like an inflicted nuisance in his small, dainty fingers with perfectly manicured and gleaming nails.

"Then, of course, you are no doubt well aware," Sam continued in a confiding tone of the man of the world, "how essential it is these days for anyone who intends to do business with the world to speak English. You can reference any of my students who will tell you how it's helped them. They will tell you that I am an A Number One, first-rate teacher."

The man setting the card spoke English slowly. "We have many teachers here in Nagasaki. Schools and universities—"

Sam didn't accuse him of not being able to pronounce the Western L. "Ah, but you see, I myself come directly here—to your offices."

"Sorry. We have no more time to talk. Thank you."

"I do have references." He was back to lying. "I didn't think I'd need to bring them with me, but I can return with them." Sam was surprised how quickly, and with little more than a perfunctory nod instead of even modest bow, they disappeared. "Please keep the card," he urged. "I will call again tomorrow morning."

On his way out he passed a line of flawlessly dressed businessmen holding their winter hats, candidates for employment. "I teach English," he announced cheerfully and offering cards. Every man in line cringed in mortification. Clearly this bumptious, young gaijin had no idea he was egregiously breaking every rule of business and social Japanese life.

Outside the Hotel Bellevue he screwed up his courage to dare to invade the lobby on his way to the washroom, his impromptu headquarters for reconnoitering—sponging a smudge of coal dust off his celluloid collar and slicking down his bronze hair. After a brisk nod in the mirror, he approached the front desk with his identity firmly held in two thumbs. The Japanese hotelier, smoothly professional, bowed without accepting the card, asking the young gaijin if he had a reservation. Sam, two thumbs still clamped, bucked up his courage with a quick, "Not today. You see, I'm here in Japan to teach your staff English. I'm an expert teacher. I have references—"

"Sorry," the clerk answered in near-flawless English as he traced his fountain pen down a list of guests.

Sam raced from the hotel to the largest Western-style department store already enthroning Santa Claus and decorating its windows for Western-style Christmas sales. Long lines of women and men applying for positions, and dressed fashionably in hats and gloves, waited with Buddhist patience outside the store. After he'd put in his own three-hour stint, with a bow, he presented his card to a crisp little Japanese employment personnel man with a white carnation in his lapel and a look as sour as his Bremerton grammar school's photograph of President Woodrow Wilson. Sam began his sales talk, but was interrupted. "Yes," the employment officer agreed in Japanese. "English is very important these days. That is why we have already established the highest connections with the university."

Sam risked a sudden shift in tactics. "But you're getting ready for Christmas and I could start right now helping you with your English-speaking customers. As an employee."

The man glanced past him at another executive. Without looking at him, he said, "For that you would have to be a Japanese citizen." Anything that smacked of passports terrified Sam, but he fought on. "As a matter of fact I was born right here in Nagasaki."

It was dusk, lanterns were beginning to glow, by now it was too late in the day to make any more calls. He hadn't eaten a bite since this morning's rice and persimmon and hunger clawed at his stomach. With plenty of pluck his first day, but no success, he held off spending even one sen for rice.

It was beginning to drizzle. Here on the sidewalk, without an umbrella, he was dodging crowds of Japanese hurrying home from work. How fast, how confidently everyone moved. Tonight in Nagasaki the world seemed so sure of itself, with every one of them with a job to return to tomorrow morning.

CHAPTER TWENTY-THREE

Back at the hotel two drunken Danish sailors brawling out in the hall jolted him awake before daylight. Lying in the dark on his narrow bed, it took him a long moment before he realized he was no longer a prisoner in the mission's whitewashed cell.

He bounded up, brushed his teeth vigorously, ignored the gray dawn beyond the torn window shade and gloried in his second day of freedom. "Hallelujah, Brother and Sister! No more Snyders!"

He lathered up and shaved, listening to the horns and whistles of ships out in the harbor coming and going from the world's seven seas. Nagasaki. All those ships. The U.S. Navy. His father, a lieutenant on the Abraham Lincoln, had twice sailed into this harbor.

His father. Was that face in the small, cracked mirror looking back at him anything like his father? Here, right here in Nagasaki, he'd found proof that his father had married Butterfly, his mother. He'd deserted her, and heartbroken, she'd taken her life. Kate, his father's American wife, picked him up, two years old, from the tatami and took him away from the house with the tall pine. The Showalters said that back in the States she'd planned to pass him as her own. Heartbreak, not Butterfly's samurai knife, ended her life.

And Benjy, like Sam, he'd been too young for the Great War. He was a Showalter, fourteen now and living a rich kid's life in Baltimore on the other side of the world. Today his breakfast wouldn't be persimmons or rice. No, he'd dig into a hot, glorious breakfast of fried eggs and ham along with hash-brown potatoes served by a black servant. After breakfast a uniformed chauffeur was waiting to drive the young master off to some fancy, private school.

Sam was talking to himself in the cracked mirror. "You ever think of me, Benjy? Ever wonder what had happened to Sam?" He studied the face in the mirror. "I'm over here in Nagasaki—an English and Japanese teacher living in my own home town. Not Japanese, not a true descendant of the Sun Goddess. All alone, Benjy, but I'm free."

Enough of Benjy. Today, in his own home town all he needed to succeed was plenty of Horatio Alger's All-American pluck.

Struggling to put the stud in his collar he winced at finding the blotch of persimmon juice stain on his shirtfront. Damn! He should have washed it last night. Dabbing at the spot only made it worse. His suit, moist and wrinkled from yesterday, needed pressing. His boots were still damp. The broken mirror on the wall was too small to see himself head to toe. He could only hope he was presenting himself with the crisp and clean professional look the world expected of English language teachers.

He was without a raincoat, but with a broken umbrella he'd fished out of a trashcan. His first call was back to the American Consulate where the best he was able to do was to leave a stack of his cards. From there he found some kind of college where he pinned five cards on a bulletin board.

By noon he was out in the rain, still with no breakfast, hungry, lonely, and scared, a seventeen-year-old with nowhere to go but trudge back to "that lousy flophouse" to get in out of the rain.

By now he was drenched. In the lobby the desk clerk, gobbling up steaming noodles, ignored him. Sam hesitated, but had no choice but to break into the man's slurping to ask for his key. The clerk didn't look up from his noodles or reach down to get the key from its hook. Feeling a chill colder than the outside December rain, he realized his two paid days at the hotel were up. Anyone could see that big pay-in-advance sign posted above the desk, but surely the clerk would trust him for one more night.

No. He'd been locked out.

"But my things—"

The man reached for the telephone. "Do I call the police?"

Being illegal, the mention of the police paralyzed him. All he could prove about himself was that flimsy paper, that document recording the baptism of Lieutenant Benjamin Franklin Pinkerton and Nakamura Eiko's son. Then it struck. "Oh, God." The floor opened up under him. That paper was in his dictionary locked away up in his room.

Cold and shaking, he fought panic with one blazing hope—a sudden inspiration—that charged him back to the street to run all the way along the waterfront past Deshima Island to that church he and Sato-San had visited. They'd have a record of his baptism. They'd help him find some way to stay alive, establish some kind of citizenship—U.S. or Japanese. Even better, they might even give him temporary work. They were

Christians in a way the Snyders never were. That Mrs. McKie was really kind. She'd help.

The church was locked. He rattled the front and side doors. In a street stall near the door a woman behind a stack of white radishes supplied the news. Reverend McKie had died five years ago and the congregation was still waiting for a new minister to arrive.

A steaming cup of tea for the last of his few precious sen bought temporary shelter and the warmth of his hands around the hot cup brought his only cheer against the cold, wet world.

"Get back to Asahi-Mura!" Like the tea, the thought warmed him. Never in his life had he felt more welcome anywhere. Still, he told himself to face the truth. That first visit he'd come among the priests and villagers as a stranger. That farm family had taken him in, shared the best they had. For a day and a night they'd treated him as an honored guest. No one had to tell him that life among those rice fields was desperately hard. Go back? Even if by some miracle he could climb on a train and get back—the truth was he'd be a beggar. Even if he became the most devout believer in Shinto he couldn't live alone in the forest.

CHAPTER TWENTY-FOUR

In the cold December evening the train station glowed with warm light. The entrance bustled with rickshaws and travelers hurrying past a line of fortune tellers' lamps. Without sen, what possible future could Samuel Adams Nakamura-Pinkerton predict for himself?

He supposed he should look around for a place on the station floor and keep out of sight of the law. At a back wall he hunkered down. Keeping his head down, he stole looks at the other homeless. Two feet away a scrag of an old woman was cradling a jar of sake more lovingly than a baby. Two cripples had staked out their territory to pick through a little mound of garbage. A few, already asleep, thrust out bare feet black with grime. A dark-yellow man, pressing a rag to his head, mumbled and rocked with pain. A nearly naked bag of bones, spitting and scratching scabby legs and insect-infested hair, sucked on a jar of sweet-potato brandy, cheaper than sake. Sam might be starving, but his teeth didn't ache and he had yet to scratch scabs and lice.

All he'd eaten that day were two persimmons he'd filched from a tree in Urakami, leaving his stomach clawing itself. Aromas from the noodle and tempura stalls focused his eyes like those of a starving dog. Across the station others with coins were burrowing into bowls of vegetables, slurping miso, scooping rice into their gullets. Against the wall, Sam was part of a wretched band with no coins, hungry-eyed outcasts praying for scraps.

A scuffle of clogs brought a newcomer to the wall, a gray skull poking up out of a voluminous Western-style army overcoat. He dropped to a heap squatting next to Sam, locking his arms over bare and knobby arthritic knees, adding his unblinking eyes to the gallery of the starving. Sam stared like his other fellow pariahs, knowing the best they could hope for was that one of those with coins might prove extravagantly wasteful enough to leave a few noodles in the bottom of a bowl. Best of all would be a bowl empty but for the shell-end of fried shrimp. Would anyone leave a fishtail—not the head for that was a delicacy—but a fin? A few grains of rice? One or two miserable pickles?

He stole looks at the greedy eyes of the starving, knowing too well that chances were few that any Japanese in this train station would leave behind a scrap. Gray Skull was breathing hard, his glittering eyes fastened on a young mother with three children hurrying to board a train. His hope was concentrated on the mother bird shoveling noodles and rice into her chicks who might, in her rush to board a train, fail to seize a bowl from a dawdling child

Sam raced Gray Skull for the bowls left behind, and because he was young, seized the prize, a half serving of buckwheat noodles and the shell of a deep-fried prawn. Absolving his conscience, he assured himself that the old man couldn't possibly be as starving as he. Hungry as he was, in his triumph, he missed seeing a small hand emerge from a flutter of rags to snatch away the bowl. Everything about this evil little thief said he was a professional, now shoving his foxy little face so deep into the bowl that only his shaggy black hair showed. Tipping up the bowl with one hand, he scratched an armpit with the other. His rags were nothing Sam could logically accept as clothes; they were a parody of abject poverty.

Sam clenched his hands into angry fists. The shaggy black head rose from the bowl and the huge dark eyes in a sickly pale face locked on Sam's. He made a show of dangling a noodle like a worm in a bird's mouth before slurping it up with a triumphant, sucking sound.

"Give me at least some of it!" Sam demanded.

"Ask politely."

"Please. May I have some? Please?"

"No." The urchin shrieked, joyfully plunging back into the bowl. Ready to explode with rage, Sam barely resisted kicking this pile of rags across the train station. The thief's shining dark eyes rose above the bowl, looking past Sam, who followed his gaze back to the food stalls. His evil little elf's head jerked, alerting Sam to a housewife a few feet away slipping an *o bento* box into a string bag she'd left unattended while she sampled a dealer's *satsuma* oranges.

"Steal?" No. He could filch persimmons, but he couldn't steal. Ravenous and defeated, all he could do was slide his back against the wall and sink to the floor.

CHAPTER TWENTY-FIVE

Though he hated him Sam recognized a survivor in this ragged thief. He was still giggling and licking his lips. A rosy tongue swiped away the last trace of broth. "Good. I've had better, but good. You like buckwheat noodles?"

"Shut up."

The street rat rocked with merriment. "Here. Take the bowl back to the noodle man and tell him you want more."

"Go to hell."

Sam felt the bowl shoved at his stomach. He rose to his feet. If the noodle man didn't take pity, perhaps he'd reward him for returning his bowl. At the counter behind a boiling pot, the vendor, shiny as a garden slug with sweat, grabbed the bowl only to shoo Sam away from his tantalizing aromas.

He crept back to the wall to sit by himself. The urchin, whose grin uncovered missing teeth stretched wide as a jack o' lantern's, came scuttling over and hunkered down beside him. With grunts, the thief's pinky fingernail dug at his few teeth. "I usually eat good. I like Chinese best."

"Shut up."

Laughter bubbled out of the brat. "Nagasaki has the best Chinese food in the whole world. Better even than China. *Champon.* Ever eat *champon?*"

"I told you—shut up."

"*Champon's* juicy clams. Fish. Eggs. Noodles. Very tasty. Also I'm partial to crispy pork and chicken."

"You want me to kick you to death?"

"Only you won't. Because I have an idea that will make us both rich." In spite of gnawing hunger and boiling rage against the thief, Sam felt a tickle of interest. Obviously this was a clever little brat, clever enough perhaps to offer a glimmer of hope. Sam reverted to the missionary he'd been and took the moral high ground. "I don't steal."

"Better than stealing."

"If you're so goddamn smart, how come you didn't have money for Chinese food tonight and had to steal my dinner?"

"I have money. But tonight not enough for *champon.* I was puking and shitting all day today. Couldn't work. The night before last I drank too much sake and got into something—not Chinese. Bad fish I picked up."

"Stole."

The brat pulled a finger from probing his nose and refined the diagnosis. "Food poisoning."

"Good. I only wish it'd killed you." Sam had found something to feel superior about. "If you had any brains you would have smelled it first."

"I did. But after all that sake, shit would have smelled sweet." He startled Sam with a sharp jab in the ribs. Sam drew himself away, making a show of ignoring him. Another poke had him looking down at a tiny hand holding two coins. "Take it. Buy yourself some noodles."

Sam narrowed his surprise to suspicion. "How come you're doing this?"

"A business deal. With a bowl of noodles in you, you'll listen better."

This time the cook nodded at the big gaijin and ladled a bowl full of buckwheat noodles, filling it with broth—hot, steaming, tantalizing broth. He dribbled in chopped green scallions.

"More."

The hand sprinkled more scallions.

"And shrimp."

"Not enough money for shrimp."

Even before leaving the stand Sam began gobbling up the slippery noodles and sucked in the broth, feeling life surge back into him. As avidly as the street rat had licked his lips, his tongue found every drop of broth in the bowl. Back at the wall he sank down beside his grinning benefactor. "Thank you."

"Don't mention it."

More convinced than ever that this creature was a survivor, he asked. "So what do you do when you work?"

"Stupid question."

Sam huffed. "You don't work, you steal."

The urchin fluttered his rags. "My working clothes." He turned himself into an elaborate display of smudged arms and face while whining pitiably.

"Beggar?"

"The best." He scratched himself. "So where you from, Big Stupid?"

"None of your goddamn business."

"You have beggars in America?"

"Not many. It's a disgrace."

"Here we have millions and it's no disgrace. Good trade. Buddhists always give, maybe not much, but they give." He reached over, lifted Sam's filthy white shirt and patted his stomach. "Good noodles?"

Sam struck his hand away. "What did you mean about a business deal?"

"I am an A Number One Beggar. That's because I have an enormous talent for looking spectacularly pathetic." He hung his head for a second, then raised it, his eyes spilling tears. "Please, lovely lady, kind gentleman, show the mercy of the Lord Buddha. Acquire virtue for the next life." He grinned. "Not a Buddhist alive who won't give—if you do it right."

Sam shook his head in amazement, but resisted rewarding the beggar with agreement.

"Ragged clothes. Dirt. Be even better if I was crippled. I tried that. Got a little cart. Made fake stumps for legs to poke out at people. But there are too many hills and stairs in Nagasaki for a cart."

"This deal? Where do I come in?"

"Big American—"

"I'm Japanese."

"You look American. Big. Stupid. That's all right. We'll make you dumb. Deaf, too. Carry me on your shoulders—"

"And beg?" Sam spluttered self-righteous outrage.

"I'll do the begging," the professional announced.

"Not me. Never!"

"That's why you're Big Stupid—"

"Because I'm not a lousy beggar—"

Bright, sharp foxy eyes looked him over. "So what are you now?"

"I'd commit seppuku first," Sam declared.

The beggar sucked a shred of dinner from his teeth. "No you wouldn't."

"Tomorrow," Sam announced, "I'm going to find work—"

Suddenly the beggar clawed him fiercely and shrieked, "Run!" Sam sensed real danger and scrambled to his feet with the brat pushing him from behind. Around them startled squatters struggling out of a tangle of blankets, scuttled in all directions. Sam was running as fast as the beggar.

Whistles shrieked. The beggar shoved him out of the station as they kept running. "Police! Shut up! Follow me!" The beggar didn't allow Sam to stop till they were ducked down into shadow behind a line of rickshaws. Sam caught his breath, gasping, flabbergasted. "We weren't doing anything wrong—"

"Without me your ass would be on its way to jail right now. And you know why? Because you don't know shit." Here in the dark Sam watched the beggar's bright eyes peering around, more than ever a wary little fox. They could see inside the station, where uniformed police were shoving the old woman with her sake jar who was barely able to hobble. She dropped her jar and it shattered.

The urchin coolly signaled Sam to stay in shadow, not to move. Not yet. "Once they finish their sweep for the night we can go back in."

Returning to the wall, Sam glanced around to see who else had survived. Gray Skull, under his huge overcoat, was a few feet away, coughing his lungs out. Across the station, the other derelicts were still outside, waiting like forest creatures for the last of the police to leave.

"Thank you," Sam, still catching his breath, muttered.

"Without me to save you those sons-of-bitches would bust your head open like a melon as soon as look at you. Once they get you, you can kiss your ass goodbye. They run you in," the urchin's hand mopped his nose, "and whether you did anything or not, they torture a confession out of you."

"I said thank you."

"So, Big Stupid American, you listen to me from now on."

Sam had been saved. "So what's your name?"

Instead of answering the street rat gave his dribbling nose another swipe.

"My name's Samuel Adams Pinkerton. I asked you yours."

His rescuer was on his feet. "Right now we're clearing out of this shithole." Sam's new friend had Sam sprinting after him winding through the line of rickshaws out into the street and across streetcar tracks. When he'd decided he'd never learn his benefactor's name, a sharp elbow jabbed him in the ribs.

"Torazo."

"Is that your first or last name?"

"My name."

"I mean is that a real name or a nickname?"

"Who the hell do you think you are? The police?"

"I only meant—"

"You're really dumb, you know that? Stick with me or you're fly shit."

CHAPTER TWENTY-SIX

The two new friends walked for hours.

Torazo produced a crumpled cigarette from his rags and offered to share. Sam, still missionary boy enough to refuse, nevertheless was pleased to be asked to share what Brother Wendell had condemned as "the devil's weed." He'd been alone and starving on the streets of Nagasaki, now he was following Torazo. After an hour he was convinced this raggedy elf could teach him more about staying alive than anyone since Sato-San.

Torazo's cunning moved them through the labyrinth of Nagasaki's back alleys with a self-assured swagger. Torazo was proud to have Sam in tow, his new friend, this big, strapping fellow who said he was Japanese but any fool could plainly see was American.

Sam had been overdue to find a friend and heard himself opening up to Torazo about his Japanese mother's house on the hill and the family he was desperate to find. He told him about California and Washington State in the USA and baseball and his American family there before his other mother died. He even opened the wound of the terrible Showalters and the Snyders hollow years of slavery. Sharing his life and spilling over with excitement he brought him up to date on the Asahi-Mura trip and his introduction to Shinto's fire ritual and with its sex and sake—his first glimpse of real Japanese life. Torazo, however, insisted that a village—any village—even with sake, was only a shithole out in the sticks which any boy who wanted to make something of his life must get away from as fast as running from the cops.

Suddenly Torazo's elbow jabbed again, demanding his American-looking giant reveal his birth date. Sam's answer troubled him. No longer merry, he looked pained waggling his head with concern. "Very bad. I shouldn't even be talking with you."

Sam slowed, stunned that his openness met such coldness. "You were born under an unlucky star."

"That's bullshit."

Torazo spoke as one on firm ground. "You have no family—that's proof. It's the worst thing that can happen."

Sam was defiant. "I'll find them," he was determined. "You'll see."

Torazo corrected himself. "I am wrong. Worse is being an *ainoko*—a half-breed—"

"Now you can really go to hell."

"If you knew anything at all you'd know Japanese don't like people who aren't one hundred percent, totally Japanese like me."

Sam couldn't deny what he knew only too well to be the truth. "I can handle that."

The foxy little face darkened with real concern. "You have big trouble ahead."

Sam fought sounding as desperate as he felt. "I just told you, don't worry about me. I'll be all right."

"Like you were back in the station?"

"Goddamn you, shut up."

A grin split Torazo's face open on uneven teeth. "We can't all be born lucky."

Sam lashed back. "Your family's so wonderful?"

As they continued to walk, now it was Torazo's turn to talk nonstop, making it clear he was a pure and honorable Japanese from a famous, old samurai family. Not an *eta*—one of the untouchables. He held up his claw of a hand. "Stay away from them. Them and the cruddy Chinese, except for their cooking. And worse, the stinking Koreans."

"You don't like anybody—"

"At least I'm not half-breed," he announced. He slowed and rearranged his rags to present a more dignified self to the world. "If you really want to know, the truth is, I've actually got one. A shitty family—but a family."

Sam was surprised that Torazo was every bit as loquacious about himself as he had just been. Mostly, the tattered runt insisted he was blessed because he was born—according to the ancient Chinese astrology chart—a tiger, the luckiest of all signs. As a tiger he was able to survive a father who drank *mo tai,* a fiery Chinese brandy, and gambled and a mother who drank *sochu,* cheap sweet potato brandy, and did not gamble but staked her survival on the earning power of three daughters younger than him. This revelation made his dark eyes sparkle at eliciting shock from this handsome refugee from the Christian mission. Obviously, his new friend knew absolutely nothing of the world, and he clearly relished the joys of introducing this obvious virgin, a naïf in almost every phase of life, into thrilling depravity.

About women he began by explaining that, unlike most Asians who regard daughters as a burden, often to be killed at birth, his mother was raising his three sisters as sources of income. He explained: true, the oldest, and least promising, was ugly as a mud fence and scarred with smallpox. She'd be sold off as a kitchen slave. The second might clean up and miraculously turn out to possess talent enough to be sold into geisha training. The third, utterly without brains, but with an appetizing young body, his mother would rent to men to support her.

Sam stopped dead on the street. He shuddered. "That—is the most horrible thing I've ever heard."

"Hah!" Torazo, delighted to shock, danced in his rags. "I could tell you a lot worse, Asshole. And don't try to stand there and tell me even a big stupid American like you doesn't know about such things." The raconteur was relishing his startling amount of wisdom about the real world, which gave him such total command over the gaijin. "Since I don't give them a sen, how else is my cruddy family going to stay alive?"

Music squealed out of bars. Sam, still more the Bible-reading missionary boy than his new friend could guess, walked in silence. Torazo continued delighting in chattering dark news about the world which kept Sam shaking his head in disbelief. "Even if it's true, it's horrible."

"It's life—something you don't know shit about. So how are you going to live? You say you won't beg. You probably wouldn't be any good at it anyway. So, you're planning to sell yourself, right?"

Sam 's footsteps slowed. His voice dropped to angry challenge. "Just what do you mean by that?"

"You're stupid but well built and very good looking. Dirty yellow hair and almost blue eyes. Very American. A gaijin exotic for us. A lot of Japanese men would pay to fuck you."

In shock Sam locked himself rigid on the sidewalk. "What the hell are you talking about?"

Torazo chirped on. "I wouldn't mind fucking you myself, so don't stand there and try to tell me you've never heard about whorehouses with boys."

Sam's stare couldn't begin to match his utter, his total shock. No. He told himself he must have heard wrong. He'd never dreamed such things could be. What Torazo talked of so airily and took for granted seriously disturbed him. This was no friend. This little devil was Satan himself.

Torazo shrugged and hissed. "Me—I'm a skinny little runt. Nobody'd pay to fuck me. What we'll do is, I'll manage your career. You'll do very well."

Sam refused another step. "Goddamn you. Get away from me!"

Torazo snickered. "Before you'd do that, you'd grab a knife and commit seppuku?"

Sam spun from the little wretch and rushed past the light falling from a bar. Torazo lurched after him. "Hell, I'm serious. I can pay. I'll fuck you right now."

Sam kept moving, choking, scarlet with anger turning to cold rage. Torazo caught up with him, clutching his arm to slow him down and look at him. The beggar's dark eyes, up till now sparkling and full of evil, had grown wide, desperate in his need to keep his new friend. The tall American was seething with outrage. "I ought to beat the shit out of you— break every bone in your runt body right here and now—"

"You'd lose." Instantly Torazo broke into laughter, again the toughest of street kids. "I know how to fight. You don't know shit about anything. Stick with me."

Sam ground his teeth and fled down an alley. Torazo raced after him through a maze of backstreets to reach his place at the station wall. As if their last angry exchange hadn't taken place, he plopped down at his side. Sam jerked himself away. Further distancing himself, he crept further down the wall. Never again could he ever dirty himself and talk to this vile creature. No matter how down and out, no one could sink so low as let this terrible creature into his life.

"Don't American boys fuck each other?" Torazo was back at his side.

"Shut up!" His hands made fists. His face was burning.

"Lot of fun. Boys. And then they tell you who to marry and fuck a woman and after that whores and if you're rich enough, a geisha. But, like for *champon,* for that you need money."

"Get away or I'll kick the shit out of you."

"Hell, I don't sleep here. I've got my own place. You hide out here in the station tonight. I'll be back at dawn to get you."

CHAPTER TWENTY-SEVEN

With a groan Sam pulled himself to his feet, working out the kinks from his night on the station floor. The aroma of breakfast soup pulled him toward the food stalls. He was running his tongue over his dry lips with his stomach clawing like a wild animal when he spotted Torazo in his flurry of rags trotting in from the street. He was carrying a bundle under his arm which he tossed to Sam, and adding a dramatic display, offered him roasted rice paste on a stick along with a bottle of hot tea. "*Mochi* and tea! Last night I read a wonderful book. An American book. Jack London. I read all the books I can steal."

Sam ignored him but grabbed and wolfed down the gooey rice as the street rat chuckled. Why had he brought him this bundle? Torazo unrolled a worn work jacket he flapped out to full length. He unfurled a long, dirty white cloth whose use Sam couldn't guess. Torazo reached over and tossed a pair of straw sandals at Sam's feet.

"Since for now you refuse to beg or sell your ass—here—get into these."

"Goddamn you, get away from me."

"We'll talk about making real money in the future. Today I've got you a job. You'll sweat your guts out all day for a bowl of rice but not in your dung beetle missionary's suit." Sam looked at the ragged work clothes, signifying a total change in his life. "Go get dressed," Torazo ordered. No. Sam refused. He'd already yielded to Torazo's *mochi* and tea. Before sinking deeper into sin he'd have to take his stand against what Reverend Snyder often called "The Vile Tempter."

The beggar tossed the work clothes at him. "Hurry up. Get your ass into the crapper and change."

Sam made a shuffling attempt at reluctance, but broke down and carried the work clothes into the toilet. For a real job, a manual job, what choice did he have but to shuck his black but grimy Sears and Roebuck suit, shirt, tie, and shoes. Naked, he turned the dirty white cloth in his hands. Some kind of underwear? A breechcloth? If that's what he was holding, he had no idea how to wind it around himself. Stumped and staring at the thing, he sensed two weather-beaten farmers turning from their peeing to watch, amused at the young foreign giant's bafflement. Between loud guffaws, they hopped over and showed the mortified naked boy how to cover himself Japanese style. With his lower body now wrapped, over his shoulders they hung the jacket that fell ridiculously short on his tall young frame. He slid his feet into straw sandals and they showed him how to keep them in place by hooking the thong over his big toe. That much he already knew from the boys in Urakami. The farmers mocked him with a bow, and burst out with loud laughing at the outlandishness of their creation. Torazo sprang in, climbed on a bucket to tie a headband over Sam's dark yellow hair, then jumped back to assess his American in the too-short coat. "Doesn't even cover your ass." He considered his creation. "You don't look Japanese, but you look like you might be able to work. At least till you wise up and decide to make some real money selling that ass."

Sam hunched his shoulders in an effort to slide the work jacket farther down. He retied the belt. He looked down at himself in his change of clothes. "You stole these?"

"Didn't have to." Torazo chuckled. "The guy they belonged to dropped dead last night."

Back to giggling, he prodded Sam to the station entrance and into a crowd of piteously down-and-out men and a few women presenting themselves to prospective employers for work, wages, a pittance to scrape through another day. Sam felt another of Torazo's sharp elbow jabs.

"Those three over there? Stinking *etas*. No real Japanese will have anything to do with them. They live by themselves butchering animals and working with leather." Sam stared at the three pariahs, who except for being filthy, didn't look any different from the other Japanese. "What you say they are—how can you tell?"

"*Etas*. Any real Japanese can tell." Sam was wondering if the Japanese knew who he was, an *ainoko,* when Torazo jabbed again. "See those three coming through the door? They're as bad. They're here to hire guys who'll do anything for a day's wage."

"What would they have to do?"

"Burn the bodies of people who die from disease. Or clean up a lepers' camp with fire." He burst with taunting laughter. "Maybe you'd prefer to dig up rotted bodies from the old killing ground from the days we had public executions. Guys will be here hiring for that today."

"Shut up," Sam growled and drew his belt tighter, protecting the dignity he didn't have.

A train clanged into the station and alighting passengers rushed to the waiting rickshaws, rickshaws the Snyders so hated. Sam admired what he'd seen of these tough independent men.

"I'd rather pull a rickshaw. At least they're their own boss."

"Not you. Never," Torazo explained. "Rickshaw pullers think they're King Shit—Look." His nod directed Sam to a slender young man in a smartly tailored Western-style brown suit. A gloved hand twirled a silver-topped walking stick. His rakish English hat met dark eyebrows over the large brown eyes of a fawn. He climbed into a carriage and sailed off.

"He's a whore," Torazo said. "Very rich. Thinks he's in London the way he dresses. After a couple of weeks hard work, you'll be begging to be just like him."

Two stocky, dark-skinned men in worn kimonos had approached the *etas* when the little beggar's rags fluttered in a mock-cripple sprint, intercepting them. Unable to hear what Torazo was saying to them, Sam was being beckoned over to the three where Torazo parted his broad shoulders and strong legs for appraisal.

"Two days," spat a square-faced man with a black bulbous growth hanging over one bushy eyebrow. Torazo haggled, finished negotiating, and shot Sam a grin. "Very pleasant job, my boy. Not dead bodies at all but unloading nice clean hides from Argentina." As his two employers walked away telling the hired worker where to report, Sam grabbed Torazo and hissed. "But you said that's *eta* work."

"Of course," said his manager.

"But that's only for untouchables."

"You're an *ainoko*—not even an *eta*."

Sam throttled his rage and braced himself, he'd never been a stranger to hard work. That was before his day of hauling mountains of flopping stiff cowhides from Argentina on his back, staggering up from a freighter's hold, then down a gangplank, the weight all but crushing him to the deck. With every ache of his body he was convinced not even a mule could stagger under such a load. And yet, hour after hour, he fought his way up from the hold. Even though his heart was racing it went out to the smaller men around him, many only skin and bones, some old and withered, barely able to totter. Not one complained.

At the end of the day he waited at dockside. Torazo appeared grinning, carrying Sam's bundled missionary suit and demanding the paymaster fork over every promised sen owed his young worker. Ready to drop with fatigue, Sam was thrilled, waiting to clutch his first hard-earned coins when Torazo's surprisingly strong grip on his arm was already taking a thirty percent commission.

"Too goddamned much!" Sam wailed.

"Without me you wouldn't get shit."

Torazo clinked his coins. "Okay. Follow me. No more railroad station. Thanks to me now you can afford to be Lady Gray Rat's honored guest."

Sam, fighting aches and pains, walked stiffly behind the little beggar through alleys passing a miserable, bleak shamble of sheds. At the most deplorable shed of all, he rattled back broken *shojis*.

"Lady Gray Rat," he sang out, "I've brought you an honorable customer!" Sam felt himself prodded into a smoky room, black as a cave but for one smelly kerosene lantern and the wavering glow from a pot-bellied ironstove. His manager spread a welcoming arm. "Welcome to the Rat's Nest. Not that I could ever live here."

As Sam's eyes grew used to the dark he saw men and women like those in a black and white Gustave Doré biblical illustration, frightened ghosts peering out of coffins that were bunks and cubicles behind tattered curtains. This was a hovel, a flophouse even smokier, more grim and vastly filthier than third class on the *Tenyo Maru*.

Torazo elbowed Sam, getting him settled, then chirped. "Dear Lady Gray Rat, you owe me for bringing you an honored guest—"

A voice scraped like rusty metal. "Shut your trap, Dog Fart."

In the dark Sam made out Lady Gray Rat—not at all a scraggy little rodent conjured up by the name, but the shapeless tree-stump of a woman in a striped black-and-gray kimono poking charcoal into a hibachi heating a jar of sake.

Torazo signaled Sam to get out his coins. Without leaving her hibachi the woman turned and snatched up most of them. Her voice was rust. "This is only enough for one night."

"He has a job. Give me my commission."

"Keisuke's old bunk," she rasped.

Torazo led Sam through the gloom past the pot-bellied stove where shadows of men and women stirred a pot of something smelling so evil Sam stifled gagging. Something swathed in blankets that could be a man or a woman thrust a ghastly white face up close to the newcomer hissing garlic breath. "Welcome to Keisuke's bunk." Sam pulled back the thin curtain on a ragged heap of blankets and tossed in his bundled black suit. To Torazo, a few feet away, he dropped his voice to a whisper. "Keisuke's bed. What does that mean—"

"You're wearing his clothes."

A cackle came from the shadows. "Dead."

Sam stiffened and backed away. "He really died right here?" He backed away. "His clothes? No. Not his bed—"

"The only bed." The screech in the rusty voice came from Lady Gray Rat pouring herself sake. "Dog Fart, tell your giant freak—take it or get the hell out."

Torazo scratched under his rags and grinned. He had his commission from Sam's pay, now Lady Gray Rat had the rest. Trapped, Sam heard snickers in the dark that rose to wheezy laughter from inmates watching the gaijin grab the grinning beggar. "I can't stay in this stinking hellhole another minute!" He shuddered with disgust. "Live here? Crawl into this dark hole?"

"Okay. Go back to the train station and risk the police."

"But I can't stay here—"

"At first," Torazo delivered a sharp slap on his back, "that's what they all say."

CHAPTER TWENTY-EIGHT

At dawn Sam rattled back the broken *shojis* and burst out into the open to breathe the blessedly, relatively fresh air of the alley. After his first breath his spirits sank. He was facing another brutal day hauling cowhide.

He gulped down breakfast noodles and scalding tea, ran to the docks and lined up eagerly with these men of all ages, crowding together, desperate to sweat and struggle doing only one day's work, all that stood between them and dying in the street. Without a grumble they dropped down into the hold, got their backs under loads of heavy hides and staggered into action.

Sharing their struggle, Sam fought the devastating realization. Their lives were one-day's muscle-tearing work at a time, toil to earn a few coins in order to gulp down sake and flop into some hovel as filthy as the Rat's Nest, till after a lifetime of struggle they left a bunk as empty as Keisuke's.

Breathing hard he looked past the ship out to the end of the dock. Even more dreadful than the hide carriers he saw long lines of smudged, blackened beasts. Women lugging baskets of coal refueling ships putting into this harbor from all over the world. Basket after heavy basket. Nagasaki coal.

At the end of his fifth day his agent was on the spot to make sure the paymaster handed his client his full wage. Torazo was so happy today that he was all but jumping up and down. Yes. He giggled. He'd had a good day at his begging business. European tourists and Buddhists on convention had been generous. Then, in what seemed an afterthought for him he matter-of-factly announced that hauling hides ended today. Stunned, Sam croaked, "What about tomorrow?"

"If you haven't anything better to do, see you at the station."

The bottom had dropped out of the lowest depth of Sam's world. Confused and at a total loss, he watched his manager prance off for an evening of fun which he whispered was too expensive and too wicked to include his exhausted day laborer. Alone, Sam pulled off his headband, still dribbling sweat into his eyes. Wiping his brow he looked around at the others. Beyond being only half-Japanese, was he so different? Yes. He was different. From the first day with them he couldn't bear their passivity, their beaten acceptance that this was their life.

Dog-tired and scared at being out of work, he struggled back to the Rat's Nest to fall into the dead man's bunk. He repeated that Biblical injunction the Snyders endlessly chanted at the mission. "Sufficient unto the day is the evil thereof." Brother Wendell had expatiated on the verse—

take life one day at a time and trust in God and tomorrow would take care of itself.

At dawn the next day at the station Torazo paraded his giant client as the tallest, sturdiest worker in sight. An hour passed without a nibble. The foxy little face peered up at Sam. "Don't move. Wait here."

In a few minutes he returned with a wooden crutch. "Some kind of religious holiday with no regular work. Don't argue. If you won't sell your ass you're going to learn begging."

"No."

Torazo shook his head at such pig-headed unreasonableness even from a gaijin. "Begging's sure as hell a lot more honorable than *eta*-hauling-cowhide. Look, Big Stupid. With me waving my crutch from being all crippled up on your deaf and dumb shoulders we'll break their fucking Buddhist hearts."

"I don't beg," Sam declared.

"And you don't take it up the ass or get yourself sucked off." He spat between his jack-o'-lantern teeth and shook his head, defeated by Sam's stubborn, totally irrational American refusal to accept how the world works. "Okay, Asshole. Go hungry. Today I'm working the Sofukuji Temple. See you here tonight."

At a loss, Sam lingered at the station entrance watching the rickshaw men waiting for passengers. From his first day in Nagasaki he'd admired these tough men. Sam found them race horses compared to the pathetic mules under cowhides he'd been slaving with. Rickshaw men. Rough and ready, onion munching, forever pissing on walls. Like Torazo, they knew how the world works, or at least enough of the world to fight for their place and roll through life between the shafts with a certain pride.

He assessed the sky. Black clouds threatened rain. This was the tomorrow he'd dreaded. Would it take care of itself? He had the whole day to kill. Absolutely nothing to do today or tomorrow. A week away from the mission and how different life had already become from his dream of teaching. Life meant going hungry, sitting up all night in a train station, hauling hides or starving. The sky broke. In the rain he realized he was wandering back to the smoke and foul air of the Rat's Nest. He picked a newspaper out of a trash can. At least he could practice his Japanese.

At Lady Gray Rat's place the light was too dim to read even those kanji he was able to decipher. He tossed it aside and crept to the warmth of the stove with the other specters, huddled, listening to the rain. He'd read the Holy Bible in seventeen days. Since crossing the Pacific on the *Tenyo Maru*, in the following six Jacob-labor years at the mission, he'd read it four more times. Whether he truly believed it to be the Word of God, its study was an accomplishment, its discipline his only education after leaving the fourth grade. "Fourth Grade." Thinking of his Bremerton classmates, tears prickled his eyes. "In June they'll be graduating from high school. Some will go on to college. Maybe not my pal, Eddie. And there's Benjy back there in Baltimore getting the best education in the world in some high-hat rich kid's school. Little Benjy with his asthma—

His thoughts of America broke off. In the darkness of Lady Gray Rat's squalor something was crawling up his shoulder and onto the back of his neck. A rat? An insect? He scrunched around to find himself staring into what looked like the face of a ghoul. The thing was dirty white, powdery and moth-like. A face? A woman in a ragged kimono closing in on him, a white mask with a tiny scarlet mouth and hard little eyes, was kissing his neck.

"Come." At her onion breath and something worse he shrank from her. "Come," she crooned, "fucking in the rain is best. Come." She turned her head so her hard little eyes fastened on him and did not blink. Two gray claws dug into his shoulders.

This was not Jacob's Rachel in the Bible or a woman from a Sears Roebuck brassiere ad but another kind of creature from another world entirely, different from that lotus of the Shinto priestess he'd met in Asahi-Mura.

"For you only a few sen—"

"I'm broke."

She spat in his face. At the same moment someone brutally kicked her aside and she crumpled. Lady Gray Rat shoved into the glow of the stove with her sake jar. Behind her a serving girl hovered, always a sound-less wraith.

"You like sake?" Lady Gray Rat's voice was too rusty to purr.

"Yes."

"You want sake?"

"Please."

"What do you mean, please? Can you pay or not?"

"No."

"Then no sake."

The woman sprawling at their feet dragged herself up, but the landlady kicked again. "Get away." Her blows produced only a determined claw snatching at the steaming sake jar. Lady Gray Rat kicked again, this time plunging the ghoul deep into shadow.

"She sees ghosts." A man's cracked voice came from another ghoul, a phantom of an old man with a shaved head poking up out of ragged robes. Clicking prayer beads he was suggesting in another life he had been a Buddhist priest.

Suddenly the street *shojis* clattered. A voice, loud, masculine and powerful, boomed, a cry full of life. "Sake! Sake for everyone!"

This roaring, cheerful bellow came from someone throwing off an English-style raincoat revealing a Western-style suit. Sam could only guess the man, who was smoking a cigar, had blundered into Lady Gray Rat's by mistake. But no. He'd not only entered but swaggered into the smoke and hunkered down Japanese-style warming himself by the glowing stove. His enormous cigar added more smoke to the thick air. From the shadows the inmates came crawling while his eyes glittered almost as brightly as the firelight glinting on his slick, oiled hair.

"So, Gambler, you've had luck?" Lady Gray Rat patted a filthy cushion inviting this most welcome of men to sit beside her.

Gambler grinned from behind his cigar and jingled a heavy handful of coins. The landlady motioned for the serving girl to stop hovering like a ninny and get the man a cup. "The whole jar," Gambler demanded in his huge voice, "then heat up another."

Sam crept forward for a closer look at the visitor only to find the man staring at his gaijin*'s* bare torso and wide shoulders. To Sam's surprise he reached over and gently stroked the bronze hair of his forearm, considering the foreigner for a long moment. Then he announced for all the inmates, "I want to hear why Tom Brown of *Tom Brown's Schooldays* honors us with his presence."

"Tom Brown was English," Sam declared. "I'm Japanese."

The man Lady Gray Rat had called Gambler howled with laughter. "And I am Rincon Abraham!"

The man commanded all the inmates, usually such tattered sleep-walkers, to stare in near rapture at him demanding the youth explain himself.

"It's true," Sam insisted. "I'm Japanese."

"No way." The prosperous appearing man who seemed to fill the place rolled his cigar across his wet lips. "I asked what you're doing here—not in the luxury of Lady Gray Rat's establishment—but in Japan."

Instead of lying, he confessed the truth. "I'm finding out who I am. Where I belong."

"Spare us that." Gambler seized a jar from the serving girl and poured sake, first for Sam, then everyone else. "Go ahead, tell us your story, Tom Brown, but keep it short," Gambler gulped his drink and poured another. "And if you have to lie to make it interesting, go right ahead."

Several bundles of rags Sam had never seen in the glow of the stove crept close, waiting for sake even if it meant having to put up with the young giant's story. Now everyone shared Gambler's sake and Lady Gray Rat shooed the girl off for another jar. "Go ahead," Gambler prodded Sam.

"The American Consul here knew my father, who married a Japanese lady. My mother. I was born right here in Nagasaki." Sam had scarcely begun explaining when the failed whore, the mothlike ghoul, interrupted with what she felt was far more compelling news.

"I'm from Sasebo."

"Kagoshima!" The landlady declared her hometown was the best possible place to be born. "Kagoshima. Now there's a *real* town!" Sam sipped sake and was ignored as everyone chimed in. The onion-breath whore was now trying to slither onto Gambler's shoulder, but he roughly hurled her onto Sam's bare torso. She slumped against him, and he shrank from her mouth breathing at his ear. He recoiled further from her murmuring. "Did you ever kill a baby?" He pressed further back hoping he wouldn't have to slam her away. The Gambler, having no hesitation, directed her to shut up. She was still whispering. "Me, I ought to know. I killed three."

"And you've told us ten thousand times!" Lady Gray Rat didn't hesitate to give the pallid creature a powerful kick, banishing her threat of gloom from the most cheerful little party the Rat's Nest had probably celebrated in years.

The whore, however, crept back to Sam. "Three," her face pressed to his, but Gambler leaned over. "Tom Brown, fuck the bitch. I'll pay her for you just to shut her up." Raucous laughter exploded with everyone egging Sam on, but with embarrassment he went a maroon deeper than the stove's glow. His prudery was proof he wasn't one of them and probably American. Another woman Sam had never seen, a creature in shadow, breathed in his ear. "She doesn't know shit. I'll tell you how to kill babies—"

"Shut up!" The Gambler blew smoke in her face. "Leave the kid alone."

"It's easy to kill babies," she breathed into Sam's ear. "All you do is you put rice paper in your mouth till it's good and wet and then you put it over the baby's mouth and nose." She shrugged. "Then the baby goes to *Jizo.*"

"Tom Brown doesn't know who the hell *Jizo* is," Gambler spat. The hovering priest with his prayer beads and hands together shuffled close, wavering in front of Sam in bleary solemnity. *Jizo.* Sam nodded. Yes, he knew he was talking about the little stone statues of the god he'd seen standing at crossroads. "*Jizo,*" the priest explained, "watches out for dead babies and kids in the next world."

"But not us!" Gambler roared with laughter.

The ancient creature, who indeed might have been a priest, was determined to explain the Japanese god to the gaijin. "*Jizo* wears knitted hats to keep the babies warm—nursing mothers tie bibs on him and sprinkle drops of their own milk for hungry little ghosts."

"Shut up," Gambler roared.

Lady Gray Rat slapped away the possible priest. "Shut up about *Jizo* and dead babies or I'll kick both the priest and this cunt's ass out of here." She waved for her slave to pour more of Gambler's sake. "Me," she said, "I see a pregnant woman, I go right up to her belly—yell right at what's inside. 'Do yourself a big favor—don't get born.'"

Gambler grabbed the sake jar, spilling some but splashing it into cups held in eager hands. The priest held out his cup and pushed the woman who got rid of babies away from Sam. Now the priest was bending down, thrusting his gray face into the foreigner's. "I see ghosts. Many ghosts."

"After my sake he'll see more than ghosts," Gambler mumbled. "Piss on all priests. And you, Tom Brown! You call those sissy little sips of yours drinking?"

Gambler, a winner today, had performed a miracle, rousing nearly everyone from their lethargy out of their bunks, creeping over to the warmth of the stove and easing life with alcohol. Sam looked up at a nearly naked man he'd never seen before emerging from the darkness bearing a cup. In the russet light he was a startling sight, his sagging skin completely covered with tattoos of blue and red dragons. Without saying a word, his bones clattered as he squatted among them.

Gambler's heavy arm dropped around Sam's shoulders. "With those tattoos of his he wants everyone to think he's *Yakuza*—a gangster. But he's not. He's a chickenshit coward." Gambler whooped with laughter and the others joined in and the naked man ignored them, holding out his trembling cup for sake.

Sam felt the stove's warmth on his bare legs, his arms and face. Sake glowed within him. Hunkering in the smoke with these smelly, scratching, farting strangers was not the family he was seeking, but for someone who'd found no family, being among these wretched sake drinkers was better than being outside and alone in December's wind and icy rain.

CHAPTER TWENTY-NINE

. . . the thing which I greatly feared is come upon me . . . Job's words beat in Sam's brain as his straw sandals, squished, wading through blood. Here he was in a bamboo forest working with two *etas* burning corpses. He'd vomited five times before he learned his trade was not as simple as tossing a dead body on a pile of burning logs. Roaring fire devours flesh but leaves the calcium of bones untouched. One of his fellow ghouls, announcing himself an expert in sending bodies to the Buddha's Western Paradise, shared his professional trick—"wrap wet rice mats around the corpse so the flames burn deep."

Splashed red with blood from a fresh body hadn't been horror enough. Now he was a ghoul, gray with human ash.

He stumbled home to the Rat's Nest with no hope of more sake parties. Gambler had run through his winnings and Lady Gray Rat had booted him out into the December drizzle and pawned his Burberry raincoat.

A week later, Torazo, streaming with a head cold, poked in to find Sam. He brushed cremated ashes off his client's hair.

"Ready to beg? Or sell your ass?"

The rest of that bitter December Sam went on burning bodies and Torazo's winter cold wracked him with such fever he couldn't drag himself out to beg. He sank so low in the world he moved with Sam into the Rat's Nest. Two days later, driving himself fiercely and still hot and shaking with fever, he shoved his thin little body out into the bitter December wind. Never looking more pathetic, sick and shivering, by the time he crawled home, he'd scored his most profitable week ever.

On a windy evening full of needles of freezing rain, Torazo declared their spirits needed lifting. "Get your dung beetle missionary suit. We're going out for a night on the town."

"Using what for money?"

"Leave that to me, " he said recoiling. "Agh. You stink—you know that? You stink worse than shit. First, you need a bath." Knowing every back alley better than the neighborhood cats, and telling him to bring his gaijin clothes, Torazo hustled him to the public bath, the *sento*. Sam, barely able to stand his own odor, stripped off his bloodstained and ashy work jacket along with his breechcloth which Torazo flung to an attendant for laundering. The beggar hung a respectable dark-blue kimono waiting for him in his locker.

Skinned out of his own tatters, Torazo turned and saw his client naked for the first time. At the sight of his strong, young body Sam saw the look on Torazo's pale little face was close to heart-rending in undisguised love and admiration. As for Torazo, Sam wished he hadn't looked, wincing at seeing the beggar naked. Stripped of rags, naked, Torazo was pitiable, a scrawny plucked chicken, all ribs and bumpy backbone. Catching Sam's look of shock, his only friend shrugged. "A beggar can't afford to look too good."

Since this was Sam's first public bath, he whispered. "Will there be naked ladies?"

"You can't wait, can you?" Torazo jabbed his elbow. "Come on." He poked him forward with Sam quickly covering little of himself with a tiny towel. With another shove he was in a scrub room working with soap and brushes and sloshing hot water over each other till they glowed. The scrawny little beggar prodded him into a hall and along a wooden walkway into a vast, steaming pool.

"Really? Naked ladies?" Sam asked.

"Your first look?" Torazo cackled.

Sam dared only furtive glances through the steam and at first all the nakedness he saw was male. But suddenly there, sitting at the edge of the pool, were two creatures totally bare, scrawny and withered but hung with breasts, therefore female. Nothing related them remotely to the fantasy species he'd lusted after in his dreams of Jacob's Rachel or the ladies in the Sears Roebuck catalog, or on the most ethereal level, the Shinto priestess in Asahi-Mura. His first sight of a real, naked woman shriveled his sex.

Before him steamed the *o furo*. Sam shied back from approaching the steam rising from the pool. At Torazo's jab he dipped an experimental toe into what he'd been warned would be hot. Hot? This was a cauldron in hell and he leaped back howling. "It's boiling!"

"Jump! Get right in!" Torazo commanded, grinning his Jack-o-lantern grin, but Sam hung back. Gingerly he tried another toe. "Hot as hell."

"That's how we real Japanese like it." He chuckled his delight snapping his tiny towel across Sam's buttocks. "If you're Japanese you can't get it hot enough. Go ahead. Prove you're half Japanese. Start by going halfway in."

Suddenly Sam was back in Bremerton watching fishermen with their catch, green and gray crabs, dropped live into boiling water to turn them bright red. The other naked descendants of the Sun Goddess had sunk themselves here in the scalding water—bobbing heads were red but still alive. Torazo dunked himself into the pool with Sam hanging back and still alive. Torazo grabbed Sam's ankle drawing him down into this hell. Sam wailed. He caught his breath, stiffened, paralyzed, waiting for his skin to peel and drop from his body. Torazo pushed his head under the water. When he surfaced, apparently still alive, he shuddered, held his breath immersed up to his chin. After the shock he felt his body undergoing an entirely new sensation, soothed, yielding to lassitude, then a bliss he'd never imagined. He grinned at Torazo. God, this must be a terrible sin to be rejoicing in a way the Snyders would dream possible only through a life of Christian cold-water devotion.

"For tonight," Torazo said, draping his dribbling little towel over his head, "we forget all about dead bodies and fill up on the best dinner you've ever had in your life. Then—the two most beautiful whores in Nagasaki."

Sam's heart banged against his chest. Tonight—this very night, and shiny clean, was he—at long, long last going to be with a woman? Not, of course, like these bobbing in the water with him, nor as incredibly lovely as that Shinto goddess in Asahi-Mura, but a real naked woman as beautiful, as well-favored, as the Bible's Rachel?

Shining clean within his expensive kimono which Sam felt certain was stolen, Torazo looked surprisingly unbeggarly, tiny but even respectable. The *sento* had laundered Sam's white shirt and pressed and brushed his black missionary suit. First in Torazo's eyes he saw the miracle, then in a mirror as he smothered a gasp. He looked every inch the absolutely respectable, even splendid young gaijin.

Out in the cold dark Torazo challenged him to race into Chinatown, hungry and fired with joy, passing dozens of ornate restaurants spilling light and music into the night.

Torazo's goal lay ahead behind a plate-glass window, a fantasy of Ming Dynasty splendor, a dream of mandarin red and gold with fish ponds and lanterns and silken girls strolling and plinking lutes. Sam balked. "We can't possibly go in there."

Torazo passed him a cloth wallet, which looked fat with yen. "Make sure everybody sees you carrying this. Act rich and bored. And don't speak a word of Japanese. Tonight you're an English lord. Here we go." A jab pushed him into a revolving door.

Music and laughter flowed down from a second-story party Torazo sneered at as an uncivilized Chinese wedding. A sleek headwaiter, bald as a winter melon, glanced at the two, the gaijin and the tiny Japanese, assessing them, his professional look deciding if he could pass them into his celestial kingdom. Torazo elbowed Sam. "Act bored."

"Yes, young sirs—will we be two?" Formal in his black tailcoat, his smooth hands picked up menus from the cashier's desk.

Torazo spoke carefully without exposing any of his missing teeth. "This young man happens to be an English lord. His honorable parents are staying on board the Canberra tonight but he's been promised the finest—the very finest—*champon* dinner in Nagasaki. Can I assure him yours is the best?"

With a bow the man said, "Please tell your Englishman we serve the very finest *champon* in Nagasaki." Torazo turned a questioning look at the foreign visitor. Sam covered his insecurity with a bored air he hoped passed for world weariness. Torazo looked into the dining salon, a red pavilion with golden dragons crawling up pillars. After his nod, the two allowed themselves to be led while casting cool glances at all this imperial grandeur of the Middle Kingdom. By now it was Torazo and not the headwaiter who was in charge. "If we decide to stay, yes, we are two."

"Assure your honorable friend," the sleek headwaiter, now close to groveling, whispered. "Sir has come to the very finest restaurant in Nagasaki."

Their host, still bowing, escorted his guests through the diners to a table where he enthroned them on elaborately carved rosewood chairs.

Sam plucked up the knees of his trousers and sat, telling himself to look rich—rich and bored—and to allow no one to see he was struggling to gulp down his fear. Torazo was still standing, deliberately keeping the suave headwaiter waiting. Without glancing up at their host, he sighed, "Perhaps if we started with two *mo tais.*"

The headwaiter hesitated. "*Mo tai* is indeed a fine, a first class choice, but the one we usually serve for our customers of older years. It's very dear. Many of our younger but most discriminating guests actually prefer plum wine."

"Two *mo tais.*" Torazo's black eyes pinned the waiter. "Hold on. Let me understand. Are you telling us you'd prefer for us to pay for them now?"

"Oh, no, sir. No possible need to pay now. No need at all."

"Hold on, my man. Perhaps it is best we pay now. My friend hasn't entirely decided yet this place is to his liking." Torazo turned to Sam. "May I?" He was signaling for Sam to hand over the Japanese cloth wallet from which he casually drew out a five yen note from a thick stack of bills and tossed the wallet on the table. Five yen. Sam strangled a gasp of surprise.

"The *mo tais*." Torazo snapped. "And quickly. It may be, as I say, my English friend might decide we'll be better served somewhere else."

Their sleek host cringed at anything so indelicate as to even glance at the foreign lordling's money. "As to the *mo tais,* most of our guests prefer such a drink after dining."

"Not my English friend."

The headwaiter signaled over a slender shining-silk creature in a long gown, murmuring the drink order. After a moment, Sam was still unable to utter a word as two silken maidens approached with a white porcelain bottle from which Torazo insisted on meticulously pouring two cups scarcely larger than thimbles. The lovely maidens watched the young men lift their drinks to each other.

"*Kampai,*" Torazo sang out and threw the fiery white alcohol down his neck.

And Sam? One sip knocked the fake English lord speechless. Asahimura's sake had been his first taste of alcohol. This was liquid fire. "My old man," Torazo said, "calls this Dragon Piss. Not that he's ever been able afford it."

By the time the line of fire ripping through Sam faded and human life began to creep back into his body, he leaned anxiously across the table eyeing the wallet. "Where—" his voice was low, scarcely to be heard against twanging lutes. "Where the hell did you get all that money?"

"The question is, Mister English Lord Passenger on the Canberra is, do you like your *mo tai?*"

Sam, on fire with Chinese brandy and an English cigarette, grew wider-eyed at the way the glistening silk caressed the lovely bodies of the alluring maidens.

"And after dinner," Torazo wet his lips, "you will enter the Royal Door." Sam didn't ask what the Royal Door was, but guessed that it was no doubt one of the Oriental references for that raging obsession that until now he could only imagine relieving not with his hand but with a real, live woman.

"Start thinking about that now," Torazo advised. "The Mama-San's going to ask if you have any special requests of her girls." He broke off to signal Melon Head. "Another *mo tai*. And perhaps just a smidgen of *champon.* You agree, don't you, my English friend should at least try your *champon?*"

"We offer Nagasaki's very best, sir."

"After all," Torazo smiled to his foreign visitor, "perhaps we should. It is Chinatown's most famous dish. That is, if you don't want bear's paw or live brains from living monkeys." Torazo sighed looking admirably rich and bored. "For now the *mo tais* and a packet of cigarettes. English. Players."

The headwaiter vanished.

Shark's fin soup arrived, then thousand-year-old eggs. "Save room for the duck," Torazo advised his friend as platters and bowls arrived— the most expensive delicacies from far-off mountaintops down to the bottom of the sea.

"Uncle Joy," as Melon Head had whispered the Chinese called this wine, lived up to its name. Alcohol was turning Torazo's foxy little face crimson but his fingers never slowed flickering his ivory chopsticks. Grandly, he rested the sticks across a plate and leaned back in his chair and belched loudly. "Not bad, uh?"

The elaborate feast, the two *mo tais* and the wine had dissolved some of Sam's terror. After all, he told himself, he was with Torazo. Count on Torazo to twist the world by the tail. If it hadn't been for Torazo they wouldn't be sitting here dining like princes, drinking, smoking, with Sam daring to laugh. And after dinner? His heart raced, his seventeen-year-old body stirred. Yes, after dinner, and most of all, at long, long last—he would enter the Royal Door.

He wiped his chin and grinned at his friend. Who could have dreamed of such bliss as this night, dining like emperors with lovely Chinese girls in shimmering gowns moving through music and golden light? Carefully he laid his ivory chopsticks down and grinned his happiness. By now their tabletop lay before them, a battleground strewn with the leftovers that had been their feast. Torazo burped and pushed himself to his feet. "Toilet," he announced with dignity and catching himself stumbling, strolled off.

Sam wasn't so transported that he didn't stare at the cloth wallet. Glancing around to cover his surreptitious move he flipped it open. Yes, a nice little pile of bills. He fingered the one on top. Yes, but wait. Under the five-yen note was paper money like nothing ever seen in Japan. His heart jammed in his throat. Icy fear froze his happy drunken glow and he quickly shut the wallet. His intoxicated mind slowed its racing, realizing the scam that Torazo was playing.

Like a young Ming prince he glided back to their table to find Sam masking his panic, his voice betraying him with a squawk. At Torazo's signal he hushed so low as to be all but inaudible. "How much money do we really have? Goddamnit, tell me the truth."

"Don't drop down dead." Torazo smiled flicking lizard eyes right, then left. "Looks like plenty, right? Except for the five the others are crap that in place of real money the Chinese burn in ceremonies on the altar—"

Sam's heart stopped. "Jesus—you're saying the five is the only one that's real?"

"Keep your fucking voice down and smoke another cigarette."

"Oh, God." Sam felt icy sweat streak down his back. "What are we going to do?"

"One thing we're not going to do is get out of here by way of the toilet. I just looked. There's no door or window to the outside—"

"Oh, Jesus—"

The Imperial Chinese feast was fast becoming a congealed, cold lump of cement in Sam's gut. Torazo sipped plum wine. "Relax and do exactly what I tell you." He folded the wallet and slid it to Sam. "First, I signal Melon Head for the bill. He brings it and he stands right here waiting for me to lay out every sen—which I don't. Instead, I tell him we'll pay at the front desk because this dinner was a test to see if it was good enough to bring your mother and father and a party from the Canberra. For that I'll have to talk to the Mama-San over at the desk. Relax. You look like you've got mice nibbling at your asshole. Now just shut up and listen. I pick up the wallet and push back my chair. That's your signal. You get up. Move slowly but keep moving. Don't stop or arouse any suspicion—just stroll. Get out the front door. Wait for me across the street. When I come out I'll probably be in a hurry."

Sam looked over at the Dragon Lady Mama-San at the desk.

"No, asshole. Don't look. I checked this out yesterday. Her desk is right next to the revolving door. From across the street watch me through the front glass windows while I talk to her about bringing your parents.

I'll have the greedy bitch so busy making reservations planning the big Canberra Party that when I toss down the fake bills before she has a chance to look I'm out the door."

Sam was drenched in sweat. He shut his eyes and prayed.

Exactly as Torazo had set up his trick they kept Melon Head waiting to be paid while they took their time finishing their cigarettes. At Torazo's signal Sam rose and, striving to emulate the beggar's cool nonchalance, strolled in the direction of the revolving door passing through diners and tables, the dragons, the golden light, the silken girls, while music played. There was the Dragon Lady and the revolving street door three feet ahead. At this moment the wedding guests from the second floor, drunk and boisterous, were crowding the staircase to reach the ground floor's cloak-room, photographers waiting with blinding flashes. What luck! He blessed the crowd and the distraction till he was whirling himself through the re-volving door and out into the cold night.

Free! He'd escaped. The icy blast of wind was freedom carrying him across the street gulping down his terror, no longer for himself but for Torazo. He shrank into shadow with his eyes never leaving the restaurant windows and that revolving door.

Over there, inside the glass, exactly as Torazo had planned, he saw his little pal leading Melon Head to the cashier's desk but in sudden fear was crying out into the cold a frantic warning. "Torazo, watch out! That crowd's blocking the door—" Suddenly, utterly helpless, he was watching the scene playing out before his eyes, a motion picture, silent and un-changeable.

At the desk confident little Torazo was playing the silent movie, talk-ing with the Dragon Lady over an opened menu arranging the gaijins up-coming dinner. With an estimable show of indifference he reached for the wallet.

"Torazo! They're blocking the door!" Across the street a crowd was jamming the revolving door with Sam screaming his warning in this silent film with its star, the little beggar, pantomiming a man of the world. Fol-lowing his script he tossed down the wallet and raced for the door only to slam into a solid wall of guests and flashing cameras.

Sam's cold hands clamped his face. Within heartbeats police whistles were shrilling with officers plunging into the light of the Chinese pavilion.

From across the street Sam stood helplessly watching the silent film—two cops grabbing the skinny boy. Torazo fought and writhed against the law shoving him to the floor and handcuffing him to the delight of the wedding guests. The law had Torazo. Now Melon Head rushed to the window and pointing into the street to catch the other criminal—an Englishman.

Sam ran like hell.

Icy air burned his lungs as he lurched along streetcar tracks and through alleys bursting into the Rat's Nest calling to Lady Gray Rat who was warming her hands over her hibachi. "The police have Torazo! We've *got* to help him!"

Lady Gray Rat prodded charcoal with tongs without so much as a glance at him. Didn't she understand? He cried again, this time louder. "The cops have Torazo!"

"And I've got an empty bed to rent." She hissed for her pale little slave to emerge from the shadows. "Get rid of Dog Fart's filthy rags. Burn them in the stove—"

"No!" Sam cried.

The landlady signaled the girl to obey. "He won't be back and all his damned rags won't be worth a sen—"

"I've got to get to him," Sam wailed.

"Go, Gaijin. Go and get yourself arrested, too."

CHAPTER THIRTY

All night he sat staring into the embers in the iron stove, staring, praying for his friend. Not since those days with his mother in Bremerton had he agonized so deeply over another's life. He crawled into the dead man's bunk, his heart with Torazo who he'd never see again. In the morning without Torazo he'd have to face going out in the winter wind and cold and finding work on his own. No. To keep this filthy bed at the Rat's Nest and pay for his daily bowl of rice he'd have no choice. He'd have to go on burning corpses.

December was ending with his feeling himself as dead as those bodies, a ghoul by day, a ghost by night trudging alone, hollow and cold. Life was bearable only numbed by sleep. Two weeks after Torazo's arrest, he crawled out of his filthy blankets and slid back the shojis, always terrified of the cops or anyone asking for papers.

On what had surely to be the blackest night of the year he dared a return to the harbor, staring up at the ships that crossed oceans. Here at the waterfront bars and shadows where seamen were smoking and drinking he heard murmurings in languages from around the world. All of these foreigners had crossed the seas bringing them here to Japan. All of them would be leaving. Sailing. Without a passport why not take a chance and climb a gangplank?

Why stay on in a Japan that had only punished him as a slave all those years at that hateful mission and now an *ainoko* down and out in Nagasaki? In Asahi-Mura he'd felt himself most Japanese, but with no link to his mother, not even her grave. Life in Japan meant nothing but sweating out his guts at work beneath the dignity of any Japanese. Go back to the States? And lie about who he was? The States were the Showalters. The States wanted Benjy. Not Butterfly's son.

Across the harbor's icy air in the Mitsubishi shipyards, acetylene torches flared brilliantly with Japanese who had real jobs working at night. Out in the black harbor a United States Navy cruiser glowed, outlined with festive strings of red and green lights.

Americans.

On the cruiser a band was playing carols. Americans were singing. He'd forgotten tonight was Christmas Eve.

CHAPTER THIRTY-ONE

In the freezing sunlight of this, the first day of the New Year, Sam insinuated himself into a happy crowd parading across raked gravel, surging under a *torii* toward a giant Shinto shrine. Never before had he made himself part of such an enormous crowd. Every family along with visitors to Nagasaki must be here, elegant in their finest traditional kimonos, a river of silken color and happy laughter in the bright morning light of this most important day of the year.

Aching to feel himself part of the human race, he had followed the sound of drums and music to get him here, dressed in his just-washed but humble Japanese work jacket and sandals. He made himself part of the throng. Here were aged grandparents, bent double, and families in kimonos carrying babies, and flocks of kids. The adults were too polite to look twice at this young gaijin dressed as a Japanese. Gangs of boys of high-school and university age in their black uniforms were bold and stared openly, asking each other who this strange creature might be. Young women, at first demure, tried not to stare, but girls of every age bunched together in spasms of titters. Toddlers, simply overcome, darted from behind their parents to peep at him in wide-eyed amazement and run back into hiding.

He nearly stumbled over a beggar who'd crept up on him, a silent spider cupping his grimy hand and whimpering pitiably. Torazo? No. Of course the creature wasn't Torazo, but Sam dug out his smallest coin murmuring to the gods of Shinto, the Lord Buddha, Jesus—any power who might listen to him on this New Year's Day not to forget his only friend in whatever prison he was locked.

A flock of young ladies, glistening in silk like a bower of flowers, wafted toward him, sending his young man's heart fluttering. In a group and therefore emboldened, they dared glances at this handsome but strange young man. A few even smiled. One, with the shining dark eyes of a doe, dared look him straight in the eye and his face scalded.

One had looked directly at him, but that was as much as he could hope for. In that last evening together Torazo had promised him a woman. Since that disastrous Chinese dinner he could only dream of entering the Royal Door or whatever he'd called such bliss. For that joy he needed yen—far more than he could ever earn to enter even one of the lesser whorehouses they euphemistically called teahouses. Because most houses displayed galleries of photographs on their outer walls, it didn't cost to stare. So many, many times he'd devoured these pictures, fantasized what he'd do if he was ever able to peel back a kimono from breasts with pointed nipples and smooth skin curving down across bellies to young, silken hair. Indulging these fantasies he grew flush, no longer with shame, but the impossibility of knowing even love for sale. Today at the shrine with the Japanese, he was no longer the failed missionary boy but a young man aching for what was under the silk of these women making him hard and leaving him breathless.

Homeless but for the Rat's Nest, his only place in the world, he was desperate not to give up and spend his New Year's Day hiding back in that smoky hovel pulling his filthy blanket over his head. No. He couldn't go back there, not on this day when all things should be beginning. With loneliness cutting so deeply, the only refuge he could afford with his few corpse-burning sen was a movie house. He'd passed by one where Charlie Chaplin leaned on his bamboo cane up there on a huge poster.

His hope that beginning his year with Shinto and Buddhism lifting his half-Japanese heart had failed. Maybe Hollywood's Little Tramp could make him smile. From the bright cold sunlight he entered the dark. Here were no temple bells and incense and no Japanese families welcoming the New Year. The Little Tramp in black and white shadows was coaxing a few laughs out of lonely men. Sam and Charlie Chaplin were all but alone in a scattering of those who didn't belong. His eyes filled with tears. How could the world laugh at anything as infinitely sad as that poor little guy?

After the movie, he might have been the Little Tramp himself, trudging the business district's cheerless pavement, till suddenly galvanized by a clanging streetcar, he vaulted to a safety island. At the same moment a fearful screech of metal and the crack of splintering wood startled him. A streetcar went clattering down the hill oblivious of the rickshaw it had struck, its carriage toppled over in the street and wheels still spinning. Rushing close, he saw the broken shaft had pierced the man sprawled on the tracks, a broken puppet, bloody, striving to sit up but falling back. Sam rushed to him and his waving hands, crying out not for himself, but for his rickshaw.

The man's face, scraped raw as peeled peach, was oozing blood. One arm hung limp with a bone poking through the forearm's flesh. "Help!" Sam heard his own voice yelling and peering up and down the street. He leaned close. "Hold on. I'll get you to a hospital—"

A rattle from the broken man's gaping, bleeding mouth protested. "No. The rickshaw—"

"Stay right here." Sam was on his feet. "I'll get help." Alone, with no one in sight, he crouched over the victim. "Hold on." His mind raced. "If your rickshaw still works I'll prop you up onto the seat and get you to a hospital."

The fallen man's hand was still waving away help. "No hospital. The stable—" Broken words strangled on blood had Sam nodding to show he understood. Yes. He knew of the rickshaw stable across the street from the train station. He nodded again to show he'd get him there. The man was bloody and so badly injured, could he dare risk moving him? To his horror he found the victim struggling, crawling to his rickshaw, making the decision for him.

Sam righted the carriage onto its wheels that appeared undamaged. The right hand shaft had broken away from the carriage Without it was there any way to replace it and match the unbroken left shaft? What could he use? He looked to the wounded man who was struggling to untie his heavy cloth sash. "Yes, your belt." Sam cried and without waiting for any kind of answer he tied the heavy cloth to what was left of the right hand pole. He tested lifting the improvised shaft till it was level with the other. Dropping down to the pavement and nudging his shoulder under the puller, he hoisted the man up in a sprawl across the passenger seat and strapped him in.

In the empty street he positioned himself between the two shafts and drew forward. The strong belt held. Under his strength the slender wheels on their ball-bearings came alive and, with a final glance up at his bleeding passenger, he was off and running. His heart was pounding, less from exertion than fear of jolting his broken passenger. Three streets from the rickshaw stable, for one perilous moment, they swerved wildly out of the way of a horse-drawn bus without tipping over. "Hang on!"

After the five minutes it took to reach the stable and, not the eternity it seemed, he raced the carriage into the stable shouting for help. More cries brought a lone man, crouching over an inner office stove, to the door. Instead of rushing to help, the stablemaster glared at the broken rickshaw and even more menacingly at this absurdly tall foreigner invading his domain, shouting for help. Grumbling, the man who must have been the stablemaster left the warmth of his stove, a gnarled figure of middle years in greasy work clothes with gray hair bristling from his face and ears. Not until he slowly hung glasses over his animal snout did the sight of the broken rickshaw cause him more grunts as he thrust aside the young gaijin who continued to yell, demanding the stablemaster call a doctor to save the broken man up on the seat. The gaijin, fighting for breath, saw what the boss saw. The man he'd tried to save would never pull another rickshaw. His passenger was dead.

CHAPTER THIRTY-TWO

The stablemaster thrust Sam aside. The bloody corpse he shouldered down from the rickshaw seat could have been a sack of rice he dumped on the floor. Sam was shattered and told himself he'd done all he could. Still breathing hard and shaking with horror he looked around at the stable and at second glance he realized he had seen this fierce creature in many forms in Japanese folklore, the startling incarnation of Tanooki, the often evil wild badger. Tanooki in the flesh swiped his snout, a scowling forest beast, and dumped the dead man on the earthen floor. Sam was crushed that the man he'd fought to save lay dead at their feet. "What we did is we tied his belt to the broken pole . . . I ran as fast as I could. I just wish I could have got here in time to save him."

Was Tanooki even bothering to listen?

"Sir, what was his name?"

Tanooki wasn't listening. He refused to hear. He had a broken carriage out of service on this busy New Year's Day when all Japan was demanding holiday rickshaws.

Sam had done all he could. He waited for Tanooki to stop assessing the damage to the rickshaw and turn and at least thank him for fighting to try to save the man's life and returning his rickshaw. As his heartbeat slowed, his tall American-looking presence brought no more than a glance. What did the gaijin want from him? He fished a few coins out of his heavy indigo kimono sleeve. Coins, but no thanks, no acknowledgment, no obligation other than payment in full by thrusting out his hand with a few coins. For Tanooki the stablemaster it was simple as that, pay off the gaijin and get him out of his stable.

Sam had learned Sato-San's Japanese code of honor. Tanooki's refusal to acknowledge profound obligation to another Japanese would be unthinkable, but this gnarled brute was dismissing him, a foreigner of another race and therefore outside any code of honor. Sam stiffened with rage. He slashed aside the hand sending the insulting payoff across the dirt floor in a spatter of coins. Tanooki, the furious badger, bared his broken teeth in a snarl, a fierce animal growl. Under the tall, young westerner's challenging glare he grabbed up a heavy wrench. Sam stood his ground. Yes. He looked like a foreigner but he was standing here charging the creature to live up to the code of righteousness he owed any Japanese. Tanooki seethed with fury. If he didn't want money what the hell else did the bastard gaijin want? Sam, silent, resolute, betrayed no sign of backing down. What did he want? "I want his job."

Tanooki sucked rattling breath in over sharp teeth. His hairy badger head seemed to bristle into more spikes, his entire body raging that he couldn't possibly have heard right.

"I take his place as a rickshaw man."

The stablemaster tightened his grip on the heavy wrench and snarled into this foreign face that dared hold him to his people's code. Now this further outrage against his stable, the honorable trade of twenty-two men, now reduced to twenty-one. "Never! The others would hate you even more than I do. Pick up the money. If you don't want it get the fuck out!"

Sam wondered if Tanooki could hear his heart banging against his ribs. Whoever Tanooki believed the gaijin to be, he was holding his ground insisting the reciprocal code among Japanese be fulfilled. "I don't want your fucking coins. You owe me his job."

Tanooki turned from scarlet to purple, ready to explode when the telephone in his office shrilled. Rushing to the call for a moment, the stablemaster, holding his iron wrench, was all but kowtowing, apologizing profusely to the caller. The stablemaster was up against an emergency. He was struggling to explain to an important client why he'd failed to send a rickshaw. He sputtered apologies. Please forgive him. Because it was New Year's Day—every one of his rickshaws were engaged.

"Yes, Doctor. Yes." The Badger was groveling. "Yes, Sir." He was cornered, desperate to keep his stable's commitment. "Sir, five minutes. Someone—someone will be there."

Leaving the phone, the snarling animal charged from his den clawing his hair. "Fucking high-and-mighty doctor. Doctors—as bad as Geisha! Buddhist priests! All think they're King Shit! Thinks he's got an emergency—" With a glare at Sam and surprised to find himself still brandishing his wrench, he stepped over the dead body on the floor. He flung aside his wrench and strode into the dark recesses of the shed. He reappeared wheeling out an old carriage. After dusting it off he sprang onto the seat. From his perch Sam realized he was spitting orders down at him, the young gaijin—totally unacceptable ever as a true rickshaw man—but maybe, just maybe as a substitute for today. He ordered him between the poles.

Sam picked up the shafts. Taller than any of the other pullers, his first lift of the shafts hoisted the carriage too high, threatening to fling his infuriated passenger from his seat. Tanooki howled, gripping the seat handles, spewing new rage down at the wide shoulders before he hopped down.

"No. Not even if I have to go myself." Without moving, Sam watched the man's angry strides while clawing his hair. His emergency was apparent. In charge, he couldn't leave the stable. After more pacing, he ground his sharp teeth casting increasingly piercing glares at Sam. His thinking was apparent. As urgently as he needed a substitute during the New Year's rush, this foreigner could never be considered as a rickshaw man. Sam surprised him by shoving Tanooki back up on the seat. The glowering stablemaster saw him pick up the shafts, adjust them to his height and draw the carriage forward. The ball-bearings sprang into a life of their own. Sam rolled his passenger, back and forth, avoiding the dead body, till the stablemaster dropped down, still raking his wild hair.

"Fifty percent of the fare!" the Badger barked.

Sam snatched up the dead man's headband with the stable's name and tied it over his brow. "Twenty percent." He quoted the rate he'd heard pullers at the train station shout at the stablemasters.

"Get the fuck out!" Tanooki screamed.

Sam tightened the knot on the headband.

"Forty," the stablemaster hissed.

"Thirty," Sam shot back, "but you have to take me on full time."

Tanooki's red eyes blazed. "Forty. And today only." He found a straw mushroom of a hat, clamped it down over the substitute's head and tied it tight. "Keep your fucking gaijin head down so they don't see your fucking dirty yellow hair!" Tanooki rushed into his office and brushed ink onto paper—the doctor's location. "Shit. Of course you can't read—"

"If there aren't too many kanji," Sam declared.

"A doctor. He's got an emergency. He's Japanese but he lives in Chinatown."

"You know where that is?" Tanooki demanded.

"Hell, yes."

"Chinatown." Never, since his escape from the restaurant had he dared risk setting a sandal anywhere near Chinatown—the scene of his crime. Tanooki was shouting. "You hear me? Keep your devil-white eyes down under your hat so no one sees your yellow hair."

With his two hands grasping the crossbar, Sam trotted his rickshaw out into the freezing cold of dusk. He found the house in Chinatown. The physician was waiting, an unusually tall old man in a formal European dress for New Year's Day. This emergency call for a rickshaw was taking him away from family warmth and celebration. In the open doorway a birdlike wife fluttered among the New Year's decorations of pine and bamboo. Without a glance at his rickshaw's locomotion, the doctor, with his black bag, climbed up on his perch. His rugged beast of burden under the straw bowl of a hat took off, a little uncertainly at first but after fifty paces he was racing his fare through the streets, leaving noisy Chinatown and climbing a steep hill's brick-paved road, Hollander's Walk.

The bitter-cold air set Sam's lungs on fire. Though he gasped for breath his body thrilled, his muscles straining, running through the chill. This was no work for outcasts. This was honorable work. Japanese work.

CHAPTER THIRTY-THREE

Sam's fist tightened hard around his pay. His spirits flew high into the night. Gasping and wiping hot sweat in the icy darkness he'd finished his first run. If he could hold this job—his only hope of solid work—he was a rickshaw man. Without lighting his lantern to attract another fare for tonight, on his own he began his long run back to the stable.

With each slap of his sandals he told himself to be on guard. With Tanooki he had to sharpen all his instincts. As the new man on any job he'd be in for trouble, and not just from the hairy, broken-toothed Badger but from the regulars he knew took such pride in their profession. Proudest above all of being Japanese, they were bound to resent any newcomer. A tall foreigner? A gaijin?

At last, his muscles howling with pain, got him back to the stable where he wheeled in carefully, trying to make himself small in every way.

Tonight, the last thing in the world he wanted, the thing he dreaded most, was his next encounter with the potentially murderous Tanooki. Yes, there he was. Badger, red-eyes blazing, waiting for the substitute he was counting on to be too exhausted to put up a fight.

"Fifty percent," he snarled.

Though shaking with fatigue Sam summoned a long, deep breath preparing to fight. He dug his sandals into the earthen floor. Into the stablemaster's face he barked. "We agreed on forty."

Tanooki bared his sharp, broken teeth ready to tear flesh. Veins bulged across his purple face. He reached for his wrench.

"Hand it over. Fifty percent," Badger snarled.

"We agreed on forty," Sam spat back.

Tanooki's grip on the wrench was tightening when Sam sensed a rickshaw had rolled in. A powerful man with iron gray hair flopping down over eyeglasses taped to his head, was watching the two. Tanooki kept his wrench at his side. Whoever the man was, Sam could see he brought enough dignity to the stable to change the stablemaster's threatening tone of voice. "Stay out of this, Masao."

Strong Masao didn't move. He didn't have to raise his voice to stop the argument. Without glancing at Sam he said, "The kid's new. He says your deal for his first day told him forty percent. Not fifty."

With a nod to Sam he told him to pay Masao forty percent, which Sam quickly handed Tanooki. Masao was gruff. "If the kid stays and learns the ropes, he hands over twenty like the rest of us."

Shaking with fury, the stablemaster stared daggers at Sam, turned and left swinging his wrench.

Sam couldn't wait to thank his savior, but Old Masao, with his taped-on eyeglasses, rejected gratitude. "You're not Japanese. You don't know our ways. You hold back one sen of commission and you're out." He took a jar of sake from his rickshaw and before he disappeared into the stable's smoke he cautioned further. In their trade holding out on fares were reported from one stable to another. Banishment from one ended a rickshaw man's life work forever. With a rocking motion he disappeared into the dark with his jar of sake.

Watching others rolling in from the dark and turning off their lanterns, Sam was careful to stay away and park his rickshaw in the shed where Tanooki had found it. He stood at the door of the bunkhouse. No one spoke to him. No one told him what to do. He trailed into the rough but decent living quarters where he found a bed already stripped and open. Another dead man's bunk.

He lay wide awake in the smoky dark listening to every word mumbled by this band of men he was determined to join. Through the smoky gloom he recognized a few from the train station. Not one was as young as he. Some were old and gnarled as oak trees. To a man they drank. Two were playing Go. Was there one who didn't smoke? He listened to their talk—trade-talk—he'd have to learn. One group, apparently single men without families or homes other than the stable, carried on deeply serious talk comparing the talents and prices of whores. He listened hard. Others had been soldiers. Some had lost ancestral farms or had been to sea only to return to Japan, hauling rickshaws, and by doing so their standing within the infinitely complex Japanese hierarchy was forever determined. Three or four, deeply devoted to their trade, worked late into the night tuning and polishing their carriages by lantern light.

Before sleep came he'd searched through the smoke for some sight of Masao, his champion who'd defended him, but caught no sight of the tough old veteran. Perhaps the older man didn't bunk here, he told himself falling asleep in the smell of honest sweat, sweet-potato brandy, ball-bearing grease, cigarette and pipe smoke, and the sounds of not a few farts.

The next morning Sam kept to himself, slurping up his miso and digging into his rice. Tanooki had been wrong about his reception among his men. While it was true no one spoke a word or welcomed him into their band, no one seemed to hate or reject the gaijin, but simply ignored him. He was an outsider among a special brotherhood of Japanese priding themselves on their independence, rough and bold, rising this morning ready for tremendous hard work out in the city with a light snow falling.

His first assignment on New Years' Day had been that doctor in Chinatown, a one passenger run. Today, he dodged Tanooki and simply trotted his carriage out into the snow looking for fares. He kept his straw hat down over his light hair.

Did his straw mushroom and the falling snow hide him from his passengers? None of his fares tucked up under the snug carriage cover seemed to guess that other than being unusually tall and broad-shouldered, their rickshaw boy was only half a full descendant of the Sun Goddess.

His first full day racing around town blistered his feet and tore his muscles until he lit his lantern in the cold dark afternoon praying for the strength to drag himself and his rickshaw home to the stable.

He owed his job to Masao and kept looking around for a chance to thank him. In the encounter when the gruff old man defended him against Tanooki he sensed he'd witnessed something deeply Japanese in the man. Here was honor and dignity standing firm against the money-grubbing greed of the stablemaster. He'd heard the others talk of Masao with deep respect. Was it possible he was a samurai? He'd never known a samurai—now banished by the government—but he knew of their tradition. Warriors so fierce, so proud, that even out of work and with empty bellies and starving they'd swagger down the street working a toothpick, telling the world they just dined on roast duck. Rock-hard Old Masao, with his eyeglasses taped to his gray head, was that kind of man.

At the end of the day he waited for his champion to roll in with his rickshaw. Because he didn't live in the bunkhouse he rolled in and cleaned and shined his rickshaw for the night. When he was leaving Sam tried to stop him long enough to express his gratitude. Masao nodded, brushing off thanks and hurried alone out into the night.

Night after night in the smoke-crowded, roughhouse intimacy of the bunkhouse no one offered a cigarette or *sochu* or sake or considered including him in a happy band rushing off to a whorehouse. He went alone to the *sento* and sank into the scalding water Torazo loved so much.

Masao took no part in bunkhouse life crowded with stablemates in the smoke and reek of sweat and those salvos of farts. Sam felt increasingly alone at night amidst the loud laughter and joshing, watching the men pull on leggings and jackets to race out into the day and coming home late, drunk and falling into sleep. How long, he wondered, could this go on before the Japanese, rough and decent men, would break down and show some gesture of humanity, share a friendly word, a drink, a cigarette if not the full brotherhood of being a rickshaw man? Here, between two worlds, he didn't exist. With that chilling thought haunting him, he had to ask himself if this was what the rest of his life would be like. Then he'd tell himself to shut up and stop complaining. Cut out the whining. He had his work. Tough as it was it was, honorable work. That meant he existed.

CHAPTER THIRTY-FOUR

January had been freezing. February was bone-rattling cold with the wood and paper houses of Nagasaki groaning and shaking in the Arctic blasts howling down from nearby Siberia. Through the drizzle and snow he was skillfully dodging streetcars and roads glazed with ice, with his passengers tucked in with a robe under the carriage hood. With his sandals slapping icy streets how surprised would his fares be to learn the strong young man speeding them through the city of his birth was a gaijin?

On and on he ran through February till one morning in March a vast snowfall of blossoms spangled the hills frothy white reminding him of Bremerton's starry dogwood trees. But here was a whole country full of blossoms.

Late in the month, if not accepted at the stable by now, at least he felt he was tolerated. Then came the day when he felt he'd arrived, when he helped his first geisha onto his passenger seat.

A geisha!

Thrilled and honored, he raced with his geisha like a young buck through the spring day with the sun shining on them, hoping all Nagasaki would see his elegant passenger. In Sam's years in Japan he understood a geisha was not a white-faced, brilliantly painted little doll. Those were girls in training, *maiko*—apprentices to geisha, decked out in colorful silk and elaborate, propeller-shaped and lacquered hairdos. This goddess now sitting up on his carriage seat was a lovely woman whose hair was coiffed in a soft dark halo, setting off her flawlessly handsome face with only a hint of lip rouge. Her innate dignity, her skill and charm, up there in his carriage had raised her to a position among the very few women in Japan who enjoyed any control over their lives. At her age, perhaps an unlined forty years, she might be married to a rich man of her choice. More likely she was keeping her independence through a lifetime liaison with a powerful man in government or industry.

Or she might get married to an American navy officer. The thought struck while his sandals pounded on the asphalt street—a street his mother must have known. Had she lived she'd be younger than this lovely geisha. No. Cho-Cho-San was no geisha. Before entering her training as a *maiko* she had left to marry Lieutenant Benjamin Franklin Pinkerton. He could still hear the cheery Scotch voice of Mrs. McKie back in the church office. "Nakamura Eiko. Such a lovely thing. Barely seventeen when she came here to have her baby, the Pinkerton baby, baptized—"

A streetcar clanged and Sam dashed ahead hoping he hadn't jolted his passenger. From under his hat he stole a glance up at her, serene behind a pale green fan. He dodged a cart heaped with white radishes and gleaming tiny purple eggplants. His geisha tapped her fan. She'd changed her mind and wanted to stop at a department store, and with his help, stepped down. No. She didn't wish him to wait. On the sidewalk several Japanese and a huge Western couple stopped in their tracks and stared open-mouthed at such exotic loveliness disappearing into the store.

His first geisha. Often he trotted with whores as passengers, but no whore had the loveliness, even with their too colorful silks and less subtle maquillage, to stop people in the street. Nevertheless, the truth was he liked running for whores. With the exception of their bossy mama-sans they giggled at their strapping young runner and were bold enough to speak with him which meant more giggles of delight, scarcely able to believe this strapping young gaijin was at their service. In their colorful silk and with fluttering fans and coquettish games with umbrellas, whores were allowed to flirt with him. They were fun and paid well.

Apparently he'd been whispered about in several of the better teahouses in the Maruyama. Rumor of this tall and strapping Western boy who was a rickshaw man had spread until he'd developed a steady clientele as a fashionable novelty running in and out of the Maruyama. Ladies in bright colors preening on the seat above him had mischievously pulled off his straw hat so that Nagasaki could see their near-blond with his handsome Western face sweating in their service.

Whores, of course, were available for money. He never left the Maruyama pleasure district rattling across the Shianbashi Bridge without counting the days until he'd indulge his fantasies with coin enough to trot his pretty little passengers through their own paces.

Sam couldn't pretend he didn't know what a surprising sight he was trotting between the poles and not always keeping his head down under his straw hat. Children never failed to point to him with startled shrieks of glee at such a strange sight. If his passengers above were startled, their innate Japanese mask of politeness kept relations businesslike. Adult Japanese were too polite for second looks and if they had comments, they were whispered. Westerners were the most surprised and without exception, openly gawked.

Imagine if the damned Snyders and the goddamned Showalters could see him now—a deep-breathing beast of burden, wiping sweat, munching onions, smoking cigarettes and shooting steaming piss against some of Nagasaki's finest buildings.

What would Benjy think if he saw his older brother trotting through Nagasaki, a rickshaw-boy? Then he thought of Torazo, that skinny brat, his only friend. It pained him to think of him rotting in some jail. How he'd love to show that evil little fox he'd survived on his own in this most traditionally Japanese way. What fun to have him sitting up there on the seat, letting the two of them lord it over Nagasaki.

And his mother? As he ran he asked himself how many of these streets she'd known. What would his Japanese mother think if she saw her tall half-American son back in the town where he was born, a rickshaw boy?

Week after week, month after month, into spring and summer he ran like the college track star he felt certain he might have been in another life at an American university.

One early summer evening with clouds of swifts twittering and circling the sky, while he was waiting for a fare and munching a particularly crispy turnip outside the Bellevue, he glanced into the lobby. Even outside he could hear harps and violins playing new American songs he did not know. In Seattle's New Washington Hotel across the Pacific were they still playing Victor Herbert? He studied the Western guests entering and leaving the front door, all huge in their spotless linen and white hats and polished boots and talking in such loud voices, watching from more than a world away in his *happi* coat, naked legs and sandals. He gave his turnip another chomp and pulled out one of his first purchases, his faithful pocket dictionary, ironically half Japanese and English like himself. Could any of the Westerners surging down the steps guess he was using his waiting time tracing these devilishly difficult Chinese ideographs that can only be learned by rote?

The doorman whistled. He snapped shut his dictionary, tossed aside his turnip, and trotted forward. His passenger, who carried an English boater in his hand, was a young Westerner as tall as he, his features aristocratic and probably European. Within the flawless English tailoring of his brown three-piece suit he raised his hand in a small wave to three Japanese gentlemen in top hats, cutaway coats, and striped trousers. He had yet to turn to his waiting rickshaw. Sam guessed the young gentleman was no more than twenty years of age, but his display of such nuanced politesse with these important men suggested a lifetime here in Japan. A diplomat? A banker? His passenger clapped on his straw boater and was in the midst of lighting a cigarette when he turned to the rickshaw. Their eyes met. His cigarette dropped. He turned from Sam and his rickshaw. He ground out his cigarette with a brown leather boot. His shoulders stiffened and he deliberately turned his back on the rickshaw boy. He was Sam's fare. Did he want him or not? The young gentleman hesitated a moment longer, then brusquely wheeled around presenting a face clamped in fury. "You speak English?" Sam recognized an accent achieved through a careful British education.

"Yes, sir."

The English voice thinned to a hiss, separating each word, making it clear he was speaking for the entire Western world. "Then, for God's sake, what the hell do you think you're doing?"

CHAPTER THIRTY-FIVE

"Rickshaw!" The sharp command, more of a bark than a woman's voice, came from a flash of red and gold silk, far too gaudy to be the kimono of a geisha. This small-faced woman with tight scarlet lips and hair shellacked like a wooden helmet, was Auntie, not the kindest woman in the world, but one of his regular fares from the Maruyama.

He'd pulled under a willow and had been gazing into the bonfires of the mid-July Bon Festival, his blood pounding with drums, that primordial pulse he'd shared with the villagers in Asahi-Mura. This was Japan, his heart beating to drumming as old as these islands.

In the night full of fire and music he watched families dancing together, moving from the bonfires to the water's edge. Here, mostly children, but adults, too, were launching paper boats folded around candle flames, each the spirit of a loved one who'd come back to their homes on this holy night, a flotilla of glowing souls returning across dark water from their visits to their families and what had been home. Sam bought a paper boat for his mother. On his bare knees, he felt her close, helping him light her candle. Here, under the willows at the water's edge, watching her paper boat crossing the dark water returning to her eternal home, her glow merging with thousands of others out in the darkness.

"You! My white-eyed Rickshaw Boy!" The second command breaking the spell was even sharper.

"She says to wait here."

"Who?" Sam asked. "Auntie?"

"You'll find out." The whisper and more giggles came from his two passengers.

From the other rickshaw across the garden, Auntie, in a flash of scarlet and white silk, shooed her two women twittering into the house.

Sam slapped mosquitoes and stretched his muscles while waiting between the poles. After ten minutes wiping sweat he twisted with impatience. Whoever had given the order was wasting his time. On this busy night he had other fares to run. What kind of silly, girlish prank was this? Was someone making fun of the rickshaw boy?

He was picking up his poles when he caught sight of what appeared to be a pale ghost stepping down from the porch into the garden. No. It wasn't a ghost, or even Auntie. Nor was it either of his giggling little whores. Whoever this was, she wasn't in silk, but in a blue-and-white light-weight cotton summer yukata and zig-zagging across the flagstones toward him, with none of the mincing gait of a young painted doll. She was taller than most young Japanese women though a head shorter than Sam. With the lamplight behind her he couldn't guess her age. Her black hair was not tortured into an elaborate coif, but a ponytail falling down her back. When the light caught her at the gate she looked young, no more than twenty. At closer range her face was not quite oval but a little wider, warmed by a soft lantern glow and shining with perspiration in the summer heat, free of rice powder. It was her eyes. Her eyes held him, enormous and glittering—a trick of the light or clever makeup? Her eyebrows were natural, full and dark, and not painted high on her brow above those remarkable eyes. Her scarlet lips glistened wide and full, nothing at all like the little heart shape affected by most of the pleasure dolls of the water trade.

She came close, openly appraising him till he felt his adam's apple bobbing. For something to do he bowed slightly. She moved close and had yet to shift her gaze. His palms dripped sweat. "So," she began, "you are the brass-haired one they all talk about." Her voice was low, but not a whisper nor even purringly feminine. "The Greek Statue. That's what the others call you."

Sam gulped.

"Hot work tonight?"

"Yes, Ma'am."

"You are not too tired?" Her low voice was unsettling as her index finger rose and began tracing his wet neck below his ear.

He wasn't able to answer.

"I asked you," the low voice said, "if you are not too tired."

His heart crowded his throat and he was forced to gulp it down before he could speak. "N-no. I'm used to it."

"Not too tired to come inside?"

Hot and streaming sweat and at a loss, he fought his confusion. No one, not even a whore, could be so bold as to actually ask him to follow her into the house. Lust roughened his throat. "No money—"

"For me," she snapped disdainfully, "you'd need far, far more than the rich old men pay any of Auntie's stupid girls."

He was trembling so violently he reached to grasp the poles. He couldn't move. His face, already scalding, was now on fire. She tossed her head in the direction of the door across the garden, an order to follow her. He still clung to his rickshaw.

"Leave it," she commanded. "Those who come here in the night do not come to steal rickshaws." When he still hesitated, still clinging to the poles, she stepped close raising her hand and closing it on the back of his wet neck. He shied like a colt and choked out an apology.

"I'm sorry I'm so sweaty."

Was she smiling? "Young man's sweat."

He was paralyzed. How long would she keep her cool hand on his neck?

He allowed himself to be led from his carriage through the gate and across the garden spangled with warm light spilling from the lattices. Laughter, soft music, and song from different rooms filled the house. She stepped up onto the low porch and slid off her getas and stood in bare feet looking straight into his eyes. Her look was a question. How long was he going to keep her waiting? He quickly kicked off his sandals and managed to line them up alongside her getas hiding them before a row of men's Western-style black leather shoes.

"Be very quiet."

He bobbed his head promising to obey any command. From the porch his feet touched the coolness of polished wood. Ahead in the dimness of the corridors he saw serving maids scurrying with trays of beer and sake. He hesitated. Should he walk in front of her or behind? The answer was her hand returning to the back of his neck.

She stopped one of the maids clad in a dark *yukata* all but invisible in the shadows. "Is the Tiger Room free?" The servant, keeping her eyes lowered, nodded. Sam's captor turned him into another long hall. "The Tiger Room. Does that inspire you?"

He struggled to find breath. "First can I take a bath?"

"Did you hear me say I didn't like sweat?" Her hand tightened on his neck. "Later," she murmured, "perhaps a bath."

A maid scurried out of the shadows, kneeling to slide back a panel and creep inside to light a floor lamp and spread a futon. Sam waited, then obeyed his young woman's hand leading him into the room where his bare feet touched the tatami.

He was scarcely aware of ink paintings covering two walls with tigers, hot with passion, in ferocious coupling. He flinched, feeling her hand slip under his jacket. Staring down at the golden mats he didn't dare move. She untied his belt.

The maid stood ready to help her strip her man, but his young woman ordered her aside. She would do the undressing herself and slid the rickshaw boy's *happi* jacket down from his shoulders. It was picked up by the maid. Sam stood stock still, holding his breath as she unwound his *fundoshi*. The servant took the breechcloth leaving him standing hot, naked and fully aroused, ready to explode but shaking with uncertainty. This was what he wanted and ached for so desperately for so many years with every fiber of his young body. Scarcely able to breathe, he told himself however impossible, his blood raging, he must wait for the woman to drop her *yukata*. Wait and pray and hope that his fierceness wouldn't break him in two as he watched her untie her cloth belt as the light cotton robe opened and fell from her. She presented her body, naked, wet and gleaming.

"You see? I, too, sweat—a little."

His hands at his sides felt ridiculously huge. In the soft light, her nakedness was more ravishing than his most lurid fantasies. He flinched under her hands as they held him for her pleasure, her eyes telling him they were both here to look at each other. She gloried in her nakedness— perfectly smooth tea-colored skin, small high round breasts with apricot-colored nipples. Her torso curved down to a nest of soft dark hair between strong but slender legs.

"I have long legs," she said without a trace of self-consciousness. "Most Japanese women do not have legs so long."

She smiled. Yes, she gloried in her body. Nothing of what he'd known of life had ever hinted that a woman could want sex as much as a man. Though she loved being naked, she held up her hand telling him to wait. "You have seen many naked Western ladies?"

His throat had clamped shut. His nod was a lie.

"I myself have seen many Western statues," she purred. "Am I not as beautiful?" Her hands cupped and lifted her breasts for both of them to appraise. Then the hands slid down caressing the curve of her stomach. "Beautiful? Yes?"

"Y-yes."

"You are beautiful, too. The silly ones here in Auntie's house swear you look like a Greek statue. That is why I brought you here. To see for myself. Not many Japanese men are so tall with such strongly muscled bodies. Few of the men of my race look like statues. Don't move. You must stand still." Her fingers pinched a nipple as she drew closer with the other hand sliding down his belly.

"I saw a motion picture with Romans and Greeks. Big men like you. Greek statues—"

"I'm half J-Japanese," he blurted, but a hand sealed his lips.

"No. You are a Greek statue and very beautiful even if you do have hair on your arms and chest and legs." Her fingers caressed hairs glinting on his forearms. Exploring him she held both his wrists out from his body. "Beautiful. But, of course, I am more beautiful, for my hair is only in places proper to have hair."

She reached back, loosened the tie of her ponytail, and shook out her mane till it fell in a black cascade. "When I first came here Auntie taught me a girl does the things men tell her they like. No. I told you— don't move. I'll tell you when. Always, I did what men like to do. Now, with you, I will decide what I like to do—"

She was on him, nuzzling his shoulder, licking his sweat with his manhood raging. His hands, fired with their own life, pulled her close.

"Slowly. Slowly." Her purr was a command but now for Sam there could be no slowly. Not now. He clasped her, sinking them down on the quilt, but before he could throw himself onto her, he exploded, semen gushing out of him in milky gouts. He drew back clutching himself. He was scarlet with humiliation as spasm after spasm gushed into his hot hands. In agony, naked and trying to cover his shame, his horror became complete shock as he heard smothered giggles. Shame turned to panic. Feverish and confused, unable to hide himself from the mocking laughter they were hearing from the slid back hall panel. His woman took his hands away from any attempt at modesty, stroking him, gathering his offering, amusing their audience.

"Save it for Auntie!" a woman's voice cried. "She uses it for her complexion—better than nightingale shit."

Sam shrank from showing himself to those at the panel. How many gleeful spectators were out there crowding, watching the young gaijin with his amateur performance delighting the entire house. He turned his back to the panel and bent himself double trying to hide his humiliation. Leaning close she patted his backside. "Show's over. Now we have all night." She kissed his ear. Their audience applauded. She licked his neck, murmuring loud enough to inspire more applause.

"Truly, this is your very first time?"

"N-no," he lied, only adding to his shame. She took his shoulders and dropped him on his back. Her teeth nipped his breast. "Then we still have your first time to look forward to—"

He twisted away from her hot body and scrambled across the cool tatami sliding the panel shut on the snickering, but not before a tattered book came flying onto the futon. The sliding wall closed. She picked up the book and crawled to him, flipping pages. "While you calm down— look." She was showing the missionary boy unimaginably shocking pictures. His astonishment at the line drawings of men in endless ways of penetrating women delighted her.

"A pillow book," she laughed. "Never seen a pillow book?"

"No." Instead of calming down he sprang at her, but she held him off.

"No pillow books in America? No?" She flapped the pages at him. "You have much to learn." Her smile promised education was possible. He didn't need inspiration. His arms went around her, his mouth on her neck. She whispered, "I am better than any book. When I am able to calm you down, I have many ways to sharpen pleasure for both of us. Some ways are Chinese. Some come from Hollywood in California in the U.S.A."

With a coarse, unladylike laugh she tossed the manual to the tatami. "I can see you need no stimulation. What you need is careful training. First we slow you down." She kissed a nipple. "Lovemaking is not a rickshaw race." Her tongue flickered down his chest, his belly. "If I allow you to stay, you must do exactly as I say."

CHAPTER THIRTY-SIX

By now she'd tied a tight green bow around his genitals, handling him in a way the missionary boy had scarcely dared touch himself. Stroking his buttocks with one hand, she spooned cooling shaved ice, flavored with wild pomegranate syrup, into him. He wasn't cooled, but ready to explode when she lay back and pulled him down on her. "Slowly. Slowly . . ."

He entered her and when, at last, he slumped exhausted, her fingers combed his hair wet with sweat, and kissed his neck. Because the sliding panel to the corridor couldn't be locked, this time those outside clapped in applause.

This woman, whose name he still did not know, considered her exhausted prize lying panting on the quilt. "This time they are saying you did a little better. Only a little. You have so, so much to learn." Having put on his unwilling show, he grabbed out for his *happi* jacket but found the maid had taken it so he seized her *yukata* for himself. His lover tore it from him and flung it on the tatami. "Being naked shames Americans?"

She kissed his shoulder. "In America people don't like to look?" She kissed his manhood. "We Japanese love to look. Some of Auntie's clients would rather look than do. There are old men out there in the hall who wish they had your young gaijin body."

"I told you, I'm half Japanese—"

"Shut up. If you can learn to slow down and do what I say I may permit you to be my Greek statue. Of course the rest of those stupid bitches here in this house are going to be more crazy jealous of me than ever. But not all. Some prefer other women to men. In America do you know about such women? I would be the last to say there is not great pleasure in that. Besides," she added a little petulantly, "I'm the one who should be angry. They were all looking at you and not me."

She spread him on his back with her smooth legs straddling, clamping, her young trophy. She loved to explore him, aware of their peeping toms seeing she could be as expert as a connoisseur considering a piece of porcelain or a bolt of fine silk.

"You are the first gaijin most of them have ever seen naked." She kissed his lips.

"And my first." She trailed her lips over his chin, down his neck and across his breast. She had him breathing too hard to speak, and in full control, commanded, "No more talk." Now she sat him up turning him to the floor lamp for even closer appraisal. "Japanese people wish to see how you are made—if any of your parts are different from our men's." She enjoyed her careful search of his body, and spoke over his shoulder for the benefit of those out in the hall stifling their snickers. "Everything is here, just like a Greek statue."

She ran chips of shaved ice across his skin. "Usually," she explained, "Japanese people are not excited by naked bodies. We see too many. Everywhere. At home, at the bath, farmers from the fields and their fat, muddy wives. Most are not beautiful. And in these pillow books the stupid woodblock artists use only lines for naked bodies. They don't make you hot. Our Japanese paintings are as bad. As for statues, most of ours are Buddhas and gods of Shinto. No Greek gods. Western art is full of handsome gods and beautiful goddesses—real bodies full of hot blood. I even know of Japanese women, and a few men, too, who get aroused at the sight of your naked Jesus on his cross." Her eyes looked down at his. She smothered a laugh. "Is this a terribly evil thing to say?"

Sam felt a chill. "Very." To his surprise he heard himself telling her he knew of a gaijin who'd declare that even whispering a thing like that would send her straight to hell. "As a Japanese you've probably never even heard of the Last Judgment."

Like most Japanese, the Day of Wrath meant nothing to her. Not when she was purring with sex. "More even than Western art, I love most of all Hollywood movies where men and women show off their beautiful bodies. But why—just when they're ready to drop their clothes for sex—do the pictures on the screen go somewhere else? Do they stop the cameras just when the beautiful movie stars get ready to fuck?"

"Ask Charlie Chaplin."

She slapped his face playfully. "I don't mean Charlie Chaplin. I mean movies about Rome and Greece with beautiful men and women slaves who must do exactly what their masters command. So," she ran her tongue over a nipple, "you are my Greek slave and you must do whatever I command."

Thrilled to obey, he was available, eager to let her handle him any way she chose leading him into a world exciting beyond his wildest fantasies. He gasped, "I didn't think women liked sex."

"It may be American women don't. I love sex and if my Greek slave will do exactly as I say, someday I may tell him a secret—"

"Tell me now," he begged.

"Shut up."

His two hands took her face. "Not until you tell me your name." She answered by pressing a finger against his lips. She ran her fingers through his sweat-soaked hair, the rest of him dripping, wet.

"I'm awfully sweaty. Can we take a bath?"

She pretended petulance. "I licked off all your sweat. I missed some part of you?" She rose and pulled him to his feet, took him by the hand, slid open the panel leading her prize past their audience down a dark hall. They entered the scrub room where an ancient barefoot crone in a gray ragged work *yukata* down on her knees was scouring wooden duckboards. She took one look at him and shrieked. His lover, still with no name, kicked at her and screamed louder. "Old Hag! Get out!"

Her order was so sharp, so imperious, that it made him wince for the pathetic creature she'd sent rushing with downcast eyes out the door. Once alone, they began the same procedure he had observed at the public *sento.* They soaped and scoured each other till they were glowing. Sam thrilled when she ordered him to shampoo her long hair. After rinsing themselves, under buckets of clean water, she grabbed two little towels and they entered another room with steam rising from the *o furo.*

Scalding water on one of the hottest days of summer? No. She led him past the steaming hell to an outside garden where rocks and flowers bordered a pool gurgling with running water. They sank into the cool, his radiant, gorgeous, naked creature insisting they were otters frolicking, kissing deeply, sinking below the surface, emerging to kiss and kiss again.

"Now," he whispered, "you have to tell me your name."

"Your name," she said "is 'you- talk- too- much-Gaijin.'"

"Okay," he persisted. "Can I at least ask you a question? Was it your choice to work here?"

"Not if you ask a stupid question not even the stupidest Japanese kid would ask." She was wringing out her wet towel and placing it with great delicacy over her brow before resting the nape of her neck on the side of the pool. He vowed to stay silent and wait for her to be the first to speak. From behind the towel she said, "Nobody bought me. I came here because I'm not the type to put up with those years of being kicked around in an *okiya* begging to be a *maiko*. I've worked a helluva lot harder than those little twittering birds till I learned how to make any man beg Auntie for me." She lifted the towel and looked straight into his eyes. "You. Your very first. If you knew anything you'd know I'm the best—the very best. Me—I am A Number One—"

"Like me," he cried happily. "After Masao, I'm one of the best rickshaw men in Nagasaki and believe me, pulling a rickshaw takes skill—real guts." Proud of his trade he found himself still American enough to confess dreaming of a brighter future. "It might surprise you, but I'm an English teacher. Maybe not right now, but one day I'll have my own school and I'll be rich—"

"I'm already rich so shut up." She leaned back luxuriating in the bliss of the pool. "One thing you better know right now if you ever have any ideas about coming back here again—"

"If?" He wailed in shocked disbelief. "How—how can you ever say 'if' when you know I'll never leave. I have to come back. I love you—"

"Cut all the crap about love. You do what I tell you and both of us can have a good time."

He was in the pool up to his chin, yet on fire. "When? When's the next time?"

"First, get this through your thick gaijin head. I'm the only one here in this house of Auntie's who is with just one man. Get it? Just one. Mine gives me everything I ever ask for—even one of those new radio things. When he gets back from Tokyo, I only have to ask and it's mine. He's my only one, get it? So don't you ever confuse me with the others here. Those bitches have to put up with anyone who can pay—any fat slug crawling and sliming all over them."

He wanted to ask: "Is this rich man who's going to buy you a radio as good at making love as I am?" But he didn't ask. He told himself not to risk the question, not on his first day freed from virginity, eighteen and aching for praise. He was a beginner but already blissful beyond his wildest fantasies. Just imagine, he told himself, how he'd be after the wonderful things she was going to teach him.

"He can't live without me. His wife—a bag of bones who's never given him one good fuck—doesn't know a thing about what men want—and doesn't care. He says all Old Bag of Bones ever does is lie there. He swears no other woman he's ever known, including the fancy geisha he sponsored for years, is anywhere near as exciting as I am."

"He can't love you, not like I do—"

"He's a man so he thinks only of himself and his pleasure, and believe me I know what he likes. I'll never let him leave me. He's in Tokyo right now, but as for you and me, next when he's away I might let you come here and see me. That means we can't risk anyone ever breathing a word to him."

Astonished, his mouth dropped open. "How can it be secret when everyone in the house just saw us!"

"Everyone in this house is scared shitless of him. They know what he'd do to shut them up if he even suspected they knew. No, they won't talk."

"What about Auntie?"

"He's making her rich, so she's the last one who'd ever talk. It's up to you." She lifted the towel and looked straight into his eyes. "If—and I'm only saying 'if'—I do let you come back and see me, can you keep your big mouth shut?"

"Yes! Yes!" He lunged across the water.

"Hold back. And never, ever crow about me to those assholes you work with?"

"I swear!"

She was dead serious. "Swear on your Jesus Christ?"

He nodded. "I swear on Jesus Christ I'll never tell a single soul."

CHAPTER THIRTY-SEVEN

They stepped from the pool, the rich man's young whore leading him by the hand back through the scrub room, when he felt her lips on his ear. "This time, my room." At the promise of what sounded like even more intimacy he hurried with his naked lover until she suddenly stopped. They'd both heard a duckboard creak. Alert as a woodland creature she looked around. They weren't alone. Someone hiding in shadow was following them.

Sam sprang into the dark coming face-to-face with the bath scrubber, the old, gray crone staring at him with one eye, the other dead and white. Her toothless mouth gaped, old hands flailed. "It's Old Hag!"

The naked girl rushed at the woman slashing out at the cowering bundle of rags. "She's a witch—spying on us, cursing us." Her damp hair flew as she lunged, driving back the tattered specter, a ghost hovering in the gloom but staring, hypnotized by the naked gaijin.

The enraged girl's screams brought serving maids running. Auntie herself, yanking on a gray kimono, tottered into the hall shouting, restoring order, waving back men and women eager to be part of the excitement. Auntie chased the specter off and into banishment. Sam had seen Auntie before, but never without paint here in her own house. This small-faced woman, now without her red gash of lip rouge and nearly bald without her helmet of black hair, was mistress here. Her piercing eyes held the naked couple, who backed away. His lover raced him down the hall deep into the house where she slid open a panel. Here she stopped with a signal, telling him to wait while she slipped into her room. After a moment he heard the faint hissing sound of a phonograph record, sinuous as movie music evoking the Arabian Nights, along with the scent of heavy incense.

"Open Sesame." Her voice from within the room, like the music, was a seductive invitation to slide the panel back on a room smaller than the Tiger Room and so totally exotic he could only blink his eyes. He'd entered a fantasy hung with beaded curtains, a large Moroccan screen, gleaming brass lamps, a sofa spread with a fake leopard-skin throw. His bare feet sank into a thick carpet. The Victrola with its morning-glory horn stood next to a stack of shellacked records. The walls were crowded with black-and-white photographs, shiny movie stills and posters in full color of a voluptuous Hollywood movie star naked but for a few strategically placed beads. His eyes widened as from behind the Damascene panels of the screen a hand, heavy with bangles, snaked out into the room. Slowly, she emerged emulating the screen goddess, a woman in an Egyptian-style headdress, eyes circled with black kohl, her mouth dark red, almost black. Her voice was low.

"Te-da-ba-ra," she intoned. In case her young captive didn't understand, bejeweled fingers indicated the posters and photographs of Theda Bara, a Hollywood fever-dream sex goddess, seductive eyes shining out from behind black kohl. Out of the Tiger Room and into her own lair she'd turned herself into Hollywood's Theda Bara, "The Vamp." Before him, incarnate in Japanese flesh, his idolatress struck and held a seductive pose, wordless as her silent Hollywood movie-star inspiration. The Vamp, preparing to devour her lover after allowing him her charms.

Fingers dripping with glinting costume jewelry bid him to an alcove and a shrine, a collection of more posters and photographs of Hollywood's goddess. The Japanese voice was a low, seductive whisper, a question. "In her movies you love Tedabara?" Sam nodded vigorously without admitting he had only seen posters of the wicked star—the Vamp—at movie theatres and the ubiquitous photos in Japanese magazines and newspapers.

Tedabara led him to another wall of photos of nearly naked gaijin men. He recognized her idols, Douglas Fairbanks, Wallace Reid, and the heavyweight boxing champion of the world, Jack Dempsey. The phonograph record stopped, but with Tedabara winding it, it played on. She directed his gaze to a shelf, her own art museum with cheap plaster-of-paris statues, reproductions of naked ancient Greek athletes, the Discobolous, and a standing Hermes.

"We adore the movies." Tedabara's purr dropped and in sudden enthusiasm she became an excited Japanese girl. "We never miss a new picture." Again she disappeared behind her screen. "Now—wine. Not sake or beer. Wine." She re-appeared setting a bottle and two cut crystal glasses on a table covered with a brightly fringed Middle-Eastern shawl. With bracelets jingling, she slithered her naked body onto the leopard-skin sofa and with

Tedabara's wicked eyes ordered her helpless love slave to open the bottle.

Plum wine, and Sam poured two glasses.

A gesture from his temptress commanded him to approach the sofa and kneel before her, presenting her glass. Shaking, fighting nervously to keep from dropping the glass, he waited for her to sip. "I'm Samuel Adams Pinkerton," he suddenly blurted. "Now you have to tell me your name."

"I told you. I am Tedabara—"

"You can trust me—"

"Tedabara. No more talk." Her voice sank low, cool. "You do not wish to kiss me?"

He put his glass down and sprang to her mouth, greasy with lipstick, which his tongue worked past as it ran over her teeth. She drew him to her naked body with greater passion than had seized them in the Tiger Room, then pulled back to untie a vermilion silk cord, dropping a tent of mosquito netting over them, a gossamer world in which to tangle in her long damp hair.

"Slowly. Slow . . ." She commanded while he fought his raging young body to slow himself. "Still too fast," she said reaching for a pack of Camels. "American cigarettes," she announced with pride. She lit one, drew in smoke, and held it out to him. He lay with her quietly, sharing the cigarette and listening to the Victrola and a summer rainstorm pattering the roof.

The Victrola hissed and wound down. She stubbed out their cigarettes. She pressed his hot face between her thighs from where Sam raised his eyes. "I love you," he murmured again and again. "I love you." He felt her body shake with laughter. Stung, he drew back still holding her in his arms searching to see why opening his heart so amused her. "What I just said, I swear to God I've never said to anyone but you."

"This is how all Americans talk?"

"Now I'm Japanese," he insisted.

"If you wish to stay longer you must be Greek."

"Teach me everything. I'm never going to leave."

"When would I sleep?" She nuzzled the hollow between his neck and shoulder. "It is important that I sleep or I will look like Old Hag. Then how would I please my sponsor?"

"I'm not afraid of him."

"You should be. I meant it when I told you no one here in this house would dare ever whisper of this." She slid herself from under him, and reached through the netting to pour more wine for herself. "They've all heard how his horrible men punish his enemies." She sipped the wine and licked her lips. "But I am his Tedabara. He can't get enough of me."

"I'll find a way you don't have to be with him—"

"Listen." She raised her head to listen. Sam stifled his own breathing. They both heard a soft whistle. "The soba man," she explained, as if Sam didn't know the sound perfectly well of the night seller of piping hot noodles outside in the rain. She parted his lips with a finger. "Is my statue hungry?" He shook his head, saying not for all the soba in the world would he budge from this leopard-skin sofa.

"Not even to keep up your strength?"

An hour later, with soba and rain on the roof, they turned the rest of the night to fire till kitchen sounds warned Sam the house was stirring. He glanced over at Tedabara, who'd found a pool of warmth under the mosquito netting and had no intention of rising. At more sounds indicating that part of the house was up for the day, his heart tightened, dreading the moment she'd tell him he must go.

She yawned. She patted his backside.

"I'll never leave," Sam cried from his heart.

"No?"

With a burst of joy he rose on one elbow to look down into that face he could no longer live without. She smiled. "When you are richer than my sponsor, then perhaps you may stay." He reached for her but she lifted away his arm. "Go. Pull your rickshaw."

Sam gripped her shoulders. "Please," he begged. "Right now—one more time."

She lifted the netting and turned her back to him. "Go."

"The minute it's dark I'll be back."

He crept down the dark hall and onto the porch where he pulled on his sandals. Someone else was here. He looked up. Auntie's little eyes were glaring at him. "You've had your fun, Rickshaw Boy. Now get your gaijin prick out of this house while you've still got it and never come back!" She thrust her bald head with its white face at him. "Not that I give a shit what old Kodo would do to you after he cuts your balls off and breaks your legs. You'd be no use to Kuniyo then—"

"Kuniyo? You mean Tedabara?"

"I mean the bitch!" Auntie's face hardened to granite. "If you want to keep your prick—never come back!"

CHAPTER THIRTY-EIGHT

He ran all morning. He ran under the scorch of noon. He ran through the blaze and swelter of the hottest hours of the afternoon. His headband, soaked, streamed with sweat. He shut his eyes and ran. Sundown—the earliest possible moment he could finish his day and get to her—was still hours away.

At last in the red dusk of evening, with the first lanterns winking on, he was back at Auntie's. A serving maid in the garden stifled a cry when the rickshaw boy kicked off his sandals and plunged into the house. Auntie, half-dressed and fanning herself furiously, appeared in the shadows with her glare but made no move to stop him. A snap of her fan made the sign of a knife slicing across a crotch. "And worse," she hissed. "No one runs from Kodo. Never." She called after him. "If Kodo finds out and doesn't catch you himself, his thugs will."

He sprinted down the corridor into Tedabara's fantasy of the Arabian Nights. Her tent of mosquito netting was wafting from an electric fan. Inside its film she was totally naked, her eyes blackened with kohl glancing up from licking shaved ice. Breathing hard, he prayed her makeup was proof she was expecting him. Her body that had haunted him every minute of this longest day of his life was a thousand times more desirable—here before him at last—in the flesh.

With half-closed blackened eyelashes watching him she slid her tongue over her lips shining from pomegranate syrup. "Oh, so it's you, is it?" Acting the indifference she imagined would be Tedabara's, she murmured, "Do I remember hearing you say perhaps you might come by this evening?" Her eyes gleamed over her ice, watching him fling off his *happi* jacket and tearing his *fundoshi,* in his haste to get naked.

"First," she murmured, acting as tauntingly aloof as ever, "Go wind the Victrola."

He obeyed, but when he rushed to her she kept him waiting, breathing harder, certain that his body would snap in half. She sighed elaborately, "Now pass me that box over there." Instantly he fetched the exquisite piece of lacquer she called her "box of toys." In another stalling tactic she'd lit a cigarette and through the smoke opened the box untangling yesterday's green ribbon from two marble eggs dangling on a thin chain. She pushed aside a knotted silk rope to find tiny jars of unguents and packets of powder. She ignored how hard he was breathing, looking down over her shoulder at things in the box for uses he couldn't imagine. She drew him close and tied him with the green ribbon. He gasped and suddenly her tongue was on him, a cat licking his sweat and purring, feeling his heart galloping. "You really must learn to control yourself . . . Slow . . . Go slow . . . Very slow."

Sam's breath was rattling, his body ready to explode, crying to himself, "Slow's easy for you to say." With one hand she held him off, with the other languidly plumping the artificial leopard skin cushions under the gossamer mosquito netting of her tent of Araby. She took her time sliding onto her back and raising her arms before she abandoned all her pretensions, and hot and ferocious, pulled him to her. Their bodies locked as she increased his fire, their violent lovemaking burning him to ashes. With a gasp he fell exhausted against her. She slid her face through his sweat, lapping every inch of him till she fell back and reached out to a side table to prepare another shaved ice. Pomegranate syrup on ice shimmered ruby red, and with one hand she spooned ice into him.

For five nights he returned, racing to her. This night he licked the ritual tiny ice spoon and laid it aside, his mouth exploring her exciting body. "Kuniyo," his voice was muffled between her breasts. "Please, you've never called me Sam and I want you to know who I am—"

"From the first night I've told you, you talk too much—"

"But you never ask me what it's like being half Japanese and half American?"

"See? There you go, still talking."

"Because I want you to know the truth about me and how I love you." She pressed close, every inch of herself available to him. "As for you,

I wouldn't even know your name was Kuniyo if Auntie hadn't told me—"

"Tedabara," she sighed. He was breaking the rules.

"And that guy's off in Tokyo. At least now I know his name's Kodo. Doesn't matter what it is because I love you, and I'm taking you away from him—"

"In your rickshaw?"

"I'm not joking."

"May I ask where you're taking me?"

"Away from here."

"Lucky for us you're so rich."

"I will be. You'd be surprised at all the plans I've got—" Her shrug indicated total disinterest in anything about him but conjuring his strong, young body as a Greek performing within her fantasy.

"I'm young and strong and I'm smart. I've told you. I read dictionaries—Japanese and English."

Was she listening now? No her total concentration was on her box of tricks. "Please. Listen, Kuniyo—"

Her free hand slapped his face and not lightly. "Tedabara."

He nodded. "Okay, Tedabara, but, please—you have to understand who I am."

Again he met indifference. She didn't care to hear that he'd had a mother over there across the Pacific. She was totally indifferent to America except for the Hollywood she devoured in films and magazines. As to his life, the only time she'd perked up was hearing that his Japanese mother had left the *okiya* to marry her handsome American. That his father was a United States Naval Officer impressed her, but when he'd launched into his grinding seven Jacob years at the mission, his trip to Asahi-Mura, his adventures with Torazo, and his plans to set up a language school she simply clamped her hand over his mouth.

"Just shut up because tonight's your last time—"

Sam recoiled in shock. His wide eyes asked, "He's coming back from Tokyo?"

She pulled her body away from his without answering.

Galvanized onto his feet, he was ready to act this very instant, "That means we're both getting out of here tonight—Now!"

She shifted her position under the glow of the gossamer net. "Like a Hollywood movie?" She shook her head. "No. Much as I adore movies," her retort was sharp, "I know what's real—I know what 'out of here' means." She poured pomegranate syrup over more crushed ice.

Try as he might to change the truth, she was a whore, a woman who'd suffered the world's cruelty. He'd heard his rickshaw brothers talk about their whores and he had no reason to think her life before the Arabian Nights and Kodo had been different from the others. One more little girl from a dirt-poor farm and a drunken father in some village like his mother's, Asahi-Mura, another little girl sold into slavery and prostitution. She'd been able to retreat into fantasy. Yes, she was a whore. She belonged to this Kodo. It broke his heart to admit the truth. If she allowed him another night it must be here within her private world. Loving her meant getting her out of Auntie's and away from that damned rich and powerful Kodo. He took her face in both hands. "Look at me. Tell me the goddamn truth. I know you love me or you wouldn't have told Auntie to let me in—"

"Shut up or get out!"

"I'm here. That proves you love me as much as I love you. You're mine—"

She wrenched from his arms and escaping her cocoon, sprang to her feet displaying herself more boldly naked than ever before. "Mine?" She spat the word running her hands over her body. "This? Yours? Who the hell do you think you are? No one will ever say that to me! Ever." Tedabara's anger was shining with sweat. "Get out!"

He didn't move.

"You got wax in your ears, rickshaw boy?" This wasn't Tedabara. Gone was every trace of fantasy and make-believe, exotic elegance. "You deaf? You didn't hear me tell you to get the hell out!"

"You know I won't ever leave you." By now he too had left the gossamer net and was crawling to her and pressing his face up between her legs. "Please. . . ." He was breathing hard and she allowed him her body and beating heart. His lips spoke to her skin. "I'm going to marry you!"

At his words she broke and lit a cigarette. "You'll leave tonight but before you go, I wouldn't say no to some Chinese food. That is—if you can learn to keep your mouth shut."

His silence swore he wouldn't say another word.

"With all your talk about being rich you haven't even brought me one single present. Not so much as a *castera* you know I like."

"I will. Right now. Right this very minute—"

He knew very well this Portuguese sponge cake was a test. He also knew she didn't give a damn about the cake. She was ordering him to give her a tribute purchased from one of the most expensive shops in town.

She crossed the room to the Victrola and, lifting the records one by one, pretended she was considering which to play next. For Sam, simply to gaze at her nakedness seized him with such fierce need he knew in his bones that if he had to, he'd go out and buy all the *casteras* in the world. "You're going to marry me."

Without looking at him she put the record on the turntable and wound the machine. The needle touched off a whiny American song, *For Me and My Gal.* She picked up her cigarette. "Marry you?" she scoffed. "Me? I'm not like all those other Japanese bitches—stupid wives, no better than slaves. I'll never be a wife and never again will I be like those cunts in this house. Not after I buy myself from Auntie."

"I love you. I'll always love you—"

"Shut up." She sounded hard and her eyes flashed. He grabbed her wrists and kissed both her hands. A hint of a smile melted some of the hardness from her face. For a moment she looked young, perhaps only a little older than when she was brought to the city. In her eyes he saw he was her fantasy, her Greek statue. She raised a hand to his lips and turned, lifting the mosquito net. Her look said if he would shut up and obey her, they still had the rest of the night.

CHAPTER THIRTY-NINE

Without his rickshaw he rushed to a shop so elegant it called itself a patisserie. Carefully bearing Nagasaki's most costly sponge cake and wild to reach Tedabara, he sprinted across the Shianbashi Bridge into the Maruyama.

At Auntie's gate his heart stopped. He was looking at an automobile of the most tremendous size, bigger than any he'd ever seen in Japan. Hot sweat turned to ice. This dragon—an American Marmon—was having its scales polished by a uniformed chauffeur in white gloves. His world stopped. This monster could only belong to the hated Kodo, back from Tokyo. Kodo was inside with his Tedabara right now.

"Goddamn you, Kodo—you touch her and I'll kill you! She's mine!" His bold challenge ripping from his heart reached no further than himself. He ducked into shadow, watching the porch when a restaurant delivery boy jingling his bicycle bell brought a slave rushing out to tell him where to carry his trays. She was the same pathetic little creature, scarcely more than a child, who'd been scrubbing the bath after Tedabara had Old Hag fired. Sam raised a hand signaling her. His presence so alarmed her she pretended not to see him. "Please," he hissed, "please, come over here!"

Too terrified to step down from the porch she left Sam no choice but to dare cross a few of the flagstones. "Please! Help me. I know he's here so I'll be careful. Tell Tedabara I love her—that I'll be back!"

The little child's hands covered her face and she shook her head. No. She was saying she wasn't brave enough to carry messages. Sam looked down at his enormously expensive sponge cake, tribute, but now a token of defeat. He set it down on a flagstone. "Not for Tedabara," he whispered, "for you."

Retreating into the hot night alone, locked in silence, no one in the Maruyama heard him open his mouth screaming for his Tedabara.

Four more agonizing nights he crossed the bridge into the pleasure district. Four more nights he stood alone in the dark under flickering bats cursing Kodo's monster car. He told himself that like magic, on the fifth night the Marmon would be gone. It was more than magic, a miracle.

To hell with caution. He burst in and ran down the hall. She was alone and naked spooning shaved ice into herself. The face he adored was bare of make-up. More good news. If Kodo was coming she'd be painted and ready for him. Her electric fan stirred her hair. She made no sign she was surprised to see him. He dropped to his knees.

"I thought I'd die," he gasped.

"But you didn't—"

"Is he coming back tonight?"

"If he was do you think I'd be crazy enough to let you in? He's gone back to Tokyo to buy off more politicians."

"What does he do?"

"He makes money."

"And I make love."

Her eyes told him the answer wasn't too bad and he'd be permitted to lick plum syrup from her wet lips.

"Admit it! He's nowhere near as good at making love as I am. You want me every bit as much as I want you!"

"Just a boy?" the seductress again, assessed his young body. "No expert at making love, but amusing—"

"I could kill you for that." Damn her! Yes. Maybe he had been a green kid, a fumbling boy that first night in the Tiger Room, but since then they'd made love thirty-one times. She dropped her ice and pulled him to her.

CHAPTER FORTY

Three nights later Sam rushed through Auntie's house to burst into Tedabara's Arabian Nights fantasy. Naked in the heat and mending a tear in the mosquito netting, she scarcely looked up with a glance of welcome. Undeterred, he dropped his *happi* jacket in a kind of dance, shucking his *fundoshi* to be as naked as she was and pull her to him. She didn't glance up from her sewing. "Oh," she sighed with the world-weariness she'd affected the first time he'd returned aching for her body. "So it's you again."

His arms went around her, but she didn't rise, seeming intent on the gossamer net.

"Careful you don't get stuck with the needle." He hated her when she played this damned game. Why this pretense that she hadn't been waiting, her blood pounding for him with the same fever he felt for her? Was this some new kind of Hollywood-inspired enticement? He wanted her. He knew she wanted him. "No more games. I love you and you love me and I can't get enough of you—"

"When did I ever say I loved you?"

"Then say it now. Right now." He drew her to her feet and held her tight but nothing in her lovely body was yielding to him. He lifted her chin to peer into her eyes. At a loss he breathed, "What's wrong?"

"Let go. I'm trying to mend this net—"

"To hell with the net."

She twisted from his arms.

"Tell me what's wrong!" Without answering she returned to her sewing, leaving him more at a loss than ever, staring at her pretending to concentrate on her sewing. "Kuniyo—" quickly he corrected himself to maintain her fantasy—"Tedabara, my Tedabara, what's happened since our last time? I've never seen you like this. Please, look at me." Without raising her eyes she maintained the pretense that her sewing demanded all her attention, leaving no memory of their fierce love they'd shared till tonight. "Tell me. What's wrong? Tell me."

She didn't raise her eyes from her sewing. In a voice without love, but with a trace of worry close to fear, she said, "If you knew what was good for you, you wouldn't be here—"

"Being with you—except for you, where else in the world would I be?"

"As an American or a Japanese?"

"Don't do this. This is me—Sam. Sam who loves you."

She rose and pushed past him and he thought she was going for the Box of Tricks. Instead she found a black case. "We'll see how Japanese you are when you say you love me. You'll prove it the way Japanese lovers have for centuries—"

Naked, he stood with open arms. "Don't I prove I love you every time I come here?"

"Show me you trust me completely the way a real Japanese would. That means do exactly what I say."

"Go ahead," he said prepared for anything. "I'll prove it—"

"No more talk." She pushed him down till he was spread naked on the floor. Lifting himself up on one elbow he saw her unsnapping the black leather case. She took out a shining steel needle half a foot long. She wiped its wicked point with a square of silk. "Stay down flat." He obeyed and could see enough that she was polishing the long needle, preparing for some secret rite between Japanese lovers. Holding the needle she took a deep breath and shoved him flat, holding him motionless by straddling him with her bare knees. Giving his left ear a twist she turned his head and pinned the right side of his face flat on the floor. Matter-of-factly, she announced as if this were the name of the test, "You have wax in your ears."

What kind of a ritual game was this? The sharp needle had him feeling distinctly uneasy but eager to prove his love. He was her captive. "Stay perfectly still," she warned, and her serious tone filled him with fear, his heart beating with alarm at what use she was going to make of that terrible thing.

"Don't move," she clamped him tighter. He flinched when he felt the steel tip entering his ear canal. "Don't move!" Holding himself rigid, not daring to breathe, clenching himself motionless, the needle probed deeper. One slip of her hand and steel would pierce his brain. Other than breaking out in a sweat of terror there was nothing he could do now but lie perfectly still, shut his eyes and pray.

"Don't move—"

His life in her hands, the ultimate test of intimacy, he was fighting fear to stay alive by putting absolute trust in his lover. Apparently this was a traditional Japanese ritual between lovers. Naked on the floor, how much of him was fighting to be more Japanese than American—trusting his lover with his life. He gasped, "Does he—Kodo—let you do this to him?"

"Shut up and don't move."

He felt her thigh muscles lock tighter against him, her face and breath hot on his neck. Shutting his eyes he coiled his hands into fists feeling the needle reaching deeper. Deeper. Closer to his brain. Now she was the one holding her breath.

"Jesus—" a careful cry crept out long past the moment he couldn't bear another second of such absolute rigidity against the needle. Her legs unlocked. She sank back on her heels passing before his wide-open eyes the long wicked needle skewered with a dab of amber wax.

He was alive and struggling to rise.

"Now the left." She twisted the ear she'd finished and turned the other side of his face to the mat.

"Jesus," he croaked. She pushed him down.

"Don't talk. Don't move." He held his breath feeling the needle moving deeper inside his ear telling himself in desperation to take his mind far, far away to a baseball field on a rainy day in Bremerton seven years ago. It was a misty day across the ocean from Auntie's brothel when up through the floor he sensed footsteps outside the hall panel. No maid had such a heavy tread. Pinned helplessly he heard the panel sliding open. Steps became heavy thuds. He smelled smoke. A cigar. With his face on the floor he saw a shadow crossing the room. As the cigar smoke became heavier the shadow spread. An enormous presence was filling the room.

Down on the tatami, locked between Tedabara's knees, he saw black silk stockings, a man's feet. Dark blue trousers rose above him as gigantic as tree trunks. Not daring to gasp his shock, the needle still held him, but it was not the only danger. In this moment everything he'd come to fear most in the world stood over him in this room.

Tedabara slowly withdrew the needle, unlocking her legs, settling back on her haunches. On the floor Sam's lips worked noiselessly, a muffled call on God, praying this wasn't the hour of his death. The foot in black silk hose caressed his face. Utterly defenseless, he slid his eyes up at the man looming over him.

Of course it was Kodo. He seized Tedabara's long needle and, giving Sam no chance to scramble out from under him, the man's foot pressed his shoulder down into total helplessness. Feeling the needle pricking the skin over his thudding heart he shut his eyes and waited. One thrust and he'd be dead. He felt his bowels lurch. If he was about to die he prayed to die without soiling himself.

From flat on the floor he opened his eyes and saw Kodo in a three-piece suit of blue-striped English tailoring. Broad shoulders merged into a short bullneck glistening in a celluloid collar. From below his features looked heavy, a flat nose above full lips, wide in a snarl. Dark eyes flashed under black brows in a furrowed low forehead under black hair combed straight back from the glowering face, ferocious as one of the Japanese wooden temple-guards pop-eyed with rage.

Kodo kept his captive from wrenching out from under the steel as his black stockinged foot increased its pressure against Sam's neck.

And Tedabara? From what he could glimpse she was hurriedly

pulling her *yukata* over her nakedness, while trying to creep into a corner hiding her face. Her young lover, whose trust she'd betrayed, lay naked on the floor awaiting death. Instead of striking, Kodo appeared to be drawing a white business card from a gold case and dropping it on the bare, young chest.

Kodo drew on his cigar, then speaking for the first time, an order to Tedabara. "Get over here and read it to him!"

Clutching her *yukata* around her, she crawled over and plucked the card from Sam's chest. In a small voice she read, "Koichi Kodo."

"Louder," Kodo barked.

She continued in scarcely a whisper. "Kodo Koichi, Chairman of the Board, BlackStar Construction and Bay Trading Corporations, Nagasaki and Tokyo."

Kodo sprinkled cigar ash down on his captive. "So he knows who he's dealing with." Sam clamped shut his eyes. Were these the last words he'd hear before the needle pierced his heart?

Still alive, Sam raised his eyes meeting hers glittering with tears desperately begging him to understand before she bowed her head, "I didn't tell him."

"No." Kodo intercepted her silent cry. "She didn't have to tell me. Not me. Not when a man's woman has another man's stink on her and jumpy with nerves at what she's been up to. You want proof? Tell him how I proved I knew. Bring me your Box of Tricks." Still holding the naked youth he opened the box Sam knew so well and was digging into its miracles. "So—here we have it." He dangled his proof. "This green ribbon. Not from one of our games, but here it is, still wet from use." He swung it over Sam. "Want to smell yourself?"

Proud of his powers of deduction, he indulged himself. "If you were Japanese you'd be dead by now—dead in a way all Nagasaki would be talking about for years. But you are American." He turned his head for another angle considering his prize. "You look American. And in our little test I had her put you through we found out just how Japanese you can be."

"Whiskey!" Kodo's rough voice barked. "Two glasses." His foot lifted but his needle still teased Sam's nipple. Tedabara rushed to set a bottle of Johnnie Walker Black Label and glasses on the low table. She scrambled to the ice chest, but Kodo stopped her, snapping, "How many times do I have to tell you with Scotch, no ice."

With shaking hands she poured Kodo's drink, which he held while assessing his captive. He signaled her to pour a second drink and press it into Sam's startled hand. In one surprisingly graceful move Kodo lowered himself and sat cross-legged on the floor, studying his gaijin. He clamped his cigar in his strong teeth, still holding the needle in one hand and raising his glass with the other. "*Kampai.*"

The foot rose from Sam's shoulder but the needle tapped his breast. Tedabara shot Sam a frantic look begging him to rise enough to return the toast, but his shaking hand failed to raise the glass. Before she could creep back into her corner Kodo grabbed her wrist. Now obedient as Sam had never seen her, she knelt beside Kodo and lowered her eyes. Kodo smoked. He drank. He chuckled: "Welcome to Tedabara's world of the Arabian-Nights. My Tedabara loves the movies. American movies. You like the movies?"

Sam streamed sweat. Facing that needle and instant death he couldn't answer. Kodo drank. "American and you don't like Scotch whiskey?" Sam struggled to pull in his first real breath and managed to get the glass to his lips.

"From Scotland. I prefer Scotch to bourbon whiskey from your own country." Sam could see Kodo was displaying himself as the host, completely at home and in command in a world for which he paid every yen. He raised his heavy bottom enough to break wind. A sweep of his cigar was another order to Tedabara. "Bring the bottle." Kneeling on the cushion beside him she kept her head bowed. Sam's host spoke, his voice, rough, a series of grunts Japanese men use with other men. "Tedabara tells me you are eighteen." It was a question. Sam nodded, too paralyzed to answer with his own rough form of masculine Japanese.

Kodo flicked cigar ashes. "Drink your whiskey."

Sam gulped and felt the alcohol rip through him.

"No wife?"

Sam shook his head. Kodo's steady dark gaze locked on him, demanded more. "Nothing being arranged?" He knew the answer but was so completely in control he allowed himself irony. His heavy lips spread. "Answer me. No wedding plans?"

"No."

Kodo's cigar hand reached over and drew Tedabara close and still holding the cigar reached into her *yukata* fondling her breast all the while looking straight at Sam. "Tedabara. Very beautiful, but not wife material." In his gruffness, but without malice icing his voice, he was the host and considering this situation in which the three found themselves. "Any man I respect would kill for far less than has gone on in this room." He downed his whiskey and with a nod motioned Tedabara to refresh both glasses. "She tells me the women of this house consider you exotic—handsome. A Greek statue that makes them think about sex." Sam stared at his whiskey.

"You agree?"

He was close to inaudible. "I don't know many women."

"What about young American women?"

"Don't know any. I'm Japanese."

"But Tedabara tells me you are without a *koseki*."

"Oh, God," he cried to himself, "Tedabara's told him everything." Kodo was looking across his glass, assessing his young man. "Speak English for me."

Sam held himself silent.

"Speak English!" The command was an order a man gives a child. Sam heard himself, a trained, callow schoolboy:

"Four score . . . and seven years ago, our fathers . . . our fathers brought forth upon this continent—"

"Lincoln Abraham." Kodo smiled and turned to Tedabara murmuring in Japanese. "Our *ainoko* learned that in school in the United States. Good. He has not forgotten his English." He turned again to Sam. "Tedabara tells me your Japanese mother is dead. And your American mother as well. Is it true your American father was an officer in the United States Navy. What rank?"

Sam hated himself, hearing him saying. "By now maybe an admiral."

"Maybe? Admiral or not, does that mean he is dead?"

"I don't know," Sam muttered.

"No?"

"No."

"You are proud of the name Pinkerton?"

"Of course—"

"Yet she tells me you have not heard from this Pinkerton father of yours for many years. After your American mother died you came to Nagasaki looking for your Japanese mother and her family."

"Jesus," Sam muttered to himself. Was there nothing she hadn't told him? Not even a glare of hate at her could be enough to show his heartbreak at how she'd betrayed him.

Kodo, in a businesslike way, continued. "You have no one." Over the rim of his whiskey glass Kodo was studying his every reaction. He began his assessment. "You are tall. You look healthy. You know English, but not much else. Still, if your father's an officer the family has standing and it is possible you may be intelligent. You speak Japanese—of a kind. Nothing, of course, that will ever get you invited into any proper Japanese home. You attend a university?"

"I'm a rickshaw man."

"Who reads dictionaries." Kodo chuckled. "Tedabara and I have decided no more dictionaries for you."

Sam was gathering strength to blurt out his challenge with the abandon of a man facing death with nothing to lose. "Whatever she did you made her do. She loves me."

Kodo chuckled with his hand feeling deeper into Tedabara's kimono, murmuring in a confidential voice he nevertheless intended his captive to hear. "He's asking himself how a rickshaw boy with no family, no education—an *ainoko*—can ever live in Japan."

Kodo drank. "Yes. Perhaps we can make him useful to us."

Sam moved, rocking back on his buttocks squirming away from the needle. He clamped his arms across his chest attempting to defy the man. Tedabara's low whisper, the first time she'd spoken to him, she was begging. "Please. Do what he says."

"Or he'll kill me?"

Kodo's hand crawled deeper into the woman's gown. "Tell him if he insists on being a stupid rickshaw boy all his life, he chooses not to live."

Tedabara's voice was a scrape of raw fear. "Listen to him."

Kodo downed his drink. "From now on you will do exactly as I say or my people can provide you with an unusually painful death." His hand left Tedabara's breast and he stubbed out his cigar. "For your sake it is best if we can avoid that."

From his vest he drew a gold fountain pen and picked up his fallen card and scrawled an address. "My tailor. Start with him." He wrote. "Time and place. An appointment you will wish to keep. My people will see to that." He capped his pen, and crushed Tedabara to his side. "Yes. We will see what our young man—American or Japanese—looks like when he's cleaned up and dressed like a gentleman."

With mock formality Kodo presented the card with two thumbs. Sam could only stare at Tedabara, bewildered, utterly at a loss. This elegant Japanese behavior—was it the mockery it appeared? No. Not with this powerful man. It was real. "Time and place." Kodo announced. "Now, young Mr. Pinkerton, you will leave us. Say goodbye to Tedabara. You've seen her for the last time. Tell him, my Tedabara, tell him to get out of here and do what I say and never come back."

CHAPTER FORTY-ONE

Apparently he was still alive. At least he was slowly dragging his empty rickshaw back to the stable, even oblivious of Tanooki blocking the door. The Badger, his broken teeth bared, gave a fierce animal snarl of triumph. "Leave the rickshaw right there. Now I can finally kick your fucking *ainoko* ass out of here."

Sam, still back in Tedabara's facing death, naked, heard not a word. Every step leaving her he'd struggled for some way to deny she'd betrayed him. He'd give anything to believe that, to forgive his love.

He realized Tanooki was reaching for his iron bar. Had orders from Kodo already reached the rich owner of the stable? Kodo's power would explain Badger's triumphant brandishing of this iron bar, kicking out the outlander he'd always hated, giving him no chance to say goodbye to Masao.

Tanooki's bar poked at a pile of rags and worn leggings and straw sandals. His bunk had been cleared of all he had in the world. Sam heaved a sigh of relief when his eager search among the rags found his dictionary, his last link to America. With a snarl Tanooki handed over an envelope with two yen, paying off the young gaijin who now belonged to the powerful Kodo. At that moment Kato came lurching up the alley. Eagerly Sam rushed to him. "I'm out of the stable but I have to see Masao."

"Charity ward," Kazuo grunted. "You haven't heard? Charity ward. The old boy took a spill on the Hollander Slope. Tanooki's only happy because his rickshaw wasn't hurt."

Masao in the charity ward? Damn. It was too late to go to him tonight. Picking up the small bundle of all that was his life, he forced himself down the alley to a flophouse—any flophouse would do as long as it wasn't Lady Gray Rat's. All night he lay wide awake, thrashing in his bunk, shaking with fear at the complete control Kodo suddenly had over his life, but suffering more from the heartbreak of his lover's role in trapping him for Kodo. All night was a nightmare without sleep, as he felt the terror of that eleven-year-old American boy in Puget Sound's icy water caught by that riptide sweeping him toward death, this time in Kodo's net. He'd already lost his desperately hard-won place in the stable—the only place he'd won in life. Where could he hide? Not in Japan. Not with the rich man's thugs tracking the gaijin down.

He told himself he loved Tedabara, that once back in his arms she'd explain how that damned farting, powerful Toad had forced her into setting the trap. Maybe it wasn't Tedabara at all who'd set the trap, but Auntie betraying them both. Yes, Auntie. That bitch wasn't above selling anyone, anything.

By lantern-light he studied the card ordering him to the tailor shop tomorrow. Tonight, with his mind racing, he was no nearer to explaining what Kodo wanted with a half-Japanese, half-American rickshaw boy.

Tomorrow finally came, another furnace-hot day baking Nagasaki. Hating the idea of obeying Kodo and his thugs, he'd go to the tailor shop, but the minute he could break free, he'd race straight to Masao.

The address on the card was a tailor shop on fashionable Sofukuji Street. Swabbing himself he squinted up and down the glaring August street and saw what he feared most. A hundred feet away a man certain to be one of Kodo's thugs was watching him.

The ex-rickshaw boy, still in his work jacket, took his first step and entered the quiet shop. He guessed the elegant, wood paneling was meant to look like an English gentleman's club. Brass horse fittings gleamed. The large photograph of an impossibly handsome young man he recognized as the Prince of Wales, huge on the wall. Albums of cloth samples were strewn across tables. More photographs pictured aristocratic young men, preening in front of ancient buildings flying the Union Jack, showing the world what England was wearing.

A bald Englishman, encased in London britches and a butterscotch tattersall vest, plucked at a tape measure hanging around his neck. If the man was alarmed to see this barelegged ruffian of a rickshaw boy he maintained an admirable coolness. Apparently he had no need for Sam to present Kodo's crumpled card. He'd been alerted to the challenge of turning this tall young gaijin man, ridiculously garbed in a *happi* jacket, bare legs and straw sandals, into an immaculate copy of a flawlessly tailored toff in a bespoke suit worthy of London's Saville Row.

Sam found himself holding a glass of port wine while the tailor and his Japanese assistant buzzed like bees around him, busily measuring most parts of his sweaty body. The gaijin with an English accent lifted away Sam's glass of port and with an appointment three days hence, he was released to the blazing street.

He cursed himself for turning chicken. Kodo seemed to want a gentleman. He'd taken the first step. Now he raced to Masao. With shaved ice and pomegranate syrup along with a juicy onion he slumped down beside Masao's Western-style iron bed. He winced at the sight of his old friend bruised and bloody and perhaps even broken. "Masao-San," he dropped his voice to keep his admission between the two. "I think I've got myself into a terrible jam."

"With that cunt you can't stop talking about?"

"Don't call her that. It's not her. It's that shit who thinks he owns her." Who else could he open his heart to but to his only friend in the world?

"Kodo?" Like everyone else in Nagasaki, he knew about the powerful industrialist rumored to have *Yakuza* connections. "What I don't get is that he caught you bare ass with his whore and let you live."

"If you can call it living. That goddamn Toad thinks he owns me." Masao thanked him for the ice but preferred a big bite of onion. "What's your squawk. At least you're still alive." Masao shrugged. "Don't fight it.

The Kodos of this world always get what they want. It's your fate. The gods have already decided—"

"Bullshit," snapped Sam.

Old Masao had seen too much of the world to offer his young friend any advice except to face the world and its hard facts. Sam shook his head. Sam had opened his beating heart and confessed to his only friend that he'd die if he couldn't have his Tedabara.

Masao gave him an old man's look that indicated that forbidden love didn't necessarily have to require dying.

But it was a fact, dammit. He couldn't live without her. With Tedabara there'd be no dressing up like a fake British gentleman. She wanted him naked and sweaty. Could Masao understand that his heart was breaking?

"I'm scared, Masao. Really scared. You can't run from a shit like Kodo. I know for a fact he's got his thugs following me."

Masao had fallen asleep. Sam jumped up, leaving snoring Masao while he raced back to the Maruyama, his blood pounding till he could clasp Tedabara where she belonged. Locked in his arms.

For the next three nights Kodo's American Marmon guarded Auntie's, and no one he could trust appeared on the porch. There was no way to signal and get word to Tedabara that Kodo had already changed him. At the tailors he'd seen himself as Kodo's creature, reflected in a three way mirror, standing in supple leather Church boots impeccably fitted in a dark-brown three-piece suit. His white shirt gleamed under a deep maroon tie in heavy silk, knotted beautifully in the new style favored by the Prince of Wales. A ripple in the fabric of his left shoulder was a flaw the tailor and two minions, mouths sprouting pins, attacked. At last the three in Nagasaki's outpost of Seville Row stepped back allowing themselves a severe look, then a smile of pride at their magic transformation of this roughneck rickshaw boy into a splendid young aristocrat topped off with a hat from Johnston and Murphy and doeskin gloves. The tailor climbed a stool, removed the hat. His comb carefully parted Sam's hair down the middle. Sam's abandoned *happi* jacket, *fundoshi* and sandals he ordered burned, but Sam fought to keep them. At least he'd leave with his bundled work clothes. "No. Now," the Englishman announced, "the two of us go directly to Mr. Kodo!" Sam fought this next step, but the tailor, under a

Panama hat, was already out the door ordering him to walk with him the few streets to BlackStar Construction and Bay Trading Corporations. Offices covering an entire floor of a brick building overlooked the same docks where he'd unloaded hides.

Kodo's office was vast, a wood-paneled suite, like the tailor's shop, another replica of England in Japan. Plate glass windows framed the harbor. In his kingdom Kodo himself looked even more toadlike, but a powerful toad enthroned in a leather chair behind a mahogany desk. A prissy Japanese clerk closed a stenographer's pad, bowed crisply, and backed from the room.

Without a word Kodo rose and circled his prize, assessing his young man he'd found naked on a whorehouse floor. Without rewarding the Englishman with praise, he dismissed him and offered Sam a cigar from a humidor. "Havana," he said.

"I don't smoke cigars," said Sam.

"You do now."

Sam held his cigar and watched Kodo trim and pierce his Havana with precision instruments from a silver tray. Like a trained monkey he assiduously followed Kodo's cigar expertise, especially careful, like Kodo, not to remove the band. They smoked. "Four o'clock tomorrow afternoon," Kodo announced. "Hotel Bellevue. You will meet with Mr. Ono where he will arrange an English high tea with the most highly honorable young lady you will ever meet."

With no clue to what this order might mean, Sam vowed not to leave this office till he got up his courage to demand Kodo explain to what he was being sentenced. Before he could speak, Kodo's cigar dismissed him. His second Kodo-San meeting was over.

Damn. It was still there, Kodo's black dragon of a Marmon guarding Auntie's house, filling his world. Damn this dragon of a black car and damn him for being inside with his Tedabara doing god knows what from the box of tricks he was putting her through, while holding him powerless. From the shadows he glanced around for any sign of Kodo's thugs. At the sight of Auntie crossing the porch he drew further back. She was dressed for the street and at the moment she stepped into the garden he moved from hiding and grabbed her wrist. She didn't struggle. A woman who'd been treated as roughly by life as she had was too hard to act anything but annoyed, at this tall young lovesick gaijin. She spat, "Do I have to tell you it's worth your life to be seen here?"

"Kuniyo's so scared of him he made her set the trap. Goddamnit, tell me what he wants with me—"

She wrenched her wrist from him. "Ask him yourself." She tamed a black snake of hair that had escaped her tight helmet of dyed ebony. "But you don't have the guts. Get this through your head, *Ainoko*. Stay away from Kuniyo and stay alive."

CHAPTER FORTY-TWO

It was Wednesday, the day Sam was under orders to appear at Ono-San's tea party at the Bellevue. He'd dressed at the *sento*. While staring into the mirror, he found himself close to smiling, forgetting for a moment how he feared his new life. True, he did look handsome in his splendid Western-style clothes with his bronze hair parted down the middle. "Take a look, you fucking Showalters!"

Then he turned away from the mirror. The Snyders and all good Christians railed against indulging in what he knew in his American heart was vanity. All his years of reading the Bible suggested the very real possibility Kodo, if not Satan himself, was here looking into this mirror with him.

He walked to the Bellevue in his Church shoes instead of his straw sandals. In his brown three-piece suit he was the London toff, yet a coward. All week he'd asked himself how he might escape Kodo's net. Masao, the realist, was no help. Auntie had laid down the truth. More than once he'd walked the docks considering a furtive dash onto a ship leaving Japan. But leaving Japan for America where people like the Showalters hated him was no option.

At the Bellevue's front door, handing his hat to a bowing Japanese servant, he discovered he'd lost one of his doeskin gloves. Not daring to be late there was nothing to do but to enter the lobby of mostly Japanese ladies and gentlemen, all as elegantly dressed as he and speaking in hushed voices.

A harp was playing. He was back at Seattle's New Washington Hotel's marble and palms when he realized a tiny man was standing before him in a hint of a bow, a fastidious little man, without doubt Kodo's tea-party host. A tiny hand snapped out a little white fan fluttering before a doll-smooth face with features painted on porcelain skin. Black strands of hair in rows like harp strings across his pate only emphasized his bald head.

His thin little voice used the old-style Japanese form to introduce himself. "Ono Ganjiro." He continued in his eerie kind of English. "I have honor to arrangement for Mr. Kodo."

"I speak Japanese," Sam replied, but the fan folded, prodding him across the lobby and into a small, private room, thick and overstuffed with Western-style furniture. Once the go-between had the young man alone, the fan signaled him into ramrod attention to examine his specimen from combed dark-blond hair to shining brown boots. A suit pocket flap needed turning out, the tie wanted straightening. At the sight of one large, callused hand he stifled a cry of real pain.

"Your glove. Where is your glove?"

"I only have one—"

"One?"

"I must have lost the other."

Ono-San, upset and trembling, sucked in his breath, shutting his eyes and calling on all eight million Shinto gods for intervention. He regained enough of his composure to hiss, in something like English saying, "At all times keep other hand behind your back." The doll-like factotum, having done all he could to salvage this catastrophe, continued to hiss. "Speak as little Japanese as possible. Your accent is totally unacceptable. Come!"

Sam didn't move. By resisting instant obedience he was hoping to show a modicum of independence, some way—even at this late hour— that he might still escape.

"Do not risk keeping our honorable hosts waiting." The fan, Ono-San's social compass, pointed to a tearoom beyond, sparkling with white linen and crystal with delicate flowers quivering under the stir of a revolving ceiling fan. "You are an incredibly fortunate young man that your gods, if you have them in America, have smiled on."

"Who's this lady I'm going to meet?"

The go-between ignored him and began the drill. "You will take tea but little cake. Tiny bites. Do not smoke. Say as few words as you can and those you address to the honorable mother, you must speak very softly." Ono-San and his fan kept his young charge moving across the tearoom and through mahogany doors into a private room. Here the Western style with its oppressive, heavy upholstery and thick velvet drapes was even more oppressive. Sam felt a jolt, an electric shock. Kodo was here, the last person he expected. The hated Toad in his three-piece black suit, expressionless as a Shinto god statue of Toad, was waiting behind a tea table, enthroned in an upholstered wing chair flanked by two women. Following Ono-San's cues, Sam trod softly. He stood at attention and bowed from the waist. He caught only a glimpse of a pale young woman in a soft green Western summer dress sitting beside a thirty-years-older version of herself, a woman with dark hair smoothed back from a face without color, like Sister Ellen, without a hint of make-up.

Sam held his bow. Kodo made no move and, if the two women nodded in return to his formality, it was nearly imperceptible. Ono-San's fan tapped. Sam straightened himself, waiting to be led into the next step of whatever ritual this might be.

He stole his first real look at the young woman. She was a thin little thing perched primly on Kodo's left, eyes lowered, staring demurely down at her white gloves. This meeting was clearly of enormous importance for her. He was vaguely aware of Ono-San speaking in a reverential hush. His quivering respect for the dark-haired, pale woman must mean she was Kodo's honorable wife. Could the young woman possibly be their honorable daughter?

Kodo's daughter?

Ono-San's fan tapped his sleeve, an order to sit. Sam pinched up his trousers at his knees and perched gingerly on the edge of a maroon velvet-upholstered chair. Not yet had he dared look directly at the young woman. While Ono-San chattered, he slid what glances he could. She was no girl, probably five years older than himself, although Sam had always found it difficult to judge ages in Japan. She held her slender body properly, all but motionless, enduring this ritual presentation. Even an ex-missionary lad and rickshaw boy knew enough to suspect she was being displayed in the latest Western fashion from Paris and London. Most of her black hair was tucked under a cloche hat of summer linen with silk appliquéd nasturtiums of exactly the same pale green of her dress. A swoop of soft, dark hair was artfully allowed to escape the hat across her brow softening the thinness of her face. Wispy eyebrows he guessed had been darkened to look fuller and black liner on her lashes was an attempt to make her dark, wide-set eyes appear larger. When she dared raise them, diffidently, they shone with life—her best feature. Her thin lips were blushed with red. The open collar of her pale green silk dress fell in soft folds setting off a string of pearls as white as her short gloves. Sam could see that every care had been taken to present the honorable daughter as a modern girl, artfully coifed and made up, cool and elegant and passably pretty.

Another of Ono-San's all but imperceptible taps of his fan warned his charge that a bare and callused hand risked exposure. With his exquisite politeness the go-between continued to conduct this painfully formal introduction between Sam and yes, Kodo's daughter. Apparently her name was Mayumi. Conversation was called for, but Kodo said nothing. Ono-San and the ladies tried unsuccessfully to include Sam in twittering banalities about Nagasaki's heat wave. Kodo pulled out his cigar case, but at his wife's signal, returned it unopened to his jacket. Without a sound a troop of liveried servants brought high tea on silver trays which they placed carefully on the table. The high tea began with all eyes watching little Mayumi's every move, carefully presiding over the intricacies of lifting sterling silver and filling bone china cups. Ono-San smiled as she continued flawlessly presenting an elaborate assortment of English-style cream cakes, biscuits and thin cucumber sandwiches. And here to mock him and remind him of Tedabara—a *castera*.

Kodo's unblinking frog eyes proudly followed his daughter's meticulous performance as Mayumi maintained her dedication to the imported Englishness of the high tea. Sam, as warned, took tiny bites, but a cucumber sandwich jammed his throat at exactly the moment Ono-San's fan was signaling him to praise Mayumi's beauty and exquisite skill.

Sam summoned all his powers of concentration and like the first time he pulled a rickshaw, he improvised. His requisite first words were to Mayumi, whose eyes had yet to meet his. He complimented her on the subtle color of her pale green silk. With her lowered eyes, Mayumi's expression didn't change, but from her mother he received a tight, formal smile and a slight nod.

Kodo, denied his cigar, gobbled cake.

An enormous silence filled the room. Sam squirmed uneasily. The overhead fan wasn't able to keep cold sweat from trickling down his back. The grandfather's clock across the room announced itself and beat for what seemed endless minutes. Kodo had waited out all the English elegance he could countenance and finally ignored Ono-San and his wife and lit a cigar. Sam, without the offer of a smoke, was totally unaware of the time passing in which he was pretending to make small talk, munch cake he couldn't swallow and sip tea. Unaware of any contribution he was making other than sitting on the maroon velvet cushion, he had no idea the ritual meeting was over until Ono-San's small fan prodded him to his feet. To bow seemed a good idea. The Kodo ladies acknowledged his obeisance with barely perceptible nods. Uncertain as to his next move but remembering to keep his callused hand hidden, he obeyed the go-between's fan and backed away, exiting noiselessly across deep carpets and through the mahogany doors.

Ono-San caught up with him with an order to wait among the lobby's potted palms where a shimmering harp and violin played a subdued version of "Alexander's Ragtime Band." After ten minutes by the lobby clock, the go-between returned with a slit in his face that might have been a smile. With excruciating formality he announced the Kodos were expecting him next Sunday at five o'clock precisely. "This time, their house. I shall meet you here at half-past four. You will, of course, wear a black kimono."

"I don't have a black kimono," he snapped, terrified that things were going too far, far too fast—spinning out of his control, "And besides—"

> *Come on along, come on along*
> *Let me take you by the hand*
> *Up to the man, I'm talkin' 'bout the man*
> *Mmm, the leader of the band*
> *And if you care to hear that Swanee River played in ragtime*
> *Come on and hear, come on and hear*
> *Alexander's Ragtime Band.*

By now Ono-San had vanished.

CHAPTER FORTY-THREE

Sam rushed out onto the street gulping the hot August air, wanting to rip off his Western finery. "To hell with Ono-San and the girl's mother and what's her name, Mayumi. To hell with Japan! To hell with Sato-San's four-year-ago brutal lesson about honor. Most of all, to hell with Kodo. Who did this goddamned cigar-smoking Toad, no matter how powerful or how rich or how threatening, think he was, deciding his future for him?

He sprinted to the *sento,* stripped off his hated three-piece English suit. He hurled aside the choking collar and cuffs. After a soak and a return to his *happi* jacket and straw sandals, he enjoyed a long, satisfyingly happy piss.

It had been eleven days since he'd pulled a rickshaw. He raced with the spirit of the Shinto gods of the wind, one of the *kamis,* to the charity ward carrying two onions and shaved ice and taking the stairs three at a time rushing to his only friend. Inside the shabby clinic the sight of rows of men in pain tightened his heart. He found the old soldier on his iron bed without his glasses, his face still bruised and bloody. He stepped close.

"How are you feeling?" He winced at seeing his friend in such pain. He had to say something before he sat down on the foot of the bed.

Sam was the one blinking back tears at the sight of his old friend fighting pain. He offered the suggestion, "Maybe you should be in a real hospital." He could kick himself for his second stupid remark. This grim charity ward was all the care the broken old soldier would ever hope for. Sam tried cheer. "How 'bout some shaved ice."

"You have an onion. I'd rather have that."

"I brought two. One for each of us." He wondered if any of the other men from the rickshaw stable had come to visit. Here was his only friend in the world lying here in pain, maybe dying.

"You already look a lot better," Sam began. "Hell, you're going to be your old self in no time." He hated hearing himself lying. He offered him the onion but Masao shook his head.

"Now, kid," Masao rasped, "you're going to ask what the rest of us do when you can't pull a rickshaw any more. Don't—"

"If you're not better by tomorrow I'll ask about a hospital."

"Shit. Don't worry about me. In the summer I'm going to sit in the shade and eat green onions and in the winter drink hot sake. I told you I'm set for life. I was in the Army. China. I've got my pension—"

This was the first time he'd ever heard the old soldier lie. "So don't worry about me, kid. Something's eating you. Whatever it is can't be so bad. Not for a kid your age." He reached for the onion and struggled for his first bite. "So what's eating you. Go ahead. You can tell me. I ain't going anywhere." Slowly, he was chewing onion. "This is about that Maruyama bitch who has you so hot and bothered—the one that belongs to Kodo."

"She doesn't belong to him goddammit—"

"Don't try to shit an old man—"

Sam held out for a moment, then gasped with a cry, "I'm in terrible trouble and scared to death." Masao put his onion aside and looked over at him. His only friend in the world waited for the truth that Sam could no longer hold back. He described the whole terrifying encounter with Kodo. Masao had to slow him down to make sense of the scene of being naked on the floor with a needle in his ear. Sam's breathing choked his cries. "He's got a daughter—I'm scared to death he's going to force me to marry her."

Masao offered nothing. He was considering what he'd heard up till this moment. Then he said, "Keep going."

"I met her. Her name's Mayumi."

"He needs you," Masao sounded offhand offering the simplest of answers. "That's why he didn't kill you—"

"But I can't—I can't marry her—"

"You'll do what Kodo wants."

"No. Goddamnit." He looked at Masao sucking onion out of his few teeth. He'd run to him and sought help or at least some goddamned sympathy, but his friend was blunt, telling him to face the truth. "At first I couldn't believe it. I still can't." He fought sounding frantic, trying to make sense of his life spinning out of control. "Why me?"

"Kodo's kid. Means she's rich. Old?"

"Not very. Well, maybe twenty-three—"

"That's old. Old and not married. Ugly as sin?"

"Not very pretty, but not ugly. Jesus, now they've got me roped into seeing her again on Sunday. I won't go, Masao. How can they make me marry someone I don't love?"

"Hand me the rest of that onion." Sam put it in his old hand. "Face it, kid. They're rich. When you're rich like Kodo, you think love has anything to do with getting married? Face it, kid. Not just Kodo. Ask any Japanese man of any standing. They'll tell you. If his kid's rich, don't think twice. Marry her. Forget this Tedabara cunt you never shut up about. She belongs to Kodo. Marry his kid and then get yourself some other whore but his."

"Never. Not me—"

"If that's your America talking, you're crazy. You're eighteen." Munching, he shook his gray head. "You want to be forty-one like the rest of us still hauling a fucking rickshaw? Shitting in alleys? No wife. No kids. No money to buy women." He reached across the bed and patted Sam's hand. "Marry Kodo's kid." Masao took another bite of onion. "He didn't kill you. Means he needs you. Cheer up. Kodo's so rich he can fix everything—"

"But," his cry tore from his soul, "why me?"

"You'll find out soon enough—" His friend stifled a cry of pain.

"Some of the ice hasn't melted. You want some?"

"What I want is for you to listen to me. A lot of men in this world have fathers-in-law who are shits—"

"She could marry some rich guy—a baron or a prince or even a Mitsubishi—"

"Kodo's rich but he's not in their league. Everyone knows he's done all kinds of shit, terrible things. Decent Japanese hate his guts." He winced in pain, then went on. "This kid of his. You said his kid was what— twenty-five?"

"Maybe twenty-three—"

"By that age you can bet besides her father being a shit, there's some big reason no prince or baron or Mitsubishi hasn't asked Kodo for her and probably never will. Look kid, I'm not saying she won't make a good wife—"

"I haven't asked her, and I won't." He raked a hand through his damp hair. "This is my fucking life—"

"You can thank Kodo for that." Sam saw Masao shut his eyes fighting pain. He was still with his young friend. "When it comes to life, you think any of us gets the life we'd want?"

"Maybe other guys don't, but goddammit I'm different!"

"That's eighteen and America talking. Whatever Kodo's reason, he's giving you the break of your life—"

"And don't tell me I can't go back to Tedabara—"

Masao grabbed his arm. "You're a good kid. Careful you don't get yourself worse than killed. Forget his whore. Marry his daughter."

CHAPTER FORTY-FOUR

Sam was alone again, crushed and fighting despair. Tonight he faced losing Masao at any hour. He doubted that anyone at the stable would come to say *sayonara.* They lived their lives pulling rickshaws and enduring their daily aches and often suffering until they ended like Masao, smoking and drinking and using the cheapest whores. On Sunday Kodo's tightening web threatened to snare him forever.

An hour later he was hiding in shadow outside Auntie's and cursing Kodo's Marmon, desperate for some way to reach Tedabara and keep from facing Sunday. But he remained in shadow and alone.

Sunday, as it always does, arrived. In the lobby of the Bellevue Ono-San was waiting for him, holding a black kimono. Sam stopped short and forced a deep, determined breath. "Look, all this is going too goddamn fast—"

Did Ono-San hear him? The go-between's fan was pointing at a private room where his charge would change from his brown three-piece Western suit into Japanese silk. "Mr. Kodo has decided—"

"But I haven't, dammit!"

The fan prodded him into a dressing room where, defeated, he suffered being turned into a Japanese gentleman in black silk robes and white *tabis.* Sam stared at a white fan of his own being thrust into his hand. Ono-San handed him a purple silk *furoshiki,* some kind of gift. "Present this to the honorable mother. Very finest smoked mullet roe."

No one in Japan knew more than Ono-San what was appropriate to all occasions, from smoked mullet roe, to the flicking of fans, to the proper transportation to the next rendezvous. The matchmaker insisted they arrive by rickshaw. Two rickshaws.

Sam winced while climbing up on the passenger seat, holding his *furoshiki* in his lap feeling himself a total fraud in black silk, an interloper, but thanking Western and Eastern gods the puller wasn't a man from his stable who'd recognize him.

He'd passed the Kodo mansion many times, a villa with a blue tile roof, one of the new ostentatious estates he remembered farmers out in Urakami vilify as belonging to the new class of war profiteers. Ono-San's carriage was alongside his own, close enough to allow Sam to lean over with a last desperate attempt at freedom. "Ono-San, I'm an *ainoko* and you, of all people, know that's a hell of a lot lower than that rickshaw boy down there."

Ono-San's fan waved away his charge's concern. "Mr. Kodo has decided."

Here it was again, that persistent question. "But why me?"

Their carriages slowed to a stop. Ono-San alighted first. Then Sam. "I have already told you to thank whatever gods you've worshipped up till now. You will close your young face and do exactly—exactly—as I say."

"To hell with you," he muttered under his breath. "To hell with all of you. This is my life. I'll do the deciding."

The white fan, by now the symbol of his fate, ordered him into the vastness of the villa, past a receiving line of low-bowing servants. Shoes off, they crossed what seemed like miles of highly polished floors until entering a twenty-four-tatami room opening on a garden. The fan indicated a vermilion *zabuton*. Sam glowered but sank down Japanese-style, the *furoshiki* at his side, agonized and locked in silence. He told himself that any minute he could still jump up and run. With his legs folded under him, he and Ono-San waited a couple of lifetimes which was probably only a quarter-of-an-hour, with his leg muscles tightening.

Across the room a panel painted with a gnarled pine and a snarling tiger was sliding open. Inside the room beyond were the three Kodos seated in a row, three dolls with the father in a black kimono, his wife in iris-blue silk. Seated between them their daughter seemed to float in a flowing white, persimmon, and celadon-green robe. Nothing Western today. Mayumi's hair was shellacked into the style befitting her years as a virgin, and her face was dusted white, the inheritor of nearly fifteen hundred years of tradition. Sam felt a sense of awe and found it hard, if not impossible, to believe he was playing any role in this escalating series of rituals.

Ono-San prodded Sam forward to approach a black lacquer table facing the family, where the two sank to their knees. Sam was vaguely aware that Kodo's honorable wife accepted his gift of mullet roe without a smile, but an all but imperceptible nod. Apparently the offering was correct, appropriate. Japanese tea was sipped, *o kashi* cakes worthy of the temple altar were nibbled, but little was said. Servants whisked away the tea table and placed a long koto on the mats before Mayumi. Today, without white gloves, her small hands slid back her vast kimono sleeves, taking the greatest care tuning the instrument. Suddenly her little fingers, with pearl nails, coaxed out a plangent shiver of notes.

Kodo pointed his own fan at Sam's ability to sit as a Japanese with his heels tucked under him.

"You see?" Kodo announced. "More Japanese than he looks."

Ono-San and Kodo exchanged significant glances. Silk rustled as the three adults rose, making it elaborately clear they were risking the perils of leaving the young people alone together. What had hardly qualified as conversation among the five, now sank between the two into a drowning silence which filled the enormous room, with Sam avoiding looking directly at Mayumi. The one or two glances he managed to slide in her direction found her eyes lowered. Not once had he caught her looking directly at him. Hands with those little pearl-gleaming nails lay motionless in her lap. One of them was obliged to find the flimsiest line of small talk to keep some sort of exchange afloat. At last, with what Sam felt must have taken all her courage, Mayumi spoke so quietly he almost missed hearing her. "You are very tall."

Nothing suggested itself to him as a follow up to this observation, but now it was his turn. She waited. He squirmed but suggested, "Would you care to take a walk in the garden?"

Mayumi raised her eyes, stricken, unable to hide her shock. In the instant their eyes met, hers faltered and she busied herself rearranging her kimono and dusting her koto with a square of silk. Sam cringed, abashed. Had the idea of a garden stroll been so outrageous that he'd broken some important rule of protocol? He knew enough about the Japanese to know that if he expressed admiration for this palatial house, rules of etiquette would call for protestations from the daughter, denigrating the mansion as totally unworthy. To his surprise he heard himself praising, of all things, her father's car.

"That's a wonderful sedan your father has. A Marmon."

"American," she said, apparently feeling no need to denigrate her father's foreign automobile.

"Do you like to ride in it?" he asked.

She answered. "No. I do not ride in it."

"It is a beautiful car." This girl, close to pretty in her frail way, was searching for words as desperately as he. She gathered her long sleeves and reached for her koto. If she played again, it was an admission of defeat—music being a substitute easier for both to endure than this stillness.

The notes twanged into a melody he recognized instantly. He grinned.

"My Old Kentucky Home," She whispered. "Famous American song."

"Yes."

"Mister Foster Stephen," she said. "You can sing?"

He began shakily, but soon rode the melody. "The sun shines bright on my old Kentucky home . . ." He surprised himself by remembering the words, and Mayumi skillfully matched her plink-plinks to accompany his voice.

He finished boldly. "In my old Kentucky home far a-waay."

She patted her hands together in admiration close to idolatry. "You sing very well. You have been to Kentucky?"

"No. Have you?" He reddened at the idiocy of his question. She stifled giggles by pressing her hands to her face.

"You play very well," he announced.

Her hands waved away too tremendous a compliment.

"I like music," said Sam.

She nodded. She, too, liked music.

At least they were talking. So there was a human being here, a nice pale girl he'd vowed time after time over the last two weeks never to see again. Here he was. Maybe it was his fate to marry and spend the rest of his life with this slender girl. Fate could never stop his burning for Tedabara.

Sam smelled cigar smoke. Kodo strode back into the room leading Ono-San and Mrs. Kodo. The prospective bride having been viewed, having played the koto and exchanged a few words stayed kneeling, her eyes lowered and her hands together in her lap. Sam was still sitting on his heels.

Ono-San's fan touched his shoulder, telling him to rise. Apparently he'd passed the second highly-organized test. The fan tapped again, turning him to the bows of mother. Standing, Setsu-San was taller than her husband. Her hair was jet black with no hint of white. The small face her daughter had inherited was unlined. She wore no traditional white rice powder and no make-up to conceal the dark smudges circling her eyes.

"Young man. Mister Pin-ker-ton." Mayumi's mother spoke for the first time, precisely and very quietly. Ono-San hovered but Mrs. Kodo spoke so quietly Sam leaned closer to hear. "Has Mister Kodo or Mister Ono asked you about religion?"

"No, Ma'am." he confessed.

She glanced at both men. "Then forgive me, but someone must." Her seriousness meant the question was of burning importance to her. "With your American heritage, you are a Christian?"

"I was baptized a Christian." Even speaking the words, he was back smelling calcimine and sauerkraut. Sam found Setsu's eyes peering, searching his face, seeking an answer deeper than words. He waited, sure that now she'd ask if he'd considered embracing either Buddhism or Shinto or as perfectly customary, both. Instead, she spoke with an intimacy no one else had come close to touching in their two meetings. "I have read your Christian Bible." Her small hand waved away any confusion. "Please understand, I am not a Christian. Have you read your Christian Bible?"

"Yes, Ma'am." Armed with the truth he allowed himself a smile. "Every single word of its twelve hundred and seventy-two pages and five times."

"So you are a Christian?"

The truth was he was still deeply uncertain about his position here with Mayumi and the Kodos, but about religion he spoke the truth. "I have to admit I'm not too sure what I am."

"I believe, however, you have a kind heart." She bowed. He was all but her son-in-law. He bowed even lower.

CHAPTER FORTY-FIVE

Ono-San had Sam waiting in Kodo's office in his mansion when the master thundered in brandishing papers and glowing with triumph. "Start planning the wedding." Kodo's cigar glowed red as he waved aside all doubts of the future. He thrust a paper at the old man. ""Fortune-teller's report. And here's the astrologer's. September first is most auspicious. As for the adoption they want me to get my lawyers started on it as soon as tomorrow."

Adoption? This was his life and the two were brushing him aside, deciding on the details of his wedding and now, this adoption. "Wait!" he cried aloud. "All this is going too fast!" The cry went to Ono-San, not Kodo. "Not just the wedding, but—"

The white fan signaled for silence. "You will understand later," Ono-San hissed with Kodo happily rattling his sheath of important papers. "Tell him now," barked Kodo.

"The Honorable Kodo has no son," Ono-San continued. "When you marry Kodo-San's daughter you will, of course, become a Kodo. An Honorable Kodo."

Instead of crying his dismay Sam could dredge up no voice at all. The fan jabbed his breast. "Did I not tell you?" Ono-San, performing at the very top of his profession, reminded the young man, "Did I not tell you the gods are smiling on you?"

"You mean change my name?"

The tiny man swelled with pride. "I advise thanking Mr. Kodo for even considering your entry into such an enormously prestigious and powerful family."

Without consulting him they'd decided on a life for an *ainoko* without a *koseki*—a rickshaw boy here in Japan until now illegally. "Wait!" The two men weren't listening to him. "Wait!" Sam cried. "It's my life. What I do is up to me!"

Kodo's glare through cigar smoke dismissing any further talk from the young man. He had moved on to other plans. "For the Western-style part of the wedding," Kodo was making final plans with the go-between, "the boy will need someone to stand up for him?"

The factotum was thrilled to agree. Even in the matter of the newly fashionable Western-style weddings he was an expert. "What they call a Best Man," he explained. "The groom's best friend."

Kodo chewed on a new cigar he couldn't take time to light. "Since he has no friends, leave that to me—"

"Wait!" Sam cried, "I haven't agreed to any of this—"

Kodo's dead cigar waved away all objections. "Respect!" Ono-San's thin, insistent voice was a knife blade. "Show respect to your new father!"

At his desk Kodo found one of his cards and with a smile of inspiration wrote with a gold Mont Blanc pen. When Ono-San read the card he caught his breath. "Robert Talbot. Perfect!" breathed Ono-San. "Absolutely perfect. I shall contact him immediately."

"I'll do it," Kodo announced proudly. "Young Talbot happens to be a member of my club." From Ono-San's awed reaction Sam sensed Kodo had invoked a magic name. "So who's this Robert Talbot?"

"If you must know," Ono-San was delighted to take a moment to explain Kodo's coup. "Although Talbot-San is an *ainoko* like yourself," his whisper was a hush of respect, "he is of the very highest—absolutely top standing—except perhaps for Glover himself."

Sam had heard of Tomisaburo Glover, the son of the great and powerful Thomas Glover, a Yorkshireman married to a *geisha*. Glover was a partner in the Mitsubishi enterprises. To speak of Talbot in the same breath as Glover himself enshrined him at the very top of top ranks in the Nagasaki pantheon.

Kodo chortled, "His high and mighty old man owes me a favor." He moved decisively, picking up the telephone while his wet cigar shooed the two out of the room.

Outside the office Ono-San and Sam waited in silence till Kodo flung open the door. The man glowed with triumph—"Tomorrow. Ten o'clock—"

"But I just told you, I haven't agreed. No. All this is too fast—"

"The Occident Club. Ten o'clock. Look your best. Now get out."

At the *sento* he breathed a huge sigh of relief getting out of his London clothes. Naked, he gloried in scratching himself, scratching where he couldn't scratch under his Western suit. He was getting back into to his work clothes to visit Masao when two rickshaw men, the wild dogs from the stable, bounded in. The sight of Sam had them barking, roaring with wild and derisive laughter. Sam kept winding his *fundoshi* and ignoring their idiot bursts of laughter and derision. Word of his coming wedding must have reached the stable. The idiot boys couldn't contain their glee and hurling insults. "Your secret's out," Kazuo taunted. "Found yourself what you call a woman, have you?"

"We've seen her at the stable. A really horrible old scarecrow." The wild dogs were all but jumping up and yelping happily and rocking with laughter. What were they talking about? Certainly Mayumi had never been anywhere near the stable. "Your ladylove keeps coming back to the stable looking for you."

"Talk about a hag!" Akio was doubled over with laughter. "An old drunk. Skin and bones with only one eye." The one called Akio grinned maliciously and pretended a shudder of revulsion. They delighted in heaping on more scorn. "Ugh, horrible old thing. But you can thank Tanooki for saving your ass and telling her nobody in the stable knows where to find you." Sam ignored them and took his laundered jacket off a hook. No way could they be talking about Mayumi and trying to insult her. Mayumi rarely left the mansion and would never be seen in a place like the stable. So why were the wild dogs heaping insults? The only sense Sam could make of their derision was their saying the old hag had white eyes. Were they talking about Old Hag—the old crone Tedabara had seen fired from Auntie's?

"So the next time your ladylove shows up, where do we tell her to find you?" The wild dogs were laughing so hard they had to hold each other up.

"If this is you bastards idea of a joke, go to hell." By now he was back in his short *happi* jacket that barely covered his legs. He stepped into straw sandals and left the bath sprinting off to report to Masao more incredible news. "Kodo's adopting me and has even named the day of my marriage and chosen a Best Man I don't know to stand up for me."

The charity ward was crowded. A fallen scaffold at a construction site had filled the ward with many broken and injured men who lay on the floor on filthy futons. He reached Masao on his iron bed, a gray ruin of his sturdy self. He'd brought an onion he put down knowing his friend would never eat it. Was he asleep? His eyes opened and he found Sam whispering, "How are you, Masao?"

"Not so terrible," the old soldier answered with the old words Sam and he had long shared. Masao tried to smile but failed. His voice was weak. "By now you've decided to marry the girl?"

"If I do, will you stand up for me?"

Masao reached out his rough hand and grabbed Sam's.

CHAPTER FORTY-SIX

Going up to the sixth-floor bar of The Occident Club, Sam realized he hadn't been in an elevator since Seattle's New Washington Hotel. On this day in August 1919, he was no longer Huck Finn in knickers with his little brother at his side. Dressed in his brown three-piece English suit he was greeted with low bows from the club's staff, ushering him into a room with vast windows and a view of Nagasaki's harbor.

Thick carpeting and mahogany paneling created an atmosphere that was more London than Japan. A sleek headwaiter continued to bow till his gaijin-looking guest was seated on heavy leather and presented with the *Japan Times*. Before Sam could light his cigarette, the waiter sprang forward with flame.

At the same moment the waiter excused himself, gliding off to bring in a new arrival with a bow even deeper than the one he'd given Sam. This respect was given to a young man in a flawlessly cut oxford gray suit striding nonchalantly into the room, already smoking a cigarette. Sam ground out his own cigarette and rose, smothering his surprise for he recognized the man instantly. Till his dying day he'd remember that afternoon he waited with his rickshaw in front of the Bellevue while this haughty young aristocrat glared in anger at the Western-looking boy pulling that rickshaw. He wondered if he would be recognized under these circumstances.

Sam guessed Robert Talbot to be about three years his senior. Kodo and Ono-San had identified him as an *ainoko,* one of the few half-Western, half Japanese Sam had known. At first glance, he decided Talbot looked more Japanese than he did, but, of course, that was for others to assess. The ease with which he crossed the carpet was a quality Sam considered quintessentially European, and to a lesser extent, American. He was an inch taller than Sam and with his slicked-down brown hair parted in the middle, large, brown almond-shaped eyes, and tea-colored, perfect skin he looked remarkably like Tedabara's photographs of the movie-star, Rudolph Valentino. Sam wondered if they would shake hands, but Talbot did not offer his hand.

"You play tennis, of course." His tone was English and offhand enough to sound slightly bored.

"No."

"Why, for heaven's sake, not?"

"Haven't gotten around to it." He was blunt, knowing better than to attempt to match Talbot's easy sophistication. His host offered a cigarette from a gold case and when he took it he felt sure this polished gentleman was looking nowhere but at his rough, red hands.

"Odd we haven't met here at the club."

"I'm not a member."

"The Wayfarers?"

"I don't belong to clubs." Feeling a sudden need to declare himself a non-club member he began the meeting with a pre-emptive defense. "I'm half-Japanese." Instantly he cursed himself. How could he have been so stupid, so unfeeling as to begin their contrived relationship by alluding to the shared identity, this proud young man was bound to hate.

Talbot's porcelained superiority didn't crack, indeed he sounded admirably offhand. "In your case I might twig to your background, but I doubt if many other Europeans would. As for me, as you see, I look like an English actor made up for the *Mikado.* Always have. My father's a

Yorkshiremen from Liverpool—out here donkey's years when he married my mother. Old samurai people, hers. Satsuma. All that."

Sam began his own full disclosure. "My father was a Lieutenant in the U.S. Navy when he was here in Nagasaki. He married a geisha. No. Not a geisha actually. She was still in an *okiya.*"

"Actually married her?"

"Luckily for me."

"Obviously you look more like your father. I'm told I look more like my mother. It's never been a problem for me. Not among the Japanese who set out to kill one with politeness. Westerners pretend to overlook the fact once they hear one's family owns Talbot and Company."

For all this haughty man's worldliness, Sam felt his exaggerated show of candor might well be a shield to deflect what he knew he faced as the central fact of his life. Talbot spoke through cigarette smoke. "Which doesn't suggest for a minute one considers oneself on a par with his Holiness Glover. Old Tomisaburo. You know Tomisaburo?"

"No."

"Tommy practically owns Nagasaki. Mitsubishi's partner—all that. Nearly the same background as mine, father from Scotland, his mother a geisha." At this moment a waiter brought a pot of coffee. "Take that away. Scotch." Talbot stubbed out his cigarette. "No ice. Your mother's still alive?"

"No."

"You said she was in training in the Maruyama?"

"The truth is, I don't know. Not for sure." Sam doubted he could say anything about Japan and this city Talbot didn't already know. Nagasaki was a small town. Western men, sons of geisha, or apprentices, were rare. Talbot was the first he'd met. The Scotch arrived, no ice of course, and Talbot raised his glass in his role as host, an *ainoko,* but a splendid young member of this club. "So what's this business about your becoming a Kodo?"

"He thinks I'm going to marry his daughter."

"Thinks?"

"I still haven't decided."

Talbot shot a look at Sam asking why he would hesitate. "You have met the girl?"

"She seems very nice."

"Well there it is, then. Arranged marriages. Quite usual out here. For those of us who insist on seeing marriage in the Western romantic tradition, it takes a spot of getting used to. What's the Kodo lass' name?"

"Mayumi."

"Never met her. Not at any of our shindigs. Apparently she doesn't dance or play tennis."

"She plays the koto."

"Of course. Dreadful instrument."

"My Old Kentucky Home."

"Well then," Talbot pronounced with a display of fine white teeth in a dismissively mock show of cheer, "that's a start. Out here marriages have been built on far less." Sam hoped his awe didn't show. Never had he imagined anyone could exude such effortless worldliness.

"He's even talking of adopting me."

"If the young lady has no brothers, of course that's how it's done." Talbot seemed to enjoy educating this naïf to whom he'd been assigned. "Adoption's the common practice here. Makes sense when a family has no sons to continue the name. Of course in this case all of us must treat you as a Kodo with all the perks and responsibilities of an eldest son." He smiled. "Congratulations would appear to be in order."

Talbot waved over a waiter and without asking Sam, ordered two more Scotches.

Sam was searching for some way to open Talbot up enough to ask him questions about the new family he was entering into. "You know Mr. Kodo well?"

"Everyone in Nagasaki knows Kodo about as well as they care to." Sam knew Talbot had come as close as a gentleman could to passing judgment without calling a fellow member of the club an outright shit. His prospective best man waved away a waiter leaning down to ignite another cigarette. "Let's be clear on this thing about me standing up for you as Best Man. I'm here only because my family owes Kodo a favor, and you have doubtlessly seen our Kodo is a man who will go to any length to see his favors returned—" A look of distaste smudged the porcelain face. He'd glimpsed someone entering the bar and interrupted himself with a wince. "Oh, God, here comes that fat fool, Pratt."

An unhealthily pink European was snatching up his own double Scotch from the bar and, with a wave at the two, was inviting his enormous paunch to their table. He dumped his heap of wrinkled white linen into a leather chair. His face looked burned, flamed with eczema. Talbot kept the introduction as minimal as possible. "James Pratt—Sam Pinkerton."

"Scots myself, from Clydesdale," the heavy man wheezed. "Pratt's Drydocks here. Godowns in Hong Kong."

When Talbot explained that Sam was rising in the world now that he'd been introduced to Kodo's daughter, Pratt drew himself closer to the table. "And a damned fine chap your Kodo is." He chuckled conspiratorially. "Bumper, right?" Talbot's smooth face, more a Valentino mask than ever, kept an aloof gaze as their garrulous guest heaved himself closer to Sam, a chance to establish ties with anyone close to the contractor-shipper. "Got to hand it to Old Bumper. He's streets ahead of the rest of us the way he shows the rest of the Japs how to run a business. Right now he could teach all of us a trick or two, the way he's handling those Red union shits down on the docks. Last year the Bolshies were roaring like bloody hell all over this country. In one year alone—five hundred fucking strikes. Bloody hell from Hakodate all the way down here." Talbot's gold cigarette case was already open on the table, and Pratt helped himself to one. "Mark my words, the Reds won't be happy till they ruin this port." He plopped a pink hand on Sam's knee. "Two years ago, they tried to muscle in on one of Bumper's construction jobs. The Inasa Bridge—you know those bloody-huge gigantic piers at either end?"

Talbot cut in. "Don't you think we can spare our bridegroom that rumor?"

"Rumor, hell. I give Bumper high marks for doing only what the rest of us ought to be doing." Sam decided the man's face was a radish red, and in sharing information was only warming up. "His workers were pouring cement when one of those shit Bolshie agitators chose that moment to climb up on a catwalk to wave a red flag and begin his harangue. Old Bumper was right up there behind him when it appears the union sod apparently lost his footing and fell plop into the soup. Still there. Every time I cross the bridge I always think, 'That's one less bloody Red we have to worry about.'" Pratt rumbled and wheezed with laughter. He raised his glass. "To Kodo. First rate chap. Samurai people." He slapped Sam's knee.

"Doubtless, I'll be seeing you, Pratt," Talbot rose, picking up his cigarette case and signaling the waiter to put the drinks on his bill. Sam understood his signal as an escape from Pratt and got to his feet.

"A pleasure meeting you, Mr. Pratt." Overly deferential, he was taking no chances with anyone allowed within the sacrosanct confines of this gentleman's club.

"Give my best to Bumper," Pratt, still sitting, shouted. "Oh—a word to the wise," he added with a chuckle. "Perhaps it's best not to call him 'Bumper' to his face, though he'd not deny it."

Talbot maneuvered Sam from the bar and out of earshot. "One has to be decent to people out here in the East one wouldn't think of letting through the door of one's club in London." After the elevator took them to the street Talbot removed a glove to shake Sam's hand. If he felt scraped calluses he pretended not to notice. "One day when the weather cools, tennis is in order."

"I'd like that. Of course, I'll have to learn." Then, in a sudden burst of honesty—if Talbot was to be his Best Man, and, he hoped a candidate for badly needed friend—Sam felt he had to get out his confession. "You've seen me before but we didn't really meet. I was in the street. These calluses on my hands are from pulling a rickshaw."

Talbot had lived in Japan and England too many years to betray any reaction. Nevertheless Sam caught a look in his dark eyes that said yes, from the first he'd recognized this tall, Western-appearing young man. His Best Man turned to leave but Sam stopped him. "Please, you're the only one I can really ask about this son-in-law business of Kodo's. I mean, why me? I'm not rich like you. Certainly not educated. To the Japanese I'm no one, so why would Kodo want me to marry his daughter?"

Talbot's face showed nothing. "No idea, old man. No idea at all." He hailed a taxi. "About the wedding—Little Ono-San's bound to keep us in touch."

CHAPTER FORTY-SEVEN

He felt his life spinning out of control faster than any rickshaw. Now, under orders from Kodo, he was never to appear on the street in anything other than London-inspired clothes. How could he feel more dreadfully out-of-place than entering the shabby clinic in his finery carrying his shaved ice for Old Masao? At his bed he found his thin mattress rolled up. Old Masao was dead.

With only two weeks before his wedding he was back at Auntie's in hiding from the late August sun. He was studying the house, desperate to find a way past Auntie to his love when he glimpsed the little slave he'd given the *castera* to crossing the porch to water chrysanthemums. To his surprise she saw him and signaled him to wait for her out of sight beyond the front gate. She was pretending to work till at last she was close enough for him to hear her very small voice. "Thank you for the wonderful cake—"

"Tedabara," he whispered. "Tell her I'm here."

With her act of bravery the little thing had outdone herself giving him thanks. Now her tiny hands fluttered, shooing him back in shadow telling him that helping him reach his Tedabara was out of the question. But she didn't leave. She edged closer.

She had a message. From Tedabara? No, so what message beyond her thanks for the cake was important enough for this secret meeting? "Old Hag." He barely heard her question. "Did she find you?"

"Old Hag?"

"She's been looking everywhere for you—"

"You mean that crazy old bat Tedabara had fired?" Yes, a bob of her ragged black hair said that was true.

"She lives at Futaba—" At that moment Auntie's voice cracked out from within the house. Panicked and stifling a cry, the frightened girl fled back across the garden into the house, leaving Sam at a loss with no way to reach Tedabara. Why did the little scrubbing maid think it was important enough to whisper about that crazy old bat who'd crept after him in the dark bath? And a few days ago in the *sento* those wild dogs had flung their mockery trying to humiliate him about the creature.

He held his breath as the thought struck. Old Hag! Was it possible? Could Tedabara secretly have made her their go-between? Why not? It made sense. No one would suspect her of carrying lovers' messages. Of course! What else could explain the wild dogs' jibes about the old crone coming time after time to find him at the rickshaw stable. "Old Hag!"

Where was it that little scrub maid whispered she lived? Yes. The Futaba!

Down a wretched alley, there it was—a wooden gray shack with a tattered lantern and broken *shojis* even more decrepit than Lady Gray Rat's Nest. "So this is where Old Hag goes to die," he told himself. "Hang on for one more day before you croak, Old Hag, while I pray to God you get me to Tedabara!"

He drew back the torn *shojis* on a barefoot woman coughing straight into his face. Her watery eyes were wide with surprise to see anyone so young and healthy at her door. This disheveled fury in a *yukata* flapping with agitation was the landlady. Glaring. What in hell did this gaijin dressed in Western finery want?

"I have to see . . ." Sam faltered, for he didn't even know Old Hag's name. He tried again. "I'm here to see the woman who used to be the scrubwoman at Auntie's in the Maruyama." If she'd heard him she didn't blink she'd understood. He began again, this time slowly. "She's very old. Thin. Ugly. The one who scrubbed the bath at Auntie's."

"She's drunk."

Sam yelled directly into the crumpled face. "I've got to see her! Please!" The landlady's hands waved his off, violently shaking her head, fighting him to draw shut the broken *shoji* . Sam held the doorframe and pushed another coin, then two more till she shrugged. With a thrust of her sharp chin she was telling him to wait out in the street.

How long was she going to keep him waiting? At last the sound of shuffling feet brought him to the door that slid open. The landlady was prodding a lurching gray bundle of rags. Yes. Here she was. Old Hag with her one eye and the other as white and dead as an American schoolboy's aggie marble. Old Hag who'd been so desperate to find him. Her mass of wild and tangled white hair flopped down on her chest.

"What's wrong with her?" Sam gasped.

"Drunk." The landlady scoffed, summing up a life. Old Hag's head wobbled but slowly rose, attempting to focus her one good eye on the tall young man. Without warning, in rage, she lurched, clutching at him, seething with anger. He shrank back expecting her to spit in his face. Instead, her voice rattled, then shrieked. "Go—go back to your damned ship." A hand, nothing but bones, swiped out to banish him from her one eye. "Go away!" Suddenly she bent, shaking with sobs. "More than two years she waited for you . . . now you do this to her—Pinkerton bastard!"

Pinkerton! His heart stopped. Even in the woman's slurred drunkenness, Sam realized she could only be talking to a man she remembered—a U.S. Navy Lieutenant—Pinkerton! His father! He forced himself to wait. Was it possible, really possible, she was the secret to everything for which he'd come to Japan? Again her breath rattled before she burst into tears. "Pinkerton." Her hands waved like claws, banishing his father across the sea. This crazed, sobbing old woman with only one eye was looking at his father.

He reached out to her, but at his touch lurched her wildly from him. She fell. Catching her bones, he begged, "Please—"

Her head lolled. An arm flopped. She sank in his arms. Was she dead? The landlady's shriek held them both. "Satisfied? I told you she was drunk." Holding her, Sam was crouching down to peer into Old Hag's face. "No. Not my father. You know who I am—"

The bones came to life fighting off the past, banishing his face—his father's image, from her sight. Grasping her thin shoulders, he turned to the landlady with a cry ripping from his heart. "She knew my father! She knew my mother!" Old Hag was writhing, fighting him. "Hold still," he cried, "I'm taking you to a hospital—" With a fierce jerk she slipped from his grip and plunged back into the dark house.

She was gone.

Sam slowed his racing mind enough to stop the other woman before she, too, was gone behind the *shojis*. "I'm not leaving here. Don't let her have any more to drink. I'll wait till she's sober.

CHAPTER FORTY-EIGHT

He waited all night. For the three longest hours of his life he agonized before the door rattled back and the Old Hag, crazed, rushed out at him. Her white hair that had been so wild had been pulled back tight across her skull. Her tattered gray *yukata* was a sack with bony claws snatching out at him. In such stumbling excitement she couldn't form words. Drawing her close, he led her down the alley to a hole-in-the-wall filthy tea place. At last, after two pots of tea, she was calm enough to scrape his hands and whisper that she, Old Hag, who knew his mother, had a name—Suzuki.

It took another pot of tea and more sweeping through the cobwebs of years of misery fuddled by last night's sake. In her hangover, for minutes at a time, she fell into a trance when Sam feared he was losing her altogether. Then came more stares, long, loving stares of incredulity at this handsome young man before her. Then her whispers:

"My Butterfly's son." She wasn't lost to him nor he to her. They'd both found one another.

"Last night—I thought you were—"

"I look like him? My father?"

"At Auntie's—you remember in the bath? I was seeing a ghost—"

"Why didn't you say something?"

"When everybody already thinks I'm crazy? At first I was sure that I really had to be bats. You weren't just another huge gaijin with a prick as big as his—but too young to be that bastard Pinkerton. But here! In Japan! You had to be his son." She nodded and kept scraping his hand. "I had to keep it secret before I could get to you—then your Kuniyo—that Tedabara—whatever such filth calls herself—had Auntie driving me out of the house." Her other hand, nearly skinless knuckles, rheumatoid knobs, scrubbed her good eye. She shuddered. "That Kodo. You cannot possibly know what a terrible man he is."

"More tea?" Sam poured but spilled tea putting aside the terrible feeling he shared with her about the man taking over his life. She reached out intending to pat his cheek, but her old hand dropped. He went back to the tea. "Or would you rather have sake?"

"Of course!" Then, as quickly as her cry, her hand slapped the idea away. "No. No more sake. Ever. Can you believe—can any of the gods believe—I've found my Butterfly's boy." In his hand he took hers, dry and brittle as an autumn leaf, to share their miracle. "This old woman sitting here in front of me," he told himself, "her hand in mine, has known me from the minute I was born."

"Yes." Her thin shoulders shook. She was laughing. "I used to hold you out over the garden iris jiggling the shit out of you to save on soiling diapers." Dry lips kissed his hand. "You sure you don't remember Old Suzuki?"

He remembered tatami. Perhaps even the feel of silk covering his eyes but nothing of this thin, gray old woman so close to being a ghost. The miracle was that she remembered him and was the closest he'd ever come in this world to being with his mother. "Suzuki," he began but choked back tears.

She nodded and kissed his hand. "Butterfly's Suzuki." She studied his face, wet with tears, his gaijin face searching for some sign of her Butterfly. "I was her maid, you know. More than her maid, her only friend, when she had no friends."

"Thank God—since the bath at Auntie's—you kept looking for me."

"Ben-ja-min Frank-rin Pin-ker-ton," she nodded with each syllable of the name.

"No. My name's not Benjamin. My American mother saved that to name my little brother after my father. I'm Sam—Samuel Adams Pinkerton, the name of the boat they took me to America on—I'll explain later. Now we have all the time in the world." His young hand and her skin and bones tightened on each other. More tears, happy tears, flowed.

"You couldn't forget tatami. Learning to walk, falling down on them—"

He interrupted. "What was my name?"

"You didn't have a name. Not yet. Your mother insisted we wait for your father to come back to her before we named you." He watched her smile fade and knew she was back in the house on the hill with his mother looking down into the harbor, waiting for her love, his father, to return.

"He came back," Sam's whisper sounded like a prayer.

Suzuki pulled back her hand. Sam felt her anger. "If you call that coming back—" Her face tightened with hate. "He came with her—that tall yellow-haired *kappa* with glasses who took you away from my Butterfly."

"You'd think I'd remember that," he whispered.

"You were two years old when she said goodbye to you . . ." With a sudden shudder Suzuki straightened herself and swiped her nose with her sleeve. "That son-of-a-bitch bastard Pin-ker-ton. Out there in the garden under the pine tree with My Butterfly inside the house tying a silk over your eyes so you wouldn't see what she was going to do. Seppuku. Her only way . . ."

With a gasp of hope he asked, "Do you have a picture of her?"

"Lost it years ago. Now you want to know if your mother was beautiful. Everyone said she was, but the truth is, she had a *tengu* nose like the one she gave you. Too long for a Japanese. The rest of you looks like him—that bastard."

Fired with sudden inspiration he blinked back tears. "I know where she lived—where you lived. Her house with the pine tree . . . we can look at it from that garden. Let's go. Right now. Right this minute. I'll get a rickshaw for you—"

She was on her feet, as excited as he. "Hell," she huffed, "I can walk."

CHAPTER FORTY-NINE

"I used to come here all the time, but haven't been back in years. Too many tears." With Sam at her side she stood at the gate under the tall pine tree looking at the garden. Gaijin's now. They're letting the moss dry up. And that camellia needs trimming." She turned away. "I need sake, but I'll settle for more tea."

Arm in arm he led her into the garden and they sat on the flat cushions both trying not to keep from looking across the way at the house under the tall pine tree. The day was hot and still, without a breeze. For a quarter of an hour neither breathed a word, imagining they were back in that house with Butterfly. At last Suzuki sighed and unfolded the corners of a purple *furoshiki.* "*Mochi,*" she announced. "I don't like it, but it was your mother's favorite. You liked it, too."

Sam understood. This was a ritual. His first taste of the gooey rice paste was to be his open sesame to take him back sixteen years. He nibbled the gooey blob and she watched him closely. Was he back there across the way, two-years-old crawling on the tatami?

"Good," he lied. The rice paste wasn't taking him back to that house. He was still here in the garden with his mother's friend.

"*Mochi.* Your bastard of a father wouldn't even try it." She sucked her few teeth. "Is he? Dead?"

The tasteless goo stuck in his throat. He swallowed hard. "The truth is I don't know."

"Your own father and you don't know? What kind of a father is that not to tell you if he's dead or not?" One eye was enough to tell her how stricken he looked, and she backed off, easing her attack. "And that other bastard—that molting old crow. What was his name. That other, that tall American? Sharp-ress?"

"The American Consul?" Though the *mochi* didn't evoke memories he felt he was suddenly sorting through fading old snapshots the way names on paper in faded ink were coming to life. These were people Suzuki and his mother knew, people who'd actually lived here in Nagasaki. "You really knew him—the American Consul?"

Yes, she remembered the American consul. After only a few hours with her he realized that in spite of having only eye her memory was sharp. "The first time—that American ship—the Rincoln Abraham—white as these camellia blossoms—came into port, and it was that damned old crow who brought his young Yankee officers to the Maruyama teahouse." Her hand waved away any chance of confusion. "No, I was no *maiko* or *geisha,* but don't think for a minute that even as a serving maid I wasn't always number one. Without me that place couldn't have stayed open for a week—"

"My father?"

"Am I telling this or are you?"

Chastened, Sam held himself in impatient silence.

"That old crow dragged in young officers from the ship—all gi-ants—all loud. With all their noise and clumsiness and hitting their heads on the ceiling we had to ask ourselves, "Don't they have parties and women to chase in America? Running around after the bath with their peckers out as if they'd never seen a naked woman—"

Sam broke in. "And my father?"

"That one," she huffed. "He looked like a gaijin Prince Genji. Gold hair. Tall. Blue-white eyes."

"And my mother?"

"Fifteen years old. Still an apprentice. Not even a *maiko*. Still in an *okiya*." Her one eye held him. "I shouldn't tell you this, but if you want the honest truth, she was a lousy *samisen* player, but a very graceful dancer."

"She worked there?"

"Not work like that snake Tedabara. My Butterfly was still an apprentice. No *mizuake* yet. Still a virgin."

His mother. He closed his eyes. Imagine. Sitting here in this garden only days before his arranged wedding, they were talking about his mother. One day after finding Suzuki, he still found it a miracle, he still couldn't believe this old woman knew and loved his mother and they were talking about her, bringing her alive—his mother! "But why was she there—at the *okiya*—at all?"

Suzuki turned her good eye to brushing off a maple leaf from her *yukata*.

"Suzuki—why was she there?"

"The *okiya*? Why else but her family sold her to them."

Torazo was the first to tell him about girls from poor families being sold, but the thought of such a fate for his mother gripped his heart.

"Don't look so shocked. The *okiya* in Nagasaki was better than a village grubbing for life throwing shit on rice shoots like some stinking farmer's wife."

"She actually lived in the Maruyama?"

"Didn't I just tell you?" she huffed. "She was in an *okiya* just outside. The others thought she was stuck up the way she told everyone she was from a famous samurai family in Satsuma."

"She was, wasn't she?" Sam asked eagerly. "From a samurai family?"

"Fat lot of good that did her with those old timers losing the war against the government in Tokyo and leaving them nothing to eat but grasshoppers. Proud. Those assholes are all so high-and-mighty proud that even when they're broke and starving to death, they swagger down the street working a toothpick like they've just gobbled up duck."

Masao had said exactly the same thing, but now she was talking about someone who might be his grandfather. "But she was, wasn't she—from a samurai family?"

Suzuki shrugged. "She might have been. That would account for the few things she brought from home. And you—being a man—you're probably all fired up about swords, so you might as well know, she had a blade she claimed Tenno himself had presented to her father—"

"The emperor?" Sam, wide-eyed, gasped. "Have you still got it?"

She shut her eyes and shook her head. No sword. Her memory considered the possibility. "It might have been true that sword came from Tenno. At least, she wanted to believe it did. She hung on to it as her most sacred possession—" She ended that memory abruptly. "You know how to read Japanese?" He nodded without mentioning his years of brush-strokes. She pressed on. "If you know how to read—*He dies with honor who cannot live with honor*—was written on that blade. Of course, the Yankee part of you doesn't give a shit about honor. But my Butterfly did."

"My father married her. That was honorable, so he must have loved her."

"What he did was pay a marriage broker for her release to marry him. My Butterfly—that's the name they hung on her in the *okiya*—begged me, never stopped begging me to go to Pin-ker-ton's house with her. What else could I do? A girl at fifteen doesn't know shit about the world. Especially her. Believe me, nobody in the world needed someone older, someone wiser, to watch over her more than your mother.

"You had the wedding reception in the garden?" He explained, "Did I tell you I've been to the church where she got me baptized?"

"If you're going to keep interrupting, I might as well take a snooze." She wrapped her loose *yukata* tight and gave her nose another swipe. "And if you will be good enough to keep your trap shut, I just might tell you about the wedding."

"What did she look like?"

"Your mother? Like a mud fence." She cackled at his consternation.

"I told you, except for her *tengu* nose, which you got from her, she was very lovely. That didn't mean she had a real *Fujiwara* face the Japanese like. But you wouldn't understand. Yes," she shut her eyes, "she was lovely, but at her wedding she didn't look like any picture-postcard *maiko* with a white face under stiff-hair full of metal and fake flowers. She wore a wonderful kimono—all white. And for the reception a robe of robin's egg blue, crimson with white herons."

"And the Shinto priest?"

"What Shinto priest?"

"Mrs. McKie at the church told me she had an uncle who came from her home town shouting curses."

"That Shinto priest." She spat on the floor. "How could I ever forget? Mean old fart scaring everyone out of their skins. Even now thinking about him gives me goosebumps. Your Pin-ker-ton and Sharp-ress chased him out. After that everybody said they'd never been to such a wonderful party with Japanese who'd never tasted anything but sake, lapping up whiskey from Scotland." She chuckled. "Going home, some fell all the way down the hill. Thirty-five rickshaws it took for the rest." She leaned back. "What a wonderful, wonderful party. The August Moon—very good moon—even came as guest of honor to add his blessings." She yawned. "That's enough for now. My bones ache."

"Please, what happened then?"

"Hah! That night? You happened."

"But after my father left?"

"You got yourself born long after the Rincoln Abraham sailed out of Nagasaki Bay."

"Did my father know about me?"

"Not then."

"But the next time—when he came back with my American mother."

"That old crow Sharp-ress wrote him. By that time all the money your father left ran out." She sighed. "I kept telling her to marry one of the rich men the marriage broker was always pushing on us. I prayed to the Lord Buddha and a whole shelf full of the real gods—Shinto gods— for her to get some sense. I told her again and again. 'We're broke and you're not getting any younger.' Would she listen? She would not. Her answer was always the same. She swore that one day her Pin-ker-ton would come back to her."

"He did come back—"

"That bastard." She patted his hand. "I'm sorry, but the truth is that's what he was. Before he came back, Sharp-ress came to see us. And if you don't believe me, just tell me what kind of a shit of an American consul could keep a letter to her from Pin-ker-ton for months. She didn't even know he'd married some ugly, tall American woman with glasses and wasn't coming back. You think he'd have enough honor to show her the letter? He did not. He said not one word. That's Yankee-American honor for you. What he did was tell her to accept one of the marriage broker's clients."

"But she was married to my father!"

"All the time driving me and everybody crazy with her high and mighty 'I'm Mrs. Ben-ja-min Frank-rin Pin-ker-ton.' Every single time that Yankee crow and the marriage brokers came with a prospect she threw them out of the house."

"That's because she loved my father!"

"To hell with love, stick with sake."

Dredging up so much truth had exhausted her. Sinking back on her cushion, she waved off any more questions as if they were May flies.

"Boom!" she cried, coming alive. "Don't tell me you don't remember when the cannon went off down in the harbor? There it was—just like she said—the white ship, the Rincoln Abraham—shining down in the bay. Your mother rushed to put on her white kimono and stood at the *shojis* looking down at the bay. So, so excited—waiting and waiting. The sun went down and we waited. Night filled the sky, the stars came out with the three of us still there waiting, looking down at the bay. Dawn! That's when your father cut my heart out of me! I was the first one to hear the garden gate creak open and run to the porch. That's when I saw that crow—that vulture—that Sharp-ress out in the garden signaling to me to keep my Butterfly from coming out and seeing who he'd brought with him. She came running but I stopped her and sent you both into the back room and jumped into the only one of my *zoris* I could find to go racing out into the garden. That's when I saw her. There. She was standing at the gate holding a parasol. Her. Tall. Horrible yellow hair and far too tall for any man to love. And there he was—Pin-ker-ton—holding her arm. There I was with one bare foot, so what could I do but stand there with my heart banging in me so loud I was sure it would crack me wide open. All the while those three tall *Tengus* staring at me. I turned and ran back into the house. I knew, I knew—I absolutely knew—why they'd come—"

"My father came for me."

"With that woman who could never, never be your mother."

Sam was struggling for breath. "Then what, what did my real mother do?"

"What could my dear Butterfly do? Sharp-ress kept them out in the garden where we watched her step onto the porch in her best white silk. Plain white. Her lovely hair down her back. And you? You were in your little white kimono. You knew something was wrong and hid behind your mother. My Butterfly. She never looked more beautiful even though those Yankee shits were telling her they were here for you. You know what your mother did? She gave them a slight bow but no satisfaction in letting them see tears. Not one tear. I couldn't believe hearing her wish Pin-ker-ton's tall wife happiness. She stood there, white silk, the most beautiful thing I've ever seen and wished the American bitch happiness. Then she took you by the hand and went back and set you on a cushion and put the little American flag from her shrine in your hands. She held you close and whispered goodbye."

"The silk blindfold?"

Suzuki nodded. Sam had no trouble clearly seeing what Suzuki was remembering. "Two years old in your kimono with silk over your eyes with an American flag in your hand. She told me to find her father's sword and we set up a screen she went behind so none would see." He expected tears, but her old eyes were dry. She breathed hard. "My Butterfly showed those Yankee shits what honor was."

Sam shut his eyes and in his mind's eye saw red blood on white silk.

CHAPTER FIFTY

On their way down the hill they passed the Christian church. Before Sam said a word Suzuki muttered. "I know what you're going to say. That your mother took you here to have you baptized."

"Were you with her?"

"I didn't go inside. I'm no Christian. I don't understand your gods."

"If you were American you'd have only one." He took her hand.

She nodded. "Show your god how we really look?"

Inside the hushed shadow of the empty church they found no one stirring, and took a pew at the back and sat side by side. Stained glass, not the cheap colored paper like those on the windows in Urakami, cast a spell unlike any other place in Nagasaki. He took her shoulder. "As soon as I get the money I'm moving you out of the Futaba."

"Son, don't worry about me." She turned and smoothed back her hair all the while looking at the cross. "Now, tell me about this girl you're going to marry."

"I've only seen her twice. I scarcely know her."

Here in the hush of colored shadows, he opened his heart. "I love Tedabara. I love her with all my heart. I'll always love her."

"But Kodo has you marrying his daughter."

Sam sighed deeply and had to agree with a nod of his head. "At first I didn't know what he wanted with me. Now I do. He's not only forcing me to marry his daughter but to take his name."

She added a shrug of her own which offered him no comfort, no comfort at all. "Kodo's as bad a name as Pinkerton."

"Don't joke, Suzuki. I'm scared. This is the rest of my life."

Short on offering comfort she patted his hand. "You're scared because you don't believe it's the gods who have decided—"

"It's that Toad Kodo who's doing all the deciding."

"Don't sell the gods short. Maybe not your god but our gods have been part of our lives for a long, long time."

"To hell with the gods. As for deciding, I do my own. This is my life."

"You know who you sound like? That's how he talked. He used to brag how Americans controlled their—what's the word for deciding your own future—making your own life and going your own way?"

"Deciding your own fate."

"That's what he used to tell Butterfly—that he knew better than bowing down to family and country the way we Japanese do. He made a lot of loud noise about being his own man—his own master. Most Japanese know better. You've been here five years—"

"Six," he corrected her.

"By now at least half your nature should tell that Shinto, the gods will take you the direction your life will be?"

"No. You hate him but I'm American like my father. It's my life. As for the gods it's Kodo, not Shinto and all the gods controlling my life."

"With Shinto, even Kodo, you have a fate that makes you almost one of us. Here in Japan your fate is better than being a nothing like an *eta* or a *burakumin*."

"You didn't say *ainoko*."

"How could I? You're my dear Butterfly's son. My son. I'm completely a Japanese, who already loves you and is telling you to trust our gods. Yes, they've decided who will be your wife."

CHAPTER FIFTY-ONE

"Five days. Five days to go," Sam told himself. He was with Ono-San watching as Kodo assumed the gruff swagger of a warrior planning the last details of a military siege. From the beginning he'd been out to conquer Nagasaki and what he called its 'top people,' and make Mayumi's wedding the social event of the year. Sam stood helpless in his office watching him sign Ono-San's contracts for the Bellevue fortune tellers, two orchestras, florists, photographers, caterers, bills for hundreds of wedding presents for the guests as well as press releases. Ono-San assured Kodo that Mayumi's Heian-style Shinto robes and her white Western-style wedding gown of Venetian lace would triumph over any other Japanese bride's of this year or any other year.

For weeks Kodo had been scouring the guest list for the names of top people who would attend. Ono-San covered his worry by mentioning one particular acceptance. "You will see the Honorable Baron Kuroda has accepted."

"That old drunk. What about the top people at Mitsubishi?"

"It appears many will be traveling."

"And the Glovers?"

"Regrets. Unfortunately."

"Make telephone calls."

"I have, sir."

"Don't stand there. Call again."

As Kodo started again at the top and ran an eagle eye down the list, Ono-San hurried on, "The Tokyo guests will be staying at the hotel. And—we've just heard from Kimura-San who will be coming all the way from Honolulu, Hawaii."

Sam had never felt more like a bystander, simply looking on till Kodo turned his glare on him. "Now what the hell's this problem Ono-San tells me you're giving him with the guest list?"

"I've asked Ono-San to add only one name," said Sam. "Kyo Suzuki."

Kodo's glare shot to Ono-San. "Who the hell is Kyo Suzuki?"

"A creature," he sighed with suffering, "to make a mockery of everything the Kodo family represents. "Tell him," he snapped at Sam, "tell Kodo-San. If you won't, I will. Tell him your creature's nothing but a scrubwoman from some whorehouse in the Maruyama. The creature's totally out of the question," Ono-San jabbed his fan at Sam. "Tell Kodo-San exactly what you told me."

Sam, convinced he was so totally right in this quarrel spoke with remarkable calm. "I've told Ono-San that Suzuki-San was a friend of my mother's. My one and only guest."

Kodo waved him off. "Ono will decide."

The matchmaker declared the case closed. "I've already decided. The creature is unacceptable—absolutely impossible."

"Sir, it's no secret I came to Japan to find my mother. I learned my mother's dead, but Kyo Suzuki was her best friend and is still living here in Nagasaki—"

Ono-San bared his false teeth in refusal. "A scrubwoman."

"She was with my mother when, as Mrs. Benjamin Franklin Pinkeron, she lived up on the hill near the Glover mansion." Sam counted on the mention of the Glover Mansion to raise his mother and her friend's standing I believe you know my father was a commander in the navy and likely an admiral by now. I'm sure Sir can see that this one guest of mine concerns my honor, which will become the honor of the Kodos. I've given her my word, not as a Pinkerton but as a Kodo. The lady I've invited is a matter of honor. As a new Kodo I know you would never respect any son of yours who'd go back on his word."

Sam held his breath. Kodo drew out his cigar and studied its wet tip, smiled, and turned to the furiously trembling Ono-San and his list. With his wet cigar butt he tapped the name of Sam's one guest. Suzuki would be at the wedding.

On his wedding day in the Kodo mansion, Sam was in a dressing room with the persnickety Ono-San fussing and adjusting the tie of white cord on the black silk kimono with five family crests. Sam looked down at his beige skirt with no hint as to its historic significance. The five symbols, *mon,* he knew were the Kodo family crest and probably of uncertain or recent origin. He prepared himself to face two ceremonies, the first from Japan's historical Heian Period—and no one in Nagasaki knew more about preparing a Shinto wedding as infinitely traditional as Ono-San when it came creating the ancient rite. The Kodos—mother and daughter—were being prepared in another wing of the mansion. The second ceremony would be Western style. Here, with Sam, the little man wiped his glasses and studied the too-tall groom, splendid in his traditional robes of that far-off dynasty. Ono-San had done everything possible to present him as sufficiently Japanese. At this last moment he insisted on one more drill preparing his charge for the solemn commitment he was entering. Sam understood his role but had never felt more bereft, or more alone, since the Showalters' rejection.

His Best Man wasn't even a friend he could turn to for moral support. He'd been chosen for him. The son of Kodo's top people, Robert Talbot, would take no role here in the mansion in the Shinto rites. Sam wouldn't see his Best Man till the Western-style wedding performed for a larger crowd at the Bellevue Hotel. There, Ono-San would change Sam into cutaway-Western suit and white-tie grandeur. Since the war young Japanese couples were joining the world of the twentieth century as bride and groom in black and white. *Lohengrin* was taking the place of the *samisens* and *hachibashis* summoning the gods. Ono-San, of course, hated this new style marriage ceremony but this was 1920, and Kodo insisted on the height of fashion to impress Japan's postwar rich.

Ready or not for the first ceremony, Sam felt Ono-San's fan jab him in the small of his back. He shuffled out of the dressing room in white *tabis* on the long fateful march through the corridors of the recently built mansion, the new ancestral castle of the Kodos.

Here it was, the great hall. Across the sea of golden tatami the Kodos were positioned against a long gold screen with Mayumi standing so close to her father she seemed to be clinging to him. Sam supposed the young woman—his bride, imagine, his bride—was as trembling with nerves as he. Her mother stood alone, impassive. The groom joined them against this gold folding screen of twelve panels—displayed in Heian glory with his new family. All in their ancient and formal costumes, of gold and red, they were arrayed, a row of ancient dolls.

Though he stood at rigid attention he flicked his eyes out across the guests in the most formal of dress, some men in kimonos, others in London black, their wives, every single woman in their finest Japanese kimonos. Sam could risk no more than sliding his eyes across the crowd searching for Suzuki. Out of the corner of his eye, he caught sight of her and breathed again. Yes. She was here but hanging back from the other guests. Her kimono was silk and of proper black, her white hair smooth, and her red, rough hands carefully covered by full sleeves and crossed below her gray waist *obi*. Suzuki. He thanked his Christian God that he'd fought Kodo and Ono-San. His only guest was here. As for the others, he had no idea who they were—Kodo relatives, friends, business acquaintances, city officials? Everyone here for Mayumi standing next to him, her arm in her father's, all but lost in billowing brilliant silk, flaming orange and heavy red brocade with white herons rising above peonies. Little of her elaborate, varnished hairstyle showed beneath the traditional headdress of white gauze over pink silk. Her small face looked smaller and paler than usual under a ghostly white dusting of rice powder. Her thin lips were a crimson mouth painted even smaller than her own.

The young couple and her family and a few relatives unknown to Sam faced the glint of a bespectacled Shinto priest in white and a young priestess in white and vermilion gliding across the tatami, approaching the couple waving wands of cut white paper. Sam moved only to share saucers of sake with Mayumi in what Sam had been told was the most ancient, sacred, but simple, of rituals uniting forever the descendants of the Sun Goddess.

White paper wands wafted and sake apparently made them one. The Shinto ceremony here in the mansion had ended. With considerable command Kodo and Ono-San dispatched the guests in hired cars to glide them to the Bellevue. On her father's arm, Mayumi and her mother and father filled the monster Marmon, but only after Sam had stolen a moment to reach Suzuki to see that a car waited for her. Hugging her, she tugged his head down to hers, telling him his mother was here with them.

CHAPTER FIFTY-TWO

"Red Rover, Red Rover, let Sam come over." It was a strange Bremerton memory that struck him entering the Kodo Marmon. It was too late to run. Feeling great uncertainty riding with the Kodos in the giant black car he so hated, he was trying to sort out his emotions—feeling himself a total fraud, an impostor presenting himself to the world as a true Japanese.

At the Bellevue, Mayumi seemed to float into the hotel borne by her mother and father. Ono-San corralled an enormous crowd to keep waiting out in the lobby while he finished re-staging the Heian rite from the mansion. Against more gold screens, Kodo was already announcing the ceremony to be the largest Nagasaki had ever seen. Sam and the Kodos waited for Ono-San's last inspection before his fan signaled the footmen to throw open the ballroom doors.

The flood of men in black and women in vivid kimonos surged down the aisle past tables laden with gifts from the bride's family—endless rows of boxes wrapped in white and red. Nagasaki, Japan and the world—

everyone Kodo had been able to dragoon to the extravaganza—saw the bridegroom, the new Kodo, in his black kimono with his new family monograms, tall and wide-shouldered, a dark-blond-haired man with round eyes.

Those round, gray eyes looked straight ahead only daring a few glances across the room at Suzuki's lowered head.

Photographers' explosions flashed. Motion picture cameras, the first ever seen at a Nagasaki wedding, kept the Kodos and their five hundred guests alert and in increasing awe. Kodo, newly rich and powerful Kodo, was keeping his promise—his daughter's wedding was the very last word sure to keep Nagasaki and Japan buzzing.

Once Sam spotted Suzuki his search went on till he found Talbot in his splendid Western tailcoat staring up at him. If Talbot felt scorn for this rich man's excess, the traditional Heian Period tableau swelled Japanese hearts with pride, affirming the uniqueness of their island race. *Samisens, shakuhachis,* and kotos shimmered their last ancient melodies until Mayumi's parents lifted their daughter between them, wafting her away to change for the Western ceremony.

Sam, like a sleepwalker, found himself led into a dressing room where Robert was sprawled in an upholstered leather chair. Ono-San directed menservants relieving Sam of his five-monogrammed kimono of Heian grandeur into the tight-fitting carapace of a twentieth-century black tailcoat with a choking white collar and tie. His Best Man could be heard to sigh, put-upon with boredom and suggested that whiskey would help matters. When Sam refused the drink, Talbot, in his sprawl in the upholstered chair, poked a silver flask into his handsome profile. He seemed amused watching Ono-San and enjoyed smirking at the spectacle of the old Japanese fussing over his creation. His splendid and handsome Western-style groom turned, at last, to view himself before a full length mirror.

"Ab-so-lute-ly piss elegant splendid," Talbot was overdoing a British accent. "You'll have our Kodo bursting with pride."

Ono-San double-checked to see that Talbot had the ring. "You feel any different?" the Best Man asked with a world-weary sigh, "More grand with not one but two weddings making you into a Kodo and an old married man?" Whiskey had raised his usual arrogance to slurs of open contempt. "And did you get a look at that mob out there? In case, Old

Son, you haven't guessed, that is the most dismal crowd of nobodies you are ever likely to see collected in one lifetime." Talbot's nastiness became scorn. "To give you some idea of Kodo's friends, all he could manage to whistle up as his one social lion turns out to be a seedy baron who should be in jail. No Glovers. No top people from Mitsubishi. Certainly no one from my mother and father's set—only yours truly, blackmailed to be here to appear to upgrade the proceedings."

Talbot relented enough to answer Ono-San's call to duty and heaved himself to his feet to join the last full-length study of the two of them in the mirror. "Hold still. Ono-San hasn't the foggiest what a respectable gentleman looks like." He whistled the *Mikado* through his teeth while long fingers straightened one of Sam's shoulders. Again he raised his flask in salute. "To the new son and heir, the new Kodo. Quite the young gentleman aren't we? Certainly beats lugging a rickshaw about town."

Sam tightened with anger. At this moment in his life he needed a friend like Masao or that long-gone foxy little urchin Torazo. "I count myself lucky," Talbot drawled, defining his role, "I'm only here for Kodo's command performance—to pass you off to that mob out there and then, *voila,* I'm out of here. You, Old Son, have to kiss his fat, farting sweet ass for the rest of your life." He pulled in more Scotch. "As to your honeymoon plans—I wouldn't be surprised if your new father didn't allow you to set foot out of his house."

Sam gritted his teeth as he squirmed under his tight collar, but instead of cursing Talbot he defended his future independence. "We've got our own wing."

"Of course. Keeping you under his roof—"

Ono-San's fan poked the groom and his Best Man to the reception hall, a ballroom with a hardwood floor dividing a sea of tables set with crystal and silver, where five hundred and three buzzing, excited guests strained for the best view of the grand, new-style Western marriage ceremony in black and white. The gold screens had been removed, now showing the groom and his Best Man posted before banks of white gladiolas and magnolia blossoms and a cascade of white orchids. Among the flowers Sam saw three bridesmaids, young women he did not know, take their places waiting for the powerful father to come through the door leading his Mayumi down the aisle.

Sam searched the guests. Suzuki had not crowded forward but was sitting alone by herself, hiding her hands. Music swelled. No more *samisens*. No more kotos or *shakuhachis*. A Western orchestra was pumping out *Ich Liebe Dich* and hushing the enormous room to silence. Suddenly an organ burst into Wagner's radiant shimmer of *Lohengrin*, turning every eye to Mayumi in a cloud of white Venetian lace. Covered by her wedding bouquet her hand, as before, clung closely against her father's arm. Sam squared his shoulders waiting to offer his own arm to his bride for the rest of his life. Mayumi seemed to be relying more tightly on her father's arm as they moved with slow steps into the room, approaching the altar, making their way slowly down the long aisle, their steps unable to keep to Wagner's rhythm. The bride broke her stride. She paused for a moment and tightened her grip on her father. Sam held his breath, sharing the crowd's wave of apprehension.

Another step and Mayumi stumbled. Kodo grabbed her, but not before a cane, unseen till now, clattered to the hardwood floor. A guest rushed forward, retrieved the stick and returned it to the bride. For a long, agonizingly long moment, she closed her eyes and stood motionless. She kept her head raised before half a thousand guests and Sam, who didn't dare breathe. With an effort she nodded to her father and they resumed her unsteady march down the aisle.

Sam felt Talbot's hand gripping his arm. "Oh, God, Sam. I swear I didn't know . . ."

Sam kept his gaze directly on Mayumi and prayed the world didn't see his look of shock. She was a cripple. Of course. That explained why he'd never seen her stand alone. Now he knew why that time playing the koto she'd refused his invitation to rise and walk in the garden. Yes, during the last two ceremonies her parents had presented her seated or supported between them. When Ono-San had ended their meetings she'd been all but lifted from the room. Her cane explained the truth.

Of the rest of the ceremony he remembered almost nothing. After the Japanese version of "Dearly Beloved" he stood with her for the first time, bride and groom in a reception line waiting for congratulations. Now it was him to whom Mayumi was clinging, and not her father. Who could count the number of hours it took the endless parade of men and women filing by, bowing, and the two returning bows.

Dinner, for Sam, was a blur—faces, small talk, babble from people he did not know—one old man in black after another rising, speaking empty words at a vast roomful of guests listening with utmost gravity. Did Talbot say a few words and raise his glass while the bride and groom pretended to eat a few bites of the Western-style dinner? Was there more Western music? More champagne?

At one point a bride's maid and her young escort went out on the dance floor but after a few steps, realized their gaucherie and retreated. No one danced. Sam sat beside his wife, his new world an empty blur.

Hours—an eternity later—with the guests leaving, Sam broke away from Mayumi long enough to find a silent Suzuki and put her into a cab to the hotel where he'd moved her. She kissed him. Neither said a word.

CHAPTER FIFTY-THREE

It was true as Sam had told Robert. The newlyweds had their own wing in the mansion—all the privacy, Kodo declared, any young couple could wish. New tatami gleamed pale gold under the glow of *andons.* Mayumi's mother had arranged the *ikebana*—morning glories—flowers appropriate to the season. Sam wore a summer-weight *yukata* and smoked a cigarette while maids spread the wedding-night futon. *Shojis* opened to the garden alive with the thrum of cicadas. He waited alone while a maid hung a mosquito net enveloping the futon. Tedabara would have made that a world for two, but now he was in a world without Tedabara. Another maid scurried in with a tray. Tea. The futon maid inquired if the young master and his bride wanted their bath now.

"No. No bath," Sam heard his voice close to panic, too insistent, dismissing such intimacy. Not tonight. Would he ever have the courage to admit to himself he simply couldn't face seeing any part of Mayumi naked? If he felt that way, imagine how she must be dreading the thought of showing him her crippled self.

Alone, Sam waited. His wife had yet to enter the spacious but empty room in the Japanese style, without folding screens, nothing to hide a new wife from her husband. He imagined her coming in, leaning on a cane that, of course, had a tip that had to be padded to protect the tatami. She'd stand motionless, ready for a maid to undress her. He had no idea when he took her into his arms what she'd be wearing. Still waiting, he stepped barefoot onto the cypress *engawa,* to allow his wife to enter in privacy.

The room behind him was dim with only one *andon* glowing. Hushed. He stood in the mild night looking out into the garden, his back to the room to show her he would not see her undressed. He pretended to watch the moon silver the garden as only that one floor lamp cast a pool of light in the room Mayumi had silently entered, now lying on the futon covering herself with a white crepe sheet.

He took a deep breath of the mild September night air and stepped back inside. where he stood absolutely motionless, presenting himself to a maid waiting to undress him while asking himself what, if anything, a new Japanese husband wears to bed on this night of nights. Naked for a moment, the maid answered by drawing a light cotton *yukata* over him. Thank God, he told himself. They'd both be dressed. Not naked. He was expected to forget the wild, hot delicious nakedness of two bodies exploring every inch of each other while sharing himself with his Tedabara.

No! He warned himself not to think of Tedabara or his heart would break. He nodded to the maid to extinguish the *andon* which he well knew was usually left lit all night, before she slipped out leaving total darkness.

He lifted back the mosquito net and sank down on the futon beside his bride with care, scrupulous that no part of his young body touched hers as he carefully positioned himself on his back.

He dared slide one glance. Mayumi was wide awake, but she lay still without moving a muscle. He listened to her soft breathing. Minutes passed and the silence separating them became unendurable, excruciating till he had no choice but reach for her hand. At his touch she turned to face him. Still, neither spoke.

"Please?" Mayumi's whisper was a strange little cry. "Please?" Her whisper carried on her softest breath. "I begged my father and mother to tell you."

He slid an arm under her shoulder. At his touch she hesitantly pressed her face, wet with tears, into the hollow of his neck. He drew her close and hoped she didn't feel how violently he was trembling. She spoke against his skin, "You like to dance?"

"No."

"All young men like to dance."

"I never have."

She held his hand and he realized she was sliding it under her gown, down her body past her thigh, down her leg bringing his fingers to her foot. More than ever he was trembling as much for her as for himself, imagining the courage it took for her to share with her new husband the shame she'd lived with all her life. "A club foot," she whispered. "My father took me to every doctor he could find." Sam's every instinct was to pull his hand back and shrink from the foot.

CHAPTER FIFTY-FOUR

The year of the spectacular Kodo wedding, Crown Prince Hirohito visited London as a guest of King George V at Buckingham Palace, and was photographed in Western clothes, increasing the Japanese rage for British fashions. The Prince of Wales reciprocated, returning the honor during his visit to the Islands of the Sun Goddess and donning the uniform of a Japanese general. In Washington, Japan entered into an important naval conference, which Sam attempted to follow in the papers. He didn't understand the treaty, but it seemed to him the Western world, even after the Great War, was treating Japan as a second-rate nation. No one had to explain the horror he and Mayumi and all Japan felt when Prime Minister Hata was assassinated by a railway worker. The country slumped into a postwar depression but silk, at one-third of total imports, stayed high and Kodo, the Toad, swelled his coffers with the growth of the chemical industry and ship building. Nagasaki shared the maritime boom with Kobe and Yokohama and, in spite of strikes, Kodo's BlackStar Corporation and Bay Trading was filling foreign ships with coal, bringing in lumber from America's west coast, and the hides that Sam remembered unloading with a shudder. Kodo raged the loudest against workers inflamed by labor leaders as a greater evil than inflation or the year's seventeen typhoons, three severe enough in Nagasaki to rip the hardiest persimmons off the trees.

Not a day and scarcely an hour went by when Sam didn't burn for Tedabara. As the Chinese proverb held *kanji* he'd brushed in black ink. "Idleness breeds lust."

On a cold night in the third week in December Sam and Mayumi, man and wife, side by side in their warm futon, listened to the night watchman passing outside. She asked if Sam remembered it was Christmas Eve. He lied and said he'd forgotten, which only made her beg to hear about his Christmases in America. No. Memories were still too sharp—the smell of a fir tree, decorating it, candles glowing and the smell of roast turkey and stockings hung by the fire and then, visiting other kids' families with fathers instead of his having to pretend to be Santa Claus. No. He lied. He didn't remember that last heartbreaking Christmas Eve, the next day without his father.

Mayumi was kissing his shoulder. "I have," she whispered, "a present for you."

He heard an intimacy in her breathless little voice that hadn't been there before. It was Christmas. She nuzzled her face on his and he could feel her lips smiling. "Yes. A baby." He folded her into his arms, astonished this bony little body was able to create life. Like a happy little animal returning to its home, she burrowed her face into the old place, the hollow of his shoulder. A baby. He held her telling himself he should be the happiest man in the world instead of pushing back words from his heart he could scarcely breathe even to himself. "God, if only I could love her."

He covered her face with kisses. "Have you told your father yet?"

"Not yet. Not even mother. Only you."

They shared a long silence.

"Father wants a son more than anything in the world. And mother, of course," she said. "And I."

What could he do but pretend he was thrilled with the promise of a new life, to tell her he wanted the child every bit as much as she and her family? He drew her thin body close, feeling her heart beating, and hoped she did not feel his fear for his own life. Kodo's net was drawing tighter. For a long moment they lay together without a word. She answered the terrible question she knew he dreaded to ask. "I've already seen the very best doctor in Nagasaki who swears what I suffer will not touch our baby." With her good news she tightened her body, against him hoping for deeper intimacy than they'd yet shared.

This was his Christmas night, a night for opening her heart. She surprised him with a giggle. "You have heard about *Kirasmasu Keike?*" He didn't answer. They both knew she was talking about the saying that any woman in Japan who reaches her twenty-fifth birthday becomes a Christmas cake and goes on the shelf the day after, too old for any man to marry. She drew him tighter and whispered. "Almost twenty-five and this foot. This Christmas," she kissed his breast, "I have the best gift of all—now, being in your arms everything before—only a bad dream."

"Don't," he said roughly, "we don't have to talk about it."

"I must, my Dear Sam-San. On our wedding day when you saw me come limping down the aisle you knew part of the reason my father chose you. By now you must realize the wonderful plans he has for you with the company, and perhaps one day even beyond Japan."

Of course, he told himself, she loved her father but the last thing he wanted was to be reminded of Kodo's shadow, his net drawing tighter. With a light kiss, he said, "Let's leave your father out of this, let the news of the baby be enough for tonight."

She eased him onto his back and pressed closer. Could she possibly guess that this gesture was what he most loved with his Tedabara, her drawing her breasts across him. Mayumi, a shy little animal, was nuzzling his ear. "I know it's hard for men to tell women all that they feel. Not for me. Not with you. Can you imagine, my dearest Sam-San, how much I love you and bless all the gods that I am your wife. Now, with the baby coming, I can admit what I couldn't say our first day at the Bellevue. I can't wait for the day you'll open your heart and tell me all that you feel."

Did she feel him nodding? He was trying to cut her short. "I understand—"

"Do you? That no Japanese girl of any standing would have met with you and have her family choose you? But my father knew the gods meant you for me. Your Best Man, Robert Talbot, has he told you that in spite of being rich and powerful—or perhaps because of it—people of real standing—'top people' as father calls them—here in Nagasaki—do not respect him. People like the Talbots and, of course, the grandest of all—the Glovers—and they're not even fully Japanese—do not make him welcome in their world."

"Tonight let's just be happy about the baby—"

"Now that I've told you about my father," she giggled, "our father, I can tell you who the mother of your baby is—"

"Can we save it for another night?"

No. With the news of their child she felt she could open her heart, tell him about her life before that tea with the pale green nasturtiums on her cloche hat at the Bellevue. "When I was a girl in school I was never once invited to parties in the other girls' homes. In those days I hoped, for my mother and father's sake, that the reason the others didn't include me was because of my foot. Then one day one of my schoolmates, a fat girl whose cousin is a prince, spat the truth at me—everyone in Nagasaki hated my family because my father made his money during the war. Oh, Sam-San it hurt so terribly because everything she and the others were saying I knew was true. Father is not respected here in Nagasaki or in all of Kyushu, but in Tokyo he has powerful—very powerful friends—some even in the Diet. Mother and I were in Tokyo with him once. You should see the bowing and scraping some of the most powerful people in the capital show him."

She drew aside his *yukata* to kiss his bare breast. "Even in Tokyo father engaged a matchmaker, but found no suitable husband for me. Of course, Mother and I both knew he'd never give up. He'd find someone. Then, one day you applied for a position with BlackStar."

Sam kissed her lightly. He lied with a nod. That was it. He'd come to the office looking for a job.

"His first thought was your perfect English language could be wonderful for business. And anyone can see you're healthy and the handsomest man in the world. My father," she was teasing—"have I ever told you he loves me very much and he would never have chosen you if he didn't know you were the fine, kind man we all know you are."

Could she read his thoughts? Of course not. He could never tell her the truth, so he settled for bitterness. "You think being such a fine, kind young man changes being an *ainoko?*"

He'd said the word only once before and that time she'd pressed her hand against his mouth and looked straight into his eyes lighter in color than those of any Japanese. "Never say that word again."

"Before I married you every Japanese considered me less than a nobody. Maybe they still do—"

"My father is the cleverest man in Nagasaki. I don't say that just because I'm his daughter. Being half American and working for him can be a tremendous advantage—with outsiders there are no rules."

"I said my father is clever. He says that even if your father is dead he was an honorable officer—a commander in the United States navy. Your mother was beautiful and doubtlessly had such an honorable *koseki* he married her."

Every word she said could have only come from Tedabara, who had told Kodo about their nights of fierce lovemaking. Now Mayumi was repeating what she found so heartbreaking—that terrible scene with his grandparents in Seattle's New Washington Hotel. She was still lying on top of him, he wanted nothing more than to shove her off and race out of this room and into the night, but she was kissing him.

"What other wife has a man so tall and strong and handsome. Some people hate my father because he's rich, but no one could ever hate my Sam."

He maneuvered himself out from under her. Now they were side by side. "Don't ever tell my father I told you, but the others of standing hate him because his father was a drunken carpenter—"

Sam interrupted. "He tells everybody his people were samurai."

"My mother's family. They were on the losing side during the rebellion. She was almost as old as I am when father married her—a carpenter's son who was already rich. The war made him richer. You think you know how powerful he is? You don't have any idea. I told you, you should see him in Tokyo." Leaning to him, her kisses put an end to sharing the truth about her father. She ran her fingers through his hair. "No more talk." Begging for his love she covered his neck and shoulder with her animal nibbles. "All that matters is that you and I will have a beautiful son stronger than any American or Japanese to face the future."

The next day with Suzuki he shared his news that Mayumi was pregnant and she clapped her old hands, cackling her delight, till stopped by a terrible thought. "And the foot?"

"The doctors tell her the baby won't have it," Sam said.

Always one to face facts, she shrugged as she poured tea, "Let's hope it's true. If she was poor and the baby was crippled, of course, she'd have to kill it."

The way his mother's friend faced reality so squarely no longer shocked him. Like many Japanese he'd known, she saw life for what it was. "Don't look so down. At least you have a wife that's honest. Takes courage to tell you everyone hates her father for being an uppity bully— a war-profiteer and probably worse. As for you, son, face it. Now you're a married man. A Kodo yourself and soon a father of little Kodos." She gave him a nudge and another happy cackle.

"He wants me in the family because I speak English and know America and that could be good for business. "Oh, no." He shook his head at that future. "What I'm really going to do is get out from under him and on my own teach English—"

Suzuki stifled a gasp of real fear. "You didn't tell him—"

"Not yet."

"Don't. Stay scared of him. Don't say a thing about what you want— not till you're ready and that'll be never."

"Believe me, I will." He knew better than to whine, but heard himself. "You don't know what it's like, Suzuki, being adopted, a goddamned Kodo. I'd give anything to be back pulling a rickshaw instead of eating his shit. Sorry about the language."

"It might have shocked your mother but not me. Anyway, you wouldn't. You told me what happened to your friend Masao."

"So how long do I have to pretend to be one of those half Japanese from one of your so-called best families—like Robert Talbot?"

"Stuck up but handsome."

"I shouldn't tell you this, but Mayumi and her mother tell me I'm even handsomer."

Suzuki patted his cheek. "Of course they do. But you are handsome, you know. I just wish you didn't look so much like your bastard father."

"Don't. You know I hate it when you talk about him like that?"

She chuckled. "Then we'll talk about your new father. No. We know all about him." Suzuki's voice found a warmer voice. "What about the mother?"

"She's quiet and arranges flowers and never stops working to make everything in all our lives run smooth."

"But you still burn for your Tedabara."

"No," he lied. "Not any more."

"You men, you're all liars."

CHAPTER FIFTY-FIVE

Their son was perfect. Sam never tired of examining every part of him, amazed at the tiny nails and little fingers and toes he loved to kiss. His baby's hair was dark, as were his eyes and, yes, what a Westerner would call almond-shaped and astonishingly large.

With the baby in her arms Mayumi's smile said she was part of the human race. He could only wonder at her bringing this vibrant, healthy, exquisitely formed human life from her frail little body.

"Your father loves you," Sam cooed, nuzzling his boy. "Loves you . . . loves you . . . loves you," Hearing himself speaking in English he raised his head to his son's mother. "You teach him Japanese and I'll teach him English. Did I ever tell you, I'm a wonderful teacher?"

She nodded with a smile. "Many times."

He flopped onto his back on the tatami and lifted his son over his face and relished kissing, one by one, each wriggling finger and toe.

Outside the mansion Kodo's loud toad croaking was heard all over town. The Chairman of BlackStar Corporation and Bay Trading was bursting, boisterous, proud and thrilled. Though Tatsuo arrived three days after May Fifth—Boys' Day—he closed his office for the day, rushed home to his mansion and hoisted a bamboo pole with a fifteen-foot red balloon carp swimming in the spring wind high above the neighbors' tile roofs. "Screw them," he roared. "Bumper Kodo has a son!"

Bumper Kodo, the grandfather, pushed the father aside as if Sam had nothing to do with Mayumi's miracle. Full of Japanese rituals he laid a wooden blade alongside his heir, heaped the *tokonoma* with an ancient helmet and armor, and lined a shelf with small porcelain images of feudal generals to give the child strength. He made a great fuss cutting up sword-like iris leaves with his own hands and sprinkling them in his bathwater, green blades assuring the lad a bold, warrior-like nature. From beyond Japan, in Hollywood movies, he'd seen proud fathers handing out cigars. At the office and the club he emptied five boxes of Uppmann's from Havana.

The mansion had never seen more of Kodo and day by day Sam watched how little Tatsuo was changing their lives. Setsu, no longer remote and solemn, scurried about happily performing every task she could do with the smiling skill of a grandmother's love. Mayumi lacked milk and Setsu brought in a wetnurse, an overflowing, flat-faced farm girl the thin little mother allowed in no way to usurp her suddenly dominant role over the house. She was emerging from a passive bride to an honored mother, expecting, even demanding, honor. No longer ashamed of her cane, she stood proudly, holding her son in one arm.

Sam was in a rush to bring Suzuki to the house to meet his boy when Mayumi, a supposedly humble, diffident Japanese wife, surprised him by opposing the old woman's visit. She remembered her from the wedding. At that moment Sam coiled with fury but held himself back from striking her. He was slamming out the door when Setsu stopped him. She'd overheard his friend's banishment and, to his immense relief, he found an ally who'd help slip his guest in a back door.

Three days later when Mayumi discovered the plot and caught sight of Suzuki with their son, her innate kindness triumphed. No. She had to agree, the old woman did not smell of sake and the young mother thanked her for bringing Tat a paper maché rooster. She smiled as Suzuki explained its significance to Sam. "For the Year of the Rooster." Suzuki repeated what she'd memorized of his horoscope. "He's a Double Rooster—born at the Rooster Hour." His mother's friend continued to chant his blessings. "He's trustworthy, kind, and warm-hearted and will never intend to hurt anybody."

Sam glanced over at his wife and saw she understood what Suzuki meant to him. Nevertheless, this was a special occasion. She was here today, but even if she was his mother's friend, she must never be allowed to overdo her visits to the mansion.

Sam sensed another change in the life here in the mansion. With the Kodos doting so completely on Tat and his mother, he'd been pushed aside. He'd had nothing to do with the Kodo's having an heir. It struck unmistakably on the morning of his son's thirty-second day when he angrily challenged being shunted aside in his role of young father. This was the second time he'd stood up to the Kodos. His second triumph he shared alone with Suzuki over *castera* and tea. "On the day Tat was thirty-two days old and I came home and found the whole house dressing my boy up in the fanciest kimono and strapping him to the wet-nurse's back."

"Yes, for his *miyamari*," she said, reminding him he was talking with someone totally Japanese.

"Hell, Suzuki, if I hadn't been there, they wouldn't even have told me what they were doing and where they were taking him. Can you believe it? Not one of them bothered to tell me—his own father—that my son was being presented to the gods at the local Shinto shrine—"

"His *miyamari*—"

"Mayumi knew all about it and she wasn't even going to tell me—" He drove a fist into his hand. "That's when I told them all—'Goddamnit, and whether you want me there or not, I'm coming with my son.'" With a gulp of tea he washed down too big a hunk of *castera*. "Then they made me feel stupid being at the shrine with nobody bothering to tell me why they were waving all that fringed white paper and chanting."

"Rites of purification—"

"More and more they treat me like some kind of outsider." Sam realized he was dangerously close to self-pity, but to who else other than Suzuki could he unburden himself? "They don't want me there. It's as if I'm in the way . . ."

"You've been married over a year."

"At work it's even worse. Kodo acts like he owns me. He won't give me a damn thing to do. Everybody in the office knows what's going on and they either show me no respect or ignore me. Some even call me the '*ainoko*'—not to my face, of course, but I know those bastards do." He gobbled more cake. "Sometimes at that office and then coming back to this house, I tell you, Suzuki—if it weren't for Tat—it's all I can do not to break through the last *shoji* and run like hell and keep running."

"If you did that I would hate you as much as I still hate your father."

The nineteen-year-old husband sluiced down more *castera* with tea. "I wish to hell this was sake."

"We both do." She was silent, thinking. "In bed your wife tries to please you?"

"Now that Tat's here she just lies there all night listening in case he cries."

"Of course."

"You're going to tell me it was like this when I was born?" He looked to her for an answer.

She held him with her one eye. "When you were born your father— Lieutenant Ben-jam-in Frank-rin Pin-ker-ton—was not there . . ."

CHAPTER FIFTY-SIX

With no one else he could talk with he swallowed his pride and asked his Best Man to meet him at the club. At least the sleek Talbot showed up and in his supercilious way motioned him with his cigar across the roomful of leather chairs.

Talbot displayed the Uppmann. "One of Kodo's. First-rate Havana." This was their second meeting at the club and, as before, Sam was in awe and more than a little resentful of Robert's indolent ease. The man really was insufferable.

"The way Old Bumper crows about your son," Talbot said through cigar smoke, "and flings out these cigars, you'd think he was the father. Of course he is, in the sense he's got himself a brand-new Kodo in you and now a grandson to boot to carry on the infamous family name. Still, you did the deed." He raised his Johnnie Walker Black Label. "Congratulations."

Sam ordered a second Scotch and stopped himself from complaining, but dammit, didn't anyone seem to remember that he had something to do with Tat's arrival?

"What do you call him?" Talbot drawled.

"Tatsuo."

"No. I'm talking about Kodo. You call him 'Father'?"

"Kodo-San." Sam said.

"Simple. Certainly preferable to 'Bumper.'" Talbot drew slowly on his cigar. "Tatsuo's a Kodo family name? Scarcely seems to go with Pinkerton."

"Damn you, Talbot! Even if people have hurt you for being an *ainoko* you don't have to take it out on me." Of course Sam kept his mouth shut, drank his Johnnie Walker Black Label and said, "I'm a Kodo now."

"And so you are. Your son look Japanese?"

"How the hell would I know?"

Talbot raised his glass. "So now everyone at chez Kodo can be happy." They drank their Scotch. They smoked. "So—being an old married man agrees with you?"

"If you can call nineteen old."

Sam slid a look over at his Best Man. God, how he wished this haughty creature was someone he could trust to tell how he'd felt trapped into marrying a woman he didn't love the way he ached to love. He stared into his Scotch. Married for almost a year, he ached to cry out to someone that he'd never for a minute felt he belonged in that house. What would happen if he yelled out that all the while he was with her he was burning for another woman's body. Sam drank his whiskey and said, "What about you?"

"What about me what?"

"Marriage?"

Talbot was protected by smoke. "Out here in the East it's bad form to challenge the gods by allowing them in on one's plans." There it was. Talbot was shutting the door on any intimacy while he signaled the barman. At least he was drinking with him. Talbot made a minimal effort. "Things going well at the office?"

"Kodo doesn't give me a damn thing to do. But I'll change that. I'm still learning the ropes. And I've got my own plans."

"What is it exactly you do for him?"

"Translate any cables or letters that reach us in English and take a few telephone calls. Can you believe the Japanese actually bow to the phone while talking?"

"Likely one of our eight million gods of Shinto."

Sam could enjoy Talbot's mockery when it wasn't directed at him, and yet, with his only prospect for friendship, he felt himself in a vulnerable position. Forever they'd live between two worlds. Would the day ever come, he wondered, when this London-clad toff—this high-and-mighty Talbot—could disarm himself enough so that the two of them could talk about the central fact of their lives?

Sam carefully dared a first step toward friendship. "Even though we both know it was returning a favor to Kodo, I've never thanked you properly for standing up for me at my wedding. And as for your speech and good wishes, I heard everyone say you hit just the right note."

"The keynote," Talbot smiled, "was insincerity. It's the sort of thing the English taught me. I did my duty performing for your new father and his business chums though they're not at all the sort most of us look forward to seeing here in the club."

He wanted to stop talking about Kodo and be talking man-to-man as he had with Masao back at the stable, talking about the world and how Japan's military was building and thrusting against China. Did Robert know or care that their country's troops were already deep in Korea and Manchuria? Young men were off fighting wars. He and Robert were young. "You hear anything about the draft?"

"What about it?"

"Aren't men our age being drafted right and left?"

"Not to worry. Tenno—Our Emperor—isn't exactly looking for exotics like us serving as two officers for his Imperial Army or Navy. You'll simply have to prove your devotion to our god and emperor staying at home here in Nagasaki with Kodo and your wife and kiddiwinks." Talbot finished his drink. "Right now my sworn duty is to be off to my other club for my Tuesday-night poker game." He signaled the barman for the bill.

"No," said Sam. "Let me, Talbot. I'm a member now."

"Now you can be proud of yourself."

Sam tried to smile. "Thank you for not blackballing me." Sam was surprised he felt American enough to hold himself back from smacking Talbot's arrogant face. "Tell me," he said, "was it because having another *ainoko* in the club makes you feel less different?"

Without a word Talbot left for his poker game.

CHAPTER FIFTY-SEVEN

Though Kodo gave him little to do at the office he stayed through the empty days without leaving before the others, an act he knew fooled no one. Dutifully, since marrying Mayumi, Sam had come home to dinner every night. Walking home he detoured past Auntie's. Yes. There it was. The Marmon. As he continued to walk in his English leather shoes, how could he bear the thought—Kodo fondling every inch of his Tedabara?

Home. And dinner—sashimi, raw sea bass, abalone, and octopus, exquisitely presented, chilled for the hot summer night and presented on black-and-dark-red lacquer. He heard the soft tap of Mayumi's padded cane, a sound like nothing else in the world. At the open panels she bowed to her husband and took her place at the low table. She did not eat. She was here as the dutiful wife, pouring sake, moving tiny dishes, silent, keeping her husband ritual company.

"Where's Tat?"

"With mother."

"Did it occur to any of you I might like to see my son?"

He watched her slide a lock of hair back from her brow. He'd sensed her unease from the moment she'd slid open the panel. He knew only duty kept her here, that she'd leave the instant he laid aside his chopsticks. When that moment came she did exactly that, but he stopped her. "Don't go. Maybe I have something to say—"

"Tat's with the nurse. Mother's alone."

"So am I. When do I get to see my boy?"

He heard his voice, not at all the Japanese husband roughly commanding. "Today I went to the club looking for Robert Talbot, because I needed someone to talk to. I hadn't seen him in months. He congratulated us again on Tat and asked how things were going at BlackStar and here at home. Naturally I didn't tell him the truth." Mayumi folded her hands in her lap and waited. He looked at her. Was she listening? He surprised her by sliding an arm around her, longing to feel more than bones. "May I tell my honorable wife what I couldn't tell my honorable friend? Or isn't a Japanese husband allowed to confess, even to his wife, that he has feelings?"

Mayumi very carefully raised her hands and kept them pressed on the lacquer table.

"As I said, Talbot asked how things were going at the office." He reached for a cigarette, which Mayumi, with an old-fashioned stick match, was quick to light for him. "I found myself telling him that after all this time your father keeps me doing nothing but make-work that has everyone in the office snickering at me behind my back."

Sam didn't expect Mayumi to answer. By now he understood her silences and most often any problem between them went unspoken. He'd watched both women bend to Kodo. He'd learned enough about this country to know that when Japanese men talked about plans for the future—big, grand plans about all that mattered in the world—Japanese wives were required to listen. Even if the plans their men talked about were overblown dreams that didn't make sense, the proper wife listened. He'd watched Mayumi and his mother listen, and listen and never ask where the head of this family went nearly every night.

Mayumi's hands were together on the black lacquer table. She hadn't moved. He poured sake for himself, a lapse on her part that wrung out a startled apology for failing to pour his drink. "As for the office, if your father doesn't intend to bring me into the business don't think for a minute there aren't plenty of other things I can do." He reached behind him for his tattered dictionary. "I know that here in Japan, a man in my position isn't supposed to even dare imagine trying to make a living on his own.

Mayumi wasn't looking at him or making the slightest move.

"At least look at me when I talk, Goddamnit!" He wanted to shake some response out of her. "We never go anywhere. You and I never leave this goddamned house. And it's not just your foot—Jesus—Okay—I finally said it, 'your foot.' It's not just that keeping us here—we're his prisoners." He leaned to peer into her face for some kind of reaction. Her eyes were shut.

"You've got Tat. What about me? I'm Tat's father but do I ever see my own son? Like right now, where's my son. He isn't here. He's always with that stupid, mudface wetnurse or your mother—And don't act like you don't know what I'm talking about. You know I'm right! When do I see my son?" He gulped sake. "Dammit, say something!"

When she didn't answer he grabbed her cane from the floor. "Get my son. Now."

Mayumi lurched from the room.

When she returned carrying his whimpering boy in one arm, the naked baby's amber skin was pebbled a fiery red. Stricken, Sam cried. "What is it? What's wrong with him?"

"A heat rash. Mother says it is not serious but if he is with us he will cry and keep you awake—"

"What the hell do you mean not serious!" Sam pulled his son to his breast. Tat wriggled and squalled.

"Mother says—"

"Why haven't I been told? Do all of you think you could keep my boy from me and not tell me? Why isn't anybody doing anything for my son?"

"Mother was putting cold tea leaves on him—"

"To hell with your mother's tea leaves, I want a doctor—the best doctor in Nagasaki and I want him now!" His outburst kept him from hearing Setsu slide open the panel. Her hair was down in a way he'd never seen it.

"No doctor," Setsu said firmly.

"You're not his father," Sam snapped. "I said a doctor for my son and I said right now!"

Without a word the grandmother lifted the howling baby from his arms. At her touch Tat's shrieks faded to whimpers and burrowing against her, he hushed.

"No doctor." Setsu turned her back.

"Leave him here!" Sam shouted.

Setsu glided from the room. "It is best," Mayumi suggested.

"To hell with all of you!" Sam sprang to his feet, knocking over a sake flask, got to the verandah and into wooden getas and clattered out through the garden in a frenzy of anger directed at himself, the Kodos— the whole goddamned world.

CHAPTER FIFTY-EIGHT

Kodo's black dragon of a car was still there, gleaming in the lantern light outside Auntie's. Seething and locked within his own angry world, it took the jab of a bamboo cane to call his attention to a small man nattily dressed in a white linen suit grinning at him.

Absorbed in cursing himself and damning his adopted father for keeping him from Tedabara, it took a few seconds before he recognized the little man's grin full of missing teeth and emitting a peal of laughter. "Ready for Chinese dinner?"

At first Sam was speechless. Then he flung out his arms. "Torazo! Torazo, you goddamn son-of-a-bitch!"

"Yes. Torazo." His resurrected friend was presenting himself with a theatrical bow and a magician's sweep of hand displaying the miracle time had wrought. The ragged beggar now gleamed in white linen. Instead of a crutch he twirled a silver-topped bamboo walking stick. His hair, slicked down, gleamed with oil. His eyes, always huge and dark in the pale, little fox face, sparkled even brighter than Sam remembered. Most of all there was that smile, even more wicked, lacking several more teeth than at their grand and disastrous Chinese dinner.

Sam locked his little friend in a second bear hug until Torazo slipped free, and hopped back a few steps both arms urging. "Come on. *Campon!*"

Sam was grinning, wild with joy. "Where we left off two and a half years ago."

"Two years, seven months, and three days," Torazo declared. "I've been looking all over hell for you, worried that without my help, you'd be dead long ago."

"But you found me!" Happily pounding on each other's backs, Sam, in an indigo *tansen* and getas and Torazo in Western highly polished leather shoes took off sprinting side-by-side across the Shianbashi Bridge. Striding into Chinatown Sam had never been happier, so thrilled he constantly turned to make sure this truly was his long-lost friend back at his side. For a moment he slowed, for what he had to say was serious and came from his heart. "Torazo, you do understand I didn't dare try to see you in jail but, God, Torazo, you'll never know how many times I've thought about you."

"Not once did I ever give a thought to you, Asshole. Only that you're so stupid that without me you'd probably have died back at Lady Gray Rat's and got eaten by dogs." He grinned his wicked grin. "Hey, that's a great *tansen* you're wearing. Plenty expensive, uh?"

"Holy shit, I've so much to tell you I don't know where to begin. I'm married now. I have a son—hey, how long have you been out?"

"Three months and five days. But no more questions till we dig into *champon* and down buckets of ice-cold beer."

"The same restaurant?"

"Of course. This time no fake money. For two years I've been waiting to see the look on fucking Melon-Head's face."

Sam dropped his voice to dead seriousness. "Torazo, was it terrible? Jail?"

"Wonderful! Met some real people with real contacts here on the outside."

In the restaurant Torazo cursed his disappointment that their headwaiter was not Melon-Head, the son-of-a-bitch who'd packed him off to jail. "Okay, tell me—" Torazo began, and Sam knew he was opening the conversation with uncharacteristic generosity only because, whatever his news, Torazo was only waiting to top him. "So what's this about a son?"

"Can you believe it? I have a wonderful little boy. His name's Tatsuo. Fifteen months old."

"No money for an abortion?"

"I told you, you little shit, I'm married. Not only married but adopted into a fantastically rich family."

"There's not a lousy family in Japan lousy enough to have you."

"You ever heard of Kodo? "

Now he had Torazo's full attention. "Like I just said, Kodo's adopted me. Legally I'm Sam Kodo now."

Torazo tore open a fresh pack of cigarettes. His eyes locked on Sam's. "Then what I heard is true."

"You know the name?"

"Bumper Kodo? You kidding? Who doesn't know that shit?" As he spoke of the tycoon his face hardened, but he offered a cigarette, for the moment absolving his friend from association with the hated brute.

Sam couldn't rush fast enough, telling him about the love of his life. "Her name's Tedabara. She's in that house where you found me. If only she could be here with us now, life would be perfect. You'll be crazy about her."

Champon arrived. Torazo snaffled like a duck, but was listening to the story of Kodo bursting into their love nest. Torazo, who'd never been a listener, was hanging on every word about Sam's adopted father. He kept him going back to the first interview in the BlackStar office—even to descriptions of Ono-San and the tailor-made suits and kimonos with the Kodo crests and Robert Talbot—"

"Talbot—that's that piss-elegant rich *ainoko*—"

"We're members of the same club. Can you believe it, Torazo—me actually a member of a rich man's private club?"

Torazo dug the nail of his little finger into his back teeth.

"This wife of yours. She beautiful?"

"She's a fine person."

"Fine person means skinny with no tits."

Because he could admit anything to Torazo, he whispered, "You'll find out sooner or later, she's got a club foot."

"What did I tell you about needing my help?" The realist didn't hesitate. "Good in bed?" The instant he asked, he waved the question away. "Of course not. Scarcely married a year and where do I find you? Hanging around outside a whorehouse—"

Torazo bit a shred of duck from his fingernail. "You know why I was there tonight?"

"Thank God for the coincidence—"

"No coincidence. Not when I've been keeping an eye on your Kodo and find you sniffing around his whore—"

"She's not his—" Sam pushed away his *champon*. "Okay, I'll explain later, but for now, Torazo, goddamn but I've needed you, a friend I can tell anything—"

Torazo's eyes never unlocked from Sam's as he hurried him through Kodo's trap and his marriage in no time. "Now that they've got Tat they don't even need me—"

"Except to turn your futon into a workbench for making more tricycle motors—"

"I don't belong to them, Torazo."

"You just told me—you're trapped."

"But isn't this exactly what every Japanese man of any standing does? He gets the most prestigious wife he can in an arranged marriage? Right now you look like the king of the hill in that white suit of yours. You look great!"

Torazo's face suddenly darkened. "This fucking suit? Strangling me, but tonight I had no choice but to wear it to get me in to bargain with some big shots—"

"So tell me everything about what you're doing."

"We're not through with Kodo."

Sam was bursting to tell his friend everything. "It's just that I never guessed things could happen so fast."

"Kodos are rich. Goddamned capitalist shits. You don't belong there, but you ain't got the guts to run—"

"I can't. It's not just that he's got goons everywhere, now I have my son. You expect me to go back up into the hills and burn corpses? Swamp out bloody slaughter-houses?"

"You did once and it didn't kill you—"

"Do I have to tell you? You know I'll always be grateful to you. You saved my life—"

"A life named Kodo and belonging to a private club?" They both waited while lovely waitresses in gleaming silk brought a white glazed bottle of *mo tai* to the table. Torazo downed a tiny cup of the fiery alcohol. "You told me yourself about your father, your smart American father— he ran away."

"Just shut up about that."

Torazo raised his tiny cup. "It's your fucking life, rich boy." He nodded for Sam to pick up his cup. "I know you inside out, Sam Pink-er—" He corrected himself. "Sam Kodo." He twisted the name into a sneer. "I know your secret. You know your secret?" Sam knew enough to wait. "Life scares you."

"Maybe. It doesn't scare you?" Sam held out his cup for more *mo tai*.

The price for Torazo pouring was more advice. "You read too much—"

"Believe it or not I've been reading philosophy, Torazo." He proved it with a quotation. 'The unexamined life isn't worth living.'"

"Who said that?"

"Aristotle."

"That asshole's dead. Like all history except for Marx."

"Karl Marx?"

"You haven't read him, right?" Torazo spat. "You just sit on your ass. Don't get involved. You know why? You're not just scared, you're scared shitless."

The last thing Sam wanted was the talk turning to Karl Marx. "Hey, whatever you're up to I've got to admit you sure as hell got out of jail looking like a million dollars."

"What I look like right now is a fucking pimp. I told you, I'm dressed up in all this crap because I had to go lie to some rich people to get money for the cause. After tonight you'll never see me in shit like this again."

Sam considered the bottle and decided against another drink. "You were going to tell me about jail."

"I told you. It was wonderful. A fifty-year-old hundred-kilo *Yakuza* covered with tattoos thought I was cute."

"He helped you?"

"Fucked me raw. I loved it—an honorable Japanese tradition going back to the samurai. They didn't even have to go to jail to fuck boys."

"That's not true—"

"And your baby boy popped out of a peach?" Torazo hailed a lovely waitress and switched to beers. "He took good care of me. Powerful, with contacts on the outside."

"Where is he now?"

"Still inside. Tonight I met with some of his contacts."

Sam stared at Torazo. Yes. Under that white linen suit, he was still the same foxy, hard driving Torazo of the old days. "If you're talking about the *Yakuza* I hope that doesn't mean you."

"I'm too small to be good at breaking bones. Still, what I do's better than being married to a woman with no tits. What I am—when I'm not dressed up like an asshole—is I'm a labor organizer."

"Don't tell me you're a communist?"

"You want to hear me sing the *Internationale?*"

"A Red?"

"Drink your beer, comrade."

"Kodo says all labor union men are Reds."

"Bumper Kodo, uh? Do you know that every time a good union brother goes past that pier of the Inasa Bridge we bow to our comrade buried in Kodo cement? Every time we go past that mansion of his—of yours now—we piss."

"You're drunk."

"Of course. But not too drunk to remember that after our last Chinese dinner we didn't get to the best part of the evening, the ladies."

"I'm a married man."

Torazo roared with laughter. "Who do you think keeps all the whorehouses open?"

CHAPTER FIFTY-NINE

Torazo hustled Sam to a slum and two Korean whores. Whores, but in no way women to compare remotely to the glorious Tedabara. But they were hot naked flesh. Sam discovered that for all of Torazo's enthusiasm for men and boys in jail, he jumped on top of his whore like a crazed monkey in heat.

They shuffled off into an alley and wound up in a bar downing more cold beer. Sam admitted to his pal he'd never been away from Mayumi and Tat so late into the night. Or been with another woman. What the hell, he was with his only friend in the world except Suzuki. "Torazo," he confessed, "you don't know what I'm up against."

"Then get your balls out of the wringer," the little fox, the realist, spat.

"Easy for you to say."

"Look, Big Stupid, everything's perfect. What you're going to do is you're going to stay right where you are and help us fight the bastard."

Sam studied his beer and said nothing. Torazo moved closer as if he was about to share all the wisdom in the world. "Make him need you."

"I just told you he won't give me a goddamn thing to do—"

"He uses the docks doesn't he?" Sam nodded at what was clearly the truth. Both knew few men held more power over Nagasaki's shipping. Torazo's face was close, almost touching his. "Every day my men on the docks brag how much they steal off Kodo and the others. You think those ships Glover refuels get every chunk of coal they pay for? You think when a load of lumber comes in from America your turd has any idea how much of it gets stolen?"

"That's where you're wrong," Sam insisted. "I know for a fact he's got people he pays to be down on the docks who do nothing but check for him."

"While some other guy's paying them even more not to check."

"You think he hasn't got spies?"

"Again, taking bigger kickbacks than he pays. You seem to forget who you're talking to, Big Stupid. Me. Remember? I know the docks!" From the old days Sam had been in awe, seeing how sharp little Torazo always had most of the answers.

"So far you haven't said you're a Red, but you sure as hell talk like a Bolshevik."

"I talk like I know how the fucking world works. Something you better wise up to fast." Torazo looked at his beer and enjoyed a long burp. "Give me a couple of days and I'll find out who's doing most of the stealing. What you do is you tell your rich turd you know all about lumber. Hell, you told me that when you were a kid you lived in the States where they cut down the trees. Perfect. Convince him you know lumber and can prove a bunch of highbinders down on the docks are robbing him blind and you're just the man to tighten up on control."

Sam caught fire. "Right—instead of sitting in the office—"

"That's it. Get your ass down on the docks. Better still, get over to Fukuoka where they're robbing him right and left and you say how you can stop it. Save him money—a piss pot full of money—"

"But aren't you supposed to be on the workers' side?"

"Leave that to me—just do what I say."

Sam had never chugged so much beer, but he was ready for more, fired up about getting down onto the docks, even Fukuoka, and into battle. "Now he'll have to listen to me—"

"No. You listen to me. You're going to have to play him like a fish. Make him think everything you come up with is his idea." Sam burped and stared at the raised hand cautioning him, a hand he'd forgotten was so bony and small. "I'll get back to you in a couple of days. In the meantime, get to the docks up at Fukuoka. Show some balls, but never forget, whatever you do—always make that turd think it was his idea."

CHAPTER SIXTY

The Korean whore was his first time being unfaithful to Mayumi. Though he felt that emotionally his unfaithfulness didn't mean a thing, he was more a missionary boy than a Japanese husband. Performing penance, he began planning a special night out for their first anniversary.

That evening, September first, was sweltering, but he'd dressed in black London tailoring, putting on his gloves and taking them off, waiting for Setsu to help Mayumi through the intricacies of donning a new traditional kimono in celadon with a russet and white sash. After her mother added skillful finishing touches to her hair, she was ready to leave the house, but kept him waiting, while rushing back twice to kiss Tat.

Nagasaki was gasping in the September heat but inside the opulent Russian restaurant the fashionable international crowd in both Japanese and Western style were cooled by fans revolving overhead. Mayumi entered, disguising a gray-green cane, the color perfectly matching her kimono. She clung to Sam's arm carefully making her way through candlelight and red plush, past white linen tables and gleaming brass samovars to their table. Three huge Russian Cossacks strolling and strumming balalaikas nodded their welcome.

"Happy?" Sam asked, taking over from the Russians to seat her himself.

"Oh, yes," she lied.

"Now aren't you glad we came?"

He knew she'd been reluctant, but hadn't realized that leaving the house would so terrify her that it would take a half hour before she relaxed enough to accept her role as a beautifully-dressed young wife celebrating her anniversary with her husband. She leaned close. "Everyone says the headwaiter is a cousin to the last czar. You know what he whispered to me on our way in?" Her lips touched his ear. "That you looked exactly like a Romanov—a Russian prince." Her hand reached across the table to her prince. "Yes, Sam-San, I'm glad we came."

"If we weren't in public I'd give you a kiss," he said leaning across the table with his fingers brushing her cheek. "I just might anyway. We need some wine. Later I have a surprise."

By now he had her dark and beautiful eyes, her best feature, sparkling.

After beef stroganoff for him and chicken kiev for her, it was time for dessert and coffee. He surprised her by helping her rise from the table. Taking her by the arm he lead her up a flight of stairs. The suave Russian prince, who may have been a Romanov with all his innate dignity, opened the door of a private second-floor salon. Mayumi looked up at Sam with wide eyes. Heavy brocade curtains, rosewood furniture, the inevitable samovar, glowing candles, masses of fresh flowers set off a chaise lounge waiting in a curtained alcove. Their host wound a phonograph with a horn like a morning glory. Before he could put the needle to a record, Sam stopped him. "No. Not yet. I'll do that."

"The other gramophone records you ordered are here, sir." The prince who was headwaiter hovered. "Is everything to Gospodin Kodo's satisfaction?"

Sam frowned at the otherwise resplendent private room. "Didn't the restaurant get my order to move back the table and chairs and roll up the carpet?"

"It will be done instantly, sir."

Sam restrained himself from helping the busboys bare a hardwood floor. Mayumi sat on deep blue velour sipping her coffee and nibbling charlotte russe, wide-eyed, awaiting her husband's next surprise. He pushed away his dessert and rose to put a waltz record on the turntable and crank the Victrola. With overdone formality Sam had seen in the movies, he presented himself before her clicking his heels. "May your husband have the honor of this dance?"

Dance? She stifled a gasp but not her look of horror. Before she could escape the music, he raised her to her feet and held her close. On his strong arm there was no way she could stumble. Yes, he was asking his wife to dance and looking straight into her eyes telling her to draw on all her courage to face the truth—that young men liked to dance.

Music swelled the room with Western romance. Both studied the "How to Waltz" manual he'd brought without moving, swaying together, thrilling to the sweep of the music. He cleared his throat and announced, "Here we go!" They moved together, "One . . . Two . . . Three. One . . . Two . . . Three." She came close to faltering but he caught her, and on they went. "One . . . Two . . . Three. One . . . Two . . . Three."

By the time the record hissed to the end both were holding their breath in surprise. Both blinking back tears. They'd been dancing. Mayumi stood alone as Sam sprang to the Victrola winding it, waiting for her signal to start the music again.

This time they didn't count, nor did they dare breathe. Something wonderful, wonderful beyond belief, was happening. Two bodies unlocked and pressed close, sharing each other in an intimacy they'd never given way to in bed. She smiled. Her wet eyes shone. So this was dancing! Every step grew surer till suddenly she laughed, no Japanese giggle to hide embarrassment behind a fluttering fan, but a laugh of triumphant joy.

CHAPTER SIXTY-ONE

Sam startled his Japanese father by walking into his office and brandishing five-feet of a North American Douglas fir two-by-four. With a new firmness the adopted son had never mustered before he announced, "Sir, as you know, I grew up in the part of America where this Douglas fir comes from. I know lumber."

Kodo ignored him but heaved himself from his desk snatching the offending piece of wood. With an intent look to prove himself not only knowledgeable but an expert, he turned the two-by-four in his hand, grimacing at its sticky resin. "Piece of shit is what this is. Wide grain. Green.

Full of pitch." He spat, "What the hell are you jabbing it at me for?"

"You paid for the best, Sir. I'm afraid this is what we got."

Kodo hurled the offending two-by-four across the office. "Where the hell did you find this."

"Our latest shipment. This two-by-four was on its way to the Okamoto job."

Kodo, already enraged, rumbled thunder. "I pay people down there good money to check shipments and make sure those highbinders don't try and get away with shit like this." His eyes narrowed to slits, a sure sign suspicions were coming together. "Someone down there," he muttered darkly, "has to be buying them off."

"Looks that way, but I'm sure that Sir will know what to do."

"Find out where this shipment came from."

Sam was already unfolding a bill of lading.

Kodo took his position at his desk, flamed a cigar and drew deeply. "You probably think this comes as a surprise to me. Oh, no. I've been smelling a rat for some time—I've just been giving those bastards time to hang themselves—"

Sam fought a smile thinking of Torazo's advice. Sam had proof of fraud. His fish was hooked, and now claiming the discovery of fraud as his own idea. Sam smothered his satisfaction, enjoying watching the tycoon's face darken till furious determination spun him on his heel. Brandishing the offending two-by-four and shoving Sam with him out the door, Kodo hurried from the office.

Bumper Kodos's surprise appearance at the dock struck terror into his own people and brought defiant stares of hate from Torazo's workers. Down here on the waterfront he was a Jeremiah from the Old Testament in his fury. Sam's only disappointment was that Torazo wasn't here to revel in his adopted father's Biblical wrath.

At Kodo's side, Sam kept his voice low, careful to never be more than suggesting, playing his fish so that they might uncover even deeper crime. "I doubt sir has to worry about that big shipment coming into Fukuoka at the end of the week. I'm sure we can trust our people up there absolutely."

Kodo wheeled in another eruption of self-righteousness. "Don't stand there and tell me not to worry. You think I have time to be everywhere to check on these cheating bastards?"

"With all you have to worry about, sir, you're too busy, of course, to go up there yourself. Before the Fukuoka people add on the rail freight before hauling it down here, would it make sense if you called someone up there you can trust—someone to see we're getting what we're paying for?"

"So why are you hanging around here when you could make yourself useful? Dammit, do I have to think of everything!"

In Fukuoka harbor for the first time in over a year, Sam breathed in fresh air at last out from under the mansion's roof. For two full days and nights he was free in this city, letting his spirits soar.

Sam telephoned Torazo. "Get your ass up here. I owe you a beer. Besides, there's a big sumo tournament."

In the lobby of the best hotel in Fukuoka Sam waited for his old friend, wishing he didn't look so much like a toff in a beautifully tailored beige English suit, but he was here, an important executive of the Black-Star Construction and Bay Trading Corporations of Nagasaki and Tokyo.

Torazo swaggered into the lobby unmistakably a labor leader in rough indigo-dyed work clothes blazoned with a red scarf.

Not even a hello. "Didn't I tell you I'd get you out from under Kodo?"

Sam didn't hold back. He gave him full credit for his temporary freedom. "Kodo should put you on the payroll as my new manager."

"Fuck all Kodos." The brat who was now a man of the workers of the world had no time for banter and was back out the door with Sam rushing after him explaining his triumph. "It's Kodo's own people up here on the docks who are stealing him blind. You can't believe the amount of fraud I've already turned up." Sam hurried to his friend's side. "I've just telephoned him and he's already fired two of the worst thieves. Thanks to you, old buddy, I've already saved BlackStar a bundle."

"I'm not doing this to help that shit." He shoved his tall friend into the street. "Come on. We're already late—"

"But I've got tickets for the sumo tournament—"

Torazo waved aside any idea of entertainment, though sumo to the Japanese is close to religion. No. He was hurrying Sam to the docks and into a packed union hall raucous and surging with raw energy. Dockworkers wearing red bandanas like Torazo's jammed the place, filling the air blue with cigarette smoke. Feeling ridiculously overdressed in his suit, Sam slid off his silk tie and roughed-up his hair. The instant the crowd saw Torazo cheers exploded for their special guest from Nagasaki. "Watch," Torazo snapped back at Sam with his eyes blazing. "Watch, Mister fake Kodo, and learn."

Sam, the capitalist enemy, shrank down by himself at the back of the hall and did as he'd been told. He watched Torazo bound onto the stage taking his place with four other men at a table under two flags, one Japan's rising sun, another of total blood red. A voice raised the first notes of a song that swelled, bringing the crowd to its feet and roaring. Even Sam recognized the *Internationale* without knowing the words, but everyone in the hall was singing and none more lustily with waving arms than Torazo. The song ended. A battle cry. Up on the stage in noise and smoke a Caucasian and two Japanese in work clothes like Torazo's strode forward, facing the excited crowd now yelling, demanding first-hand news of their brothers on the Vladivostok and Nagasaki docks.

Torazo, thin little Torazo, was a giant. The hall rocked with cheers. Sam marveled at the excitement his thin little friend radiated. His cries invoked the Party with a ringing faith Wendell Snyder had never been able to reach calling on the Lord.

"The Party," he shouted, "is on the march!"

The hall stamped and cheered. One sweep of his hand silenced them instantly. For a little man his voice on a megaphone matched the crowd's roar. "How long, comrades, before the working class breaks its chains and throws out the bosses? How long, brothers, before we kick the foreign capitalists' asses out of Japan?"

Sam felt his own heart beating, his blood pounding with every man around him on his feet and thundering the cry Torazo assured them was rising from every dock in Japan. In Nagasaki the battle was against Kodo's docks and here he was, in their midst, Kodo's son. He rose to his feet as if he were one of them. "Thank God," he told his battering heart "at least this isn't Nagasaki but far-off Fukuoka."

Torazo was solid flame. "You want to know about Nagasaki? In Nagasaki—to a man—we're ready to die for the cause. What about here in Fukuoka?"

The crowd stamped and yelled.

"Do I have to tell you up here," Torazo demanded, "how to live on seventy-seven cents a day?" Another blast of answering thunder rocked the hall. "Do I have to tell you we are up against the military and every corrupt capitalist baron's stooge they send to the Diet in Tokyo? Do I have to tell you the time has past when any workingman who calls himself a man can hang back from giving his heart and soul and balls—his life— to the revolution?"

Sam stayed low and held his breath.

Torazo dropped his voice preparing his bombshell. "Do I have to tell you that tonight here in Fukuoka and Nagasaki we stand shoulder-to-shoulder ready to close down every port in Japan?" His call to arms sent the crowd wild. Huge red banners rippled down behind the speaker. Then a black-and-white portrait of a figure Sam did not recognize but the workers seemed to worship. With a fierce thrust of his fist Torazo shouted his loudest shout of all. "Strike!" The single word, like a thunderclap, flashed over the hall like a solid sheet of flame. In the roar Torazo rushed to the front of the stage reaching down to the crowd surging toward him, eager to shake his hand.

The night was still, quiet but for the hoot of a ship out in the harbor. Two hours after the massive rally the two old friends were alone, side-by-side, silently walking the waterfront. "My God, Torazo, you are really something!"

"I always got work for you, didn't I?"

"And didn't I always pay you your commission?" Sam hoped his joking answer covered his awe. Torazo, however, was clearly in no mood for sharing pride or banter. Whatever he'd been through in prison had intensified his fire, his fierce determination. For another long moment neither spoke as they walked on. In awe and respect he waited for Torazo to leave the crowd and speak of their friendship's future. He wasn't encouraged by his next words.

"Kodo's your father, right?"

"You know that."

"Do you know that if I wore this red scarf in Nagasaki his goons would smash every bone in my body?" Torazo was continuing his endless blast of hate against Kodo. Sam slowed to a standstill, looking down at his small friend who was staring straight up at him. It was clear. Torazo wanted blood. He was a demonic force with the power to raise men to their feet and follow him into hell to get that blood.

Sam sank back into silence. What could he say? Everything Torazo was accusing him of was true. Yes, he was a Kodo and therefore Torazo's sworn enemy. He'd seen that this silent man at his side was as powerful in his way as Kodo. They walked on. Sam broke the silence by acknowledging his old friend's power. Again he expressed his gratitude—he'd broken free of his adopted father and was here in Fukuoka only because of his old friend.

Torazo huffed. "With that monster turd of yours claiming it was his idea."

"You were right, and I want you to know how grateful I am."

"You'll have a chance to prove that."

Sam went ice cold. Prove what? He'd thanked him for this respite from Kodo. What—besides continuing their friendship—did he owe this fierce little man? Ducking that thought with the hope of keeping their meeting on the basis of their old friendship, he offered, "What say, right now, we go for another Chinese dinner?"

When Torazo didn't answer more than silence separated them. Out in the harbor ships' bells clanged, lights gleamed and reflected on the dark water. Beer, Sam decided, was acceptably proletarian and he pulled Torazo into a bar, determined to hang on to whatever was left of their friendship. "Hey, after watching you tonight, I sure as hell hope reading Marx doesn't mean you've lost your sense of humor with your oldest pal."

"I lost it while you were kissing Kodo's ass."

Sam steeled himself against the insult, another riptide in which he was struggling for common ground. "The other night you didn't say much about prison. To hear you talk, you made it sound like just another adventure—like letting that *Yakuza* screw you."

"Inside I met a guy from Vladivostok—that's in Russia in case you don't know. This guy had heard Lenin—" Torazo was in his own world indulging in talk of places and events he knew were beyond Sam's ken, reducing everything about Kodo's adopted son and his life as a continuing fraud. "That guy from Vladivostock actually heard Lenin speak." Shining dark eyes glittered looking beyond Sam at the future. "I take it even you have heard of Lenin."

Sam was ready to shout in his face that he wasn't as stupid or uninformed as Torazo was making him out to be. Torazo was in charge. "This guy was in Russia with a crowd waiting for Lenin outside a mine with cars coming out loaded with coal. When Lenin appeared and finally got the crowd shut up enough you want to guess the very first thing he shouted at them?" Sam didn't like it, but he knew he was under orders to keep his mouth shut. Torazo didn't want an answer. He had it. "Lenin asked them just one question. 'What comes out of that mine?' The crowd roared back, 'Coal!' 'No,' Lenin told them. 'Men—with coal'!"

Sam had little hope another beer might ease the tension between them, but even to his audience of one Torazo was fierce, smoldering. "You'll find out. Reading Marx changes everything. All of a sudden, everything I already knew by instinct was right there in print, right in front of me. Read it. Marx will tell you—even you—the way the masses get ground down deeper every day so shits like your Kodo can get richer."

Sam held himself in check instead of grabbing Torazo and shouting in his damned little fox face that if they had any chance left of staying friends, then goddammit shut up and lay off his father.

Torazo was on fire burning with his cause. "I've talked to a lot of guys who've been to Russia. To a man they'll tell you they've seen the future and it works."

"This isn't goddamn Russia," Sam grumbled, "this is Japan."

"Then you better open your half-Japanese eyes and you'll see Marx is talking about the world sweating its guts out, barely able to keep families alive. Are you so goddamned rich you've already forgotten about hauling those Argentine hides?"

Suddenly Sam couldn't bear another minute of this little bar. He rose. "Come on. Let's go. The beer's on me."

"Paying with Kodo's money?" Torazo made it clear he wasn't leaving. For a long moment Sam stood at a loss with no idea what his next move might be.

"Tonight, goddammit, you've been rough on me, Torazo. At least twice I thanked you for this trip and getting out from under him. Maybe it's the American in me, but my life won't be Kodo. I've got my own life to live. I've told you, I'm going to teach—"

"No. You're going to stay with Kodo. You're more valuable to the Party right where you are."

The Party? Making him a brother to his dock workers? "Hell, no." He knocked over a stool jumping to his feet. "I'm not Kodo and I'm not one of them—"

"Sit down, shut the fuck up, and listen. You know damned well every single word I told my workers with you sitting out there in your fancy suit was the truth. We're closing down the docks in Nagasaki. Life and death. Kill or be killed—"

"You're talking to me—not a hall full of your men—"

"It's Kodo and his shits or us!"

Sam was on his feet. "Leave me the hell out of this—"

Torazo jumped up and grabbed him. His hold was as fierce as his words. "We've got to get someone in his office besides you to work from the inside." Sam was flinging down coins to get out of this beer joint. "Your fake father. You hate him? Yes or no?"

"I have a son of my own."

"Then give the kid a better world. I watched you from up there on stage. You stood with the rest of them—"

"I was an asshole—too scared to do anything else."

"That's my Sam. Like a year ago you didn't have the balls to tell Kodo to go to hell so you married his cripple with no tits—"

"Shut up!" This had been his first and only friend in Japan who'd saved his life. He managed to find a calm voice. "Whatever happened to our friendship?"

Little Torazo, so much smaller than Sam, eyes darker than his were glaring up, on fire. "Until you come to me saying you're going to help the cause, stay the fuck out of my sight!"

CHAPTER SIXTY-TWO

The next morning Sam hurried straight from the train to the office, reported on the Fukuoka shipments and pilferage without, of course, saying one word of Torazo and his strike plans. That his success in that port digging out fraud and crooked shipments brought no praise from Kodo wasn't surprising. Still, the man stunned him when he grumbled, "Now we see if I can make you useful in Tokyo."

Tokyo?

Did he hear right? Could he be talking about taking him on his next trip to Tokyo? Imagine, finally he'd have the chance to see the capital of his adopted country!

He bought homecoming gifts for Mayumi and Tat, still excited with his thrilling news. "Tokyo!" Apparently her father had told her of Sam's Tokyo trip and if facing their first long separation darkened Mayumi's joy, she covered her hurt, smiling and appearing to share his excitement. She put Tat in his arms while she opened the carefully wrapped gifts in red and white from the smartest department stores in the Fukuoka's *Tenjin* district.

Mayumi spread wide an apple-green fringed Spanish shawl and flung it over her shoulders in delight. Tat hugged a Teddy Bear and kissed his father.

Soaking in the blissful *o furo* with his wife and son he related his adventures, his days of travel. There was no reason to mention an old friendship he'd always kept a secret part of his life and had ended so bitterly. Torazo. His first, his only friend in Japan. Torazo, who found him work on the docks. Torazo, who'd saved his life, his only joy in those dark first days. After their bath she dressed him herself in his *yukata* and oversaw a welcome-home dinner with plenty of sake.

Glowing with drink he sensed Mayumi had her own secret which she couldn't wait to share. Carrying Tat on her hip and taking Sam by the hand she led him into a back room with a brand-new linoleum floor replacing the tatami. In the corner a shiny new Victrola displayed its gleaming self. She signaled Sam to hold silent, settled Tat giggling in a corner and placed a record on the turntable. A waltz flooded the room. "Tales From the Vienna Woods," she whispered. Taking his hand in hers she moved with such grace Sam realized she'd been diligently practicing the steps.

"You've been taking lessons."

Mayumi couldn't hide her smile. She often surprised him. She might be the daughter of a fierce thug and ruthless father, but her sensibilities were as finely tuned as one of those silken court ladies in ancient Japan he'd read about in *The Tale of Genji*. Hadn't old Masao said she might turn out to be a nice kid? No. Mayumi was far more than nice. She was uncanny, with an innate sense for the feelings of others. He marveled how her feelings for her mother, the wetnurse and servants, the gardener, the driver, and, yes, even her father, went deeper than the mere politeness expected of most Japanese. Since none of this came from Kodo, her extraordinary sensitivity must have been inherited from her mother. Perhaps being crippled gave her deeper insight into what others were feeling.

They danced. He drew her close. "You and your secret lessons."

Against his cheek she nodded. "Like those tennis lessons you take."

That's supposed to be a secret so if the day ever comes when Talbot finally asks me to play I can give him a good game."

"Why wait? Are you afraid to ask him?"

The song ended and he changed the record. Another waltz. She was in his arms.

"Sam-San. Ask him."

"It's not that simple. It's touchy. We're both *ainokos*."

She waved a small finger but big in disagreement. "You're a Kodo."

He kissed her. "You probably think everyone's as kind as you. Our Robert's a terrible snob. Maybe being with me reminds him he's an *ainoko*—"

"Don't wait for him to ask you about tennis. Go ahead. You ask him."

At the club Sam seemed to be enjoying sudden respect. Members sought him out to congratulate him on his triumph uncovering corruption on the docks. Apparently Talbot had heard and offering a cigarette, Rudolf Valentino admitted, "Seems you've made yourself something of a hero." With a smile behind his smoke, he said, "Tennis on Wednesday?"

It was late in the afternoon when they played their first game in brilliant sunlight under a blue October sky scoured clean by what everyone hoped was the last typhoon of the season. The court was clay on a terrace above Chinese graves at the Kofukuji temple. As Sam suspected, Talbot was a graceful player before he turned fierce. He won, but Sam was triumphant. He'd made him sweat.

"Not too bad for a rickshaw boy. Your serve is first-rate. Backhand needs major work. Of course you took lessons."

"Of course."

"Carry on with them."

They finished with a beer. Tennis and sweat and sunlight had made Talbot less aloof. "Now that you're our club's resident expert on the docks, what do you hear about a strike?"

"Only what you hear." Sam didn't lie. He'd heard nothing since his breakup with Torazo.

Talbot's long fingers eased sweat from his eyes. "Word seems to be the workers are mounting up for a big one. I imagine Old Bumper's looking forward to giving those sods a time they won't forget."

"Like your father, I imagine," said Sam.

"Could be a rough show."

"Worse than last year?"

"Filthy Reds. Well, they shan't turn Japan into Russia, I can tell you that."

By now the two were playing twice a week. Tennis was a game with no ambiguities—in or out—long or short—the same rules for Englishmen or Americans or Japanese or *ainoko*. On the court Talbot played hard and seldom reverted to his earlier nastiness. After their games, when they drank beer in the sunlight, Sam allowed himself the hope they might become close, real friends.

On a bitter night in late October, when the mulberry tree trunks out in the garden had been wrapped in straw for the winter, Mayumi and Sam, in silk *yukatas*, were chasing their naked and giggling Tat across the tatamis. Neither heard the maid slide back the hall panel. All three were on the floor when they looked up at Robert Talbot, a totally unexpected guest. Mayumi was the first to recover and, with her infinite grace, even with her twisted foot, was bowing to the young gentleman. A *castera* in one hand, and a little carved rooster for Tat in the other, explained his excuse for his visit.

Sam was all smiles, so pleased he was nearly at a loss welcoming their aristocratic caller. Mayumi, bowing and accepting the *castera,* expressed how touched they were at Talbot-San's thoughtfulness honoring their child born in the Year of the Rooster. She hurried the maid off for hot sake and tiny cups. She found a dark-green *zabuton* for their guest onto which he lowered himself, supple as any Japanese the way he tucked his heels under his backside. Mayumi was already opening a box of cigars, testing them for freshness, insisting her two young men smoke.

Robert was a master of Japanese decorum but seemed uncertain how to cope with giggling Tat pummeling fists into his waistcoat. Sam stifled a smile. Their guest appropriately pronounced the boy's vigor was that of a little samurai and allowed Tat, enchanted by his Cartier wristwatch, to poke further under his French cuffs. The two men smoked their cigars and, in deference to Mayumi, refrained from reviewing their last tennis game as the conversation relied on the tiny cups of sake Mayumi poured with unfailing smiles.

Sam talked baseball and Babe Ruth's phenomenal season with the Yankees. Robert insisted nothing compared with cricket. They agreed to disagree with more sake.

They even toasted King Tut in Ancient Egypt and the Englishman who'd discovered his tomb that year.

After an hour and a glance at that Cartier wristwatch, Robert rose and Mayumi, with Tat and Sam at her side, walked their guest through the corridors of the mansion to the front porch. She handed Tat to Sam and with a shoehorn knelt and helped Robert slide into his highly polished oxfords. The couple, holding Tat, waved at Talbot's Packard carrying him into the cold and windy night.

Mayumi took Sam's hand and looked up at him. He nodded. "Yes, I'm glad you insisted I call him."

Three nights later Robert returned with a picture book for Tat of Japanese fairy tales by Lafcadio Hearn and two bottles which represented East and West equally—the finest sake and Johnnie Walker Black Label. Mayumi coaxed their guest into a *yukata* identical to their own, and kissing Tat as the wet-nurse took him off to bed, the three sank into the wonderful informality of living on the floor on rice mats. Robert lay back with his arms under his head. "Nothing, absolutely nothing in England is as good as this."

The mud-faced wet nurse brought Tat in to say goodnight and laid him on a quilt in front of the three. Robert, kneeling Japanese style, presented the picture book to the baby and holding it patiently, turned the pages at which Tat stabbed with a pudgy finger. The little boy stared at the pictures, his eyes shining, then giggled and butted his head into the guest, who carefully raised his glowing cigar over his head to keep from singeing the lad's fuzz of dark hair.

Mayumi took the cover off her koto, which Sam knew Robert detested. Their guest bore the plinking, which startled cheers out of him when he and Sam recognized *Alexander's Ragtime Band.* Robert startled them not only by bursting into song but knowing all the words. As the three sang, Tat waved his arms and chortled and then turned to discover a new game called "flinging the picture book across the room."

Robert's *yukata* flopped open, which he modestly drew back over his bare legs crawling to Mayumi at her koto, adding Japanese words to her traditional *Sakura.*

After they sang Mayumi poured her men Scotch and for the first time Sam and his wife of two years, and their Best Man, all sprawling on the floor, sensed it was past time to open their hearts. Both men looked at her to go first. Without any giggling preamble she spoke simply. Although she was not a Christian she told them about going to the Sturges School—Umegasaki Jogakko—for proper young ladies here in Nagasaki. Tonight, as a married lady with a child, she was able to tell Robert she'd been the only cripple in her school.

And Robert? They didn't ask, but waited. Had being the only Eurasian among all those British boys so far from home and Nagasaki been difficult? The proud man inferred that those years were more than difficult. Their guest studied his cigar. "I think that probably I wasn't any more lonely than the rest, but I was definitely the furthest from home and the taste of sushi. For a moment he was silent and Sam pictured him among gray stones with starchy headmasters offering discipline. The man lying on the floor with his cigar explained his other world. "Boys' schools in England are called public but are private and always cold and damp, made even damper by homesick boys wetting their beds. Mine was Winchester. I must have told you, Sam, that I wasn't all that keen to be chosen the lead in *The Mikado.* The headmaster said it was perfect casting and they assured me incessantly that there was absolutely no need to feel uncomfortable, and even if I should, it would develop my character."

The mood threatened to grow so serious Mayumi suggested Sam's adventures could wait for another evening when she laughed and reached for his cigar. "May I?" She drew in the tiniest pull of smoke and handed it back and sent out a wisp, astonishing her men into such speechlessness that fell backwards with laughter.

From that evening on Robert was family. He'd arrive for dinner laden with books and magazines from England and the States and the newest gramophone records. Some evenings they went out to the movies and nothing was better than rushing home out of the cold, nothing more cozy than pulling on identical *yukatas* and ordering Chinese food which a bicycle boy with a bell would deliver. No evening was long enough to talk about the songs of the day and new books and arguing about H. G. Wells's view of the future, and Mark Twain, or Booth Tarkington, whose books Sam said might be about Indiana, but described exactly how it felt to be a boy in Bremerton. World politics? Robert appeared to understand the new Five Power Treaty, but was at a loss to explain to the young Kodos why Japan's Navy was limited to half that of Britain's. As open as they'd become about their pasts, neither man talked much about their days at work—Sam in Kodo's office, Robert with his father, managing the Talbot factories and godowns. Unlike most Japanese men, they shared their feelings with Mayumi, a rewarding listener who entered their world with appropriate diffidence, expressing her own thoughts, but smoking no more cigars.

As the winter winds grew colder and rattled the *shojis,* they shared quilts and drew close around the *kotatsu,* the middle-of-the-floor sunken fire pit. These three who knew something about being outcasts—two *ain-oko*—a word rarely spoken by proper Japanese to describe their otherness—and a skinny Japanese wife dragging a clubfoot—had found one another. All three were Asian enough to know better than to challenge the gods everyone knows are jealous and snatch away such blessings. At times of heart-filling happiness, Sam was silent. Could either Mayumi or Robert guess he was thinking of his younger, All-American brother? Strange. Over the years it seemed to him the times he was nearest despair, or like tonight, at his happiest, was when he thought of his brother. Since his marriage he'd written twice, care of Johns Hopkins Medical School, where his grandfather was a famous surgeon. Both letters had failed to reach Benjy, and after months and months and covered with stickers and notes, had been returned to Nagasaki.

One November evening Robert arrived positively glowing. On his last trip on the P&O coming out from England he'd met a young English rose from Kent. Her father, who looked the part, was in banking in Hong Kong. The Clendenings, apparently, approved of any young man who'd gone to Winchester and to Oxford. In the middle of the Indian Ocean they declared their love for each other.

"Green eyes. Truly, I swear, actually emerald green. Radiantly beautiful with the most glorious auburn hair and a lovely figure. The most marvelous sense of humor. Not that she doesn't have a serious side. Not that you'd ever twig to anything serious when you're dancing with her. The most wonderful, wonderful laugh. She knows every line of Rupert Brooke and lives in Hong Kong half way up Robinson Road on Victoria Peak and can't wait to give the slip to her tiresome family. Did I tell you her name? Victoria Clendening. I chant it like a sutra a dozen times a day. Right now I've passage in my pocket to go down to Hong Kong and bring her back here for a Christmas wedding." Mayumi and Sam looked at each other. Their friend's almond eyes were shining, the happiest man in the world. "Can't wait for the two of you to meet her. Naturally, Sam, you have no choice but to return the favor and stand up for me, and be my Best Man."

Mayumi watched the two men solemnly seal the bond by shaking hands like the most proper of Anglo Saxons, then pouring sake for each other like Japanese. Sam raised himself on an elbow and knew he'd remember as long as he lived these three sharing such looks of happiness— his wife, his friend, and a few feet away on a blue quilt, even his sleeping son was smiling.

After Sam walked him to the front gate and his friend drove home in his Packard and the last of the lanterns were dimmed and the house was dark with the futons spread on the floor, Sam knew his wife was waiting. Did she know how many nights he rose and walked their wing of the mansion alone in the dark? Away from this wife, out in the frosty garden and alone, how he ached to smell cheap incense and lick the sweat off his burning Tedabara.

CHAPTER SIXTY-THREE

The first week in November Robert sailed for Hong Kong on the Orsava to bring his future bride home to Nagasaki to meet his family. Sam counted the days till he'd stand beside his friend as his Best Man. Before Robert's return, a hand-delivered invitation arrived, engraved on heavy stock. The two young Kodos were to grace a formal dinner at the Talbot mansion welcoming the young couple and her parents.

"Look." He showed her the engraved invitation with its return envelope for their answer. "You know what this means? The Talbots your father thinks are so high and mighty are practically making us one of them."

She turned away with the pretense of being too busy running the house to glance at the invitation. "Not now. I haven't time. Tat needs me."

"Your mother or the nurse can take care of him. Come on. We're answering right this minute."

"No." She seemed determined to resist what so excited Sam. "Besides, I hate Western clothes—"

He thrust the card close. "Look right here. 'Japanese style is preferred for Japanese ladies.'"

"Nothing I have is right—"

"We're rich. Buy something new."

"No." She waved away the idea. "You go. Not me."

"What's all this about? Are you crazy? I'm Robert's Best Man. He's your friend every bit as much as mine." She turned away to leave. "What the hell's wrong with you? Not only Robert but his family wants us with them—"

Without looking at him or the invitation, again her small hand waved away his words. "You go. Now I must see to Tat."

Anger sharpened his voice. "Don't give me that, and don't try to run off like this. We're his best friends and we're going to be there."

Still without looking up at him she offered more resistance. "You told me yourself you have that trip to Tokyo with father—"

"You think I'd miss being with Robert? Not even for Tokyo. No. We're going and we're going to have the time of our lives—Wait right there, dammit, don't turn away from me . . ."

The following evening he was surprised at her fierce refusal until, for the first time in their marriage, she broke into tears. "Don't you know?" She sobbed. "It's about Father." So there it was. Of course. How could he have overlooked Kodo's rage that the Talbot's doors, forever shut to him, were opening only enough to welcome Sam and his wife.

Kodo was fast on the attack, roaring into their wing of the mansion. "You tell your goddamned high-and-mighty Talbots I go—my wife and I will be there with you or no Kodo goes." Kodo ordered his son to reach the Talbots and straighten out this insult immediately. Sam could only remind Kodo that he'd yet to meet Robert's parents and for now was unable to reach his friend who was still in Hong Kong.

"If your famous Talbot is still in fucking Hong Kong, cable fucking Hong Kong. Do I have to think of everything?"

Neither Sam or Kodo foresaw that cabling Robert from the office as Kodo insisted turned out to be the most unfortunate move Kodo and his son could make. Robert's answer shot back, coming in on the office teletype, seen and whispered about by everyone in the office. SAM AND MAYUMI—ONLY YOU—STOP—LOVE—ROBERT AND VICTORIA.

Ten words. The turndown from the scion of the exulted Talbots exploded Kodo into a roaring fury. After heavy breathing he commanded. "One way or other you see to it," he rumbled, "that I'm included. That's an order!"

Which meant that if Sam didn't get Kodo invited, his father would insist on the trip to Tokyo. By now Mayumi had committed to joining Sam at the Talbot's. Sam, knowing Robert would never yield to his father's strong-arm methods that broke strikes on the docks and bumped workers from construction sites, chose his words carefully and went as far as he could go. "Sir, Mayumi and I are only invited because I'm Robert's Best Man."

"How the hell can you be Best Man if you won't be there?"

Five days later Sam slipped away from the office to join the crowds at the pier welcoming the Canadian-Pacific's twenty-one-ton Empress of Japan. Robert, waving from the first class rail, never looking happier, his arm around a lovely woman in a cloche hat. The two middle-aged *Hakujin* at the couple's side, Sam assumed, must be Victoria's parents. Though the day was not bitter cold for December, the mother was bundled in a heap of gray fur and wore a wide-brimmed Queen Mary hat with a veil. She had a tight grip on a small pink-faced banker under a Homburg hat, bundled in a tightly-buttoned overcoat with a fur collar.

Robert's smiling lady came with an easy stride down the gangplank. It was her radiant smile that first had Sam catching his breath. Robert's Victoria was sleek in a white fur, showing lovely slender legs. She was exactly like one of the mythic creatures in *The Saturday Evening Post's* illustrations, one of F. Scott Fitzgerald's "flappers." Sam rushed forward and took her gloved hand, offering East and West greetings by alternating standing straight and bowing along with an enthusiastic, "Welcome to Japan."

"Thank you, Sam. I won't even bother to call you Mr. Pinkerton. Robert has told me so much about you and your Mayumi and Tat."

Robert's Victoria, his "English Rose." With her lovely coloring and lilting accent, why wouldn't his closest friend in the world be completely charmed, head over heels in love. No wonder Robert was grinning like an idiot. Robert had been right about her eyes when he'd sworn they were emerald green. She had freckles, uncovered by Lady Esther face powder.

The senior Clendenings looked like the China Sea had proved fatiguing. Victoria's father took Sam's hand with barely a nod, going directly into Robert's Packard. Victoria insisted the three friends would go in another car to the hotel and would find the bar to raise glasses of champagne. Robert said little. He seemed totally content simply to gaze adoringly at Victoria, allowing her to do the talking. Unlike most Westerners she spoke quietly and leaned conspiratorially close to Sam. "Prepare yourself, Mr. Pinkerton Kodo. I know all your deep, dark secrets. Robert never shuts up about his Best Man Sam, the rickshaw boy."

Robert grinned. Sam nodded.

"I can't wait," Victoria cried happily, "for my first ride."

"Rickshaws became illegal last year," said Sam.

"Why for heaven's sake?"

"The government considered the work demeaning."

"When you were a rickshaw boy did you feel demeaned?"

"Not for a minute."

"There, you see," she said. "Let's find a rickshaw and break the law."

Sam had only to see Robert and Victoria together and their ease in touching and light kissing for him to feel something akin to loneliness. Kodo had chosen Mayumi for him. Robert had chosen Victoria. He was a married man looking at love.

Sam left them still drinking champagne in the middle of the afternoon, walking slowly back to the office. The goddamned office. This was the last feeling in the world he expected to overcome him, darkening this beautiful winter day. In spite of being such close friends and sharing so many feelings, out of deference to Mayumi he'd held back opening his heart to Robert about Tedabara and admit how he burned for his father's whore.

Robert returned to his parents on the hill. Victoria and her family were at home in a suite at the Bellevue. Sam, at home in the mansion on a sharply cold early December evening, was watching Tat tearing up a *Saturday Evening Post* with Mayumi pouring Sam's hot sake when he sensed her delicate feelings had her sounding too offhand to dare admit what she was thinking. "Sam-San, you haven't forgotten to invite Robert-San and his English lady here?"

"They can't spare a minute," he dismissed her thought, "not with all their family things they have to do."

"Yes, of course." He knew she'd say no more. She'd already gone too far, but he knew exactly what she was thinking and it pained him. After a week with Victoria had his best friend been avoiding bringing his English love to their home? As much as she loved him would she feel as relaxed on tatami living Japanese style? Was Robert hesitating to bring Victoria? Was sharing their life on the floor still too soon, too Japanese for his English bride?"

In the second week of December Kodo called him into his office. On the way in he passed Ono-San and his white fan, whom Sam hadn't seen since his wedding. He was with a gaunt scarecrow of a newspaper journalist employed to plant stories for BlackStar. Alone in the office with Kodo, he sensed that his father was being too pleasant. A bad sign. Kodo offered him a cigar. Another bad sign. He announced with phony cheer that he was not only postponing their Tokyo trip but lifting his ban on the young Kodos attending Robert and Victoria's invitations to the Talbots. Sam knew there must be a catch. All Nagasaki knew Old Bumper had not only been excluded from the Talbot's world, but had long suffered their stinging rebuke. Now he was practically cooing, encouraging Sam and Mayumi to pursue the Talbots. He even insisted that he would pay for an overly extravagant wedding present which Sam dreaded would be in bad taste.

The next morning Sam was summoned into to his office. The black scarecrow was dribbling cigarette ashes taking notes. Kodo commanded, "You'll give Minoru here any articles you can find in your Western magazines and papers about powerful men in America—Rockefellers, Fords, Carnegies, Vanderbilts, Fricks, Morgans—all those top people."

Minoru, the journalist, another modern man, understood how those powerful Westerners had shaped their image. Over there in America it was called "public relations" and so common it was known as "PR." Within the week Sam was holding a Nagasaki newspaper with an article and photo in which Kodo never looked more important, yet human, evincing a care for the poor.

A SAMURAI IN JAPAN'S POSTWAR WORLD
When he isn't in Tokyo, Nagasaki's Koichi Kodo, in his 20th Century castle overlooking our harbor, employs the instincts and boldness of his Samurai ancestors bringing Japan into the modern world. While modestly admitting his BlackStar's success in shipping and building has been remarkable, he stresses his concern that true success comes only when we share with our fellow citizens in Japan's remarkable march forward—

"Bullshit!" Sam flung the paper aside. "Nobody's dumb enough to believe one word of this." Then he picked up the scattered pages and finished the rest of the nonsense about the Japanese Rockefeller. In Kodo's office he'd heard the cigarette-ash dribbling Minuro's Rule One. "The world believes anything it sees in print."

Sam didn't need to be told his father's Trojan Horse relied on his two infiltrators—Mayumi and himself.

CHAPTER SIXTY-FOUR

On a chill December evening cold air carried the cheerful sounds of the privileged alighting from chauffeur-driven cars at the Talbot's house on the hill. Ono-San prepared Sam with a guest list of those he and Mayumi would meet. His own instincts about these top people prompted him to sense that they'd hate the sight of Kodo's ostentatious American Marmon. He and Mayumi arrived in a rented Model T Ford.

The Western-style home brought memories back to Sam of the two-story clapboard houses he'd known as a boy across the Pacific. At the front door a smiling woman, tall for a Japanese, in a simple kimono of deep aubergine, welcomed Robert's friends warmly. From her shining eyes and smooth skin Sam could see where Robert had gotten his striking good looks. Harumi's Talbot's oval face shone with her son's large and dark almond eyes, his full lips. She greeted the young Kodos in Japanese, then switched to English in a low voice with only a trace of accent. She took Sam's hand and told him how very glad she was that at last she was meeting Robert's closest friend and Best Man at last.

Robert's father, a generation older than his wife at seventy, was tall and impressive, a thickly muscled man straining in his dinner clothes. Sam recognized his ruddy face from photographs on the wall of the robust young railroad engineer from Leeds, who'd arrived in Nagasaki forty-five years ago. Robert Talbot Senior was one of Nagasaki's "top people." He held himself like a soldier. His manner was direct and gentlemanly, but not as warm as his wife's as he shook Sam's hand firmly. He led the Kodos, Mayumi on Sam's arm, across a hardwood floor deeper into the house to introduce them to the guests of honor from Hong Kong. The old Yorkshireman started the Clendenings off with small talk. "Robert tells me that you met our young Mr. Kodo at the boat. And this is Mrs. Kodo," Talbot Senior announced.

Mayumi bowed to the Clendenings.

Mrs. Clendening, short and plump, showed little resemblance to the lovely and vibrant Victoria. Sam had seen English women like Mrs. Clendenings from a distance in his rickshaw days, women away from their flower shows in Kent, with powdered red faces they'd brought here—Out East—as they called it.

Her husband's expertly tailored dinner clothes almost camouflaged his paunch. His face glowed alarmingly scarlet suggesting high blood pressure or too much Johnnie Walker Black Label. Though Sam was no expert on English accents, the man's way of speaking struck him as less effortlessly upper class than Robert's, but acceptably proper for an officer of a British overseas merchant bank. By this time Robert's mother and Victoria were at the young couple's side when Sam overheard Mrs. Clendening whisper to her husband, "Why, for heaven's sake, is Robert's Best Man married to a Japanese?"

Quickly Victoria led them aside. "Since I don't speak a word of Japanese and likely never shall, may I ask if your lovely Mayumi speaks English?"

"She's learning," Sam said

"Then you must tell your Mayumi for me," she suggested, "that she's married to the second handsomest man here." Victoria laughed, continuing to smile at Sam's wife. "Of course, lucky me, I can tell the truth since I'm about to marry the first." Victoria linked her arm through Sam's and Mayumi's, her lovely smile telling Sam's wife they were not going to let not speaking each other's language keep them from becoming the best of friends. "I've urged Robert to bring me to your house to meet your little boy Tat, he says is such a darling."

Several couples arrived at the front door occupying Sam as he sorted out their identities and relationships. The first was an English couple with loud voices. The second, middle-aged and Japanese, seemed nearly paralyzed in their old Meiji formality, which Sam later learned came from their years in the world of diplomacy. A third, another Japanese man and wife, smiled at the Kodos as the husband presented cards that proved he'd studied ophthalmologic surgery in Vienna. A fourth twosome entered from another room, a slender Japanese man wearing an Episcopal priest's white collar along with a pretty wife. Reverend Eliot Wada, with his hair glued down Western-style, held a flute of champagne to the plump lips of his pleasant, unlined face. His pretty wife's smile hinted at only a judicious touch of lip rouge.

"Ah, our Best Man." Reverend Wada shook Sam's hand vigorously. "Kodo—the tennis player."

The Reverend chatted a few words in Japanese to Mayumi before going on to others, leaving Sam glancing over the guests and comparing how different this round of parties was from his and Mayumi's achingly traditional betrothal ritual managed by the pernickety Ono-San.

Sam slid a glance at the Clendenings. Surely this matter of race could not be easy for this woman who'd be happier at home in England at garden shows. Sam thought it probable the merchant-banker stood in awe of a family as rich and powerful as the Talbots and may have foreseen advantages in the alliance.

Sam and Mayumi didn't have to be told that they were socializing among many of those in Nagasaki to whom Kodo was laying siege. Tonight the Japanese and the Europeans smiled incessantly, exchanging small talk, pleased to be holding flutes of champagne. The women, like his own Mayumi, did not touch a drop. The men were already onto politics and cursing the Bolsheviks for goading the dockworkers into another strike they predicted would destroy Japan.

Mrs. Talbot, the consummate hostess in her aubergine kimono, eased her guests through rooms with hardwood floors, imposing pieces of Victorian furniture, velvet drapes, cut-glass chandeliers, and sepia portraits. Sam's arm steadied Mayumi across the treacherous hardwood, entering a dining room with a long table glinting with silver and sparkling with crystal. At each place an engraved card nestled within a chrysanthemum blossom displayed names in both English and Japanese.

Servants with more champagne filled flutes so Robert could raise his glass. "To my love, my English rose." Victoria met his toast, the free-and-easy postwar girl, the only woman at the table to drink.

Sam, seated across from his Mayumi, kept a close eye on her as his guide, taking his cue from her manners, the sometime rickshaw boy lost among the intricacies of the elaborate English table settings she'd mastered at the Sturges School. Slowly she unfolded only half of her damask napkin which she trailed across her lap. Within minutes, following her moves, he was able to pick up a round spoon and dip it into turtle soup laced with sherry.

Determined not to be defeated by the fish fork, he heard the Reverend Wada speaking. "Robert, all of us have known you for donkey's years, and it's high time you told your guests about our Best Man and tennis player." The Reverend, smiling his benediction, had put the conversational ball clearly in the bridegroom's court.

"No. First, if I may," Victoria, seated next to Sam, interrupted with a mischievous laugh, alerting the table with her bright, younger generation informality. Sam glanced at Mayumi, who allowed herself to show none of the shock most of the table of important people was feeling that a woman could thrust herself forward in such a manner. Robert beamed with pride. Robert Senior smiled. The very English Clendenings appeared unsurprised.

Victoria sailed on. "Sam, I absolutely insist you confess your deep-dark secret to everyone here." She smiled and reached for the Best Man's hand to prove she had only his best interests at heart. "Ladies and gentlemen," she announced, "our Best Man seated on my right and looking devastatingly handsome was—once-upon-a-time—a rickshaw boy." She patted his hand approvingly. "Can you beat it?"

All eyes were on Sam. "It's true," he admitted. He smiled at Mayumi as she gave her attention to her damask dinner napkin. Knowing the modern woman Victoria was he sensed what she was up to. In bright table talk she was introducing as a lark what later could prove an awkward discovery about Robert's Best Man's irregular background. Sam glanced at Robert. Robert's smile assured him that Victoria, in sharing the news so light-heartedly before the top rung of Nagasaki society, and under the blessings of the Talbots, was removing any stigma and even adding considerable panache to Sam's reputation.

Robert rose and announced that Sam was his closest friend. Smiling and proud to have him as his Best Man, he raised his glass promising the table's two young couples a lifetime of friendship here in Nagasaki.

Victoria tapped Sam with a small Japanese fan. "I mean—everybody, isn't it absolutely marvelous? I mean a Rickshaw Boy—now our very best friend?"

Robert chuckled and reached for her hand. "Don't get carried away, my dear Victoria. He was only doing it because he was poor."

Most of the table responded with uncertain polite laughter. If there were those who didn't share Victoria's bright young modern views they remained silent. This dinner, they must have felt, was not the place for elders to challenge the young and risk appearing out of step with the new and, to some, deplorable, easy, democratic ways of the postwar world. Robert translated Victoria's disclosure for Mayumi who did not giggle in Japanese embarrassment, but raised her untouched wine glass to her husband. After Sam smiled at his wife he cast his eyes down the table where the Clendenings sat unsmiling and clenched in their chairs. Mrs. Clendening held her lips tight. Her husband's red brow pulsed with a blood vessel.

Robert's father explained to his guests of honor. "Rickshaws nowadays are illegal here in Japan. Do you still have them in Hong Kong?"

"No Englishman would think of using them," Clendening successfully annulled any further talk of Sam's background. His wife's thin lips made it clear she shared her husband's abhorrence to much of what one found out here in the Orient. With gruff dignity Talbot Senior steered the table talk back to safer waters, along class lines, on which they could all sail unruffled. "And the labor situation in Hong Kong," the old Yorkshireman asked. "How goes that?"

"Better I should think with the Chinese, than here in Japan." At last the banker found himself on enough home ground to be able to speak. "In the colony we're a good deal firmer with our Chinky Chongs." The Japanese held enigmatic smiles at what the banker didn't think to be a slur. The banker blotted his lips with damask. The table waited for more clarification on China, but the banker supplied no further financial information. Conversation, in spite of the spirited Victoria, stalled until Mrs. Talbot and Mrs. Wada developed an innocuous speculation as to the December weather after a November that had been glorious in a burst of scarlet maples. The winter ahead, they all agreed, looked to be mild.

The table was cleared of the fish course. Victoria reached across a setting of flowers and patted Robert's hand, a signal for an announcement she seemed bursting for him to share. Sam could see his friend hesitate, and she spoke first.

"As some of you know, my Robert was the Best Man at Mayumi and Sam's wedding. He's told me all about the wonderful new and up-to-date, truly modern things they did, and what more and more people are doing nowadays even here in Japan."

"Darling," Robert suggested, "why don't we leave that to our Reverend Wada?"

The Japanese heard her interrupt him. "Robert, I think Sam should tell us all about his and Mayumi's double ceremony."

Sam, who'd been exposed as a rickshaw boy, now felt trapped into more talk about his life. He murmured to Mayumi he'd speak in English in order to include Victoria's mother and father, their guests of honor from Hong Kong. His wife lowered her eyes. Everyone waited. "We began," he said, "with a more or less private Shinto ceremony at my bride's house— as you know—the traditional Japanese way of marrying here for more than fifteen hundred years—"

"In traditional Heian-period robes." Robert added. "Truly magnificent."

As he spoke Sam had the feeling that not all the guests shared the postwar feelings of the more adventurous young. "Then, at the hotel with Mayumi and myself still in our ancient robes, we were presented to all the guests."

Victoria cried, "Robert tells me five hundred and three guests! Can you beat it?"

"After that Robert got me through quite an ordeal changing into a black cutaway, a starchy white-tie rig—totally Western clothes. Mayumi all in white."

"Venetian lace," Victoria corroborated the elegance. "Robert tells me, a ravishing gown all Nagasaki's still talking about."

"Mayumi," Robert said, "was truly a vision, beyond lovely, spectacular in—as Victoria just said, Venetian lace. All this to *Lohengrin* from a twenty-piece full orchestra. The works." Robert shook his head to impress his guests with the lavishness of it all. "Her father spared no expense."

Victoria, pink with excitement, turned to the Church of England. "Reverend Wada, is there any reason Robert and I couldn't do the very same thing? I mean, honor Mrs. Talbot's people with a traditional Japanese wedding but then, of course, go on to a real ceremony?"

Sam winced. He couldn't bring himself to look at Robert. He understood the brightly enthusiastic Victoria hadn't intended to sound patronizing in her inadvertent demotion of the ancestral beliefs of most of the table. More than ever Sam returned to an earlier thought, the sense that these differences between the families had meant Clendening arguments in Hong Kong. Yes, perhaps the banker had allowed himself to see the advantages of a union with the powerful Talbot family, but from the day Sam had met the ship he could see Mrs. Clendening was fighting losing her daughter to Japan. Here, at this table, the already tight-lipped mother clearly was stiffening at any suggestion of a Japanese life for her daughter.

Robert reached across the table and took his love's hand. Sam could see he was warning her against her enthusiasm carrying her away in her eagerness to prove her love for him. Victoria, in her besotted excitement, felt inspired to follow Sam and Mayumi's lead and prove her love by combining Robert's Japanese ancestry with hers.

Reverend Wada, apparently seeing his mission at this dinner as bridging Japanese and Western worlds, gave an ecclesiastical chuckle. His smile at the Clendenings assured that his blessings would be purely Western.

Sam was growing concerned that Victoria wasn't sensing Robert's unease. She was enthusiastic. "Padre, Father Wada, can we do that?"

"Indeed, the Shinto ceremony our young Mister Kodo has described has been traditional in Japan for perhaps fifteen hundred years. Nowadays any number of our young people insist it's the modern way to combine the two by adding Christian vows with the bride in a white Western gown and the groom in a black cutaway coat Mister Kodo described."

"Wonderful," she cried. "So if there's no problem with the church why don't Robert and I do just that?"

Reverend Wada folded his damask napkin and set it aside. "If, dear young Victoria, you're asking if I myself might preside over this kind of double ceremony for your own wedding, I'd want to be on the safe side and should be happier first to chat with your bishop in Hong Kong—"

Robert Senior looked straight at Rikio-San, from the world of diplomacy, who'd said little. "Rikio-San, you're up on these things. So where does the Imperial Household in Tokyo stand on Shinto-Christian ceremonies?"

The diplomat adjusted his teeth and finally replied that the question involved the Imperial Household and required considerable thought. While Rikio-San spoke, Sam watched Mrs. Clendening's already tight mouth hardening. She was breathing so deeply she seemed about to burst. Before the diplomat could fully answer the Senior Talbot's question, Mrs.

Clendening signaled her husband she would need his help rising. "That will not be necessary, sir. And Reverend Wada," she hissed each syllable to avoid any possible misunderstanding, "the Clendenings do not happen to be Shintoists nor Buddhists, nor anything but Church of England." Each syllable of each word was a separate sliver of ice.

"No. Most certainly not, Mrs. Clendening." Reverend Wada said at his most ecumenical. "As I, like you, look only to Canterbury for revealed truth in all matters. My view—here in Japan—Our Church of England view—has always been not to regard Shinto as a religion as such."

Victoria's mother had clearly taken more than she could bear of Asia. Her husband reached her chair from which she was struggling to rise. "For God's sake, Arthur. Take me out of here! This minute!"

A waiter rushed forward and before her husband had her on her feet Mrs. Clendening shot a look at Victoria, an order. Robert Senior and his son, along with Sam, rose while the deep-breathing Englishwoman dashed awkwardly from the room. The banker managed his own chair and with a father's fixed gaze on Victoria repeating his wife's order, went hurrying after his wife. In silence the men remained on their feet. Sam didn't dare look directly at his friend and his fiancée. He'd read the expression "shattered" in English fiction. No other word could describe Victoria. With her happy radiance drained, she was trembling, staring at Robert's hand holding her wrist. Then she looked into his face.

"Victoria!" from the parlor came her mother's sharp command.

Sam and Mayumi shared a quick glance. "Victoria!" Her mother called again. She didn't move. Sam found himself looking at a different Victoria and saw a new truth. For all her easy laughter, her insistence that she was a new kind of woman, she'd fought her parents into leaving Hong Kong to come here to Robert's people in Nagasaki. Robert stood behind her chair with an expression Sam had never seen on his handsome face.

"Victoria!" This time it was her father. "Your mother and I are leaving. We're waiting for you."

She rose. Without a word she brushed Robert's face with a kiss. For only a second they looked into each other's eyes before she ran from the room. Sam saw in his friend the boy he must have been in some damp English school, heartbroken but determined not to show tears. He'd never beg. His Rudolf Valentino face, Japanese and English, was now a mask showing nothing. Sam couldn't bear looking at his friend.

With dignity Robert gave his guests a curt nod and strode from the room. Sam turned to Robert Senior standing behind his wife's chair and holding her hand. For a long moment the eyes of the guests still seated at the table seemed unable to know where to look. No one ventured a word. Robert's mother looked up at her husband, but showed nothing. Reverend Wada's lips moved in silent prayer. His stricken wife had closed her eyes on tears. The diplomat and his wife, though exquisite masters of ritual politeness, sat motionless as chastised children, as much at a loss as the others exiled in this dreadful silence. Sam stood behind Mayumi's chair.

Robert Senior pressed his hand on his wife's shoulder and left his guests. The enormous hush that had filled the dining room was suddenly shattered by cries from the parlor, indistinguishable words crackling with hurt and anger. Sam listened but heard nothing from Robert. From his angle standing in the dining room he caught a glimpse of Robert Senior in the entrance hall looking up at his son climbing the staircase alone. Footsteps rang out from the parlor's hardwood floor. Sam moved three steps to gain a partial view of the parlor and catch sight of Mrs. Clendening rushing Victoria to the front door. None of the guests still at the table moved. Then, at the dining room door, they looked up at Arthur Clendening's red face, the man standing for a brief moment with his arms full of winter coats, scarves, hats and gloves.

"Terrible mistake—the wife and—and—our Victoria thank all for your many kindnesses here in Nagasaki. Her mother and I are taking Victoria home to Hong Kong, then on back to England where she belongs." He fumbled with his armful of wraps and dropped a hat. Sam, without a word, picked it up and added it to the man's bundle.

"Thank you. All my fault." Sam wanted to shout at the banker to shut up and go. "Gone too far," Clendening mumbled. "Should have stopped it in Hong Kong." He turned from the guests to make his way out the front door under his burden of heavy coats.

Sam heard car doors slam and engines roar and fade into the night. From his angle on the parlor and the stairs he saw Talbot Senior rush up the stairs. "Robert!" He heard the old man call. "Robert?" Sam shut his eyes. He was frightened of how his closest friend in the world would answer. He wanted to run, but could not move. The house rocked with a blast of gunfire.

No one seemed to dare speak and the silence filled an eternity until he saw Talbot's slow steps coming down the stairs. Without a word to his wife in the dining room, he took her hand.

CHAPTER SIXTY-FIVE

Under a gray December sky three days before Christmas, in the Sakamoto International Cemetery, fifty people in black stood at an open grave. Reverend Wada read the Church of England's rites over Sam's closest friend, who was being lowered into the cold earth.

Mayumi gripped his hand, her silence telling him she could only guess at how his heart was breaking. The Talbots cast earth on the casket. Sam watched the others, one by one, drop their handfuls and turn and leave in the bitter wind. Overwhelmed with sorrow, he led Mayumi to the Ford and sent her home alone.

With only two cemetery workers at the open grave, he dropped his handful of Japan and looked down on Robert before the earth closed over him. The bitter wind chilled the hot tears streaming down his face. He looked up at the gray sky. His only friend he could open his heart to was gone. After a long moment, he whispered, "Goodbye—*sayonara*—friend—no more living in two different worlds for you."

He dropped another clump of earth into the grave. Whether he was English or Japanese, Robert was now forever in Japan.

CHAPTER SIXTY-SIX

A private car brought the Kodos, father and son, to the Imperial Hotel—"the Old Imperial," as Tokyo was now calling it—for its days of old-fashioned grandeur were numbered. A new Imperial was rising, already detested as the work of a crazy American architect Kodo cursed as "a madman in a cape."

He was not alone in his hatred of this foreigner and his new building. Japanese engineers and contractors denounced the new hotel for violating basic Japanese construction codes as unsound and worse, downright dangerous. Even more hateful the design of the new hotel insulted the unique spirit sacred to the Japanese, a spirit only the descendants of the Sun Goddess believed they could feel. If that weren't damnable enough, worst of all, this Frank Lloyd Wright creature dared the most flagrant insult—the effrontery of his monstrosity daring to face the Imperial Palace, Tenno himself.

Kodo's first steps alighting from the car and crossing the old hotel lobby proved that in Tokyo, he was one of the "Top People," triumphantly commanding a new world. A tiny man in striped trousers, more formal than any diplomat, rushed toward them with all the speed commensurate with dignity. He intercepted Kodo in a grove of potted palms and, while bowing low and hissing, he was also quivering with apologies, begging a thousand pardons. Mr. Kodo's regular suite had been pre-empted by a member of the British Royal Family.

Of course Sam knew his Japanese father was thrilled, but watched the Toad recoil, pretending outrage. Speaking loudly enough for everyone in the lobby to hear, he demanded to know how he was expected to suffer such an outrage. Best of all, it gave him the chance to prove himself magnanimous, yielding, sacrificing his comfort to Japan's guests—England's royalty.

In their suite, Kodo unfolded a list of powerful names. Kodo explained. One was a baron and a cabinet minister, another a baron, two were members of the Diet, another a general, a shipping-line owner, three contractors, and two insignificant types, members of the press.

Tokyo was waiting, but Kodo blocked his escape, putting him to work laying out a table full of gifts carried from Nagasaki and double-checking the three waiters setting up an elaborate sushi bar along with chafing dishes of hot Western hors d'oeuvres.

Sam had to endure hanging up uniformly black overcoats from men in Western suits bustling in bearing gifts and bowing with a respect Kodo would never receive from members at the Occident Club. Sam discovered one aloof exception, a baron in a black kimono with its five *mon* bore only a trifling gift. He'd never seen Kodo bow and scrape so low. Sam took his cue and bent himself double. The baron did not smile.

Sam worked with the list and detected the two members of the Diet and another baron with a broken arm in a sling. One heavy, thuggish man whose eyes Sam found disturbingly reptilian was keeping his right hand in his pocket. Was he missing the last knuckle of his little finger, the stubby amputated badge of a Yukuza?

Kodo was bubbling over with a bonhomie Sam had never seen him waste on anyone of his business peers in Nagasaki. Here among some of the most important men in government and industry he was close to sweating, working hard, too affable, with little gift to charm. After an hour Kodo had shooed out the Japanese waiters and reduced Sam to a barman serving drinks. None of these powerful men bothered to glance at the gaijin, and because Kodo did not introduce him, no one spoke one word to him.

The host never stopped apologizing for the suite. "Sorry, gentlemen," he sighed, pretending to be abashed, "to bring you to such an unworthy meeting place, but the hotel begged me to give my regular suite to a member of the British Royal Family. Japan-British relations. What could I do?"

Whiskey drinkers to a man, they raised cheers to their powerful friend from Nagasaki and what they agreed was certain to be his successful stay in the capital. Sam even heard a banzai. An egg-bald Tokyo contractor hushed the room raising his drink in mock-salute to a colleague unable to be present. As to their smirks of suppressed laughter, Sam learned the truth. Their absent friend, it turned out, was the contractor involved in the gravel scandal." Even Sam had heard about the brand-new bridge in the just-opened Meiji Jingu shrine that crumbled due to inferior cement. The mayor of Tokyo had resigned. The contractor was in jail. If any of these important men had played a role in the debacle, they were here. They'd survived.

"Most important, gentlemen," a plump, rosy little man with cigarette holder, raised his glass, "is our gratitude to our Honorable Kodo-San for bringing all of us together in the sentiment we all share tonight. Gentlemen," he raised his glass higher. "Fuck all labor unions!"

Kodo beamed and waved his cigar for silence. "Gentlemen, we'll have time for fucking the Reds later. After we do some fucking of our own. Who's interested in moving on to the Yoshiwara?"

Laughter exploded and rippled over the promise of this traditional Tokyo joy. An old man with a head of iron-gray hair cried, "Wait!" Shaking his leonine head in dead seriousness he drew a breath in over gold teeth. "This morning when I left Yokohama I saw more red flags. How about Nagasaki? Kodo, can we count on you and your people down there to smash another strike?"

"That's like asking Kodo if he knows how to get rid of shit. Hah?" With a rumbling chuckle Sam watched the Toad herd his powerful guests to the door. "Gentlemen and barons," he urged, "our ladies of the Yoshiwara are waiting. Let's get out of this dump of a hotel suite!"

The Yoshiwara? Sam held his breath. This was far, far more than Sam had hoped for his first night in town. Not only was he in Tokyo, he was about to visit the world's most dedicated pleasure district—"The Water Trade." He performed his duty helping Kodo's guests into winter coats as they surged toward the door. Holding his father's coat he throttled his excitement. It was at this moment his Japanese father acknowledged him. "Gentlemen, did I tell you? This is my new son, in case you didn't know. Looks like me, yes?"

Kodo grinned at the big laugh he knew he'd get based on the racial anomaly. "Since he's only been married to my honorable daughter for two years, and is the father of my grandson, it's only fitting he stays home tonight."

The guests, in a moment of propriety, since it annulled none of their own pleasures, applauded such propriety. The grandfather, going out the door, hissed his last command. "Call Mayumi. I'm worried about Tat's runny nose."

CHAPTER SIXTY-SEVEN

Sam was still up when Kodo burst into the hotel room at a quarter past three in the morning. He'd seen the Toad drunk but never the all-but-falling-down drunk he was tonight. Red-faced and loud, he was cuddling a little wooden toy rooster he placed with great care in the middle of a table.

"For Tat. Year of the Rooster."

In spite of himself, Sam had to smile. Imagine loud, farting, hard-drinking Bumper Kodo in the Yoshiwara, thinking about his grandson. Kodo grabbed a bottle of Johnnie Walker Black Label and shoved it at Sam, an order to pour. Sam obliged and poured two fingers for himself.

With a long sigh Kodo rejected the Western-style bed in the next room, flopped down on the Persian carpet and signaled Sam to pry off his shoes. "You have any idea who those men were? How powerful they are? Hell, two of them are in the Diet. The baron's in the cabinet. The tall one's a general. That one with the scrawny little mustache? The biggest ship owner in Yokohama. All top, top people. To a man, all out to stop those fucking Reds before they tie up the docks."

Kodo thrust out his glass for a refill.

"Not all top," Kodo admitted. "Two newspapermen. Reporters, but with top papers. For them all it takes is the best Scotch and women they could never afford, and they can't wait to write that my shit doesn't stink if I tell them to. All of 'em backing us against the Reds one hundred percent." He closed his eyes and concentrated on exploding a fart. "I told 'em, I told 'em to tell the country how the foreign Bolsheviks never stop working day and night to bring this country down. Day after tomorrow when their papers come out, we'll have every decent man in the country ready to stomp on those shits."

Not since the birth of Tat had Sam seen Kodo so relaxed, so unbuttoned. The grandfather gulped his Scotch. "Kid, the thing you gotta get straight, is that we top people talk the same language. This is Tokyo, not your chickenshit Nagasaki. You think for one single minute men like these would put up with the social crap your high-toned, fucking Talbots dish out? No way. Gimme powerful men every time. Tokyo men you can talk to. Talk and they listen!"

"I'm happy to hear things went well—"

"Why wouldn't they? Me, I come to Tokyo, they listen. The British Royal Family's only in my suite right now because I gave them my permission." Sam wondered if Kodo needed his glass filled. Never forgetting Torazo's advice, he'd ended his own drinking and was going to make sure every idea he proposed seemed to come from Kodo.

"Sir, I need you to tell me how I can best help you here."

"You'll know when I tell you. Shit—when my father needed help he never had to tell me a fucking thing. Didn't have to. I had eyes. I had brains. I saw. If you knew shit about anything, you wouldn't have to ask . . ."

Sam said, "Before I went out for a walk and saw the Ginza, I called home to see how Tat's cough was—"

"I even had to tell you to do that—"

"He's fine. He misses his grandfather. Everyone in Nagasaki misses you—"

"Now hand me that phone and get out of here. And close the door."

Sam went into his bedroom and shut the door, but Kodo's voice was so loud he was convinced he was meant to hear every word. Whoever was on the line his adopted father had suddenly become a different man, purring and chuckling. "I gotta tell you, Tedabara, you sure as hell could teach those Yoshiwara cunts a thing or two."

Sam went ice cold.

"Yeah, I don't have to tell you, you know what I'd love to do right now . . ."

Sam clamped his hot face with his hands. "Sam!" Kodo had rung off and his call was loud and fierce. "Get in here!" His adoptive Japanese father was demolishing his Western-style brass bed, flinging the mattress onto the floor improving a futon.

"Who do you think I was just talking to?"

"I wouldn't know, sir."

"You didn't listen?"

"Of course not."

"Yes, you did."

"Sir, it's past three in the morning, I'm going to bed—"

"Three guesses who was sitting up waiting for me to call? Te-da-ba-ra." His wet mouth twisted her name into a lewd act. "Remember her?"

"Yes, sir."

"Never tried to see her again? Don't answer. I'd know damned well if you had." Kodo pulled off his clothes and needed help unwrapping his stomach warmer. "Just so you know—whatever happened back there in the Maruyama between you two is long dead and buried."

Sam finished improving Kodo's Japanese bed and Kodo slumped down. "Kid? Isn't it about time you thanked me for the finest wife in the world any man could have? And my Samurai name. And my grandson. See to it I get plenty more . . ."

Sam didn't dare show his face on fire with hatred for this farting old thug, who was rubbing in how he was with his Tedabara month after month, year after year. Better than risk Kodo seeing how he felt, he turned to leave.

"Come back here." Kodo held out his glass. Sam obeyed. He poured. "You claim to know all about lumber."

"Those Fukuoka shipments came from the Puget Sound country in the States where I grew up."

Kodo dropped his *fundoshi,* stripped bare. The two didn't bathe together, so this was the first time Sam had seen his father totally naked. He was a bull of a man, thick with muscles. Though Kodo kept scratching his balls and drinking, Sam gave him his attention and continued. "I grew up watching loggers fell trees and getting the timber to the mills. I can tell you how it's cut and graded." There was no way he could cleverly ascribe this knowledge to Kodo by telling the truth, and he was surprised how easily his old talent for extending the truth was coming back.

"Tomorrow at two," Kodo grumped, "when I take you to the biggest lumber yard in Japan, you better goddamn well know what you're talking about."

CHAPTER SIXTY-EIGHT

Before their lumberyard visit Kodo met with five contractors and three government men determined to fight the current surge of foreign architects currently building in Japan. The nine had pressured a cabinet minister and three members of the Diet to see for themselves the most outrageous of the current foreign invasions—Frank Lloyd Wright's detested, sacrilegious, Tenno-insulting, new Imperial Hotel.

"You're coming with us," Kodo growled at Sam. "I might need to talk English with those American construction bastards."

The party of fourteen, including Sam, met in the building site hut facing Hibiya Park. Here the Americans were raising the New Imperial that had the temerity to look out on the park, daring to face the Imperial Palace beyond.

Though Kodo rumbled with hate, the Japanese call on Wright's bastards began with traditional politesse covering what Sam knew their visit to be—a war party. More than a simple courtesy call, a cabinet minister was in their party, demanding that this Wright himself receive them. The architect, they were told, had returned to the United States. Paul Mueller, his construction manager, introduced himself. A large and balding man, he had a thick moustache which Sam thought made him look uncannily like Mack Swain, the villain in Charlie Chaplin movies.

Mueller was unguarded, open, an American patiently explaining that it would be September of next year before the hotel opened for guests. Before offering them tea, he suggested showing them one section that had been completed, long halls under low ceilings. Now tea was served at the top of a staircase. Sam smiled to himself. Everything in Japan begins with tea and these Americans didn't know enough to serve until the tour was half over and it was too late to satisfy the proper formalities. He found himself thinking a little superciliously. "Americans. They have much to learn about the Empire of the Sun."

Outside under a Tokyo sky of cloudless bright blue, Mueller and his assistant, a thin Japanese with unusually long black hair, brought them to the entrance of the new building. Sam listened to the Japanese talk among one another, small talk that would seem polite enough to the

Americans, but that he knew to be hostile. Still, not one of his group had actually broken the pretense of exquisite manners.

The cabinet minister, the most exquisitely polite of all their group, led subtly to the first veiled attack. "One hears the project has not always been an easy one."

Mueller was blunt. "Sir, I've yet to be on any project that was easy."

"Still—in this case, would you not say work has been unusually slow?"

"Yes," Mueller answered flatly. "There've been interruptions."

Mueller's Japanese assistant made a point of showing his loyalty to the American architect by reminding their guests and fellow professionals that delays in any building, especially such innovative buildings as Mister Wright's, must be anticipated.

"Labor trouble?" asked Kodo unable to mask his hope of bad news.

"Of course," Mueller was unguarded. "There are always problems." In translating Sam had forgotten since his Bremerton days how outspoken Americans can be. Kodo moved close and Sam could see he was hoping to hear these Americans had been plagued by labor troubles. "Problems between socialist Western workers and Japanese?"

"Nothing we can't handle," said Mueller, "thanks to our very able Japanese staff and crew."

"Technical problems?" a contractor from the Shinjuku District and a respected engineer, suggested.

"We've had our share, yes."

Sam sensed these Japanese thrusts, beginning as thinly disguised as questions, were edging close to the confrontational. The plump man with the cigarette holder, Sam deduced, had something to do with finance, used his holder to jab at a report emphasizing the project's enormous financial problems. "And the bankers?"

"There've been problems." Mueller was American again, never anything but frank. "Your newspapers over here have had a field day harping on our financial setbacks." Mueller's young Japanese had been interpreting along with Sam, but turned to him for help on the word "field day."

"A celebration," Sam said, pleased with his succinctness.

"Ah, so," the Japanese nodded. They understood. Sam had performed admirably.

"One hears," the stubby man's cigarette holder went back to prodding the report. "The project's gone several times over budget."

"Three times over," Mueller said flatly.

The Cabinet Minister disguised his attack as a more polite question. "There is now talk of a new owner?"

"I'm certain all of you know Baron Okura," Mueller said as he cautioned them to watch their footing through broken concrete and the dust of a basin he explained would be a lily pond. "Still, in all, I'm pleased to be able to say Mister Wright has every reason to be happy at the way things are turning out." He faced the group to the front of the building with the morning sun casting the fresh-cut stone into sharp relief. The Japanese shielded their eyes and studied the long, low lines of the three stories and an entrance façade. Sam thought the decorative motif, carved so idiosyncratically in concrete blocks, looked to him more like what he'd seen on Ancient Mayan design than Japanese.

"*Oya* stone?" Kodo pretended to be surprised, but Sam interpreted this as damning the cheap building material as totally unacceptable.

"That's right. *Oya* stone," Mueller answered.

"Unusual choice," Kodo was laying the groundwork for his five builders to mount their offensive.

"Curious." The cabinet minister picked up the thrust of Kodo's backhanded challenge. "Here in Japan our building traditions have never considered such low quality stone suitable for construction."

"Mister Wright," Mueller said, "carves his designs directly into the blocks themselves. For that we have over a hundred masons."

"Japanese?"

"Many Japanese."

"And the roof?" Kodo looked to his countrymen, a glance that said only a damned fool would choose this material they were looking at. "Am I right? Can that be copper?"

Mueller offered no defense for Mister Wright's unorthodox building materials. Sam slid his eyes to the Cabinet Minister gazing across Hibiya park at the blasphemy of facing the granite walls of Tenno's palace grounds. In a tracking gaze the Minister swung back to the hotel linking the two buildings. "Sensitive location. Facing as it does," he made the challenge clear, "the Imperial Palace."

"Mister Wright is well aware of the honor," said Mueller. "He's the one who suggested it be called the Imperial Hotel."

"But not in Japanese style." The Cabinet Minister kept Tenno, the Emperor himself, central to his attack. Sam glanced at Mueller. Was the man's insight into the character of the Japanese deep enough to realize what the man was doing? By evoking the god-king coupled with bitter criticism of the American architect's blasphemy, the Minister had now proved how far the American had dared thrust his building outside and beyond the bounds of Japanese honor.

Mueller's Japanese assistant spoke quietly, with a humility approaching reverence, moving on from the question of location to the radical design of the building itself. "The differences in style may not be as pronounced as one sees on first viewing." He was scarcely whispering. "Mister Wright himself has always been deeply respectful, a great admirer of traditional Japanese design. Mister Wright considers his building a bridge between East and West." Kodo and company were listening but Sam knew every word they were hearing about bridges between tradition and barbarianism grated on their Japanese souls. Mueller continued, "Doubtlessly you know of Mister Wright's famous woodblock-print collection. He is a great admirer of things Japanese. Many times he has stated to the world that with this building he is taking off his hat to Japanese traditions."

Not one of the Japanese pretended to be impressed at hearing of Mr. Wright's love of *ukiyo-e* or his doffing his hat to things Japanese.

Mueller flung a wider gesture with his arm than a Japanese would make, again urging them to step carefully across the rubble of the dusty lily pond into the front entrance of carved concrete blocks. Sam sensed he was crouching into a cave. This feeling of being in a grotto was even stronger inside the lobby with its exposed concrete in angles and shapes he'd never seen in Japan or America.

"Mister Wright," Mueller explained, "has designed all the fixtures, every stick of furniture, every note of the décor."

An hour later, in an improvised setting on the mezzanine, Mueller again offered his visitors tea from a pot and cups the American Mr. Wright himself had designed, incorporating to the smallest detail the integrity of design reflected through what could only be called a highly unusual building.

Sam knew the look on Kodo's face. The Toad had been waiting to launch his biggest samurai attack. "Do we understand this building is not supported by pilings?"

"That's right," Mueller said. "Your press has been telling Japan a great deal about Mister Wright's innovative foundation. I expect we'll be hearing a great deal more."

Tea chilled. The Japanese guests glanced around unhappily, no longer pretending to find any rationale for such American insanity. Kodo's attack struck at the sheer lunacy of a building unsupported by piles, yes unsupported and actually floating on mud. "Madness," Sam heard him grunt to the baron. Only with massive payoffs at the highest levels had this American tea-set designer and collector of wood block prints managed to get his work past Japanese building codes. "Not on pilings?" Kodo repeated, making certain no Japanese missed this total proof of the lunacy of the man.

"Floating? Like a ship?" The cabinet minister spoke very slowly, stressing his point that, reasonable man that he was, he was making every reasonable effort to understand the experiment this Western madman was foisting on Japan.

Mueller didn't disagree. "Admittedly it's somewhat innovative, but Mister Wright calculates that his new treatment of the foundation makes this building far safer—"

"—than anything built by Japanese?" the cabinet minister interrupted sharply, as sharp as his glance to the others. By now he'd suffered more than enough of this American madness. He buttoned his black cutaway jacket, rose and with inadequate words of withdrawal, was the first to leave the others and the hateful building, adding a last glare at the architect-designed tea set.

CHAPTER SIXTY-NINE

Less than one year before, fire had destroyed twenty-five hundred buildings in Tokyo's Kanda District. Now its lumberyards were back and busy. After driving into the yard with its scent of fresh lumber, Kodo kept Sam in the car, laying down his last orders. "This thief Yamada deals with American brokers. He doesn't speak a word of English and I'm not telling him you're my son. You're some American bastard named Pink-er-ton, a gaijin I hired from the States as my own lumber man."

"Do I speak Japanese with him?"

"Don't overdo it. Make plenty of mistakes so you sound like an outsider, but when it comes to lumber, convince him no one knows more than you. Got it?"

A short man of sixty with a pockmarked face and a bald head spiked with bristles heaved himself from his office. Politeness played little part in gruff Yamada's nature, but he was Japanese enough to greet the Nagasaki builder with something like a bow and an offer of tea. Sam made his own bow awkward enough to show himself a clumsy Westerner unfamiliar with Japanese customs.

"I've brought along this young American from the state of Washington in the U.S.A. where most of your Douglas fir comes from," Kodo said as a staff member poured the requisite tea. "The kid knows his stuff so don't try to pull any of your shit on him."

Yamada turned to Sam. "You speak Japanese?"

"Only a little."

No one touched the tea. Yamada led them into his warehouse and Sam breathed deeply of the smell of still freshly cut wood from North American forests. Nothing said Bremerton like this. He crinkled his nose. Did he detect pitch? While he sniffed again Yamada managed to find a two-by-four with clear grain, free enough from resin that he was able to run his hand over it. "Very best Douglas fir." Sam, the less-than-polite American, grabbed it and turned it slowly in his two hands. The two older men looked on like well-behaved children awaiting his verdict. Sam tossed it aside as unacceptable and moved toward stacks of two-by-twelve planks.

Although NO SMOKING signs warned in bright red, Kodo flamed a cigar. "I hired this Pink-er-ton kid because what I'm getting in Nagasaki is shit. If you've got anything better Yamada, show him your best."

"The best, of course," Yamada assured with a cry, eager to maneuver Kodo and his young expert from America away from stock he feared the young man would continue to judge inferior. Kodo's young expert insisted on taking his time and refused to be pushed. Yamada scrabbled through his merchandise to pull out his best plank. "A-Number One."

"Mister Pink-er-ton?" Kodo was waiting for his expert.

"This?" Sam allowed contempt to thicken his voice.

"A-Number-One-Best," Yamada declared.

Sam shook his head. "Piece of shit."

Yamada stood guilty with what Bremerton kids would call a shit-eating grin. "Best we can get."

"Sorry." Though the plank was clean Sam made a show of scrubbing pitch from his palms. Kodo signaled that they'd seen enough. They were leaving. "You're wasting our time, Yamada. Come on, Pink-er-ton. I can get crap this good through anybody in Nagasaki and Fukuoka—"

"Wait." Yamada, no longer defending his lumber, brightened, a man struck with an idea he was bursting to share. "When does Mr. Pink-er-ton go back to America?"

"When I tell him to." In a huff Kodo strode toward the door. With Yamada dogging the two Sam smothered a smile at his successful imposture. Yamada clawed at Kodo to draw him aside. "How well do you know this gaijin kid?"

"I know everything about him."

"He can be trusted?" Yamada asked.

"Why else would I hire him?"

"Listen, Kodo-San. Listen—don't go. Now, just hold on for a minute and listen. What I'm saying is—since your kid comes from over there and knows lumber people—he could buy direct from their mills for both of us. Maybe make him a silent partner . . . Because he's American he'd even be allowed to buy us our own mill. It's perfect."

"No way." Kodo had reached the street door and the car while Sam hung back listening to the Toad at his best, dealing.

"Don't you get it?" Yamada had become close to frantic and grabbing at Kodo. "Our own mill in the U.S.A. It's perfect."

Kodo barked at Sam. "We're getting out of here."

"Kodo-San, wait. Hang on—Don't you see how great this could be for both of us?" Yamada ran his thick fingers over his stubbly head. He was pleading.

"What's this 'us' you're talking about?" Kodo snarled. "How much ownership do you have in this yard?"

"Considerable."

"How much?" demanded Kodo.

"I have the backing of powerful friends."

Kodo said, "I see you've still kept your little finger. Do your friends have all theirs or tattoos?"

"Look, Kodo-San, we both live in the real world," he grabbed Kodo. "Just hold on for a fucking minute and listen. "He can make us rich—"

In awe Sam watched the way his father continued to play the man, shaking his head. "I'm already talking to your competition—they're a lot more honest than you—"

"You and me. Partners." Yamada's urgency had him sweating. "We send him back to the States. Make him our man in America. I'm good for half."

"Keep your money." Kodo puffed out cigar smoke. "I'm already setting him up over there."

Sam held his breath. Was he hearing right? Kodo was actually talking about the possibility of sending him to the States? His heart was banging in his ears so loudly he could scarcely hear the two as Yamada pressed on. "I'll get the money. We send him over. Japanese can't buy property in the States, but he can. He can buy us our own mill—"

"I told you, for that I don't need you." Yamada all but pushed himself into the car with them. "The Old Imperial," Kodo commanded, heaving himself onto the seat. Sam followed. The driver closed the door on Yamada.

In the car, side-by-side, neither father nor son said a word. Kodo was wallowing in his triumph, easing himself back, lighting another cigar. Hard rain was drumming the roof, but the car was warm and blue with smoke. Sam was already in another world—across the Pacific. Kodo had to poke him before he realized he was being offered a cigar.

"Let that be a lesson to you. You see how I made Yamada take the bait? Before I leave Tokyo he'll come crawling, begging me to make a deal." Sam nodded, pretending he was listening, but he wasn't in the car, but back in Bremerton. Sam took a deep breath in an effort to smother his wild excitement. He told himself to slow down his pounding heart so

Kodo wouldn't see he was already on the boat and half way there.

Kodo was dead serious. "Of course a trip like this means being away from Mayumi and Tat for a while."

The States! Yes, it could happen. It would happen. Since Kodo had given him legal status in Japan he could get him a passport so he could be free to travel. Just think, all these years away from his other world—the other half of himself—were over. He'd go back in style. "To hell with the Showalters!" He was shouting inside. This time in Seattle he wouldn't be a scared kid. He'd go back a grown man in an English suit and London shoes and hat. The first thing he'd do is reach Benjy. All the years apart would fall away. Benjy would know about their father. Benjy and the Showalters knew his secret, but over there he'd look as American as his brother. After all these years he'd find out how American he was. In America he'd discover what Robert had learned too late—who he was and in which world he belonged.

A jab in the ribs brought him back to Tokyo. "Wait and see," Kodo was gloating, "the minute we walk into the hotel Yamada will be waiting on the phone. He was so excited he pounded Sam's knee. "My own private American. My *ainoko*. My legal son. All mine, but Yamada doesn't know that. Hah!" Sam's cigar had gone out and Kodo tossed his lighter at him. "Hah! Didn't I tell Tedabara I always knew one day I'd get more than future Kodos out of you? America. No arguments. You're going to America!"

Sam bit down on his cigar, held his breath and told himself that from this hour on, like Torazo warned, America must always seem to be Kodo's idea and he always the subservient Japanese son. In the car he was launching his future but feigning regret. "But I could never go without taking Mayumi and Tat with me—"

"Not possible."

Perfect. How could Kodo know the last thing in the world he wanted on his pilgrimage was a Japanese wife and son. "Sir, I'm grateful for your confidence, but, sir, don't ask me to leave them. If Mayumi and Tat can't go with me, I could never think of going—"

"You'll do what I goddamned well tell you. Her mother and I will take care of things here—"

"But Mayumi's pregnant again—"

"She managed Tat without your help."

The British royalty had departed the hotel and Kodo was elevated to his rightful domain. Exactly as he'd said, a telephone call from Yamada was waiting for him. "Let him wait." The Nagasaki tycoon, still chuckling over his triumph, threw himself into an armchair and ordered his son to pour him a Scotch.

"A tall one."

The telephone shrilled.

"Didn't I tell you?" he chuckled. "Let Yamada stew." He drank, then seized the telephone, listened, and said nothing. Whatever was being said Sam saw Kodo snarl with such rage that he was holding his breath, ready to face any change in plan. Was Yamada calling off the American deal?

"Yes, I fucking heard!" Kodo barked. "I'll be on the next goddamn train." He slammed down the phone. "The fucking Reds are going out on strike."

CHAPTER SEVENTY

In the middle of the night the Marmon met the train and rushed them straight to the BlackStar office. A dozen of the city's most powerful businessmen, two newspaper editors, three government functionaries, and one military officer were waiting up for news from Kodo and his powerful friends in Tokyo. Turmoil on the waterfront had temporarily eased social differences. Even Robert Senior, with his black band of mourning, was here scanning a batch of Tokyo newspapers. Exactly as Kodo had said, the Tokyo press was outdoing itself printing statements from the baron, the cabinet minister and members of the Diet, charging the lawless dockworkers with taking their orders direct from Moscow.

Talbot moved to the window and gazed through the night down on the docks lit by flaring lanterns. "There they are," the old Yorkshireman's burr announced, "putting all their faith in their rabble-rousing leaders. The poor sods can't wait for morning—"

"Colonel, are you ready?" Kodo wasn't asking, but giving orders to a bald army officer, a strong, horse-faced man rolling one of his host's cigars wet in his mouth.

"Sir, I've had my men on standby for a full week."

In Tokyo Sam had seen how his father was listened to as a force among Top Men—some of the strongest powers in the country determined to stop the strike. Here in Nagasaki a skinny little Mitsubishi man in a black kimono had been waiting eagerly among the port's power brokers for Kodo's return and his news from Tokyo. The Mitsubishi Man's worry turned him to the others. "We have to make absolutely sure the country sees them for the bastards they are, waving plenty of red flags."

Pratt, fat Pratt from the club, hogged the window. "Not only flags, but big red banners. Look! See that? See what it says? 'Get Japan's imperialist claws out of China!' Proves right there they're taking orders straight from Moscow." A smile split his plump face. "Not precisely the sentiments a country at war expects from Tenno's loyal and patriotic dockworkers."

Behind him Talbot lit a meerschaum pipe with a kitchen match. "One of my chaps tells me that there'll be thousands by morning." He turned to the colonel. "Any last chances we can still avoid violence—that is if the bastards are orderly?"

"They won't be," the prospect seemed to please the colonel, "not once they start flapping their red flags in our faces. I'll give you law and order but a few heads might have to get cracked."

Sam saw that these important men could say, as an accepted fact, that the morning would see the docks running with blood. Confident with their crushing force, they were as unassailably certain of the righteousness of their cause, as Torazo's blazing crowd had been in that union hall in Fukuoka.

Sam shrank inwardly feeling as out of place here as he'd been as the enemy among Torazo's workers. Was he the only one here in Kodo's office who didn't agree with the colonel? Were they all so eager that heads be cracked, that the docks run with blood? He told himself that both sides were wrong. He was no spy of Torazo's here among Nagasaki's leaders, but was determined he had to convince Torazo to hold back workers from rioting, from raising red flags and marching into the blood bath trap these men were setting.

The hour was late. Time was short. He was in agony, desperate to reach Torazo, but Kodo's meeting didn't break up till nearly one in the morning. He raced out into the bitter night. On a public telephone, gasping for breath, he was kept waiting before Torazo came on the line.

"I have to see you—"

His former friend said nothing.

"Torazo, are you there? Torazo, I swear to God this is life and death—"

"You've been with Kodo."

"Yes, those you call the bosses have just had their meeting—"

"Get over here and tell the committee—"

"I can't do that. Torazo, I can only see you alone—only you—"

"You know where I am."

"No. It has to be some place nobody will see us together—What about that all-night bar near Lady Gray Rat's?"

Torazo was shouting orders to someone in the background, reminding him of that night when they shared the smoke of the union hall and the rage of a thousand workers.

"Torazo! You still there? Stay on the line. Please!"

Torazo was back. Sam could only pray that enough was left of their friendship to convince him to keep his men peaceful and present themselves as a legitimate cause, loyal to the Emperor. Wave red flags and show they were taking orders from the Red Russian communists and Kodo's colonel would mow them down and all Japan would cheer. "I swear to you, Torazo, this is their plan. This is life and death and only you and I can stop—"

Torazo was fighting noise, yelling to others. Did he hear? In his rush he yielded—they'd meet for five minutes. Sam raced to a shabby bar and waited in agony before his onetime friend raced in, his face as red as his scarf—a man gasping, without a moment to spare. He was aflame with demand. "One question. Yes or no. Are you on our side?"

"I'm on no one's side—"

"Then you're wasting my fucking time!" Torazo spat and was halfway out the door when Sam grabbed and slammed him against the wall.

"Goddamnit, listen to me!"

Torazo bared his crooked teeth. "Listen to the fake Kodo?" Torazo wrenched away violently. Sam, twice his size, had to fight to pin him to the wall. "In spite of everything you think, you and Suzuki are my last friends left in the whole goddamned world. I can't stand by and see you and your men cut down."

Torazo spat bitterly. "That's exactly what your shit father wants."

Sam had brought the Tokyo newspapers he'd had on the train for Mayumi and rattled them in his face. "They're setting you up to make Japan yell for your blood."

Torazo slapped the papers away. "Lies."

"I was there," Sam cried, "in Tokyo and here in his office. They'll have the whole country convinced you're disloyal—worse—that you're traitors taking orders from Moscow—tying up the war effort in China."

"Not when the country hears the truth—Get out of my way!" Torazo pushed against Sam who blocked him as he saw a flash of light catch a blade. Torazo had drawn and flicked it open. Sam grabbed his arm.

"Jesus, Torazo." Eye to eye, both were breathing hard. "For God's sake listen to me. They're taking no chances—they've got their own goons to infiltrate your ranks with their own red flags and banners. Stop them and your own men or the minute things get out of line—when the military sees any flags but the Rising Sun, they've got orders to fire. They will, Torazo, they'll mow you down—and all Japan will cheer."

Sam and the fierce little man threatening him with his knife stared at each other. "No, Torazo hissed. "Kodo sent you here to try to scare me off." Torazo spat his contempt. His black eyes glittered like the flashing blade.

"No. I swear to God, Torazo, this is only you and me. In Fukuoka I saw how men will follow you anywhere. You have the power. Control them tomorrow. I beg you. Don't give Kodo and the others the excuse to mow you down!"

"You don't scare me—"

"It scares the shit out of me—"

"Because you don't have anything worth dying for, because you don't believe in anything—"

"Don't, I swear to God, don't do this—"

"Whose God? Your God in your American Bible? No? Just you?

Who are you to swear to anything, you weak, shit of a nothing! You're Kodo's boy. Go kiss his fat ass and live your fake life."

CHAPTER SEVENTY-ONE

Before dawn Sam was back in Kodo's smoke-filled Marmon parked alongside the old customs house, watching the docks and the massing workers. He was in front with the driver. In the back seat Kodo, Robert Senior, Pratt and the Mitsubishi man waited. Robert Senior, bundled in an afghan and fighting a head cold, was mopping his prominent York-shireman's nose. "Look at that sign, 'World Revolution.'" He shook his head. "As if those poor sods out there knew what the hell that was."

"So far no flags." The nervous Mitsubishi man swiped his window with his silk handkerchief. "Where's the colonel?"

With a thrust of his head the driver pointed behind their car into a street massed with soldiers. Sam searched the crowd of organizers blaring into megaphones, lining their men four abreast in parade formation. Suddenly there he was in his indigo work clothes but no red scarf. Torazo! Thank God! Sam thought did this mean he'd listened to last night's warning? He watched him dashing to and fro holding his men in parade, wet and freezing in the rain. Sam could only pray he'd hold back, demonstrating peaceably for a living wage.

Here, in the cigar smoke of the warm car, he glanced back at Robert's father. From him at least he hoped for some streak of decency. Surely he must know these men in the rain had families with nothing between them and starvation but what the Kodos of this world begrudged them. How could Robert Senior, a man so superior to Kodo in every way, sit here denying Torazo's men the right to a contract, set wages, some kind of compensation for injury on the job, payment for their families if they were killed?

Robert Senior's face showed nothing. Kodo's eyes were narrow, eager, searching to catch sight of those first red flags. Suddenly Robert Senior blew his nose and reached for the door handle. He was opening the door, going out into the rain. "Before they take one bloody step," he growled, "they're going to get it damn well straight from me what the buggers are in for."

"Don't go!" Pratt shouted.

Kodo grabbed his hat. "Hold on. I'm going with you—"

The old Yorkshireman waved him back. Sam realized that the old man had no intention of being seen in any way with Bumper Kodo. "Even if they won't scare off," he declared, "I won't have it on my conscience that I didn't warn the bloody sods." He flung aside the afghan and pulled on his top silk hat. Sam winced and stifled a warning cry that the top hat made him look like a caricature of a capitalist boss. Unable to bear Robert's father facing the crowd alone, Sam sprang from the car. Rushing toward him he stopped a pace behind the tall figure, a giant here on the docks of Nagasaki. Sam's heart beat full of pride to be his friend. If anyone could hold the strikers in place in order to bargain, it was Robert's father.

The sound of the crowd rolled like an ocean wave coming toward them, breaking into a roar. The crowd was stirring. Was the first rank beginning to march? Suddenly there was Torazo, pushing in front of the column, waving frantically for his men to maintain order. And the red flags Sam dreaded? Thank God that so far he hadn't yet seen one. Torazo had believed him and had taken his warning. Clearly his wily ex friend understood newspapers, photos and newsreels, and was showing the world loyal Japanese workers assembling peaceably, willing to talk terms with the bosses.

Newspapermen with cameras rushed forward, lead by Kodo's Minoru, his PR man, eager for all hell to break loose. Here in the rain Torazo was frantically holding his men in place. Just then Sam spied a worker breaking free and snatching up a chunk of two-by-four. Letting out a shriek, piercing the wet air, he sent it flying. Hurtling out of the crowd it was coming straight at Robert Senior. Sam leaped forward, shoving him aside with the weapon missing him by inches and clattering across the pavement. At shrill whistles Sam spun around. To his horror, soldiers were marching down the street.

And Torazo? Waving frantically, he was fighting to maintain order and give the military no further excuse to fire. His men cheered, turned into a mob seeing Talbot's top silk hat, toppled from his head and rolling on the street—the very symbol of capitalism. A fiery young worker dashing out of the crowd clapped the hat on his own head and put on an act prancing to thunderous applause.

The old man, his gray hair blowing in the wind with Sam at his side, faced the mob ahead. From behind, the colonel's army was marching forward. Sam wiped rainwater from his eyes. Where was Torazo? Was the frantic little man losing his fight to hold back the roaring tide?

Sam dodged a stone, but a rock the size of a fist struck Talbot's shoulder. His thick overcoat padded the blow but sent him lurching until Sam held him and placed him into the car's back seat.

The workers' parade was now enormous and out of hand, filling the street, thundering and marching toward the car. Torazo was still in front of his men looking very small in the rain. With his arms flailing, fighting to hold his men four abreast in parade rank, most of his workers were still marching in peace. Were they singing? Sam listened hard, dreading hearing the *Internationale.* But no! Smart Torazo. He had his men singing *Kimigayo,* which had Pratt in the warm car screaming with rage. "Bastards! Pretending to sound loyal to the Emperor."

Sam was rolling down his window to lean out to hear the song, but Kodo was roaring in triumph. Kodo had what he needed, a red flag held high and waving. More flags rose in the rain. Banners stretched out demanding Japan's withdrawal from China. In the excitement, the singing of a thousand men changed. The anthem of Red revolution out-thundered the loyal Japanese. Blood red flags and placards rose, waving wildly while the marchers broke ranks, scattering Torazo's parade into a wild group now out of control and charging straight at the Marmon. The engine gunned. Wheels spun on the wet pavement. Sam was halfway out the window fighting to find Torazo. There he was, still racing, waving, desperate to hold back the rushing sea of red flags.

Rifle fire cracked the wet air.

Kodo heaved a sigh of triumph and sank back as the Marmon began its escape from the riot. Sam's hot face peered into the icy rain, searching the wild disorder. He scrubbed rain from his eyes. Torazo was ahead of the mob and racing beside the car, signaling the charging horde back from the rattle of soldiers' gunfire. For an instant their eyes locked. Time stood still. This wasn't the look of hatred Sam dreaded. Glancing straight at

Sam, he was still fighting to stop his workers, still running, but stumbling. He was clutching his side with his thin, white hands red with blood. His last look at Sam was a blank look he'd never seen before on that little white mug. The powerful Marmon plowed out from the howling mob. A brick struck the back fender. Another smashed the rear window. Gunfire rattled. From his rain-streaked window Sam saw Torazo lurch, sprawling, out of control. He grabbed for the door handle to rush to him, but the roaring sedan jolted him back. In one last look he saw his first friend in Japan dead, smashed and bloody in the wet street. Sam—Sam Kodo—was safe and warm in Kodo's car with powerful men cheering their victory. He closed his eyes on hot tears haunted by the little runt's last words.

"You're a fake Kodo. You don't have anything worth dying for. You don't believe in anything."

CHAPTER SEVENTY-TWO

That dark winter, with the *shojis* rattling in the wind, each day was bringing him closer to his sailing to the United States. He knew Mayumi's heart ached at the thought that he'd be away in another life, perhaps even dreading he might never return. Japanese wife that she was, she never said a word. That didn't mean his wife, so unusually sensitive to the feelings of others, didn't understand that except for his love for Tat, this last year had been a dark time for her Sam-San. First, of course, there was Robert's death. As if that weren't enough of a blow, he finally confessed his secret, telling her about his first friend in Nagasaki, his Torazo smashed to the street in the bloody strike. "He died," Sam said, "for what he believed in."

She knew that every day at BlackStar he felt ground under Kodo's heel, and her heart went out to him. On his darkest days, she knew he wanted nothing more than to crawl off by himself into the dark. But he was a husband. A father. In their silences, when he'd catch Mayumi looking at him, he wondered how deeply she was seeing into his soul. At these moments, without a word, he'd reach over, lift back her black hair and brush her cheek with a kiss and hold her close. Feeling her beating heart he asked himself if a man anywhere in the world had a more loving, more sensitive wife. He knew in his heart that for her sheer goodness, her dedicated effort to be a wife and mother, for all her devotion to him he felt everything but love.

Love—that burning, aching love of wild naked bodies was always Tedabara. He dreamed of her. He prayed that in his sleep with Mayumi he never cried out her name.

One early April evening, with rain glistening the garden and Tat with Robert's rooster asleep on the tatamis Sam worked to help Mayumi read a story in the *Saturday Evening Post*. He closed the last page. Neither spoke.

Tat woke with a happy gurgle and crawled onto his lap sharing the cartoons in the *Post* when Sam turned to Mayumi at his shoulder and said, "I've decided and I can't put off telling you any longer." He forced in a breath. "I can't go on with your father."

Carefully, slowly she set down the sake flask. He waited. He wondered if she'd heard his words intended to change their lives. She held back a gasp, smothering a little cry of hope. "You're not going to America?"

"Yes," he said, taking her hand, "No matter how I feel about him I'll make the trip. I'm not only going because I'm the loyal son. I'll do this last thing he wants from me because this is my chance to find out what of me I left over there. Can you understand that?"

He waited for her to raise her eyes and when she didn't look at him he took her chin in his hand. Her eyes opened, glistening with tears, telling him she understood what he was saying, but they were tears full of fear. Was he saying he might not come back to her?

"When I get back—" His words came in a heartfelt rush. "I can't live this way. It's our life, yours and mine and Tat's. Not your father's. What I'm going to do is I'm going to teach—Japanese and English. Yes, I know full well when I come back, it's going to be hardest on you—the hardest thing anyone ever asked you to do. We won't live in this house. We'll have our own place and it won't be anything nearly so grand, but it will be a place of our own." He looked down at Tat ripping pages from the *Saturday Evening Post*. Mayumi took the magazine from him and their eyes met. "Aren't you going to say anything?"

She drew Tat to her.

"You understand what I'm saying?"

"Yes, I understand."

"I mean it when I say it'll be even harder for you than for me, but I'll be twenty-one in two more months and I can't put off how I'm—how we live the rest of our lives." She said nothing and he struggled on. "I've agonized over this. I've prayed over it, and it's the only way if we're ever going to have a life." Tat grabbed at the magazine. Mayumi drew the boy close and Sam leaned to her, looking for more of a reaction.

"I understand." She looked up at him with dark, shining eyes full of trust. He could only wonder if she could possibly imagine the profound changes they'd face breaking from Kodo for the rest of their lives.

"I need more than that, Mayumi. For God's sake, tell me what you think."

He was asking the finest person he'd ever known, who loved him with every last breath of her life.

"I am your wife," she said. "I love you."

CHAPTER SEVENTY-THREE

Suzuki's cane prodded him up a hill to a small Buddhist temple. "Your mother's temple. Did I tell you before?" She croaked out her broken gasps.

"But she was a Christian."

"Fat lot of good that did her." She rolled prayer beads in her bony hands. "Before the wedding to that bastard we always came here. Afterwards she brought you a few times. Me, I never stopped coming."

He helped her light incense. They both rang the heavy rope bell to tell the Lord Buddha they were here. They faced the altar, clapped and bowed. Today, with his U.S. passport in his pocket, everyday sights and sounds came into sharper focus. Students in a school room in back of the altar were droning a sutra. Birds chirped and the low, steady hoot of ocean liners filled the harbor. This last spring morning in Nagasaki with Suzuki he was open to comparing East and West, or more precisely, in his case, West and East. He'd lived in America eleven years, and here in Japan almost ten. Not only blood, but the years and time itself, had almost equally divided his life.

She was fiercely insistent they go to the outdoor teahouse across from the pine tree and Butterfly's home. The May day was blue and gold and full of white birds. They drew cushions up to the table's scarlet runner. Suzuki, silent and far from her usual chattering self, arranged her kimono and dropped her hands into her lap. Sam put aside his hat, remembering how Sato-San's panama had blown into the iris bed. In his three-piece gray flannel suit, appropriate for climbing the gangplank to board the Cleveland, he gazed at the tall pine and the tile roof both knowing they were sharing each other's thoughts, of being together on the tatami over there when he was Tat's age.

She put down her tea and took his hand in hers. "Something I never told you." He waited, sensing this was close to his mother's and her hearts. "Your mother and I called you 'Sorrow.' Yes. Sorrow, because we were waiting for your father to come back to her. 'On that fine day,' she said, 'we'd change your name to 'Joy.'" She tightened her thin, little hand on his in desperation. "No. Don't go to America."

He kissed her hand. "You know, Suzuki-San, I must."

"You go to America—you'll never come back. Like your father."

"You know the truth, that I don't love Mayumi with all my heart, but I love my son."

She studied her teacup. "How's she taking all this?"

"Of course she's being brave. Brave, and did you know she's pregnant?"

"Think I don't know that? Due in June. All the astrologists say it will be a girl."

He sipped tea. "That would be nice—a little sister for Tat. You'll see my baby before I do." Neither had to tell the other that they both knew this was likely the last time in his life they'd see one another. He took her bones in his arms. "Setsu promises me she wants you to come to the house anytime."

"Good heart, Setsu." She picked up her teacup, but put it back down. "What about the Bitch?"

Sam, still fighting the memory of their last night of lovemaking two years ago, failed to sound off-hand. "Tedabara?"

"Foolish name for a foolish woman."

"I don't think about her any more."

"Lie to Mayumi, son. Not to me."

CHAPTER SEVENTY-FOUR

On the Fourth of May Kodo had presented Sam with a U.S. Passport—Samuel Adams Pinkerton. Born June 12, 1902, Bremerton, State of Washington. It looked real, but his adopted father, the Toad, breathed no word of how he came to have it. On the Fifth of May he'd be sailing on the President Cleveland for Seattle from the Port of Nagasaki.

The day of the sailing he kissed his wife's swollen belly and felt his new baby stir. "Keep thinking about the new lives we'll have when I get back," he said. He finished his goodbyes and, without being able to tell her he loved her, but with a hug and a kiss and another, with all his heart, for his bewildered, whimpering little boy.

Kodo insisted on bustling with him up the gangplank. In his stateroom a young American steward, alarmingly huge and pale, unpacked Sam's bags and hung his new dinner clothes in a closet, and was attempting to introduce himself when Kodo bumped him out the door. Father and son stood in silence with the ship full of the sounds of hand-bells clanging and shouts of bon voyage drowned out by a brass band's *Auld Lang Syne.*

"Three minutes, ladies and gentlemen," blared a megaphone voice. A purser with a face so ash-white Sam wondered if all Americans were so sickly pale poked his long *tengu* nose into the cabin at Kodo. "Sorry, sir, only passengers now. We'll have to ask you to leave."

Kodo kicked shut the door still giving orders. "First thing you do is you go over the passenger list and find out who's on board—who's important." He ignored the insistent bells calling for visitors to leave while filling the cabin with more cigar smoke. From his own flask he poured

Scotch, of course Johnnie Walker Black Label, into two glasses. "After Yokohama you'll have two weeks, plenty of time to meet top people. See that each one gets my BlackStar card. Make every contact you can. I'm paying good money for you in first class."

Obediently Sam raised his glass to his father. *Kampai*—more than a salute from a son about to cross the Pacific, this was his secret valedictory as he was leaving to complete his final assignment for Kodo and BlackStar. He was Japanese enough to understand the honor involved. Over there he'd look American but he would be Japanese fulfilling this one last duty.

"Guard that damned passport with your life. I paid plenty for it." Kodo commanded, as he sank his bulk into a leather armchair studying Sam across his whiskey. "Over there see that you look more like a Pinker-ton than a Kodo and don't be surprised when you find out your high-and-mighty United States of America doesn't like us Japs."

Kodo thrust out his glass for a refill. "See that you pull this off and it'll be bigger than anything your high and mighty Talbots—even Glover's—got going." He signaled his son for more whiskey. "You don't have to tell me you're doing this because you like me. Tell yourself you're doing it for Tat. It'll all be his some day."

He studied Sam. "That suit. How much did I pay for that suit?"

Sam didn't answer.

"Plenty, I know that. And that panama hat." Sam knew he looked like he belonged in first class, splendid in his gray Saville Row suit with the new fashion, a soft collar and thick silk pale blue four-in-hand tie. Kodo was saying he'd created him and continued cutting him down to size. He drank and wiped his wet lips. "I took a big chance on you so don't ever kid yourself. You'd be nobody without me—an *ainoko* rickshaw boy. Back then there wasn't a decent family in the entire country who'd let you within a mile of one of their daughters. The day Bumper Kodo found you bare ass I only let you live because a certain party told me you knew English and your father was a U.S. navy officer." More bells rang. Sam wondered if Kodo, drinking and staring down at the glowing tip of his cigar.His voice dropped. "It was always about her foot." He shook his head at an old sadness and a still smoldering anger. "My little girl's foot." He looked into the amber drink. "You'll never know how I cursed the gods for that. Even Lord Buddha. Of course if I'd been a Talbot or a

Glover—in spite of that damned foot—Mayumi would have married into a top—top family. The gods weren't kind so I said to myself, fuck 'em all. Bumper Kodo makes his own rules like I made you a Kodo and now I have a grandson and another kid on the way. Now you're so high-and-mighty proud of yourself—even a friend of the Talbots. And as for the lumber business, don't think you've got me fooled. You don't know anything near what you pretend to, but your fucking Americans don't need to know that. Over there you learn the ropes. You buy me the best sawmill money can buy and come home the minute you can to my Mayumi and Tat and the new kid."

The loudest rumble of all shuddered the vessel. The purser poked his pink face in the door. "Sir, your guest will have to leave this minute. And hurry—" Kodo made an executive decision, heaved himself up and slammed the door in the man's face, locked it and pushed his face, punctuated with the cigar, into Sam's. He pulled the wet cigar out of heavy lips and considered the glowing end. His eyes locked on Sam's. "You still think about her, don't you?"

Sam's eyes didn't move. He stared straight into his father's dark eyes. "No."

"Tedabara. Yes, you still think about her." The wet cigar slid between wet lips. "She's the kind of hot bitch every men thinks and dreams about. As for my Tedabara you can stop now. By the time you get back she'll be dead." He took the cigar out and rolled it between two thick fingers. "Some woman's disease."

Sam prayed for a still heart. For a moment she was with them here in the cabin. Sam could see her licking pomegranate ice, her naked body that still thrilled him. The way Kodo had broken the news he'd been blunt, too blunt, a man covering his feelings. Kodo was relying on studying his cigar to show nothing and looked through the smoke into the future. "You have Mayumi."

Kodo ran his hands over his oily black hair. "It's time I left that Maruyama dump anyway. I'll miss the bitch but I've got a geisha in Kyoto. Not top, not *Gion* but *Ponto Cho,* top enough she's been with the head man of his electricity and power syndicate for years. Now he's in jail for life—without even the guts for seppuku. She knows everyone worth knowing in Japan. With her I don't have to eat shit waiting for the high and mighty Talbots. Not with her friends in high places. Real connections."

Heavy pounds slammed the door.

"Sir, unless you're coming with me, they're telling you to leave the ship—"

"On board and over there you'll be Pink-er-ton, but don't let that give you any fancy ideas. Just so we understand each other," Kodo continued to ignore more thuds on the door. "I've never liked you any more than you like me. Let's not kid ourselves. Tall. Blond. Big pecker. Like one of Tedabara's Greek gods. But I made a Kodo out of you with a wife and son and baby on the way. You're mine. You make this deal, you do right by this family, and I'll treat you proud when you get back."

At last Kodo turned to the door, stopped and thrust out his hand in a too-conscious Western-style gesture, not as an equal, but as a superior deigning to show he could be decent to an underling. Sam stared at his father's hand. Was he still American enough to reject the new ritual— now popular but meaningless among up-to-date Japanese? He intended this to be a formal goodbye and he bowed.

Kodo was gone. He was alone in the cabin whispering goodbyes from his heart, to Tedabara who was dying and Torazo, and dear old Robert, both gone forever.

CHAPTER SEVENTY-FIVE

He was running. No rickshaw this time. He couldn't race fast enough out of Seattle's New Washington Hotel over to First Avenue and down to Colman Dock to catch the first ferry to Bremerton. It shuddered and chugged, wonderfully reassuring like always. Inside the saloon the air was hot and heavy with the greasy smell of frying hamburgers and onions.

Hamburgers! He hadn't smelled a hamburger or sniffed the tang of mustard on a hot dog for over ten years. He climbed to the ferry's top deck to stand at the rail watching Seattle's skyline recede under Mount Rainier looming, more grand than ever, but without the resident gods who lived on Fuji. Beside hamburgers, he was breathing the whiff of salmon from the fishing boats, the acrid stink of creosote, the smoke from the sawmills.

Back in Bremerton. Six-feet tall, handsome in his gray Saville Row suit. Could anyone guess this was a rickshaw boy from Japan, his eyes stinging with tears, looking at his old brick grammar school and kids outside at recess pushing, shoving, shrilling happily? His heart stopped. There it was, the crack of a baseball bat on a ball. A bell rang and his heart raced with the kids spilling back into their classrooms to sit at varnished desks under the American flag, but no longer under the portrait of gloomy President Woodrow Wilson, but the handsome new president, Warren G. Harding.

He fortified himself for the navy's little white house last seen in that heavy March rain. More than ten years had passed and enormous firs and cedars along with maples crowded the front and back yard all but hiding the house. His house. So why was this white fox terrier racing out at him, yapping a strident warning for the stranger to keep off his property and stay out on the wooden-plank sidewalk. The dogwood tree he and Benjy had planted was now taller than the house and spangled with white stars. Down the driveway was the basketball hoop waiting over the garage door, but the rubber tire swing that hung from the madrone tree was new. So was the glider on the front porch.

He went to the shortstop Eddie Conklin's house, but the new people who were living there didn't look like Siwash Indians. At the door he found himself at a loss for anything to say when they told him Eddie had been killed in the war in France. "Chateau Thierry," they said.

He turned back to town. Eddie, with his blue tooth, a crackerjack shortstop, his best friend, his own age, dead. Sam had been spared America going to war. Unlike Eddie, he had a life to live, a life in which to find out who he was.

On Bremerton's main street he went to the Owl Drug Store and at the counter dove into a hamburger, a dill pickle, and a cup of coffee. Next door he couldn't resist Ferber's ice-cream parlor, but almost gagged on the richness of a chocolate malt.

There it was down on the water—the naval station and the BOQ where he and Benjy had tried not to cry through those last dark and rainy days before the chaplain took them to Seattle.

Before he left the hotel he'd put in a call to Baltimore and now hurried back in case his brother had returned the call. Lucille, at the switchboard with her big breasts, yellow hair, and the overpowering smell of perfume, reported no calls. She was friendly as if they'd known each other for ages. She tried Baltimore a second and third time till he said, "I'll be here in the hotel. In the bar."

Lucille didn't try to cover the strange look she was giving him. Why was she smiling this way? "I guess, Mister Sam Pinkerton, living over there in Japan Asia and all, you don't know. The country's dry. No alcohol anywhere. Now we have prohibition here in the States."

"What kind of shit was this?" he growled, but only to himself.

He bought the *Seattle Times* waiting in his room in case Lucille reached Benjy. He read that President Harding was in Alaska and Babe Ruth had outdone himself with three more home runs. A dock strike threatened Tacoma, where the local timber barons called for stronger measures against the Reds. That news, he told himself, would gladden Kodo's heart, hearing America's "Top People" shared his worry about world revolution.

The telephone jangled and he jumped out of his skin as the operator put through a long-distance collect call, not from Baltimore, Maryland but from Princeton, New Jersey.

"Samuel Pinkerton?" It was a man's voice, but hesitant. "Sam?"

"Benjy?"

"Wow." Silence. Then another gasp. "Talk about surprised. I can't believe it's really you—"

Sam would not have known this voice—husky, strong and without an English accent like Robert's, but American like he hadn't heard in years. "Wow. Sam—is it really you? Give me a sec to get this straight. You're in Seattle?"

"This afternoon I was in Bremerton. Remember the dogwood tree we planted?"

"I guess—"

"You should see it. It's taller than the house and in full bloom. The basketball hoop is still over the garage."

"All this time—Jesus H. Christ, Sam, I didn't know whether you were alive or dead . . . What happened? Where were you all this time? The

Showalters said the navy had tried to put you in a foster home. I tried every way I could, Sam, but I could never find out where you were—"

"I've been in Japan all the time—"

"Japan? Over in Japan all this time?"

"Just got back to the States this morning."

"Wow. Sorry to keep saying that, but, gee—with a surprise like this, you could knock me over with a pin. Man, oh man, oh man, oh man. I still can't believe I'm talking to you, Sam—my own brother—"

"Got news for you, Benjy. You're an uncle—"

"No kidding? You're married?"

Three thousand miles away Sam felt Benjy could see his smile. Before Benjy stumbled around the central fact of Sam's life, before he said anything else, the older brother spoke. "They were right, the Showalters. I'm half-Japanese. My wife's Japanese."

Benjy moved to safer ground. "You say you've got a son?"

"A boy going on two. His name is Tat. Tatsuo. Means dragon."

"Dragon?"

"Dragon."

"No kidding. Hey, I mean that's grand. Wow!"

"Are they with you now there in Seattle?"

"No. At home in Nagasaki. But what about you?"

"I guess you know, since Baltimore put the call through up here that I'm at Princeton. My first year."

"What are you studying?"

"It'll be medicine. Surgery. Like granddad. He died four years ago. Grandmother's still going strong as ever. And Martha—the maid—you remember her?"

"Tell me. Have the Showalters treated you all right?"

"Grandfather and Grandmother? They sent me to Culver."

"Is that a school?"

"Military prep school. Then Princeton . . ." Benjy's voice dropped. "Sam, what they did to you . . . I'll never get over that. Jesus. As good as they've been to me, I'll never ever forgive them for that—"

Sam outflanked him by managing to chuckle. "I'm fine."

"You'll have to give me a minute to get this straight—you say you live in Japan? I mean all this time?"

Sam explained he was over here as a lumber agent for his father-in-law. He left out the fact the man was his adopted father, but confessed what only his brother could be trusted to know. "I'm over here to make this deal. But since you know I'm Japanese you've got to keep this a secret."

"Lumber?"

"In the morning I have to start finding out everything I can about timber—forests and lumbering and mills and shipping—"

"You coming East?"

"Afraid not. But now that we're back in touch we can write all the time."

"Gosh, Sam, that would be grand—but this call is costing you an arm and a leg, let me at least pay half—"

"Don't worry about that. I'm just thankful we found each other."

For a long moment neither spoke. Then Sam asked the most important question of all. He hesitated, then began, "Benjy—"

"I know what you're going to ask. No. The answer's no. All these years the Showalters have never heard word one from him—no word at all. How 'bout you?"

"In Japan, how would I hear? I found out how he met and married my mother, but I'd better write that."

"Maybe I know, well I think I know, what happened to him."

"Go ahead."

"All I really know is, it was about four years ago, some woman claiming she was his widow got in touch with the navy department telling them he'd died in the influenza epidemic and she was entitled to his pension. The navy found out our mother was his first wife and because he'd left the navy under some kind of a cloud he wasn't entitled to a pension. He'd been living out there in San Francisco where he died. That would have been 1919."

Sam shut his eyes, surprised at how little sadness he felt about a father who'd walked out on their mother and the two of them on that Christmas Day. With no more word about Lieutenant Commander Benjamin Franklin Pinkerton, neither was asking himself what kind of man he was. His sons fell silent.

"Sam? Still there?"

Sam said, "I guess that's it then for our dad."

"Guess so."

"What about your asthma?"

"Not for years. Hell, I'm out for the Princeton crew. Leaving for practice right after we hang up—"

"Before I go back to Japan I'll call again."

"Sam you can't possibly know what a surprise you've just handed me—how grand it is finally to hear from you . . . Sam?"

"Still here, Benjy."

"Sam, are you absolutely sure there's no chance of your getting back here?"

"Not this trip—I'm at the New Washington."

"Jesus H. Christ, Sam. Write me and tell me everything. Send me a picture of your wife and son. What did you say their names were?"

"She's Mayumi. He's Tat. Tatsuo."

"I promise I'm going to write, tell you everything, starting right after we hang up."

They exchanged addresses and double-checked to be sure they had them right. Was it time to hang up? "Sam, I've never stopped thinking of you."

"Me, too. So I guess it's so long—at least for now."

After Sam hung up he sat for an hour staring at the phone. Memories crowded in. Little Benjy with Woodrow Wilson glasses like their mother. His asthma. That humidifier humming all night. Benjy with his new *Oz* book to take on the train. Now Benjy was eighteen and at Princeton. Turning out for crew. From F. Scott Fitzgerald stories in the *Saturday Evening Post* he knew Princeton was a college for those in America Kodo would call "top people." Benjy. Benjy at Princeton and going to be a surgeon like that grandfather of his.

CHAPTER SEVENTY-SIX

Sam unfolded his letter of credit in front of a blond, six-foot-two Swedish car dealer on Seattle's Olive Street. He'd been offered a chew of tobacco, which he took, feeling for the *sake* of business relations here in the States that it would be a mistake to refuse. With the man's friendly hand on his shoulder he climbed behind the wheel of a chestnut-brown, four-door Pontiac sedan with bud vases, and even more remarkable, fresh roses. The dealer sat beside him in the passenger seat checking the documents till he handed him the keys. "She's a beauty and all yours now, Mister Pinkerton."

"And when I want to sell it back?"

"Right here's your place. Guarantee you top dollar."

"One problem," Sam admitted. "I don't know how to drive."

Three hours later, after several perilous moments on Capitol Hill, he was crossing the Montlake Bridge to the University of Washington's School of Forestry. Before leaving Japan on a Tokyo newspaper letterhead, he'd written to a Professor Einar Lofgren. Except for missing his left leg from his lumberjack days, Lofgren, without the use of a cane, was as tall and strong as one of his tall fir trees. Sam presented himself as a newspaper reporter for his Tokyo English-language newspaper, here to write a piece he'd been assigned on logging in America's Pacific Northwest.

Lofgren took him to lunch at the faculty club with two colleagues, world experts, happy to share their remarkable knowledge of the green world of the Pacific Northwest. Since that morning with the Swedish car dealer and now these Paul Bunyans turned professors, Sam found himself wondering if all Americans were so tall. Slicing into his massive, blood-rare sirloin steak, he fought wincing at what lay there before him—to a Japanese so bloody and obscene. All three hearty and open men treated the journalist from Japan as a long-lost friend. One after another they apologized that they couldn't offer at least a beer, but the Land of the Free had forbidden them alcohol. "Do they drink in Japan?" When Sam explained that indeed they did, he added, "German beer."

The Americans allowed that from all they'd heard, Japan was a pretty modern country. No one overtly expressed his amazement that a fine young American like himself could, or would want, to get along with the Japs. Sam tried not to appear too worldly, explaining that his work as a writer made it necessary that he be open to different ways. They nodded. They supposed that was so. Perhaps flattered that he looked to them for expertise, the three outdid themselves. No men could be more open and helpful than these three. After almost four hours of his crash course on forests, timberlands, mills, and logging in the Pacific Northwest, he admitted a problem. In some ways he'd lost touch with the States. Going deep into the woods he wondered if he should wear the gear and try to look like the timbermen. "I have a hunch," he was trying out what he'd already decided, "that if I showed myself out there in the rain and those mills wearing a suit and looking like a total greenhorn—if I told them I'd gone to some Eastern college like say Princeton—I could ask the dumbest, most unprofessional questions. Maybe that way get a real, first-hand look inside the lumber business."

Lofgren considered the reporter's angle. "Go out in the woods dressed like some Eastern dude and play the greenhorn?" All three saw his point. "Not try to out-Paul Bunyan them? Give them a laugh but treat them with respect and you bet they'll tell you anything you want to know."

"One thing," Lofgren spoke for all three, "a word to the wise. I sure as hell would never tell any of them you're working for the Japs."

Within an hour his Pontiac was bouncing on a rutted road through the brightest green timberland to creep down along a logging trail. When the biggest truck he'd ever seen came thundering straight at him, loaded high with cut logs of gargantuan immensity he'd never seen in Japan, he scooted over into the bracken. He took the Pontiac into a dark green cathedral, pillars of trees towering overhead in this wettest corner of America, mostly firs standing uncut since Columbus arrived. Kodo had sent him into these wet forests till he knew enough about lumbering to wind up his journey finding a mill for sale.

He swerved the Pontiac to dodge a black bear cub tumbling across the trail. In the deep green and flickering light he caught his breath, entering a grove so breathtaking in grandeur he pulled his Pontiac over and climbed out to wander through enormous ferns, and rhododendrons billowing with pink blossoms shading shy, delicate wildflowers. A gurgle led him to a stream and a mossy log to sit upon and unwrap waxed paper from a ham and cheese sandwich. He stopped, in awe that this place was too sacred, too holy for ham and cheese. He pushed the sandwich back in his rucksack.

His heart lifted up, up through the towering trunks to swaying fir branches murmuring high above in the breeze. He was back in America with magnificent forests still uncut from time immemorial. This was the same deep thrill that so moved him in that other forest across the Pacific. Never had he been so overcome, so inspired by the wonder of life as that night he entered into the fire ceremony in that other forest grove. That was the night he knew in his heart he could never find that thrill within the calcimined walls of the Snyder's mission.

Surely some kind of Western spirits must dwell here in such a holy place. In this rustling and murmuring forest with birds singing and this stream purling over rocks, this sacred place, his soul, Japanese or American, was here.

The next day, back in his Pontiac lurching through the rough road of this deep green world, a sudden terrible metallic scream, louder and fiercer than ever heard by the gods of Shinto, sent birds flapping in panic up through the trees. Ahead, the last cathedral columns of tree trunks ended in blazing sunlight and he heard the crack of axes tearing apart deep green glades where the glare of day had never entered since the beginning of time. This was what they called clear-cutting, a kind of lumbering Lofgren and the others had talked about. Clear-cutting left this green world bare. Lumbermen had left scarred acres of slash, stumps parching, streams drying to dust where salmon would never find their way here again.

The Pacific Northwest. This was where Japan and Kodo and much of the world got its lumber. For the next few days his awe increased at the power, the fierce hard work of bands of strong young lumbermen attacking the wilderness, felling these giants, ripping the most enormous logs in the world out and onto exhaust-bilging trucks and trundling them to the sawmills. The bigger mills were sending two hundred thousand board feet a day off to railroad sidings and onto docks and overseas.

He drove for three weeks. He wound through forests as far south as the Willamette River in Oregon before he circled the Pontiac back up along the wet Pacific Coast through Hoquiam and Aberdeen. Here he was alongside the opposite shore of the Pacific Ocean where, even in the month of June, these coastal timberlands spun with mist and gray sheets of rain. The lumbering towns built around mills were made of wood. Houses were wood. Sidewalks over the mud were wood. The air was thick, choking with smoke from burning wood. In dingy cafes, full of smoke, loud hardworking men bantered with waitresses as rough and ready as themselves. Day after day he faced white plates heaped with thick meat, potatoes and gravy thick as mud. Vegetables? Maybe cabbage. Always, plenty of loud talk about lumbering fired with hate against the Chinks and Japs whom these Americans swore had come over here to take their jobs away. Sam hunched as he ate his apple pie, sucked up his coffee, and kept his mouth shut about himself.

Every night alone in some grim room after he finished writing up his firsthand report of forests and lumbering, more than anything in the world, he wanted the comfort of Johnnie Walter Black Label or at least an ice-cold beer—both forbidden, not by the gods, but by the freedom-loving United States of America.

CHAPTER SEVENTY-SEVEN

"You're much younger than I expected, Mr. Pinkerton."

Mitchell Hedrick, opening his lawyer's office door, had come from a visit with the dentist and was pressing a towel filled with ice against his jaw. In spite of the obvious pain he was in suffering a wisdom-tooth extraction, Sam found the man unusually dignified and impressive. He was about forty, with sharply-cut features, shrewd gray eyes under dark brows, and graying hair brushed forward on his brow like a Roman senator. Tea was not offered.

"You're twenty-one years of age?"

"I will be, sir. Before I return to Japan."

"Please sit down. Would you care for a cigar?"

"Yes, sir, I would."

"Good man. Let's see if I can baby this jaw enough that I can smoke while we talk."

Sam liked the man's style, easy, informal yet clearly a man of considerable education, probably from the Eastern United States, maybe even Benjy's Princeton. He was certainly more straightforward than the European members of Nagasaki's Occident Club. Sam felt confident. He knew he looked his best in his brown, English-style suit dry cleaned of fir needles and mud.

"First, Mr. Pinkerton, may I ask how you learned about me?"

"I've been reviewing reports and papers from the University of Washington School of Forestry."

"Good people. We can talk about them another time. For today let's keep our exchange down to your letter. After this damned tooth quiets down, you and I will have a better chance to get to know one another. Bremerton. Your letter said you grew up in Bremerton."

"Yes, sir."

"Navy family?"

"That's right, sir."

Mitchell Hedrick opened a black-leather dossier and drew out the letter Sam had posted from Chehalis, Washington. "Before we can even begin to open any discussion, I must ask you straight out if you've made yourself and your employer in Japan current on our land laws here in the U.S. and the State of Washington?"

"In a general way, yes, sir."

"This corporation you represent, this BlackStar Construction Limited and Bay Trading in Nagasaki, is held by a Japanese citizen?"

"Yes, sir."

"Your employer is aware that U.S. law forbids a Japanese national to hold title to land in the United States?" Before Sam could answer, Hedrick grimaced. "Damn this tooth. Sorry." He rattled an aspirin out of a tin and returned to the letter. "You wrote this?"

"Yes, sir."

"I've got to hand it to you, Mister Pinkerton. You write a good letter. You make succinct what you and your employer have in mind. Maybe a little too succinct." Hedrick's eyes fastened on Sam. He attempted a friendly smile, but his mouth twisted into another show of pain. "Black-Star as an entity may appear solid enough. However, as a word to the wise, if I were in your boots I wouldn't overstate your role as being employed by a Japanese." He folded the letter.

"I thought you should know, sir."

"I appreciate your candor, but that's best kept between you and myself. In the time we have together today suppose we start by your telling me about your Mr. Koichi."

"His name is Kodo, Sir. The Japanese put the last name first."

"Thank you." Mr. Hedrick was saying he wasn't too old to learn. "This Kodo of yours. He's a rich man?"

"A very rich man," Sam said.

"By Japanese standards?"

"I'd have to say, sir, by any standards. Besides a construction company he owns a shipping line and several other businesses in Nagasaki and Tokyo."

"And he wants you to buy him timberland and a mill over here." Mitchell Hedrick, his ice pack in one hand, held up the other for silence. "This is our first meeting and you don't need to answer. From where he sits over there in Japan, from his point of view, what he's attempting makes real sense." He winced. The aspirin didn't seem to help. "I've traveled a bit, Mister Pinkerton. Not to Japan, of course, but to England and Hawaii. My wife and I love the Islands. Did you know there are even more Japanese in Hawaii than there are in the State of Washington?"

He took the cigar out of his mouth and leaned into the chunk of ice within the towel. "I say this because we'd be wasting each other's time if the two of us didn't go straight to the matter of race. Obviously being, as you are, in the employ of a Japanese citizen, I take as prima facie evidence that you hold a wider view of the world, as do I, from most of our citizens. I feel confident the two of us, who know something about the world, view outsiders—foreigners—other races—without the prejudices of many of our fellow countrymen. Am I correct that your Mister Kodo is aware of the laws we have about Asians here in the State of Washington, indeed on the entire West Coast?"

Without waiting for an answer he snapped open the tin of aspirin, but closed it again, deciding against additional medication. "It's important that we both share a full understanding of what I am talking about."

"I believe I understand, sir, Mister Hedrick."

"I don't have to tell you the way our Mister William Randolph Hearst goes on and on in his press about 'The Yellow Peril.' He plays to readers who feel the Japanese are the wiliest of the Asians and would like nothing better than to take over this country." His cigar dismissed Mister

Hearst. "All this you and I understand. Still, if we decide to talk further, it's best to get it out of the way. Of course, you'll need to be brought up to date on the newer laws which totally prohibit immigration and restrict the purchase of land by Japanese aliens already living here. You and Mister Kodo are aware of these new laws?"

"Not, of course, to the extent you are, sir. That's why I'm here."

The attorney attempted to smile around his painful jaw. "I already have the impression you're a young man who's done his homework. So let's both agree that you and I are not indulging our personal feelings about the world we live in. You may detect my thrust is leading me to mention the client you write about. My client is a family, actually. They are, indeed, holders of considerable virgin timberland as well as Forest Service leases along with a mill and the dock you mention in your letter. However, I must tell you that my clients share Mister William Randolph Hearst's feelings about the Japanese. Under this new law, do you care to hazard a guess as to the number of Japanese who will be allowed to immigrate to this country?" Sam knew the answer but allowed Hedrick the pleasure of telling him by making a circle of his thumb and first finger. "Goose egg. Zero." The lawyer rattled the aspirin tin in his elegant fingers. "How long, Mister Pinkerton, have you been in Mr. Kodo's employ?"

"Twenty-one months."

"*Entre nous,* Mister Pinkerton, do we totally trust our Mister Kodo?"

"I work for him—"

"Understand," the lawyer said, "this isn't a cross examination." Sam showed nothing, but understood that cross examination was precisely what this was.

Mitchell Hedrick continued, "Would you say our Mister Kodo is a man of his word?"

"Japanese men have been known to take their lives when they believe their behavior to be less than honorable. Let me phrase it this way. Would you say our Mister Kodo would regard his word to an American as being as sacred as to another Japanese?"

The lawyer opened the towel and repositioned the ice.

"Sir, I wouldn't be here otherwise. I've never known Mister Kodo to break his word. I've also never known him to fail to get his way."

"Bravo for Mister Kodo." He slid the letter back into the dossier. "That's in Japan, of course."

Clearly, Mitchell Hedrick was skilled at presenting unpleasant truths as pleasantly as possible. Sam had already suspected that in Japan, as well as here in America, the more successful the euphemism, the greater the world rewards successful insincerity. He'd found himself a hell of a lawyer, which meant this was a man with whom he must proceed very, very carefully. He was back in the States and even though the year was 1923, he knew the lawyer was alluding to American feelings about the Japanese.

"You'll be staying with us here in Port Angeles for some time?"

"For however long this takes, sir."

"You realize, of course, that at this time this office can't be overly encouraging. However, I owe it to my clients to pass along your interest."

"Thank you, Mister Hedrick."

"The hotel treating you all right?"

"I have a beautiful view of the Straits. They tell me I can rent tackle and go out trolling for salmon."

"The chinook are running. I only wish I had time to go with you." Mitchell Hedrick rose and Sam remembered to shake his hand firmly while he picked up his new Panama hat.

"Mister Pinkerton," the lawyer's tone changed. "My daughter's having a few young people in for dinner this evening. It might amuse you to see what Port Angeles offers in the way of social excitement—such as we have."

CHAPTER SEVENTY-EIGHT

Mitchell Hedrick's three-story house on a hill was larger and far more impressive than the Talbot house in Nagasaki. America's extravagant use of wood was apparent—porches and towers and cupolas made possible by jigsaw into gingerbread trim, gleaming whiter than a wedding cake in the evening light. The vast lawn under Sam's polished English shoes was a carpet of emerald velvet. Was there a single lawn like this in Japan? Even in the Emperor's palace?

Mitchell Hedrick was on the front porch talking with a plump young woman in lavender organdy and an athletic man in white flannel slacks, white shoes, and blue blazer. A Victrola behind the screen door was bouncing out "Ain't We Got Fun?" a song Sam had danced to on board the ship.

Mitchell Hedrick had said people his own age would be here at this dinner party. That worried him. Young men on board the ship never hesitated to ask straight out, directly, demanding to know who he was and where he'd been educated. He didn't know enough about these people to decide whether this was simply an American trait, open and friendly, or whether they were judging him. Mitchell Hedrick crossed to the top porch step and held out his hand.

"I hope your tooth is giving you less trouble, sir."

"Taking a little medication for it at the moment." The lawyer presented evidence, raising a drink of pale gold. With an arm he drew the young lady to him. "Mr. Pinkerton, this lovely creature is Olive McKenzie. Tom Haas here is in Stanford Law."

Mitchell Hedrick turned and called into the house loud enough to be heard over the music. "Nicola, your guests are arriving." He held up a bottle of Johnnie Walker Red Label. "Yes?"

"Yes, please," Sam answered. "No ice, please."

The next two guests bounded up the stairs, a blond and an extraordinarily tall and square-jawed fellow named Dean, introduced as stroke on the crew at the University of Washington. In spite of his American perfection the Arrow Shirt Man was awkward trying to explain to Sam that the pudgy Mary Ellen Swanson, with braces on her teeth, was not his date. He made it clear that his date was their hostess. He spied another young woman hurrying across the lawn. Louise Trott was not so slender that her white silk sheath dress was becoming. In tribute to her hostess's mother she carried an offering of pink roses. Her face was round and pretty and her hair was cut short in soft brown waves. When they met he wondered why she avoided smiling. Later he saw that she, too, wore braces.

Dean stepped to the screen door and yelled over the music. "Hey, Nick, shake a leg. We're all waiting."

"Hold your horses." The voice, strong and gay, came from somewhere within the house. Sam couldn't imagine a young Japanese woman calling out in such an offhand way, easy in her command, with no thought at all of maintaining her hushed and humble role with a man.

The screen door banged open. Their hostess struck an absurdly theatrical pose that even Sam knew was overdone, a parody, while she held the door open for a plain and scrubbed Scandinavian maid to trundle out a cart clinking with bottles. Instantly he saw a lovely young woman who might have been the sister of Robert's Victoria Clendening. Dressed in coral silk with a long strand of pearls, she struck another extravagant pose for her guests. She was as gay and exciting as her voice. Her hair was not as auburn as Victoria's, but cut short and a gleaming light brown. Her eyes, large and green, looked out at the world from within a heart-shaped suntanned face. Her Western nose was a bit *Tengu* compared to the Japanese norm, but chiseled and slightly retroussé. Her full lips, gleaming with coral lipstick the shade of her dress, rose over even white teeth in a radiant smile. She was as tall as Victoria and her body moved with an athlete's grace, every inch suggesting a strong tennis game and a frank sexuality.

"Ta da!" Providing her own fanfare, the posing young lady twirled her long string of pearls. "Anyone notice anything?" Louise clapped her hands and squeaked a happy little cry. "Dean's Phi Delt pin!" Tom pounded Dean's wide shoulder. "Hey, lucky guy!"

Nicola brushed Dean with a kiss and held out her hand to Sam. "So here's our young gentleman of Japan." She made a show of eyeing him up and down. "Mister Pinkerton, I presume?"

"Sam." He suggested the informality. After all, he was an American.

"Nicola Hedrick," she announced, "and absolutely perishing—desperate for a coffin nail. Of course, Dean doesn't smoke or drink." Tom Haas sprang forward offering a Camel. "Tommy, you know I loathe Camels. Anyone got a Sweet Cap?" She was looking straight at Sam. Would he fail her?

"Camels. Sorry." He hoped he sounded as offhand, as much at ease as these young Americans. Nicola Hedrick seemed a girl straight out of F. Scott Fitzgerald's stories in the *Saturday Evening Post*—young, scantily dressed, practically naked by Japanese standards, and striving to appear totally carefree, ready for dancing and drinking—out for a good time.

She waved at another couple crossing the lawn. Harriet and Rupert

Schramm clearly belonged with her other guests. He was tall, but not as tall as the crewman, and parted his sleek brown hair down the middle. In Japan his wife would tower over any Japanese woman, buoyantly healthy, dressed in very little, a sheath like the others of shining apple-green silk. Her face was gleaming with lotion which covered a flaming sunburn on which Nicola applied a gingerly kiss.

Hands were shaken. Sam guessed that by now he'd met all of Nicola's guests. Mitchell Hedrick crossed the porch, leaving the young people, and opened the screen door. "Mrs. Hedrick and I," he announced with a suggestive smile that said he was no old fogey, "are under the strictest orders from Nicola. We're being sent to have our dinner at the club and leave you young people to your illicit pleasures." He turned to Sam. "Mr. Pinkerton, please notice these last two are wearing wedding bands. Ergo, Harriet and Rupert, I appoint you chaperones." The Schramms, already helping themselves to lime rickeys, laughed at the false severity of the role. "And, Nicola," Mitchell Hedrick called halfway through the doorway, "for Pete's sake, get our young Mr. Pinkerton another Johnnie Walker—no ice." With a wave, the Roman senator disappeared into his villa.

Nicola faced Sam squarely. "Yes? Instead of tea, which I imagine you get more than enough of in Japan. What will it be? Gin? Rye? Oh, yes, Father did say Johnnie Walker." Sam failed to cover his surprise at the array, a display of alcohol on the cart. The others laughed, delighted at his amazement, as he stretched his plight a bit. "I haven't had a drink since I got off the boat."

"Dean," Nicola ordered her wide-shouldered crewman, who drank only ginger ale, to tend bar. "No ice. He's not Japanese and takes his drink like an Englishman. Whiskey, without ice."

Tom Haas, whose precise tone suggested his final year in law school and some kind of inherited superiority said, "Of course, you realize you're breaking the law of the land."

"To tell you the truth," Sam picked up what he took to be American banter, "I was wondering where you managed to get the hooch." It was a new word he'd picked up from a young lady from a milling family in Minneapolis.

"Confess, Nick," giggled Louise with her pudgy hand trying to hide her braces. "Tell him."

Nicola swept a lovely bare arm, rattling with ivory bracelets, indicating the sweep of lawn in the direction of downtown Port Angeles and the harbor shining in the sunset. "Canada's only a skip and a jump across the Straits. We call it my gin run."

"It's true." Rupert Schramm explained. "The minute she got home from Vassar she was over there loading up." With a smile of coral-colored lips over white teeth, his hostess took the drink from Dean and handed it to Sam. With a nod of thanks he raised a silent salute to the others.

"Bottoms up," Nicola commanded Sam who grinned and sipped. "The Japanese don't have prohibition?"

"No."

"Over there you drink—what is it—sake?" She didn't wait for him to nod. "But I see you prefer whiskey." Nicola, set aside a lime rickey to pour herself a whiskey. She interrupted herself. "Damn! I nearly forgot." She poked around the drinks cart till she found what had been overlooked, tiny Japanese paper umbrellas. She opened one in sky blue and plinked it into Sam's drink. "In honor of our Mister Sam Pinkerton of Nagasaki."

Soon every drink blossomed with a paper umbrella in tribute to Japan, with everyone asking him questions he found close to stupid about the Land of the Rising Sun. Had he seen Mount Fuji? Did the Japs really eat raw fish? Did he?

"Surely not," Louise actually winced, recoiling.

"Like the *Mikado?*" Mary Ellen Swanson ventured.

"And *geeshas?*" asked Nicola.

Without correcting her pronunciation he was vague in order not to betray himself as being too knowledgeable about the foreigners across the Pacific. About geisha, he said that as far he knew they were lovely and highly skilled.

"I'll just bet," Stanford Law snickered lewdly.

He was with F. Scott Fitzgerald's bright young things, Americans who knew, with the exotic umbrellas in their drinks, all they needed or cared to know about Japan. Nicola's guests would have been surprised if he'd told them how very different he found them from people his age at home. This was a band of healthy, exuberant young animals, huge, tall creatures, most of them with strong athletic bodies, smoking and, except for the University of Washington crewman, drinking.

Tom Haas, inquired with more of a demand than a question. "What ship were you on?"

"The President Cleveland," said Sam.

"Would that be first class?"

"On this trip, yes."

"You're awfully young to already be in business." Apparently Tom had brought cross-examination home from law school. "May one ask what business might that be?"

Mitchell Hedrick had cautioned the visitor to avoid any mention of being in the employ of a Japanese. This Stanford lawyer-to-be wasn't waiting for this newcomer to their group to explain why he was here in Port Angeles. He was driving to get to the truth. Sam decided his best defense was a pre-emptive admission of that truth. "Lumber. I'm a lumber agent for a contractor in Nagasaki." He decided this was not the time to pull out his card case and distribute proof of his identity.

Olive McKenzie seemed confused and confessed disbelief. "You actually live in Nagasaki?"

"Yes."

"Full time?" Nicola joined in. "Nagasaki's home?"

By now everyone was staring at him, but far more politely without the frankly prosecutorial line of the future lawyer. "Let's get this straight, old man. You actually work for a Jap company with Jap officers?"

"Japanese, yes."

Tom crumpled his noble brow, shaking his head, making it clear such a thing might be possible but highly suspect. It was clear to Sam that none of these young people of Nicola's set could conceive of life in any way different from their own. Tom clarified where America stood. "We have a few Japs at Stanford, but they keep pretty much to themselves, which suits us fine." A seeker of truth, he turned to their guest. "Since you say you work for them, I for one, would like to know how you really feel about the Japs."

The Victrola hissed off and the evening hushed enough to hear the sprinklers and a lawn mower down the street. A dog barked.

Tom, impatient for an answer, continued his cross examination. He was blunt. "You actually like the Japs?"

"Isn't that like my asking if you like all Americans?"

"No. I think I've made my question perfectly clear. Do you like the Japs?"

"Some Japanese I like, some I don't—"

"In this country," Tom said crisply, "most of us would like them a good deal more if they stayed in Japan under their wicki-wacki bamboo trees where they belong."

Nicola slid her arm into Sam's. "Don't mind Tom. His father's in congress."

"And the law of the land," Tom stated, "for very good reason, happens to be—'Japs stay out.'"

"Enough Stanford Law, Tommy." Nicola patted his cheek.

A half-hour later they went in to dinner, where Sam found himself honored to be seated to the right of his hostess. Louise Trott, on his other side, unlike Tom Haas, had no further questions, which led him to hope these young Americans had finished with all idiot talk of Japan.

Because this was the first dinner party of their summer vacation these true-blue Americans were clamoring with much catching up to do. The animated, boisterous way they talked so loudly of their different campuses was bewildering to him. They were rich kids, but where were their manners? They kept interrupting and bursting into wild laughter, swapping stories about the college year. Nicola swore them to secrecy and treated them to a too-intimate account of her recent three-day train ride home in a private compartment from Vassar. For no apparent reason verses of different college songs burst out and rocked the table. Stranded in the middle of this strong current of brash, boisterous song and talk, Sam felt marooned. Quiet Louise, sensing how isolated these attractive, handsome young people might be making the stranger feel, threw him a lifeline. "Of course, you went to college in Japan?"

"Something like that," Sam was evasive, but Tom Haas fired more cross-examination.

"And the name of this college?"

"I was privately educated."

"Let's get this straight." Tom made a display of being patient but insistent. "You didn't even feel the need to come home for college?"

"My kid brother goes to Princeton, but no, in my case, no."

Wild laughter erupted over how funny Harold Lloyd's last movie was, and Young America speculated loudly if Lloyd did his own stunt work hanging from that skyscraper clock. Sam felt himself on an ice floe drifting far out at sea while the others plunged into their plans for the summer, their choices among favorite dance bands, with snatches of songs he'd never heard rocking the table.

Silent Scandinavian girls cleared the dinner away while Nicola prodded the men into rolling back Oriental rugs from the hardwood floor. Plump Mary Ellen Swanson cranked up the Victrola. Even though he lived in Japan the women could see he loved to dance. They discovered he'd learned to tango on the Cleveland and clamored for an on-the-spot whirl. Quickly, after catching the cold glint in their men's eyes, accusing him of showing off, he retired to make conversation with Louise Trott.

The party broke up at two in the morning with Nicola ordering him to drive plump Mary Ellen home. He was leading her across the wet lawn to his Pontiac when Nicola, leaving Dean on the porch and pulling off her shoes to save them from grass stains, came racing to him. "Hold up, Mister Sam from Japan. If you're still here on the Fourth, maybe you'd like to help me break the law of the land."

Mary Ellen explained. "She's talking about the Schramms and another gin run on their cabin cruiser over to Canada." Why was she asking him and not Dean whose Phi Delt pin she was wearing. "What about Dean?" he asked, "He chicken out?"

"He'll be in Seattle," Nicola said. "How about it, Sam?"

The idea of being with this glorious, wild creature out on the Straits of Juan de Fuca crossing to British Columbia was too good to be true. It was irresistible. About breaking the law, surely this whole charade about rum-running could only be a joke. "Sounds wonderful," he said, careful to hold off any actual promise to join in on what might prove a criminal act. The Fourth of July, that most American of holidays, was still a week away.

CHAPTER SEVENTY-NINE

"Stormridge Lumber is privately held by one family." Mitchell Hedrick was working with papers from his dossier lying across his desk from Sam. "One might think that simplifies things except for three items. One—a recent death in the family, and two, a particularly squalid divorce. And three, the oldest son is devoted to tequila and disappears deep into it at inconvenient times." He summed up other papers. "Persuading all the Falkenbergs to agree that now is the opportune time to sell is like herding cats. Is our prospective buyer from Japan available to this office during negotiations?"

"I'm enjoying Port Angeles."

"Port Angeles is enjoying you. Nicola says you tango. Did you learn that in Japan?"

"Coming over on the President Cleveland."

"As for your tennis date this afternoon, I must warn you, she'll beat your socks off. But then by now you've guessed our Nicola's tops in everything." Hedrick rose and came from around his desk and put his hand on Sam's shoulder. "Naturally," he added with a smile, "a father makes a highly prejudiced witness."

On a hot Friday Sam and Nicola fought out a sweaty game of tennis under a China-blue sky. He won but wiped sweat. "Your father said you were good."

"You learn that serve in Nagasaki?"

He nodded and tried not to think of Robert. "What do you say to a stiff lemonade?"

They sat watching other young men and women in tennis whites looking very healthy, very athletic, very American, moving quickly on the courts. Again, for a moment, he was back in Nagasaki with Robert when Nicola broke in. "What are you thinking, Mister Japanese Sam?"

"Do me a favor and don't call me that."

"You prefer Sam-San? Isn't that what they say over there?" She waited with a smile for his answer.

"No. Just Sam. You want another lemonade?"

"I didn't want the first one and now you're still not telling me what you're thinking."

"I see you're not wearing Dean's fraternity pin."

"Not on my tennis shirt."

She reached for his hand and led him to another table within the shade of a latticed pergola. "Right now you're thinking that you'd like to kiss me."

He was still at a loss at picking up the free-and-easy talk of the young American women he'd met. Now, alone with Mitchell Hedrick's daughter, he knew very well she was asking him to kiss her. He also told himself that without knowing the new American rules between men and women, for now he'd hold himself to a noncommittal smile. She was leaning forward, smiling. "So I'll do it for you." She kissed him lightly. The friendly American kind of kiss she and her friends so easily exchanged. "So tell us, Mister Sam, is there someone waiting in Japan?" When he didn't answer she tilted her head to change her angle looking into eyes. "Yes? Go ahead. You can tell me about her."

He broke her gaze and looked down at his tennis racket to show her he was off in another world and intended to keep his distance.

"Why so secretive? You can't have that many secrets. Not at twenty-one."

Realizing he wasn't going to answer, she sighed and smoothed back her dark-gold hair. "And don't sit there with those big gray eyes full of hurt like you were suffering from weltschmerz or some goddamn thing. Okay, first my secret. Away at school and living in the East, I lost my heart—that's how we say it over here—to a Jewish boy from Brookline, Massachusetts, who wrote poetry and tried to talk me into running off to Paris with him this summer instead coming home. Over there in Japan you don't write poetry, do you?"

"No. I don't write poetry."

"Just as well. So now you find me with my friends here in the deep woods with absolutely nothing to talk about. My father went to school back East and he tells me I've come back a spoiled brat."

Again, she was looking straight into his eyes. She'd put the ball in his court and it was up to him to return her serve. She'd told him her secret, now it was his turn. When he offered nothing, with another sigh she continued. "Am I, Sam—a spoiled brat. You know other places, other ways. Tell me the truth. You think I am?"

He returned her serve with what she could accept as a compliment, if she chose. "I think in Japan you wouldn't last a single day."

"Where Japanese women all walk three feet behind the man?"

"I don't remember—"

"Come on. Goddamnit, open up. Give a little."

"How they walk? Women? I guess they do, walk behind men."

"And you approve?"

"Would what I approve make any difference to the Japanese?"

"Do you realize I don't even know where you're from? I don't mean Japan, and before that Bremerton, but where you're really from. The other night Tom Haas put you through the third degree. I watched and you didn't break. Now it's my turn. So where are you from?"

"I told you, Nagasaki—"

She sighed a deeper sigh of defeat. "You're absolutely impossible. Okay, just tell Nick, with your big gray eyes and dark blond hair, do the Japanese ladies go crazy for your All-American look?"

"You're embarrassing me."

"Are you virgin, Sam?"

"You're a spoiled brat who likes to shock people."

"Answer me. Are you?"

"That's my business."

"A lot of American boys your age are." She grinned. "The trouble is it's too easy to shock the dumb clucks around here. That's why I've got to get back to New York. My Warren Morgenstern, who's in Paris, isn't shy." Her pale blue eyes held him.

"I thought you're what your friends call 'pinned' to Dean. In America doesn't that mean you're engaged?"

"He's sweet and I probably love him madly, but I could never marry Dean."

"Is that a secret you keep from him?"

"Touché. If I were honest, I'd tell him all about New York wouldn't I? Dean's my summer beau. Someone for Port Angeles. No, don't turn away. I'll tell you something else. I'm honest, but I'm not always sincere. I need a duggan. Have you got a cigarette in that tennis bag of yours?"

He opened a new pack of Sweet Caporals and lighted one for her. Over the flame their eyes met. She smiled. It was no secret he'd bought that brand of cigarettes because he'd heard her say it was the brand she preferred. She patted his hand. "And if you're getting the idea I'm interested in you, you'd be barking up the wrong tree. You're not the type I go for."

"Are people types?"

"Of course, and you're dangerously close to being the Dean type. Two Arrow Collar Men. You know the ones in the magazine ads?" She looked at him through her smoke. "Ask me if I'm a virgin."

"You told me all about New York and that guy who writes poetry."

She was back to tilting her head to study him. "You know what I think? I think you're afraid of women like me."

"Terrified." He tried to laugh to cover the truth. Not since Tedabara had he wanted any woman so much. He shifted himself to ease the strain growing within his white tennis shorts. His face burned.

She frowned. "You're a funny duck, you know that? Something strange about you." Still holding her cigarette her pinky traced his brow. "What's going on in that brain of yours, Sam? Why do I get the feeling you're standing off to one side, watching all of us—that you don't altogether approve of my set."

She waited for him to answer and when he said nothing she filled the silence. "Don't you know your Nick is waiting to hear how you've never met anyone like me? Well, have you?" She betrayed herself with a smile. "I expect you to say no. I want people to think I have loads of secrets. Wonderful secrets that make me oh so special. What if I told you my secret plan for the Fourth of July? Mom and Dad want to take me down to Seattle for the Fourth. If I had a reason to stay here I wouldn't go." She waited. Sam understood exactly what she was saying, but he said nothing. She stubbed out her cigarette, rose and picked up her racket. "So, are you ever going to answer my question? You've got someone back in Japan?"

Sam, still silent, hoped he was convincingly playing the role of a gentleman who doesn't talk about such things.

CHAPTER EIGHTY

The game was far from over. The ball was in his court. Nick, as she called herself, wanted him. Her loveliness, her long, tanned legs in white tennis shorts, the way she ran her hand through her dark gold hair moved and thrilled him. She held him with her eyes and, when he made no move, she let him know that for the next three days she'd be leaving Port Angeles with her family to visit Seattle, which would mean seeing Dean. She was letting him know that one word from him and she'd stay.

The day before the Mitchell Hedricks left for Seattle the lawyer gave Sam a telegram to read. "Seems our Eddie Falkenberg down there in Guadalajara is strapped to pay his tequila bills and needs to sell." He slid the message into the Stormbridge dossier and closed it. "That's one down. As for the rest of the Falkenbergs, I wouldn't be surprised if we heard from them right after the Fourth."

The two men took another moment with their cigars. "That means," Mitchell Hedrick said, "you'll be on your own for a few days but there's plenty here in Port Angeles to keep a young man busy. Why don't you go out in the Straits and catch yourself a twenty-pound chinook? Or hike one of the trails on our Olympic Mountains."

The attorney rose and walked his client to the door, the older man's hand on his arm. "By now you know my Nicola likes to shock. If she comes back from Seattle early and tries to rope you in on one of her Canadian rum-running expeditions with the Schramms, that, of course, is up to you. If you succumb, just see to it you don't run into the T-Men and get yourselves caught."

Because Sam didn't stop her, Nicola had gone to Seattle. The rest of her friends had scattered with their own plans for the holiday. No one called him at the hotel. With Nicola never out of his mind, he tried to make his room less lonely by writing Mayumi and Tat. He did a hundred push-ups every few hours between reading the *Saturday Evening Post*. When he went down to the desk and asked the Lutheran Bible-reading clerk where a man could find a drink in this town, the Bible reader offered nothing more than a reminder of the law of the land.

While trying to sleep he burned for Nicola. In the night she came to him in different ways, like the first time he saw her on the porch in that shining coral silk swinging her strands of beads. She came to him again at that tennis game with both of them glowing with perspiration. Alone in this double bed, his empty arms sought her smooth neck, shoulders, those lovely pointed breasts, and every inch of her down to those long, long American legs.

With Nicola in his arms how long could he keep up his lies? Could her he was Sam Kodo and half-Japanese here in Port Angeles, U.S.A. with a fake passport and lying to her father to make a deal—a criminal act for his powerful adopted father, a Japanese named Kodo. No. How long with her in his arms could he lie and keep on lying before he dared open his heart and tell her the truth. "Nick, in Japan I'm what they call an *ainoko.* I have a Japanese wife and a little boy I love more than anything in the world and a baby on the way—"

Would his love, his American girl, his Nick turn on him? A Showalter. Nick, calling him a Jap and a liar, would she run to her father with his secret that would have him arrested, imprisoned here in The States never to return to Japan?

With Tedabara, a boy off the streets, he didn't have to lie about who he was. He was literally no one, she used, wild to explore with him every pleasure two young and healthy animals can discover. Tedabara was a whore, firing him with her naked, pagan lust. Tedabara. He stopped himself. What was it Kodo had said on the Cleveland about her health? Was his love still alive in Nagasaki?

Nicola, American adorable, moving so beautifully into his dream, glorying in her athletic body, laughing, so free and open, wisecracking in her modern college-girl way, sharing kiss for kiss, drink for drink with young men.

The crackle of firecrackers woke him to the overture of America's proudest, noisiest day of the year, the Fourth of July. American sunshine flooded the room. A cannon boomed and kept booming. Band music blasted the morning with a triumphal "Battle Hymn of the Republic." *Mine eyes have seen the glory*— He remembered every word. Naked, he sprang to the window on what was for every true American the most glorious of glorious days. Below the yacht basin was already alive with red, white, and blue flags and banners rippling against the warm All-American bright blue sky. Beyond, sunlight spangled the green water of the Straits of Juan de Fuca, bobbing with cabin cruisers and sailboats.

His telephone rang. "It's the desk clerk, Mister Pinkerton. It's a call for you to go to your window and look down at the docks till you find— it's called the Geoduck—Someone named Mrs. Rupert Schramm wants to wave to you. That's all the lady said."

Of course he went to the window. There was the forty-one-foot cruiser and the two Schramms on deck and another woman. His heart raced. Yes, it was his Nicola. Nicola here and radiant and lovely in the sunshine, waving up at him. Nicola, in white slacks, sandals, a blue chambray workshirt and a red, white and blue scarf tied over her hair, one hand shading her eyes, the other hand urging him to come down.

She brushed him with a light kiss—what these Americans called a friendly kiss, but grabbed his hand and put him to work readying the Geoduck to shove off. She was here, radiant and lovely in the sunshine. He didn't need prodding from Rupert to jump on board and take the line from Harriet which, he guessed, without any experience, meant he was to cast off. Nicola, still dockside lifting her line from the cleat, was grinning at him. The boat was free. At the wheel Rupert called. "Hey, Sam. Don't just stand there like a bump on a log. We're off to Canada. Give Nicola a hand."

Casting off, she didn't need help springing happily on board. She took his hand and raised her face for a second, a more serious kiss. "Wait!" Sam's worried cry stopped all three who were looking at him. "My passport. I mean if we're going to Canada—"

His shipmates answered with whoops of delight. "For a criminal act," Rupert shouted, bringing the auxiliary engine to throbbing life, "no passport is necessary."

Careful not to sound a note of panic, he said, "In Japan breaking the law is serious."

"Here, too." His All-American, red-white-and blue girl was smiling radiantly. "Rupert can still dump you ashore. Want to chicken out?"

Was there another woman in the entire world this wild and free? Rupert slid an arm around her waist tugging her to share the wheel. "She's made this run before so she's in command." He saluted her as he called out over the throb of the engine. "In case you haven't noticed, Sam, our Nick's the criminal type."

Nicola accepted his praise. She proved her command. "Sam, look. See all the sail and powerboats out today? All over the Straits for the Fourth? Gives us cover. If you see the Coast Guard or any T-Men, don't worry, just smile and wave."

After bouncing across a patch of choppy water the Straits are famous for, they tied the Geoduck up to a pier full of seagulls on Vancouver Island. "British Columbia," Sam told himself. "Canada" Apparently there was no need for a passport. Rupert and Nicola bargained with a cheery dealer who looked like a sweaty Santa Claus in overalls, proving Canada, unlike the land of the free, was the home of perfectly legal hooch—Scotch, gin, and rye.

Nicola's rum-runners, Rupert and Harriet, put Sam to work and like professionals stowed two cartons of clinking bottles below deck under a bunk. Her friends joined Nicola with a small round of applause for Sam's help. "See?" Nicola reduced their criminal act to a lark. "See? Nothing to it."

Sam was worried but surprised at how easy it was to break the law and tried to return his crewmates' big smiles. With Canada behind them Nicola turned the wheel over to Rupert and fit herself to Sam's side. "You look worried, little boy. You're with Nick. Relax. You're not in Japan. You're with us. What the hell. Live dangerously, Sam. Stick around and I'll give you lessons." She enlisted their shipmates. "Kids, tell our honorable Japanese gentleman that if the worst were to come to the worst—that is if any of us gets caught, rule one—no rats on a rat."

"Rat?" The would-be English teacher didn't know this use of the word. He doubted if any of his English dictionaries said the rodent word could be used as a verb.

"As to squeal on another rat—another criminal," Harriet, a reader of *Black Mask* detective fiction, explained. "Now the four of us are forever bound by the criminal code."

Nicola added, "Till death us do part. Not Japanese honor, Sam-San—American honor—honor among thieves."

Out in the Straits, sailing among so many craft, power, and sailboats, the warm wind carried brass bands oomp-pah-pah-ing across the water—

Americans at play, skylarking on this red-white-and blue All-American day. Sam told himself, his hand holding Nicola's hand, that he should be the happiest man in the world. He hoped his sweat would be attributed to the hot summer day. Once they were back to Port Angeles with their loot stowed on shore he'd relax.

In command, Nicola ordered Rupert to sail them down to Dungeness to feast on the port's famous crabs—"Better, Sam-San, than anything you've ever tasted in Japan."

"Please, I asked you not to call me that."

Her arm slid through his. "Sorry." She sealed her apology with a light kiss. "Like I can't help notice you never call me 'Nick.'"

"I prefer Nicola. Is that all right with you?"

Under the hot July sun the international criminals reached Dungeness where they sprawled on deck, cracking and breaking crab claws and legs, hungry savages digging out the meat which Sam, in order to please his American friends, declared more delicious than anything in Japan. Harriet, as deckhand, brushed the heap of crab shells into a gunnysack commanding Sam as deckhand to the side, to pitch overboard. Nicola was sneaking up behind him to topple him fully dressed overboard.

With his shipmates laughing and cheering, he surfaced. Grabbing the side of the boat he leaped and pulled Nicola down into the icy water beside him. Coming up with her own happy sputter, she plunged his head underwater. Climbing back on board she brushed his wet hair back from his brow with her face close to his. She whispered, "I've broken off with Dean."

They anchored while Sam and Nicola stripped off drenched clothes and slid into the new-style bathing suits. Sam borrowed his from Rupert, who had gone below, where the last thing he needed with Harriet was something to wear. Sam and Nicola, lying side by side and glistening in the sun, couldn't ignore the married couple's thumpings coming up from the cabin below. Sam snuck a look at the lithe, athletic, nearly naked woman's body worshipping the sun. A fresh summer sea breeze tingled his skin with every inch of him fired with that fierce ache that had always sent him wild with Tedabara. Today in full sunlight he turned his head and found this American girl looking into his eyes, searching across his chest and down his belly to his trunks without pretense. She took his hand. Her round-eyed blue American gaze telling him they were wasting time till they could ditch the Schramms and get back to his hotel.

Rupert and Harriet erupted from the hatch without bothering to smother their look of satisfied love. He'd brought up a bottle of rye whiskey with them, declaring it was time, with the sun over the yardarm, to sample their loot. "Well, somewhere in the world it is."

Harriet peeled the seal from the precious Canadian Club rye. Nicola raised the bottle in a toast. "To President Warren G. Harding, long may he wave." She took the first shot, and handed the bottle to Harriet, licking her lips and running her fingers back through her ruffled hair. Sam watched her move, enchanted, by this simple gesture, the easy freedom he loved in this American girl he couldn't imagine in his Mayumi. Harriet stopped her with a frightened gasp. "The bottle! Hide the bottle!" Her panic turned the others to a fifty-foot cruiser under a big American flag bearing down on them. "Jesus," Rupert's cry was raw fear. "T-Men!"

A horn blasted an order warning them they were coming alongside. Without daring to be seen tossing the evidence of their crime overboard, Nicola slid the bottle under a seat cushion while she deployed them to the cockpit, exemplary young Americans patriots who didn't need forbidden hooch to celebrate their nation's birthday.

As the law cut their engines and approached, rocking the Geoduck in their wake, Nicola jumped to her bare feet, outdoing Betsy Ross patriotism waving her red and blue scarf. "Happy Fourth, officers!" Her hand, hidden from the law, signaled the others to fake merriment and back up her act. Sam, no brave samurai from Japan, but courageous enough to stand with the brave, joined her, forcing out his own happy wishes for the Fourth of July.

Close now, the officers looked stern and indicated every intention to board. A heavyset man with a belt that barely held his bulges together moved forward with an athletic young man, probably an ex-football star at the high school in Port Angeles. Both meant business. "You folks been over to Canada?"

"Close." Nicola awed Sam chirping away "But they don't celebrate the Fourth over there so we sailed straight on by."

The thick-bodied officer was craning to one side in an effort to read the name on the stern. "This is the Geoduck?"

"Out of Port Angeles," Rupert announced with a reasonably steady voice.

Dark glasses glinted at the Geoduck's skipper. "Appears we better have a look."

"Come right aboard," Nicola in her bathing suit sang out her welcome with all the confidence in the world, even an admirable ring of sincerity. "May I ask you officers to give us your names?"

Dark glasses flashed in the late sun staring straight at her. She didn't hesitate. "For the record, I'm Nicola Hedrick. This is Rupert and Harriet and our friend Sam Pinkerton who's visiting from Japan. Welcome aboard." Her three shipmates, her three accomplices, scarcely dared open their mouths and betray alcohol breath.

Neither officer moved. The heavy man wasn't taking any chances. "Your father Mitchell Hedrick the lawyer?"

She nodded. "I'll bet you know my dad. On the city council and a number of committees and he's death on drinking. Imagine if we had done anything illegal how awfully surprised he'd find himself, going into court and defending his darling daughter—on what charge?"

A sailboat under full white sails flashed by. On shore a band was playing "Darktown Strutters' Ball." The senior officer lighted a cigar, which apparently helped him think. He scratched his neck and gave his young partner a long look. On board the cruiser the four couldn't hear a word of their exchange. Nicola shouted, "We've got some Dungeness crab left over from our picnic if you want to come on board." Sam was in awe. Nicola looked as larky as her cheery invitation. Her shipmates held their breath. The junior officer never took his eyes from Nicola.

The heavy man took the cigar out of his face. "Miss Hedrick, I know your father and your family." The law seemed to be considering a law higher than any of them. "Now if you'll give us your word."

Sam watched her solemnly raise her lovely, lying hand. The officers ended their investigation with nods, the law looking more like two servants bobbing their heads and returning to their wheelhouse. The cruiser exploded into life. No one on board the Geoduck moved save Nicola, who was still gaily waving her goodbye.

With the Geoduck rocking their walk, Sam drew their first breath. "See?" A pleased and triumphant Nicola brushed Sam's face with a kiss.

"No sweat. Nothing to worry about. We didn't get caught so you don't have to commit your honorable Japanese hara-kiri." But he was sweating. How could this lovely girl make so light of what could have meant jail and the end of any life for him. With a kind of off-handed ease this American girl he loved had saved the day. She had her own secret. She could lie with such assurance, such insouciance, because she knew who she was. She didn't have to live in two worlds.

They were still in their bathing suits tying up at the yacht basin when he felt her hand taking his, letting him see she was looking up at his hotel window. The Schramms graciously told the two they'd swab down and see the Geoduck's precious cargo safely stowed on shore. Stepping onto the dock Sam caught Nicola's whisper. "I'll run on up to your room for a shower to get off the salt. Give me your room key."

"I don't have it." His lie was a pathetic croak explaining why he seemed to be hanging back. "The thing is, they make you pick it up at the desk. You have to be registered."

At least she was smiling. "Criminals and rum-runners, my darling, don't register in hotels like other people. Hurry up. Give me the key."

He took her hand and in a soft voice utterly wrong for the excited girl, he murmured. "Wait."

Without more words he took her by the hand and led her to a bench where he brushed off some fisherman's discarded and snarled leader line. He took her bundle of deck clothes and set it down beside his own. Wordless, unable to mask her confusion , she stared at him. He slumped with his hands covering his face. In silence she sat beside him with the evening breeze carrying a song he knew from home. Japan, where he'd heard the American song:

I'll see you in my dreams, hold you in my dreams—

She broke their silence with scarcely more than a whisper. "Sam, my darling, you want to tell why we're sitting here?"

His hands still covered his face and he was shaking his head. "We're not going up there."

"What are you saying?" Her cry choked with disbelief. "You've wanted me from the minute I opened that screen door—and I've wanted you—"

His hands muffled his already nearly incoherent words. "It's my fault. I've let myself go too far. Yes, right now—more than anything in the world—I want you up there in my arms—" She moved closer. He felt her body pressing his and he didn't draw away. He took her wrist while she sat enduring silence as long as she was able. "Darling—"

From a dance stand down on the docks, a tenor voice reached them. *Someone took you out of my arms, still I feel the thrill of your charms—*

"No. Please don't say anything. Just listen." He shook his head with one hand still covering his face, slurring his words. "All I can tell you—" he forced in a long breath before he could continue. "You don't know who I am—"

"Up there—that's what you're going to tell me—" With a cry from her heart she pulled his hand from his face. "My darling, darling, whoever you are, I know all I need to know about you. I love you and you love me. I love you so very, very much and I'm going to marry you. You know that, don't you?"

When he didn't answer she leaned her face close to his, searching beyond his hand and looking straight into his eyes. He wrenched away and turned his gaze on the boats coming in to the docks.

"My Darling Sam, don't you know there's nothing—nothing in this world you can't tell me? Look at me. Please—please, for God's sake at least look at me. Have you been over there so long with all that politeness and bowing you don't know how free and open America is for people our age?" Her words were coming in a rush, a frantic rush. "It's a whole new world. Back East in college studying Freud we can open up about everything— our deepest feelings. As for secrets you think you're the only one in the world with a secret?" Her face pressed his. "You know mine. You've seen through me already. Nicola Hedrick, swinging a rope of pearls? Some kind of good-time girl dancing on tabletops, pretending life is all cocktails and laughter racing off to Canada to smuggle in booze? There's more to me, Sam. Let me show you my real self. No? For God's sake this is 1923 and whatever's keeping us apart—I love you." She lowered her head and buried her face in his shoulder. "Tell Nick."

He pulled away trying to rise. "Please," he whispered, "it's my fault, not yours, and believe me my heart's breaking." Their eyes met before he turned away. "I can't do this to us—"

"Us? You know who I am." An edge crept into her voice. "Who are you, Sam? What has being in Japan done to you?"

CHAPTER EIGHTY-ONE

In late July Mitchell Hedrick handed a telegram across his desk to Sam. "You'll be pleased to see I've managed to line up Drunken Eddie down there in Guadalajara." Sam had never seen Nicola's father more pleased. Surely that meant Nicola hadn't breathed a word of their breakup to her family. "I'm meeting with him at the end of the week." Pleased at their progress, he continued, "I'm going down to Seattle to dig out Falkenberg's widow in the Eastern Star Retirement Home."

Sam had followed and understood the deal. "That leaves only Myra Falkenberg?"

"Fortunately I grew up with Fat Myra here in Port Angeles. She's back from Europe with her new husband and my bet is they can't wait to sell and get back to Antibes. That's in the South of France," he explained. "In her last letter she goes on about how she wants me to guarantee Stormridge only goes into the hands of the right people. What Myra means by 'right people' is no Jews." He wrapped Sam in a sly smile. "With a name like Sammy you're not Jewish are you?" His hand waved off any need to answer. "No, I think you'll suit our Myra just fine. By the way, when did you tell me you'll be twenty-one?"

"I became twenty-one exactly thirty-two days ago."

"Do you have your passport on you?" Mitchell Hedrick, all business now, took the document and glanced at it. "Fine." He opened his desk humidor. "Congratulations on your birthday." Sam helped himself to a cigar. Hedrick still held his passport. "I'll need to hang onto this for a few days. I'll keep it in my safe." From the Stormridge dossier he handed over draft copies of contracts to take back to the hotel and study.

"Thank you, sir." That Mitchell Hedrick was so pleased meant Nicola's father was sniffing real money in his role putting the deal together. Later he'd read the draft carefully, and knew he'd find the attorney was cutting himself in as counsel and probably a shareholder of the front corporation he was setting up here in the States.

"Look this over, my boy, and we'll be able to let our Mister Kodo of Nagasaki, Japan, know that things here in Port Angeles are looking very promising indeed."

This looked like the breakthrough for which they'd both been waiting. For Sam, after his breakup with Nicola, eleven more days in Port Angeles had been a punishing eternity. He was alone. Nicola's loyal friends totally avoided him. He'd fought to keep busy fishing for chinook and king salmon and hiking Olympic Mountain trails, but every day without her was unendurable. Instead of using his old ink-brush study of kanji to distract him he forced himself to write reports and cables to Kodo and send postcards, always in English, to Mayumi and Tat.

Finally, the evening came for his command performance with the Stormridge heiress. He dressed to meet Myra Falkenberg for bootleg cocktails at the Hedricks'. He knew, of course, that there was no way Nicola would allow herself to be in sight. The Falkenberg heiress, home from Antibes, was no longer fat, but big-boned and fighting middle-age with carefully coiffed hair and elegantly gowned in Prussian sky-blue silk, Sam could only assume it to be in the latest style from Paris. Allen Blake, ten years younger, slender, originally from Spokane, wore a spiffily tailored summer suit of Milano silk and a fixed smile under a pencil mustache. Yes, they lived in France where everyone talked of nothing but Doctor Freud in Vienna. The smart set in Paris was no longer kicking their legs to the Charleston, but had gone mad about American Negro music— jazz—and Doctor Coué, who was making everyone feel better through "auto-suggestion." The party moved from the Hedricks' porch to the country club dinner dance and the best table on the terrace glowing under yellow Chinese lanterns.

Sam held his breath. Was it possible Nicola might be here? Hardly daring to look around his surreptitious glances across the dance floor had caught no sign of her. He waved to Rupert and Harriet only to get what Americans called 'the cold shoulder.' Obediently he rose from the table and danced with Myra, who moved easily and laughed heartily and overdid waving to old friends. Her whisper, too close to his ear, confided that her heart was on the Cote d'Azur rather than here where her timber came from. As she'd made clear in her letter to Mitchell Hedrick, if she was ever to sell, she felt it was important to see that the family business pass into the hands of only the right people.

She clutched Sam too tightly and chattered on. He didn't hear a word. His world under yellow Chinese lanterns stopped. There she was—

Nicola, dancing with a little, short-haired, clean-cut navy ensign from a visiting destroyer. She'd spotted him, but was making a show of not having seen him, but giving her act away by laughing too much and too loudly. Oblivious to Sam's inattention, Myra was singing along with the snappy beat of the band:

'*I'm the Sheik of Araby*
Your love belongs to me . . . '

"When we left Antibes simply everyone and his cat was singing this." Myra snapped her fingers and burst into a pretty soprano.

'*At night when you're asleep*
Into your tent I'll creep . . . '

Myra sang and pulled Sam close until, flushed and dabbing at her moist temples, the heiress happily tugged him back to the table announcing—"He's young, God knows, and I have the feeling if I gave him half a chance he'd talk my arm off about Douglas fir, but the answer, Mitchell, is yes. It's a deal."

A polite round of applause trapped Sam at the table till Mitchell Hedrick had performed his duty and returned Myra to the dance floor. This was his chance. With no idea what he was going to say, he was on his feet threading his way through the dancers, now moving slowly to an Irving Berlin love song.

'*What'll I do when you are far away*
And I'm alone, what'll I do?'

The clean-cut young ensign who'd nicked his chin shaving was overly-deferential at Sam's cut-in tap on the shoulder, taking it as an order and stepping back and surrendering Nicola. To her ensign's surprise she pulled him back to her increasing her abandon, dancing, turning her back on Sam.

Instead of surrendering the dance floor to the navy he deliberately blocked the two. The polite little ensign, again surprised by this civilian maneuver he failed to understand, withdrew with a polite nod. Nicola wheeled around to rush off, but Sam clamped her into his arms. He felt her body seething with anger. She stiffened, but he was forcing her to dance, as she wrenched back in fury. He pulled her close. His lips sought her ear. "For eleven days I've thought of nothing but you—"

"Go to hell!"

Suddenly the Schramms came alongside, a rescue team with sturdy Rupert ready to thrash Sam. Shaking her head Nicola assured them she was perfectly capable of handling him. Under her breath she hissed, "God-damn you, get away from me!"

His lips found her ear. "I love you, but in Japan I have a wife and two children."

'What'll I do when you
are far away and I am blue
What'll I do?'

With a quick intake of breath she shut her eyes, continuing to dance. The truth brought a sob. She dropped her head on his shoulder. He moved them through the dancers across the floor till they stepped out onto the grass of the golf course. She pulled off her white satin shoes and they walked wordlessly hand-in-hand away from the music. The silence between them was as vast as the night.

She was the first to whisper. "Is your car here?"

"No."

"I've got mine."

In the parking lot they sat in her Packard for a quarter of an hour while far-off dance music played on. Abruptly, Nicola roared the roadster into life and hurtled them through the dark. Sam didn't slide his arm around her. He didn't ask where she was taking him. Within minutes they were out of town, driving through dense forest. They drove in the silent night till they approached a lake gleaming silver in the moonlight under black mountains. Only a few lights shone along the opposite shore. They alighted from the Packard without a word. She led him under a stand of cedars to the front door of a cabin in the woods, a summer house. She reached for a key hidden behind an oil-lamp porch light. She pushed open the door, but stopped. They weren't entering. "No. Not yet."

From the dance floor under yellow Chinese lanterns she'd led him to a bench facing the glittering lake. They sat. He reached for her hand. Neither moved. In this silver moonlight he couldn't get enough of look-ing at her. At this moment she seemed to be in her own world. "My fa-ther and I made this bench when I was nine," she said. "It's bent willow branches. Before I go in I always come here first." Her head went to his shoulder. This bench with its view of the lake he could feel seemed almost sacred to her, a holy place. Her American sense of Shinto?

He waited for her to share her thoughts. "As I told you, I talk a lot about being wild and free, and I will be, Sam, even after we're married. Not just the good-time girl, but really, truly alive—free—what we're feeling right now."

With all of his deep respect for Shinto, he was asking himself how soon could they rise from this bench, leave the lake and rush inside and make love? She didn't move, but shifted herself, pressing her body so close he could feel her beating heart. Across the lake winked only a few gleams of light and without a soul within miles she spoke in a hush. "My only time was with a brilliant guy from Yale who read Proust to me, which I have to admit, I didn't understand. Did I tell you about him? He took me home to Brookline, Massachusetts. Jewish. His family didn't like me. He's in Paris now and I never think about him anymore. Now, there's young Sam whom I can never stop thinking about since the first night I came through the screen door onto the porch and saw you. God how I wanted you. When I plunked that stupid little Japanese umbrella in your drink I was saying to myself, 'I'm going to marry that man.'" She raised her head studying his profile, kissing his cheek. "So young. Who'd ever guess you were married."

"You're the only one over here who knows."

With no need to whisper, her voice was still small. "Is she—your wife—Japanese?"

"Yes. So am I."

Her hand tightened on his. Before they could enter the summer house he had to open his heart, tell her the truth, his secret. With her head on his shoulder she listened without saying a word. She heard about Nagasaki and his father in the Navy and his Japanese mother who'd been training to become a geisha. Eleven years took only a few minutes for her to know about Kate Pinkerton, who died of a broken heart in Bremerton, and how he managed to return to Japan with the Snyders. Now an American knew about Torazo. Tedabara. Kodo. Robert. Mayumi with her club foot and Tat. And there was the baby he'd still had no word of yet.

Her face pressed his. He was here. "So my love is Japanese."

"Half. Your father doesn't know. My passport, locked up in his safe, is like me. Fake as well." He fully expected her to ask him how he could allow others to arrange his marriage, adopt him and dictate his every move for the rest of his life. Instead she told him a secret of her own. She spoke of something that seemed at first to have nothing to do with them. "I'm not supposed to know this, but for three years my father's been having an affair with his secretary. She's a friend of mine—older, but a friend. Very pretty in a Blanche Sweet sort of way. She told me the only reason she let it happen was because my father swore to her my mother didn't understand him." She raised her eyes to Sam's. "Swear that won't be us. You saying what all married men say."

"Not me." He was so open to letting her know everything about him, he said, "Mayumi understands me. She sees right through me. If I tell you she's an incredibly fine person, please don't think I'm sounding patronizing. Her instincts are so incredibly true—decent. She's so totally unselfish that sometimes I wonder if being crippled doesn't give her a special feeling about people. I cheated on her only once. With a whore. In Japan, a husband doing that's nothing, but I felt so rotten about it I took her out to a special anniversary dinner in a fancy Russian restaurant."

"Do you love her?"

"Not the way I love you."

"Sam Kodo." Her eyes shone catching the light. Both turned to the gleams across the lake. A night bird sang three notes. "Sam Kodo," she said, "married and Japanese."

He nodded. That was the truth he lived with.

"Whatever it takes, I can get used to that." She surprised him by laughing. "In case it's slipped your mind, my darling, we still haven't made love." They sprang from the bench and raced to the cabin where he took her fiercely into his arms, his mouth opening hers as they sank down on the floor.

In the middle of the night, lying on an afghan in front of an unlit fireplace, two young spent animals, sharing cigarettes, were too exhausted, too much in love to whisper of the wonder of finding each other. He smiled at the thought of her willow bench and the lake. Even if Americans didn't know it, the gods of Shinto were with them.

She found the courage to break the spell. "When are you supposed to go back to Japan?"

"If we wrap up the deal I'm scheduled to sail on the seventeenth of August."

Her gasp of disbelief filled the night. "Next month?" She raised herself on her arms to look down into his face. Was he as stricken as she? She searched his shining eyes. "So here we are, my love," she whispered. "You're the one who's going to have to tell me what we're going to do."

CHAPTER EIGHTY-TWO

Every evening they raced in the Packard to the cabin. Their lovemaking so filled Sam's heart and mind that he marveled that he was still able to concentrate enough to read the fine print Mitchell Hedrick was putting in the Stormridge contract. After wrapping up Kodo's deal by day, his nights were so on fire with Nicola that he'd all but forgotten Japan.

Japan hadn't forgotten him. A stiff little packet arrived in the mail at the hotel. Addressed in Mayumi's careful printing in English, he knew it was certain to include a photograph of his new baby. With his heart full of Nicola there was no way he could bear to open it, and he thrust it into the top bureau drawer.

One night, though it was still August, it was so chilly at the lake that the naked lovers edged close to the fire. Nicola had bought him an expensive gift, a pair of cufflinks in red, white, and blue enamel. "Now," she whispered with a kiss, "you're American."

Moving even closer into each other's arms they stared into the flames. "Dad tells Mother," she said with a courage Sam knew she didn't feel, "that as soon as our Sam Pinkerton wraps up the deal, he'll be going back to Japan."

"Will I?" He drew her close. "Half American. You're the rest of me. My missing American half."

She stared into the fire. "Have you changed your ticket yet?"

"Not yet, but I will."

Their eyes met, reflecting the fire's glow. They'd banished almost all secrets between them, and he considered not telling her about that packet from Japan. There it was in the drawer without his daring to open what he knew would be pictures of Tat, Mayumi and the baby. Even if he'd never been able to tell Mayumi he loved her, he'd do anything for her, anything not to break her heart. Did he himself know what kind of a man he'd become? Was he that kid from Bremerton, from the Urakami and the Snyders' mission, faking it with his Bible, an *ainoko* adopted by Kodo, an American here with his forged passport? What more did he need to know after feeling this American girl's warm lips on his?

The following evening they were making love only because of Nicola's elaborate lies to get herself out of Harriet Schramm's baby shower. Lying together in each other's arms before the fire, they traded sips from one of their forbidden bottles of Canadian Club. As they stared into the flames he could feel her studying his profile. "You know my father and mother, the Schramms, all my friends—there's not a soul here who thinks you're anything but American—"

"With a fake passport."

"Don't joke. I mean you look so American. Does anyone in Japan who doesn't know about you think you're Japanese?"

"In Nagasaki all it takes is one look and they know I'm not one of them. I'm what they call an *ainoko*." He'd used the Japanese word with her only once before. She raised her hand with her fingers on his lips banishing its cruelty, but he continued his blunt assessment. "Here in the States you say 'half-breed.'"

"Don't ever say that. You're Sam—not that other horrible thing."

"Samuel Adams Pinkerton Kodo?" He shrugged. "I guess."

She drew back, still intent on his face. "What does that 'I guess' mean?"

"It's not how I look, my darling, Nicola, it's a question of where I belong—"

"You belong to me. You belong here. I love you."

"And I love you."

"Say it again and again and again," she begged.

"I love you."

"I can't hear you say it too many times."

"I should get you a Tibetan prayer wheel. You spin the thing and it repeats endlessly whatever prayer you want to say. In our case it says—'I love you . . . I love you . . . I love you . . . ' I'm like one of Mister Irving Berlin's songs. I love telling you I love you." His mouth covered hers. They sought each other deeply for a long moment and drew back only to share a bit more Canadian Club. "Nicola?"

"I know what you're going to ask," she said.

You think your father knows about us?"

"That we're in love?" The firelight played on her smile. "How naïve can my Sam be? One look at that goofy grin on your face and the whole world can see you're madly in love with me."

"I mean has he said anything?"

"He's dying to ask how far we've gone, but trying to be a terribly modern father he's holding off from butting in. You know, don't you, it's not just the Stormridge deal, but Father likes you. He respects you. I quote, 'that's a fine young man you've got yourself.'"

"And what does your mother say?"

"Mother says next to my father you're the handsomest thing she's ever laid eyes on. That doesn't mean before she'll set the wedding date she won't put you through your paces." He turned from her, looking too long and hard at the fire. She wasn't through with her mother. "Naturally she wishes you'd gone to college—preferably Princeton like your brother. As for me I'm scratching off my senior year at Vassar. I marry you and they keep their one and only precious daughter in Port Angeles instead of their Little Snookums tootling off for New York."

"Sometime I'll show you New York."

"Nothing we can do in New York we can't do here." He put down the bottle so both moved, feeling their bodies merge. They'd live forever, love forever and always be the way they were tonight. "I love feeling my heart beating on yours. Listen. You hear mine?" He nodded. He felt her lips moving across his naked breast. She drew him close. "No more talk about where you belong. You belong right here. You belong to me now and forever."

"And when they ask about my mother?"

"My mother and father? Why would they ask when you don't look the slightest bit Japanese?" A finger traced his features. "Not even your eyes. Maybe it's because I know—maybe a little—no, not even that." She kissed his eyes. "Say it. Ask me to marry you, Sam."

When he didn't answer instantly she studied his gray eyes looking straight into hers. "Go ahead."

He broke their locked gaze and looked into the fire. "I can't ask you before I tell your mother and father who I am."

"That's ridiculous. No, Sam! No. You're not marrying them, you're marrying me."

"It's not just the two of us. I have to tell them the truth."

"No!" Moving closer still she knocked the bottle over. She let it lie. "Give me time. First I tell them I love you, then some day if we have to, we both tell them who you are."

"No." He drew away to add a cedar log to the blaze, his glowing face lit by the firelight. "Leave this to me. I mean it, Nicola." She waited, knowing he had more to say. "Mr. and Mrs. Hedrick, I may not look it but I happen to be a Japanese traveling on a fake U.S. passport. When I first arrived I couldn't tell you who I really was or I'd have killed the Stormridge deal. Now that there's a deal it turns out I love your daughter—I want to marry her, but in Japan I have a Japanese wife and two children—"

"No!" She drew back and cried, "Just you shut up. Goddamnit, no." Tears stood in her eyes. With a poker she prodded an alder log into flame. "Over there, whoever she is she's not really your wife. You said yourself the wedding was arranged and in their Shinto religion. Not ours. Face it, darling, I love you and I'm going to marry you. Together, after we're married, we'll Mother and Father, and if that's a problem for them, they can go to hell like everyone else."

CHAPTER EIGHTY-THREE

In the first photograph a baby girl, his baby, was in Mayumi's arms. In a second photograph Tat wore a black kimono with all five of the Kodo *mons* establishing forever who he was and who he would be. Mayumi's note in English, printed in Roman letters, made his heart tighten. His English pupil must have written the difficult words again and again in her painful struggle to please him.

FOR NIGHT AND DAY I THINK OF WHEN WE LEAVE HOUSE OF MY FATHER FOR ALL OUR LIVES. YES, FROM MY HEART I TELL MY SAM—MY DEAR, DEAR SAM-SAN—NOT LIKE OBEDIENT JAPANESE WIFE— BUT IN MY HEART I KNOW YOU ARE RIGHT, HAPPINESS FOR US AND OUR CHILDREN NEEDS WE DO THIS.

A rap on the door startled him, and stricken with guilt he thrust the photographs and the letter in his breast pocket. The skinny desk clerk, the law-abiding American who didn't drink, calamine lotion on his red pimples, reporting he, finally after trying all day, had the call from Baltimore, Maryland.

"What about my call to the Hedrick house?"

"Nobody answers except for their maid who only speaks Norwegian."

"Keep trying. It's important."

Sam ran downstairs to the phone and the transcontinental connection with Benjy that faded in and out before they caught up on each other's news. Sam brought him up to date on this last phase of his trip through the Northwest. And before going back to Princeton Benjy was going to Europe with his grandmother. For a long moment across three thousand miles they felt they'd lost one another again but were reconnected. His fully American half-brother, all the family Sam had in America, was asking his half-Japanese married brother and father of two when he was going back to Japan. Sam confessed that the date still had to be decided. Without a word about Nicola he asked Benjy, only eighteen, about his own future. "It's definite, Sam. I'll be a doctor." He sounded resolute. "I'll have to catch up with you and get myself married—but, hey, you already are. You've got a son."

"And a brand-new little girl."

"That's grand. Your boy's name is 'Dragon'? What's hers?"

"We haven't decided yet."

"Sam. If you're going to be out there much longer I could try to ditch Europe with Grandma and get out there to Seattle." Sam felt his eyes prickle with tears but thanked his brother and told him he wasn't sure where he'd be next. "Sam, we have to promise each other to get together one of these days."

"We will, Benjy. That's a deal."

Static made the promise something that didn't require too much thinking, not today. Benjy shifted from future plans to news he was eager to share. "You remember that photograph the chaplain had at the New Washington Hotel—the one of Mom and Dad just married and coming out of the marriage chapel at Annapolis? I still have it and I'll send you a copy."

Sam took a long moment. "I hate to say this, Benjy, but I don't want it. Not of him. If you've got one of Mom alone, I'd give anything for that."

"Sam?"

"I know we're both thinking the same thing—about that Christmas—"

Benjy's voice caught with emotion, and Sam heard tears. "How could he do that to her? And to us. Our own father. We were just little kids." Sam didn't trust his own voice so he let Benjy continue. "Of course I read what you wrote about—what he did to your own mother over there in Japan." After the long pause that comes nearing the end of a conversation, Benjy repeated his concern that this call was costing an arm and a leg. They awkwardly prepared their goodbyes, adding more vows to keep in touch.

Sam left the desk and climbed the stairs. He didn't come back down till close to six, this time carefully dressed in his brown Saville Row suit made in Nagasaki. He'd chosen a deep maroon silk tie that Mayumi had given him. The spotty-faced clerk was all apologies. "About your call to Miss Hedrick, Mr. Pinkerton. I haven't stopped trying but I only get that maid who barely speaks English. I managed to leave a message. You want to try yourself?"

His fashionably-dressed guest looked troubled, shook his head and left the hotel, stepping out into the early evening. The Hedricks' home was a short two blocks. On his right, rising in back of the town, the Olympics, even this late in the summer, still glowed with snow. The Straits glittered in the late sun. He stopped at a florist's for an armful of coral-colored gladiolus for Nicola's mother, though he knew the American would only jam them into a vase. Mayumi's mother, Setsu, would spend hours arranging them, honoring them through the art of *ikebana*.

A few minutes later he was crossing the freshly-cut green lawn when Mitchell Hedrick, in a rattan chair on the porch, picked up a bottle from a little side table to signal their ritual Johnnie Walker was waiting for him. Sam climbed the stairs. Nicola's father held out the glass.

"Thank you, sir." He took the drink, but didn't raise it in a toast nor did he drink. Instead he returned the glass on the table. "Before I can say a word, sir, I have to see Nicola. Is she home yet?"

"Five minutes ago. Getting spiffed up for you, my boy."

"I've been trying all afternoon to reach her by phone. I should have come over myself, but your maid said she wasn't here."

"Shows you how much you have to learn about women. She and her mother have been at the hairdressers all day. Our Norska Birgit isn't very good with messages."

"Can you tell her right now that I'm here?"

"Give her a few minutes—"

"Sir, I have to see her."

Hedrick rose and took the offering of gladiolus which he laid across the rattan chair. "For her mother," Sam said.

Sam felt himself taken by the arm. "Very thoughtful. Helen loves gladiolus. And I salute you for always being Johnny-on-the-spot. Good. Before Nicola and her mother join us we two men need to have a chin—"

"Sir, I can't talk about anything till I see Nicola."

Hedrick's arm was steering him into his home office.

"Sir, what I have to say to Nicola can't wait—"

"Waiting for women is something all we men have to get used to, my boy. First, we talk. You and I."

Marched against his will into the lawyer's office, Sam was again struck at how this room declared this man's identity. He was an American and he knew precisely who he was. Along with trophies and twenty-two-pound mounted king salmon, here was American Legion. Rotary. Commendations from the bar association. Diplomas in Latin with gold seals. A gallery of photos lined the walls including the marble pillars of the U.S. Supreme Court where Hedrick stood with a robed chief justice.

"Please, Sir, before we talk it's terribly important. Will you please call Nicola?"

Mitchell Hedrick drank. Sam did not, and found Hedrick staring straight at him as if he'd never seen him before.

"First, isn't there something you have to tell me?"

"This is about Nicola."

"This is about you." Hedrick's eyes never moved from the young man as he reached back to his wall safe and drew out the passport. "For instance, this Samuel Adams Pinkerton—is he an American citizen?" Hedrick held up his hand holding off any answer. "As far as the Storm-ridge deal goes I'll keep this in the safe just as you and I keep what we say here strictly between us. Whoever you are, you owe me the truth. You can start by telling me who you are."

Sam swallowed hard. Hedrick waited. Sam took a breath. "Has Nicola told you what she knows about me?"

"Full disclosure requires me to tell you, my daughter's told me nothing that answers my question."

Sam felt his hands go ice cold. A fortifying breath didn't help. "Sir, this is why I have to see Nicola. This is between Nicola and myself."

"This is about you."

"Nicola and I will both tell you."

"Tell me now."

"When I first came here you told me about a life in the law. You told me a lawyer in cross examination never asks a witness a question he doesn't already know the answer to."

"Yes. Go on."

"Mr. Kodo is my father-in-law. I'm half Japanese. I'm married to his daughter. I'm his legally adopted son."

Hedrick's Roman face might have been carved in marble for all the change it showed. "Thank you for telling me the truth. Nicola hasn't told me or her mother a word of this. I've wondered if there haven't been times you've found me staring at you a little too closely because I couldn't help but wonder. In spite of what my daughter calls your Arrow-Collar-Man look—I've asked myself if what you've just now told me could explain any number of things. For instance this passport."

Sam was cornered. Did he have to admit it was forged?

"Your Japanese did a good job. Very clever, the Japanese. As I said we'll keep it in my safe." Neither man sat as Sam told Nicola's father the outline of what he'd told her of his Japanese life. His marriage.

"Christian ceremony?"

"Shinto and civil."

"Two children?"

"A boy and a baby girl born five weeks ago."

"Your Mr. Kodo got what he wanted."

"Yes." Sam attempted to explain. "No family of high-standing in Japan would consider marrying a son into the Kodo family."

Hedrick sipped his whiskey. "Back in June I decided to see you because your letter convinced me that your proposal made a kind of perfect sense. I believe I suggested at that time our Mister Kodo is no fool. And you. By now I'm certain you and your adopted father will agree that my handling of this matter has been, if I say so myself, unusually adroit."

"I've cabled Mister Kodo about how much help you've been—"

"More than help. I'm sure our silent partner in Nagasaki will agree when you and I make it clear to him that all enterprises here in the States will be handled exclusively through this office as stated on our contract, page seven, paragraph five. Yes? So now, between us, do you see any obstacle to prevent us from proceeding with the Falkenberg signing?"

Mitchell Hedrick opened a humidor and offered Sam a cigar, which was refused. He turned his attention to opening the black dossier. "I've worked out an agreement I feel sure we'll both be happy to sign. Of course, we'll go over all this later. You're certain about a cigar? A very good cigar." For the second time Sam refused. Mitchell Hedrick rose, came from behind his desk and clamped his hand on Sam's right arm. "Now that business is out of the way, we can talk about our Nicola—"

"Sir, I'm in a terrible spot. Before I came here I haven't been able to reach her—"

"And now you're here. Good. Gives us two men a chance to talk."

"Sir—"

Mitchell Hedrick would not allow himself to be interrupted. "I realize I'm touching on a rather quaint—an all-but archaic ritual here in the States." He studied his cigar. "But would I be mistaken if I sensed you're here to ask my permission for my daughter's hand in marriage?"

"First, that's what Nicola and I have to talk about."

"Not just yet." Mitchell Hedrick had him by the arm, making it clear he was more than ever his captive and ignoring his every insistence on reaching Nicola.

"Sir, does Mrs. Hedrick know about me? That I'm Japanese?"

Nicola's father corrected him. "Half-Japanese." The grip on his arm was still as strong. "Man-to-man, Samuel Adams Pinkerton, also known as Kodo, do you love my girl enough to marry her?"

"Yes, sir, but—"

Mitchell Hedrick didn't wait for any expression of doubt. "So why don't you and I go back out on the porch and wait for our ladies."

CHAPTER EIGHTY-FOUR

They heard Mrs. Hedrick inside the house giving orders to the kitchen as she pushed through the screen door.

"Martini, Helen?" Hedrick asked.

Helen Hedrick's negative shake of her head made it clear this evening was far too important for drinking martinis or anything else. From the cart she poured herself a ginger ale and dropped in two ice cubes. Her small talk for her husband's young but important guest moved beyond the weather to the news of the day, her concern for the country over President Harding's death in San Francisco. "I voted for the man, Mister Pinkerton. The first woman in the Milburn family ever to vote and now the man up and dies on us. Did you vote for President Harding, Mister Pinkerton?"

Before he was trapped into admitting that he was ineligible to vote for the late President Harding or to take part in any American election, he heard Nicola's high heels coming down the hardwood stairs. Even before bursting through the screen door she called happily. "No more Mister Pinkerton, Mother. The man answers to Sam."

In a happy rush she was in their midst shining in a sheath of peach-colored silk, her loveliness set off with her trademark string of pearls. She'd been out all day. After her visit to the beauty parlor her dark gold hair was shorter, artfully framing her lovely heart-shaped face, radiant with love.

She brushed her mother and father with fast kisses but made the moment formal by reaching out for Sam's hand. With a long kiss on his cheek she slid her bare arm into his, claiming him. "Call him Sam, Mother. My Sam."

Mrs. Hedrick, still maintaining her position as a mother and mistress of the house, declined such informality. "Samuel will do nicely for now. I'm waiting to hear if your Samuel voted for our last president."

Looking over at the lovely young woman at his side, Sam said, "I wasn't able to vote in that election." With no further attempt at conversation or charm he lowered his voice hoping that only Nicola would hear. "We have to talk."

Helen Hedrick, however, was still waiting for Sam's answer. "Not even absentee?" Her raised eyebrows suggested a serious dereliction of a citizen's duty.

"I told you, Mother, Sam's just turned twenty one in June," Nicola explained brightly, taking the Martini her father had mixed for her. "Just the way you like it, Daughter." Raising her glass she smiled at Sam, who realized Mitchell Hedrick had put a glass of Scotch in his hand, but he didn't return her toast. Instead, he said: "Nicola, we have to talk." If she'd missed his seriousness, he added, "Alone," and with her arm still around him she allowed herself to be led across the porch to the top of the stairs. "Mr. and Mrs. Hedrick, if you'll excuse us, please."

If Nicola felt a chill she covered it with her brightness. "You see? Just like a man. Not even married and he's already trying to give me orders." She sensed his seriousness and she didn't move. She lowered her voice so only Sam would catch her concern. "Sam, what's wrong?"

"I've already told your father."

"Oh, God." She all but stumbled as a stifled cry escaped, a gasp close to despair. "Oh, Sam. Sam, Sam—" she fought tears—Her eyes found his. "After we vowed we'd tell them together—"

"Tell us what?" Mrs. Hedrick's look shot from Nicola to her husband. "Mitchell, suppose you tell me what's going on here." Her husband studied his drink and didn't answer. "Just stop." The woman cried, "Everyone stop!" She put down her glass of ginger ale. "What is it all of you've gone to such enormous pains to keep me from hearing? Just what is it I am not supposed to know?"

Nicola, still holding Sam's right hand, sank down on the top step, stunned, and unable to say a word.

"Mitchell!" Mrs. Hedrick exclaimed. Mitchell Hedrick retreated to dignity. "It's all right, Helen. Our two young people were just about to tell us."

Mrs. Hedrick's voice thinned to an icy wedge. "It seems, Mister Pinkerton, in this house no one ever tells me anything. May I hope you are an exception?"

"I'll tell her." Nicola said with her hand reaching up for Sam's.

"No." Sam was firm. "Your father already knows. I'll tell your mother—"

"Not yet!" Nicola's cry was close to panic.

"Nicola, you will be still!" her mother snapped, turning her throttled rage on Sam. "Tell me what, Mister Pinkerton?"

"I'm half-Japanese," Sam was holding Nicola's hand. "Half-American. I have a Japanese wife in Nagasaki and two Japanese children. This evening before I walked over here from the hotel I spent hours looking at their photographs and reading and re-reading my wife's letter before I decided." He was still holding her hand. "Nicola, all day I kept trying to reach you. I swear to God there's nothing in the world I wouldn't give to keep this from happening this way."

Nicola, seizing Sam's hand, came to his defense. "But he doesn't love her." Mrs. Hedrick's face was the same dead white as dogwood blossoms as she stood silent and motionless.

Nicola cried, "It's not even a real marriage."

"Hold on, Nicola," Sam spoke calmly. "I told you I was married at eighteen—an arranged marriage—but legal, and then I was adopted by her family. Arrangements like mine are common in Japan—"

"A Jap." Mrs. Hedrick, triumphant in her righteous anger, flung her charge.

Nicola lashed back. "For God's sake, Mother, the word is 'Japanese.'"

"Jap-a-nese," She mocked. "And with two children." She had all the facts she needed to crush the impostor. "He's not free to marry anybody. Will someone explain to me—whatever he is—why this creature is still here in my house?"

Nicola, standing with him on the top step, was still holding his hand. Mrs. Hedrick raked her glare from the couple to her husband. Armed with the bitter truth, she demanded total victory. "Is there nothing else I need to be told? No? A man who comes into my house lying about who he is? A man who'd leave his wife and two children for a foreign woman of another race?" Eyes glaring at her husband glinted icier than the cubes in her abandoned ginger ale.

Nicolas hadn't moved from Sam. "I love him. He knows I'll go to Japan with him."

Helen Hedrick simply scoffed at the absurdity. "Japan?" Her acid disbelief lashed past the young couple at her husband. "And what have you two gentleman worked out? Mitchell, answer me. This is a man you'd give your daughter to in a lifetime of marriage?"

Nicola shut her eyes. She forced deep breaths under her long strand of pearls, fighting for calm to go back, start again, and undo all that had been said. "Sam's half American. And it wasn't even a real wedding in a church—"

"Mitchell! Must I be the one to tell this man to leave this house?"

"He's half American," Nicola cried insistently. "Once we're married, if he can't stay here, we'll live in Japan." Turning and looking straight into his eyes she tightened her grip. "Tell them I love you and you love me and if they don't like it they can go to hell."

He said nothing. She was waiting for help. "Sam?"

"I love you, Nicola. I'll always love you but you must have sensed— felt what I've been struggling with?"

"We love each other, that's all that matters—" Still holding Sam's hand and with Sam looking straight at her mother and father, he said, "It's true. I love you, Nicola. That's what makes this the hardest thing I've ever had to do."

With a cry full of every hope in the world that would make everything right, Nicola implored. "Look at us, Mother." Her mother answered with thin eyebrows raised on her powdered brow—hadn't any of them heard a word she'd said? Nicola drew Sam closer. "Look at him," she cried. "Nobody knows he's Japanese. He doesn't look it and neither will our children."

Sam raised her hand to his lips. "Not now. Later." he whispered looking past her out at the long shadows crossing the grass. "When we're alone—"

"Mister Pinkerton, you will listen to me." Mrs. Hedrick was a monument of frozen righteousness. "Why in God's name are we even talking when there's nothing more for any of us to say?" A deep breath stiffened her and she became every mother in the world who knew what was right for her daughter. "I'm afraid, Mr. Pinkerton, I cannot pretend to be oh-so polite like your people, and since my husband seems to have his own reasons for all his kowtowing to you, you leave me no choice but to tell you myself. You will please leave my house." She turned and flung back the screen door and was halfway into the house.

"Helen!" Mitchell Hedrick's voice was as cold as hers. "Wait!"

"Goodbye, Mister Pinkerton. Are you coming with me, Mitchell?"

"Helen!" Mitchell Hedrick cracked out a command. "Hold it right there."

Mrs. Hedrick surprised them all by obeying and stopping, still undefeated. "Nicola, get in the house! I swear by all that's holy—and I mean Christian holy—you will never marry this lying man as long as I live!"

Mitchell Hedrick, with his Roman haircut, was cold marble, his voice as hard as his wife's. "Helen, you will shut your mouth—"

"Until you make your filthy deal?" Mrs. Hedrick spat. "Then you'll tell your honorable Japanese gentleman and your daughter what you really think?"

Nicola seized Sam's arm, hanging on to her love, a little girl desperate to make everything come right. "Both of you listen. You first, Mother. Sam's leaving his father-in-law, his Japanese boss he hates for trapping him into his marriage. He loves me. Tell them, Sam, whether we stay here or I go back to Japan with you, I belong to you—"

"Tell them I love you? They know that's the truth, but your mother's right," he said quietly. "I'm Japanese with two children—"

"You're mine! Whether we stay here or go to Japan, you're mine. We love each other!" She was desperate. "What else matters?"

Mrs. Hedrick, securely clenched in fury, was still holding the screen door. "You can ask what matters? Only the rest of your life, my darling daughter—"

"Sam, don't listen to her! She's old!" Nicola cried. "What the hell does she know about love?" She grasped Sam's hands and pulled them to her face wet with tears. "You told me yourself I made you forgot that creature—that whore—the only other woman you ever wanted before me. You don't love your wife! You love me! I love you!"

Mrs. Hedrick had put the world back in order and showed herself well-enough bred to go into her house without slamming the screen door, leaving Mitchell Hedrick facing the two.

Mitchell Hedrick spoke. "Nicola, I'm going in to your mother now. Before I do, Young Mister Kodo, don't forget we have that meeting tomorrow in my office—nine sharp."

"Yes, sir."

Mitchell Hedrick followed his wife into the house, leaving Sam and Nicola looking at each other. Tears stood in her eyes, and she made every effort to speak quietly in spite of crying out all that was in her heart. "You're thinking that you did the right thing that night when you wouldn't take me up to your hotel room to tell me who you are." Their eyes locked. "Sam, my darling, darling . I know and I love who you are." For a second he looked before returning his gaze to hers. "Sam, tell me one thing, do you love me?"

"Yes."

"But you're going back to Japan?

"Yes."

"You know all you have to do is ask and I'll go with you."

She waited for an answer while sprinklers out on the grass shut off. A bird on the wet grass, probably a robin, sang. Inside the house a door slammed. Suddenly she blinked back tears and brightened while her lovely hand lifted and began to swing her rope of pearls. "Then I'd better get busy and call Rupert and Harriet. Did I tell you they've been after me to drive with them down to San Francisco where we'll stay at the Fairmount? There's a terrific new speak where we'll all have the time of our lives—" He voice caught.

"Nick, don't—"

"No? Do you think you're going to keep me standing here on this goddamn porch and watch me cry my eyes out? Oh, no. Not Nick."

CHAPTER EIGHTY-FIVE

Nagasaki, August 3, 1923

I am too excited to print this Roman-style. But I can scarcely get the hiragana down on paper. Oh, my dear—truly—I cannot wait. I pray every hour for your safe, smooth crossing hurrying home to us. Yes. I will have to say it again. Our baby girl waits for us to name her. Tat and I—all of us—cannot wait for September first—not in Yokohama with Father but in Tokyo. I love you with all my heart,

Your Mayumi.

P.S. I have just read every page of Mister Mark Twain's Thomas Sawyer. In English. Every page.

A strike delayed the *Cleveland* in Honolulu and was now scheduled to put into Yokohama one to two days late. In the evening of the last day out Sam climbed back up to the radio office to make certain Mayumi had received his last message at the new Imperial Hotel.

The plump young radioman with a rosy face under a brushcut and thick glasses pulled off his earphones. He made it clear he was absolutely at Sam's service but unable to cover his confusion and worry. "Sorry, sir, but for some reason we're not getting anything at all to or from Tokyo."

"What about the hotel?"

"It's all of Tokyo, sir. Since noon yesterday, we've been totally out of contact. I can't figure what's going on. We're getting nothing."

"But three days ago we got through to Nagasaki."

"Nagasaki's a long way from Tokyo, Sir." He set up straight and assured Sam he'd keep trying. He'd do everything in his power to get through to the capital and the brand-new Imperial Hotel.

Sam stayed out on deck alone walking aimlessly. Sharing the dark, couples strolled hand-in-hand, murmuring. Others, deeper in each others' arms, found shadows.

He stopped at the rail to watch the sea sliding by. A heavy-set Canadian grain merchant from Vancouver he'd exchanged requisite pleasantries with in the past few days came to the rail carrying a Plymouth Pink Gin. His wilted shirt was soaked. "Bloody goddamned hot."

The man was no more of a bore than most commercial travelers and, replying with his minimal nod, Sam intended no encouragement to share the sweating fellow's company. He refused the offer of a cigarette.

"First crossing?"

"No."

"I don't know about you but I'll never get used to it out here. The bloody heat. The people. Two years in Shanghai. You know Shanghai?"

"No."

"Bloody goddamned hot, Shanghai. And only six weeks at home in Vancouver." He sighed. "Where's home for you?"

"Japan."

"I mean before."

"Used to be Bremerton."

"Navy people?"

"Yes."

Like all merchants of his commercial breed he obviously prided himself on being able to talk with anyone about anything. He glanced at the stern. "Look. The way the light catches the seagulls. Means we're getting close. Still a bloody twenty-four hours late—thanks to those damned strikers in Honolulu. The captain's saying noon tomorrow." He fished a card case from his jacket. "On the chance you get to Shanghai. Or did I already give you my card?"

"Yes, you did. Thank you."

"Do I have yours?"

"This trip I'm not carrying cards." Sharing thoughts about tomorrow and reaching Yokohama they both gazed out at the ocean. The heavy man glanced up at the night sky.

"Man-in-the-Moon up there looks like a cool one."

Sam could have told the sweating merchant that where a Westerner sees a man up there in the moon, a Japanese sees a rabbit pounding rice. "Can't help but notice," the heavy man said, swabbing a wet neck, "you've been keeping yourself scarce as hen's teeth this trip. Young man your age. All the ladies were expecting to get you out on the dance floor and shake a leg."

"I'm married. A wife and two kids."

"That doesn't stop most of us," the merchant chuckled conspiratorially. "You never did tell me what it is you do—why you're crossing."

"I'm changing jobs. I'll be teaching English."

"To the Japs?"

"Yes."

"Clever, the Japs. Too clever by half. They never stop trying to catch up. You get along with them—the Japs?"

Instead of answering Sam stared at the ocean, the immense ocean already leaving Seattle half a world behind. "I'm quite serious," the man prodded for an answer, "working with them and all. You get along with the Japs?"

"We prefer to be called Japanese."

Sam turned from the rail and walked, again alone in the hot night.

CHAPTER EIGHTY-SIX

In the morning the twenty-two ton *USS Cleveland* was still out in the stream somewhere East of Tokyo Bay. Had they entered the bay? It was hard to tell, for they were somewhere in limbo under a sky dark with thickening smoke that could only be coming from land. The worried passengers had had no explanation, no word from the crew or the captain. They only knew this murk was coming from land and increasingly blotting out the scorching September sun.

Passengers on the Pacific crossing could be expected to line the bow rail eager for their first glimpse of Yokohama. Not this morning. The smoke and yes, it was full of ash, growing increasingly unbearable and with a terrible stench, sent them shrinking from the rail and back inside the ship.

Sam stood alone at the rail. Since his days hauling hides on the Nagasaki docks he'd never been oversensitive to unpleasant smells, but this morning his hand was clapped over his nose, fighting the odor if it meant catching his first sight of Japan. His adopted land was waiting before him, a smudge, a stinking smudge with the overpowering stench becoming more unbearable by the moment.

Below, down on the ocean, perfectly still as slate, he spotted his first ragged sampans and fishing boats. Yes. Japan was close ahead. He realized that men down there were signaling wildly up at the bridge. Whatever they were saying they were laying off rather than returning into the foul darkness. The massive *Cleveland*, however, was heading straight into the murk.

Overhead in the ash seagulls shrieked their complaint.

"God what a smell!" It was the plump radio operator joining him at the rail sharing the thickening gloom. The man knew what his passenger was desperate to hear. "I know you must be worried about your people at the Imperial Hotel in Tokyo."

Sam waited.

"Sorry to report to you, sir, but we still can't get through—sending or receiving. Nothing wrong with our radio. It's as if the whole *Kanto*— that's the Tokyo region, sir—has been cut off from the world."

"What does the captain say?"

"'Steady as she goes.' Whatever's causing this, we're heading straight into it. Sir, I wouldn't want the other passengers to know, but before we lost total contact I had Osaka. Of course that's a couple of hundred miles down the coast but they were talking about some kind of tremendous catastrophe hitting Japan." Sensing his passenger's deep concern he felt obliged to offset his dire news. "Of course it's only a rumor. Like I say, sir, I know you've got people waiting for you. I'm on my way back up to the shack right now and I'll keep trying Tokyo." Before he left the rail he added, "Did you know the hotel was supposed to open two days ago?"

Yes, he knew. The Imperial had been scheduled to open September first. More than that, he knew Mayumi had cabled Port Angeles that she and Tat had been lucky enough to wangle reservations for the opening day. This was the Imperial he'd visited with Kodo and some of his top Japanese while it was being built. The Japanese hated it. He knew that no way would Kodo set foot in the despised place built by that madman American. He'd be staying with his "top people" down in Yokohama at the United Club. Sam was worried. Without the ship's radio he had no news of whether or not his wife and son would come down to Yokohama and meet him at the docks with her father.

Still at the rail he glanced up at the bridge where a crewman was waving semaphore flags sending signals into the smoke. Straining his stinging eyes he made out a U.S. destroyer looming ghostlike in the gloom.

Sudden silence. The incessant pounding of the engines that had powered the vessel across the Pacific for seventeen days stopped. Sam felt an eeriness he knew everyone else on board must be sharing. Still alone, he forced himself to stay at the bow with the destroyer sliding silently through the blistering heat into darkness though the sun stood at noon.

He told himself Yokohama lay straight ahead, close enough that a pilot tug should be meeting the *Cleveland* to nudge it into port. A tug? Sampans, fishing boats, small craft. No tugs. In eerie silence, with no sign of Yokohama ahead, the ship moved on. The sky at noon was darker now that the sun, if it appeared at all, was a pale disc. The stench had grown even worse. "Jesus, God." He fought the thought, but he'd burned bodies. He knew the smell of death.

He felt the enormous engines rumble back on but pitched low enough only to keep the *Cleveland* from wandering out of control in this limbo. Squinting, did his burning eyes make out something ahead? Land? Docks? Wharves? Whatever his blurred eyes strained to make out was smoldering gray like an ash heap at the bottom of a furnace. "Yokohama?" He wiped back tears. "No," he told himself. "It can't be." Yokohama's a huge port with piers and docks, a city with tall buildings. Ahead in the murk were his stinging eyes making out blackened ruins glowing red with fire?

Racing through passengers on his climb up to the radio shack he heard gasps and panicked cries. Everywhere, rumors were flying through the ship like crazed bats. "Mount Fuji's erupted and buried Tokyo in burning ash!"

"No. There's been a terrible earthquake, then a fire—"
Cries filled the ship. "Why don't we hear from the damned captain?"
"Steward, we demand you tell us what's happening—"
"Sir, we don't know any more than you do—"

"You're lying. Your radio people know, but it's too terrible and they're afraid to tell us—"

"I hear the radio's out—"

"What about the ship-to-shore telephone?"

"Sorry, sir—"

The first shout rose, a fierce demand, from all the passengers. "Someone, for God's sake, tell the captain that whatever's happening we have a right to know!"

Sam reached the shack. The radio was dead, the operator gone. He raced back to the bow where two ship's officers and one passenger were straining to peer through the smoke across oil-slicked water. Sam moved close to overhear any word from an officer with white hair who'd seen much of the world, and his share of disaster and horror. The man seemed stunned, scarcely able to find words. "Oh, God, yes, God help Yokohama." The oil slick ahead began flashing in sheets of flame. Those braving the rail at the bow hushed, aghast, realizing those lumps bobbing among the small craft were dead and bloated bodies.

From shouts on shore all they could make out about whatever this disaster was, it had struck two days ago, on September first. More horrifying evidence came floating out from burned piers, barges heaped high with corpses already rotting in the blazing September heat. With such ghastliness sliding past, those at the rail were held in stunned silence, asking what disaster, what catastrophe had engulfed Yokohama? Now, in what they could see of the city, red flames and black smoke rose from the hellish ruin ahead.

And Tokyo? What about Tokyo? Tokyo with Mayumi and Tat? Sam's fervent prayers to any god—Buddha, Shinto, Jesus—to have kept his Mayumi and Tat at the Imperial these last two days since September first without coming to meet him at this smoldering cauldron that had been Yokohama.

Smaller craft and barges dangerously overloaded with refugees fled the embers of the city, escaping by sea. Sam spotted a U.S. Navy cargo ship unloading Ford trucks from a freighter. Another, the City of Spokane, was swinging cargo nets. "Flour," the white-haired officer at the rail knew the cargo. In the smoke they made out the Japanese Army commandeering sampans and barges, fishing from among the dead bodies those still alive.

A French Messageries Maritimes liner, blasting its deep horn, passed Sam's rail, a steel wall sliding only feet away through the gloom and turning out into the bay. They heard a crewman yelling, "They can't land. They're going on to Kobe!"

Cries and rumors clashed among the panic of the *Cleveland's* passengers. "What the hell are we waiting for? Order the captain to get us out of here." Others, quietly, expressed heartbreak. "Leave? My wife and kids are waiting on the dock."

"What dock?" Angry passengers hell-bent on getting out of the smoke and stink and danger of the ruined city shouted them down. "All the wharves and docks have been burning for two days. No one's left in that hell."

No. Sam couldn't, wouldn't believe that. No. Even if by terrible mischance his Mayumi and Tat had left Tokyo to meet him here in Yokohama they'd survive—by some miracle they'd still be alive there in the smoldering ashes and smoke of the city. How could he stand here at the rail, whether they were here in Yokohama or in Tokyo he had to find them. If the captain gave the order to turn and sail on, no way could he remain on board this ship.

Panic had reduced elegant first-class passengers to a mob, clamoring nearly out of control until clanging bells hushed them in the companionways and public rooms. Megaphones commanded these five hundred first- and second-class passengers into the grand saloon where it was announced the captain would make an appearance at one o'clock. Passengers below in steerage had been ignored, sealed off, no part of the turmoil surging above decks.

In the grand saloon angry shouts demanding they turn from Yokohama and sail on brought worried whimpers from those begging to stay. Both sides quieted somewhat at the sight of the captain striding in. Three officers followed, bringing a small man, a bruised civilian with his arm in a makeshift sling, apparently a survivor from shore they'd somehow managed to bring on board. The captain, a short, powerfully built man with a red beard, who, under other circumstances, would have inspired Sam's confidence, faced the crowd lifting both hands for silence. He had to shout his willingness to hear their cries, but first he was making it clear that he, and he alone, was the captain of this ship. He and he alone would give the order to stay here in the smoke and offer what help they might give or sail on. "Ladies and gentlemen, whatever I decide—here on board you are in no danger. I repeat, no danger as long as you remain on board my ship—"

"No!" Angry shouts defied him. "Get us out of this hellhole!"

"We can't leave? My wife's waiting on shore—"

"In God's name can't someone tell us what's happened!"

Again the captain raised his hands for silence. "You deserve to know all I know. I don't have to tell you we've been out of radio contact with Tokyo. Even now—here in Yokohama harbor—we have no ship-to-shore telephone. All any of us know for certain is that some kind of catastrophe has struck the Tokyo area." He bent to the small man with his arm in the sling. "Our Mister Nyquist who's with the line here in Yokohama has just come on board. He reports that all telephones and telegraph facilities are totally out of commission in the entire *Kanto*—the Tokyo area."

"We know that," Sam snarled to himself, asking himself if he was so different from the rest of the passengers. How could he stand here and debate when Mayumi and Tat could be out there waiting for him? Again he prayed they hadn't come to Yokohama.

"Our Mister Nyquist will tell you he's only alive today because the day before yesterday, at noon, September first, he took his lunch to the park—"

"Louder!" an angry voice screamed.

The captain continued. "I'll ask him to tell you himself, and I'll ask you to please keep your voices down and hold your questions till he's finished." Sam, with the others, pushed closer. The little man with the wounded arm was speaking but no one heard a word.

"Louder!" Screams and yells came from the back of the room.

The captain, a man Sam could envision shouting down hurricanes, moved to stand beside the small broken man. His strong voice quieted the crowd. "Our Mr. Nyquist says that at two minutes before noon yesterday the *Kanto* region was struck by what some are saying is the worst earthquake in all history to hit any city. That was noon, September first. Lunch hour, with every fire burning and exploding wooden houses into flame. The city's still on fire. Anything left standing after the quake and the aftershocks is still on fire."

"That's Yokohama," a woman yelled, "What about Tokyo?"

"Yes, what about Tokyo?" Sam demanded

The captain had turned again to the clerk and shouted his answer to the crowd. "From what Mr. Nyquist hears, Tokyo is as bad." The survivor from shore had more to tell the Captain whose loud voice dropped almost inaudibly with the terrible news. "He says he's afraid that from what he's heard thousands have been burned alive."

"Not Mayumi—not Tat!" With no prayer but a vow, Sam was ready to make his move when a tall woman wearing a fur piece even on this blazing hot day, broke in with a cry, "You don't have to tell me—I was in San Francisco in nineteen 'six—our quake killed fourteen hundred. Is it that bad?"

The passengers saw the captain turn from Nyquist, pained, reluctant to relay more terrible news. "As for human life I'm afraid he says it could be a hundred times worse. So far there's no real news, no way to predict. As for Yokohama they're estimating eighty percent of the city has been destroyed . . ."

Another ship's officer arrived and the captain brought him forward for those close enough to hear jumbled words of more horror "—screaming and rushing from the fire to get to the harbor—trampling each other . . . crowding onto bridges till they collapsed . . . others trapped on the docks—burning . . ."

"What about the Bluff?" a tall American Sam knew to be some kind of diplomat raised his cane demanding news of that district where most Westerners had their homes.

"Gone," Nyquist said.

"I don't believe that!" The tall American turned furious and raised his stick pushing past Sam. "I don't want rumors from this flunky, I want to hear it from someone in authority! Where the hell's the American Consul!" His demand fired the rest of the frightened passengers to join his angry roar. Sam joined those shouting for silence so they could hear his answer. The officer confessed the truth. "The American Consul's been killed. And his family."

A shrieking woman rushed for the door. "Mine were at the pier—"

"You heard them," came a louder shout. "The piers are gone."

"That has to be it for now." The captain's shout was ending the meeting when the purser rushed to his side. More news? After listening, the man in command signaled him forward to face the crowd with his basso voice reaching everyone.

"It's reported that yesterday there were two hundred and thirty-seven aftershocks. No one knows when the next big one will hit. As for Tokyo, no railroads are running to Tokyo. No tramways. Nothing. All but one of the bridges are down. I have to warn all of you, leave the ship and there's no way to get in or out of the capital . . ." he was still shouting. "Ashore you can do nothing."

The ship, from the captain to his crew, and most of the passengers, fell silent at this crack of doom, apparently enough for the captain to announce his decision. "That's it then. We'll take on what survivors we can help, then we're back out into the stream proceeding to Kobe."

"But my family!" a man sobbed his fear shared by the frightened crowd. "But my

wife—"

"My kids! I've got to find my kids!"

"You heard the captain. He's ordered everyone—for their own safety—the safety of every man, woman, and child—not to try and leave but to stay on board."

The purser added his own shout. "Captain's orders. No one gets off. There's nothing you can do. No place to go—"

Stay on board? With the saloon packed with fright and anger Sam had already decided. How in God's name could he stay on board when Mayumi and Tat could still be there in that fire and smoke? He rushed from the saloon, shouldering his way through the panic. Racing down the empty companionways, he lunged down steel ladders into steerage and a Doré-like scene, a frenzied mob already ignoring the captain and swarming over the rail and clambering down makeshift ladders, jumping into an overloaded barge.

With the others Sam sprang from the ship.

CHAPTER EIGHTY-SEVEN

On shore, scrambling over burning timbers, he stripped off his jacket and tied it around the waist of his white flannel trousers. He lurched with his sea legs unsteady after two weeks, staggering through lung-burning smoke toward what he could only guess had been the center of Yokohama. He was on Yokohama's main street where he was picking his way through empty, smoldering rubble. The few buildings that hadn't crashed stood burned, empty shells.

He forced himself, gasping and standing still, to think of where to start looking for his Mayumi and Tat. In his mind he clawed back for some hope in her last letter. Excited as she was to welcome him home she hadn't been specific about where she and Tat would be waiting for him. With the ship's radio down he couldn't make sure they'd checked in at the Imperial Hotel in Tokyo. Kodo? Of Kodo he could be sure. The Toad detested that Western monstrosity facing the emperor's palace and would have made his stay here in Yokohama at an affiliate of the Occident Club—the United Club.

That was it, then. First, find the United Club in what was left of the city. Sam, already streaming sweat, drove himself gasping through the smoke and heat. Yes. First find the United Club and Kodo. He'd know whether Mayumi and Tat had come to meet him at the dock or were waiting for him, still in Tokyo.

This ruin had been Yokohama. Was this clutter of brick and stone all that was left of the center of town? He crunched and stumbled on what he thought was a burned log only to shrink from the sight of his first charred corpse. He kept running, which meant hardening his heart against more horror, more blackened, twisted dead all around him.

The September heat turned the wasteland into a furnace. Death was everywhere, the smell stifling. He slowed, breathing hard, to wipe his eyes and find his bearings. He blinked, looking around at the vast ruin. His heart sank. His search so far had been frantic and without direction. He was lost. Which way to turn? Suddenly, no longer alone, the street came alive with a thundering cart lumbering straight at him, forcing him to shrink against a shattered wall. The cart stopped. Two men in gauze masks, methodically at work, were lifting corpses, heaping the cart.

"The United Club," he shouted. "Where's the United Club?"

The body collectors ignored him. Their cart and the dead rumbled on. He crossed what had been a main street to the first man he saw, a walking dead man covered with ash and lurching straight at him. "The United Club," he cried, "Where's the United Club?"

Hands white with ash waved him off.

The *Koban!* Why hadn't he thought of that—the nearest *koban,* always the most reliable source of help in Japan, should be at the next crossroads, and there it was. The flimsy wood and glass box was shattered, but an improvised tarp shaded a water wagon. Two policemen were carefully ladling out precious water to a line of parched survivors clasping anything to serve as a cup. Still alive, desperate for water, but waiting their turns patiently.

Trying not to slow the work of an exhausted policeman in a filthy undershirt instead of a uniform, he begged, "The United Club?"

The Officer shook his head. Just when Sam thought he was being ignored, a gruff man pointed to a pile of rubble across the street. "Gone."

"Right over there across the street? Would there be any kind of list of who was staying there? A list of the dead?"

"Maybe." The officer thrust his stubbled chin at a pile of documents of his own secured under a scorched brick. "If you can read Japanese." Sam nodded, picking up torn pages. The always scrupulous *koban* officers had compiled a list covering the first forty hours, a partial registry. His hands shook, but here it was. The United Club. A guest list dated 10 AM, September first. "That would be the morning," he told himself, "just two hours before the earthquake and fire. Kodo was certain to have been in residence. Bold handwriting slashed across the top: INCOMPLETE LIST OF PERSONS CONFIRMED KILLED IN THE COLLAPSE OF THE YOKOHAMA UNITED CLUB.

His eyes raced down the first page where checkmarks against the names meant death. On the second page, halfway down, there it was— KODO KOICHI, Nagasaki.

He was gone. Kodo. Old Bumper. Gone forever with all his bullying orders, demands, cigars, farts. No more hating the Talbots and the rich and powerful of high standing in Nagasaki. No more using Tedabara whom he'd forbidden his son. Here, across the street, far from Nagasaki and home, Kodo was under that mountain of rubble. Kodo, smashed, blood and bone mingled with the other members of the Club—"top people" along with their servants.

Nothing was left now but to pray that Mayumi and Tat had stayed on in Tokyo. Pray to Jesus, Lord Buddha, all the Shinto gods that she was there, waiting for him at the brand-new Imperial Hotel. With every beat of his heart he had to believe they were still alive. He put the officer's list back under the charred brick. Without interrupting the officers with their endless ladling out of water, he dared ask what he feared most. "Any word about Tokyo?"

"Worse than here." The loud voice didn't come from a policeman but from one of those waiting in line for water, a businessman in a filthy, torn summer suit, his face sooty under a battered white hat. "Everyone in Tokyo was killed."

The officer in his filthy undershirt leaned to Sam with a mutter. "He doesn't know. None of us know. No telephone. Nothing. Almost forty hours now and all we get is rumors. All anyone knows for sure is the quake hit at noon two days ago. The quake and then the fire."

Sam called to the others in line: "Has anybody here heard anything about the Imperial Hotel in Tokyo?"

Not even the doomsaying businessman in the torn suit had any more rumors to offer. Sam was the only one in the line to turn his gaze on a horse plodding through the heat dragging a cart heaped with charred bodies under a cloud of buzzing flies. The officer never slowed aiding those in his line desperate for water, but glanced over at Sam, shaking his head. "So sad. Loved ones come searching but what can we do? We can only keep bodies two days for identification. Then they must be burned. Gone forever."

The cart rumbled on.

"So many dead," the exhausted officer sighed.

"But not Mayumi. Not Tat," Sam shouted fiercely to himself. "How do I get to Tokyo?" Streaming with sweat he made his dangling tie into a sweatband.

A woman waved a cane in a northerly direction. "Walk. Only way. Fifteen miles."

"Fifteen miles?" he asked the policeman.

Both officers spoke at the same time. "Seventeen."

"Which way?"

CHAPTER EIGHTY-EIGHT

Running, he was gasping but his heart was soaring. This was something he knew about. Something he could do. He was a rickshaw boy again. Seventeen miles? He'd run all the way, and keep up his prayers. Without breaking pace he wrung sweat from his drenched silk necktie headband and tied it tight. He'd decided there was no more sure way to reach Tokyo than following the train tracks. "Damn!" He cursed his English leather shoes that he wasn't wearing his old Nagasaki straw sandals. "Don't feel sorry for yourself. You're not even hauling a rickshaw. Only fifteen miles to go."

Jogging steadily down the iron tracks, he was forcing old muscles that tennis players, members of the Occident Club, never use back into life. No. He hadn't forgotten how to run. He loved running but not breathing in hot smoke. Ahead he found tracks twisted, bent or broken by the earthquake and he detoured onto paved streets, dodging chunks of concrete. Mile after mile, always keeping the tracks in mind, he raced through miles of the same gray, burned-out rubble, passing survivors digging through piles of brick, wood and rubble, smoldering ruins. Digging for what? No. He couldn't bear to answer his own question.

"Tokyo? Center?" His shouts tore from his scalded throat. "The Imperial Hotel? Please, is it still there?" He cried cry after cry. No one answered.

He pounded on through the blinding smoke and suddenly over to the west he caught a glimpse of clear blue sky and hills of bright emerald green. Did that mean the fire had spared some districts? Could he hope that miles ahead he'd sight the green of Hibiya Park? That would mean he'd reached the moat of the Imperial Palace across from the Imperial Hotel where he prayed Mayumi and Tat had been saved from the fire.

The rickshaw boy, back on the railroad tracks, was forcing a steady pace before plunging into a black tunnel. Here the cool was welcome but dangerous, running in absolute blackness. Far ahead, the proverbial light at the end of the tunnel, a sliver of an abandoned train blocking his passage. Jumping aboard the rear car, he raced forward through empty coaches. This was the way to Tokyo and if he was lucky a drop of water from a washroom. He turned the tap and held his breath. Precious drops of water, no matter how stale, dribbled into his cupped hands and onto his parched lips.

From the aisle through the train he kept that glint of light beyond the engine as his goal. He stopped. The engine must have crumpled abruptly under a stone and steel cave-in blocking the way ahead. His hammering heart sank. Must he turn and run all the way back to the entrance of the tunnel? No. Instead of losing precious time he climbed onto the engine, struggling like a mole, worming his way through tangled steel and concrete before he emerged, ripped and scraped, into the sunlight. Blinking to get his eyes used to the sooty sunlight he slowed, aghast, staring at a totally new horror. Only a few feet beyond the tunnel's mouth he saw five wild youths, howling animals with clubs, battering two terrified old men screaming and stumbling in their own blood.

"Damned Koreans!"

"Starting fires!"

"No—" a feeble victim pleaded.

"Looting!" The five raised the deadly chant. "Kill all fucking Koreans!"

"Please—" A moan bubbled with pain was smashed silent forever by death.

He shrank back. Would they take him for a gaijin—another outsider and equally guilty as the hated Koreans for causing this catastrophe? Hiding in the dark tunnel, holding his breath, he stayed motionless till the attackers, fierce dogs roaring for blood, raced off in their search for more Koreans.

He stepped around smashed blood and bone. Smoke had his burning lungs bending him double and snatching for breath. He'd left exhaustion far behind and prayed for a second wind. How much farther did he have to run, run and running till he reached Mayumi and Tat at the Imperial Hotel?

Fighting for breath and struggling to keep up his pace he scrubbed his eyes. He blinked and scrubbed them again. A mile ahead, were those the massive stone walls the ramparts of the Imperial Palace? And that dark green—the pines in the Imperial Gardens? Yes. Stone walls. Pines. Green. Not in ruins, not burned, the Emperor's Palace behind these stone walls. The sight charged him with such hope that with his second or even third wind he picked up his pace racing through the amber haze of late afternoon. Hibiya Park. Back in his schooldays he'd seen Matthew Brady's sepia photographs of the U.S. Civil War, here in Hibiya Park, forty-five hours after the quake, the emergency tent city with soldiers carrying stretchers of the wounded among survivors in endless lines seeking water and medical care resembled Brady's photos.

What he could see to the east across the park was horribly like Yokohama, a ruined, mostly flattened, city, still glowing, still smoking. He squinted through the smoke hanging over the tent city to where the Imperial Hotel should be. Was he imagining gray walls of stone? He rubbed his stinging eyes. Was that the Imperial with its gray, strangely carved stone standing alone in this vast ruin of demolished Tokyo? He blinked back the stinging tears. Yes! Yes, there it was! Fired with a blast of energy, he sprinted through the dusty park's city of canvas and across a street past crowds gathered at the hotel's lily pond drained by fire-fighting pumps and full of ash and dead flowers.

The crowds surging into the hotel made it clear. With the capital smashed and burned and in ruins, Frank Lloyd Wright's building had opened on schedule September first, only hours before the earthquake dragon shook and tore Tokyo to pieces at noon. There it was, the madman's hotel standing alone in the vast devastation. Sam, black with sweat and white with ash, rushed into that cave-like lobby he remembered so well.

Crowds from the shattered and burned-out embassies and government buildings, nobles and ministers, Japan's most powerful men, along with businessmen from all over the world, and a few visitors surviving in this hell, had turned the Imperial into the capital's nerve center—its command post. In the lobby Sam wasn't the only one soaked in sweat. Many were covered with ashes and bloody bandages—all Tokyo, bruised and torn. How many others like himself were praying in their search to find loved ones still alive?

He'd reached the Imperial but now, bewildered in this crush of humanity jamming the lobby, like so many others he was frantic, uncertain, helpless to know how to begin his search. Wait out the long line for the desk? That would take forever. Taller than most, he was able to glance around above the crowd. Surely there must be something like a message center—a bulletin board posting names and their fate. Exactly as he hoped the efficient Japanese would do, across the lobby there it was, with crowds pushing close enough to read the list of survivors, the living along with those certified dead. Elbowing close enough to read the names he heard gasps of "Thank God" but as often, strangled sobs of despair.

"Please God, Buddha, and the gods of Shinto let Mayumi and Tat be alive." Working his way close enough to read the list, he held his breath and prayed. The list was in Romanji and Kanji. On the first, the living, he found no Kodos. Nor was the name among the dead. A closer look among hand-printed message in English, one was staring at him. MR. SAMUEL KODO. PLEASE SEE FRONT DESK. Grabbing the message he struggled back toward the desk against the tide of those as desperate as he with the message beating in his brain. MR. SAMUEL KODO. PLEASE SEE FRONT DESK.

A pale young Japanese clerk's black hair flopped over eyes glittering with fatigue. Likely on duty for the forty hours since the earth shuddered and burst into flame, he was fighting being overwhelmed in his painfully conscientious duty to serve each in turn. A heavy European shoved into line in front of Sam, who justified slamming his fat Western bulk out of the way. As soon as the little clerk saw him waving the card he signaled him to another part of the desk. "I'm Sam Kodo. You have a message— about my wife and son!"

The precise little clerk seemed to take forever riffling a file till he found a record of a reservation. "Yes. Mrs. Kodo and son. A two-bedroom suite. Among the first. They checked in the morning of our opening day—"

"They're here now?"

The clerk stifled a little cry. He'd found another note. "If you are Mr. Sam Kodo of Nagasaki, they expected you the day before yesterday from Yokohama and the *President Cleveland*—"

"The ship was two days late putting our ship in after the earthquake. Tell me. My wife—my son—they've still got to be here!"

The clerk slid back his flop of black hair in his painstaking thoroughness. "Yes, Mister Kodo Koichi of Nagasaki made the reservations—"

"Yes," Sam fought on, that would be my father who was in Yokohama. He's dead. I'm Kodo Samuel—like this message says—Samuel Kodo." Close to shouting, he stopped and fortified himself with a long breath. "This message was left for me to see you. What does it mean?" The clerk bowed. "One moment please." He left his post, but quickly returned with a white-haired Japanese man whose hotelier's carnation in his buttonhole had faded to brown.

He used the Western form of address. "Mister Sam Kodo?"

"Yes. Please." Sam heard himself close to wailing. "I've been telling this man you have a message for me—from my wife and son. They had a reservation. They checked in on opening day. Are they here now?"

The senior desk clerk nodded and returned to his file. "Yes, here are their reservations. Yes. Mrs. Kodo checked in with her son but have not returned since—" he hesitated to pronounce what would be a death sentence—"since the earthquake."

"What's the message?"

Those in line in back of him, as desperate as he'd been, shoved and fought to reach the desk. The two hotel men gave Sam their concentration, totally Japanese in their devotion, even during a disaster and exhausted, striving to serve with excellence. "The message. Ah, yes. Here. You were given a larger suite for three, but when they did not return we were forced to let it go—" He slid a thin hand back across his white hair. "You can understand—"

Sam fought for calm and managed to keep his voice steady. "No, my wife and son were here in this hotel. Your records show they were here. They're here now." His smoke-burned throat closed off his voice. He could rasp. "Just tell me, for God's sake that they're safe."

"We hope so—" The man with the brown carnation lowered his voice. "It seems they have not been back since—"

"Since the earthquake. I understand. Ask if any of your people, anyone here has seen them since."

"One moment, please." The senior man waited for his assistant to retrieve another, this time a handwritten note. From the maid assigned to their suite.

"Please—" Sam struggled to keep from tearing the note from the younger man's hand, which the white-haired clerk offered, "Here." He looked at Sam. "Can you read Japanese?"

"Yes—"

The note seemed to be some kind of inside information, the property of the hotel. "Here. You will see the maid reports Mrs. Kodo and her son checked in, but left the suite before noon the first of September." He stopped himself. "The maid reports they did not return—"

"This maid—did she say where they went?"

The older man drew in breath, that wince of pain which Sam's half-Japanese side recognized when an intake of breath was preferable to announcing bad news. Sam, at this moment both American and Japanese, was fighting to slow his racing mind and form a plan. "It was their first time in Tokyo. The first place they'd go is the Ginza a few streets away. I mean, wouldn't they?"

The two clerks stood helpless against his desperate guesses.

"Please—the Ginza. Wouldn't that be where they'd go? Where I should look for them?"

The older man drew out a silk handkerchief and wiped his face.

"Help me!" Sam begged. Every impulse cried to race from the hotel out into the ruins and search. Without being able to bear standing here another moment, he demanded. "Is that where I should start? The Ginza?"

Both clerks, unable to answer, could only offer their deeply concerned silence. The younger man's eyes met Sam's. He nodded. "Yes. The Ginza is often the first place most visitors to Tokyo wish to visit." Nevertheless he couldn't withhold suggesting the futility of Kodo's search. "But this note of maid's—that was two days ago."

Frantic to begin some kind of search, Sam had turned from the desk when the white-haired man stopped him. "Sir, if I may—"

"Yes?"

"It has been close to fifty hours. The Ginza is still burning—"

Sam was breathing hard. "Where else can I look?"

The two clerks studied each other. Whatever their thoughts, they seemed in agreement, and the man with the wilted carnation and white hair spoke first. "If I were you, sir, I would first go to Hibiya Park."

"Across the street," the assistant, no longer attempting professional formality, was eager to help. Sam nodded that he'd just now raced through the tent city. "I know. That's where the army is taking the injured."

"Many from the Ginza," the older man added.

"The army," the junior clerk urged, offering all the hope he could. "The army brings them there."

CHAPTER EIGHTY-NINE

In his frantic dash through dust and smoke, now gold at the end of the day, he burst into Hibiya Park, dodging cars and ambulances. He found exhausted soldiers who'd been working nonstop close to fifty hours adding more rows of tents and setting up emergency care here below the walls of the Imperial Palace.

Here in the dust he found a command post but no one in charge. Racing, searching among the broken and wounded, his mind was chanting, spinning hypnotically as a Tibetan prayer wheel, endlessly repeating his cry from the heart—Mayumi—Tat—Mayumi—Tat. Above the ruined city the sinking sun was blood red in the smoke, leaving him only minutes to rush down the rows of canvas tents to peer inside each one. The injured and dying turned to him for help. Though his heart went out to them, he dashed on till he found a man in a blood-splattered white coat. "Does anyone have a list of those who've been brought here?"

The man shook his head. "No time for lists."

"Wait. Please. My wife has a limp and her two-year-old son is tall for his age—Please?"

"Sorry." The filthy coat hurried off leaving Sam alone in this darkening, improvised field of canvas, salvation in the middle of the smoldering city with the setting sun a deepening red. "Hurry. Got to find them before dark and the whole camp is black as night."

All the plan he could conjure was to continue a systematic search, which meant racing through the first row of tents. Rushing to the second, his heart sank at the sight of a longer row, now blocked. He stared in horror at another cart with soldiers heaping corpses on top of other corpses, rattling them off for burning.

He was Japanese enough to share this people's devastating heartbreak of never knowing the fate of these loved ones disappearing forever in death without ceremony, to be burned anonymously without formal ritual of farewell. That was the dead, not Mayumi and Tat. He hurried on, not utterly heartless but blotting out the cries and sobs of others, following these carts, desperate to identify the dead.

In his rush, frantic to find the living he stumbled but kept up his pace lifting tent fronts looking into the second row of tents stretching far ahead, vanishing in the twilight's engulfing shadows.

Fighting despair he became his own Tibetan prayer wheel, chanting Mayumi—Tat—Mayumi—Tat—his incantation reduced to gasps forcing himself to find the strength, searching in the canvas, while hands clutched at him with pitiful cries begging for water. In the dusk of evening all Tokyo seemed to be here, broken and bleeding, crying for help.

Lanterns winking on, marked another row of tents. At a water wagon he splashed his eyes to peer ahead and stopped without another step. Just ahead was a little boy Tat's age, his back to him. Yes, a little boy with dark brown hair, wide shoulders, sturdy legs. His heart leaped. He dashed forward grasping for his son but the boy who wheeled on him with a pushed-in little face full of dirt and a nose running snot, snarled and wrenched from Sam's touch.

Dusk was darkening quickly into night with more lines of tents still to be searched. A soldier passing with a cart full of lanterns offered him one, and he continued his race lifting canvas and peering inside. He'd finished one row and raced on to the next, crashing into another little boy sending his tin cup of precious water flying. Sam slowed long enough to bend down with his lantern light to help the child pick up the cup. This was somebody's little lost boy, his face smudged with soot and streaked with tears. Their eyes met. Gray eyes looked into brown. Tat.

"Tat!"

The boy, shaking with sobs, clutched his father's legs. Sam hunkered down bringing his eyes level with his son's and holding his dirty face in his hands and kissing wet tears. Through kisses he whispered, "Where's your mother?"

Tat didn't answer. Couldn't he speak? Without a word he tugged Sam's hand and insisted on completing his solemn mission to a barrel and refilling the cup. Carrying his precious water solemnly in both hands, in silence he led his father down the last row of tents to one no different from the others. With Tat bringing water to his mother, Sam crouched down and lifted the canvas. Sam drew him close. Without his son he might have glanced into this darkness and missed seeing his Mayumi. Yes, his Mayumi under the lantern's glow. On an army cot, she looked thinner than when he'd left, cruelly bruised in her torn kimono of her favorite color, pale green, but streaked with soot. Tat, still holding his cup of water, watched his father sink down and gather his mother into his arms. Inside her smudged silk Sam felt her heart beating, her thin breasts rising and falling almost imperceptibly against his own hard, sweaty body.

"Mayumi, I'm here—"

Tat's eyes, shining in the dark, looked up at his father, begging him not to let his mother die.

"No," he whispered to Tat, his father wouldn't let that happen. He raised her small hand to his lips in a kiss. Feeling her frail life beating against him he shut his eyes, thanking whatever god or gods on whichever side of the sea he'd just crossed that he was here with them. In their tent a mosquito whined. Out in the vast night Tokyo was smoldering embers. In their tiny world Mayumi raised her hand to his face.

"Sam-San . . ."

"I'm here—" He brushed ash from her beautiful, dark eyes.

"Father?" she asked. "In Yokohama?"

"We can talk later." Sam kissed her face. "Has a doctor seen you?"

"The doctor," Tat insisted, "said Mama isn't broken. It's the fire. The smoke."

"At the hotel they said after you arrived you and Mama probably went to the Ginza. It was noon. So you were having lunch—"

"Ice cream." Tat said. "Green tea ice cream. Then the whole world fell down," his voice choked in a rush of sobs and words. "Her cane. I couldn't find Mama's cane and—the fire—the smoke."

"You helped Mama out into the street."

Tat nodded.

"The army brought you here."

Tat nodded again.

"And now you and I are taking her home."

He was still holding the cup. "She's so quiet."

"Put some of your water on her lips." He drew him close. As deeply as his devotion had been in carrying the cup and not spilling a drop, Tat dipped a finger in the water and traced his mother's mouth. He looked up at his father, asking him if his touch of water would bring her back to them. Silent and searching his father's eyes, he waited. In the next tent someone screamed. They heard a cart rumbling past their sweltering canvas. At that moment Tat grabbed his father's hand, the two sharing their excitement. Her lips were moving. "My Tat," she whispered. Her eyelids fluttered. "And my Sam-San."

"Yes my love," Sam bent to her. "We're here."

Mayumi's tongue, like a little cat, sought every drop of wet on her lips. "And I am here," she looked up at the two and smothered a cough. "Yes. I am here and now I will live." Her eyes looked up. "The doctor promised—if I was strong I would live." Another mosquito whined. No one moved. The three were breathing as one. "I told him I was very strong . . . may I have a bit more water?"

Sam cradled her as Tat brought what water was left in the cup to her lips. Sam was already seeing the future. "Yes, my strong Mayumi, you will live and I will get us home to Tat's baby sister." He smoothed sweat and ash from her hair and kissed her forehead. He rose to stand though it meant bending, filling the tent. He looked down into Tat's large, dark eyes, so much darker than his own. "Son, you will have to be brave and stay here and take care of your mother just a little longer. Can you do that?"

"No!" Tat cried his disbelief that his father was leaving. He shook his head violently. "Don't go!" He shrieked and clawed at his father. "Don't go!"

"As soon as I come back we're going home."

Sam kissed his son's face and brushed ashes from his hair, then hugged him. "Stay with your mother. It'll be dark but don't be afraid. Stay right here. Mama and I love you and before you know it, I'll be back—"

"No." Small hands clung to his father.

"Tat, please. Wait—right here—be brave a little longer. I promise. Just a few minutes more." Sam tried not to hear his son's cries as he lifted the tent flap and raced off through the dark sea of canvas.

Tat held the flap staring out into the rows of tents and gleaming lanterns. He went back to kneel beside his mother. "He said he'd be right back."

Sam had promised Tat he'd be back in a few minutes but it was a lifetime, perhaps an endless half hour, before a lantern glowed again outside the tent flap and the dark sea of canvas.

"Mama's sleeping."

"Good. Come outside and see what I was counting on finding at the hotel." He lifted his lantern showing his son a rickshaw. "Yes, a rickshaw." He didn't tell his son that now in Japan they were illegal, but hotels usually keep a few on hand for visitors, a reminder of Old Japan. He gave the lantern to his son to hold. "Now we wake her up."

Tat gently touched Mayumi's shoulder. She was struggling to rise when Sam lifted her into his arms. With her head on his shoulder she murmured. "My Sam-San, my Tat," She asked quietly, "And Father?"

Sam had taken control. "Gone." He said nothing more. This was not the place nor the time to tell her that her father was dead, smashed under blocks of stone. Once he got them home to Nagasaki they'd have a lifetime to talk.

She pressed her face against his. "I love you . . ."

He returned her kiss and without another word carried her from the tent, lifting her up and into the rickshaw. Tat clambered up onto the seat next to her and Sam buckled them both in. He picked up the shafts. He turned and looked up at his wife and son.

"Ready?"

Both nodded. Between the shafts he straightened his sweatband that had been a deep maroon English tie, bent forward, and they began to move.

THE END